Tree-House Comix Proudly Presents

DOG MAN
A Tale of Two Kitties

WRITTEN AND ILLUSTRATED BY **DAV PILKEY**

AS GEORGE BEARD AND HAROLD HUTCHINS

WITH COLOR BY JOSE GARIBALDI

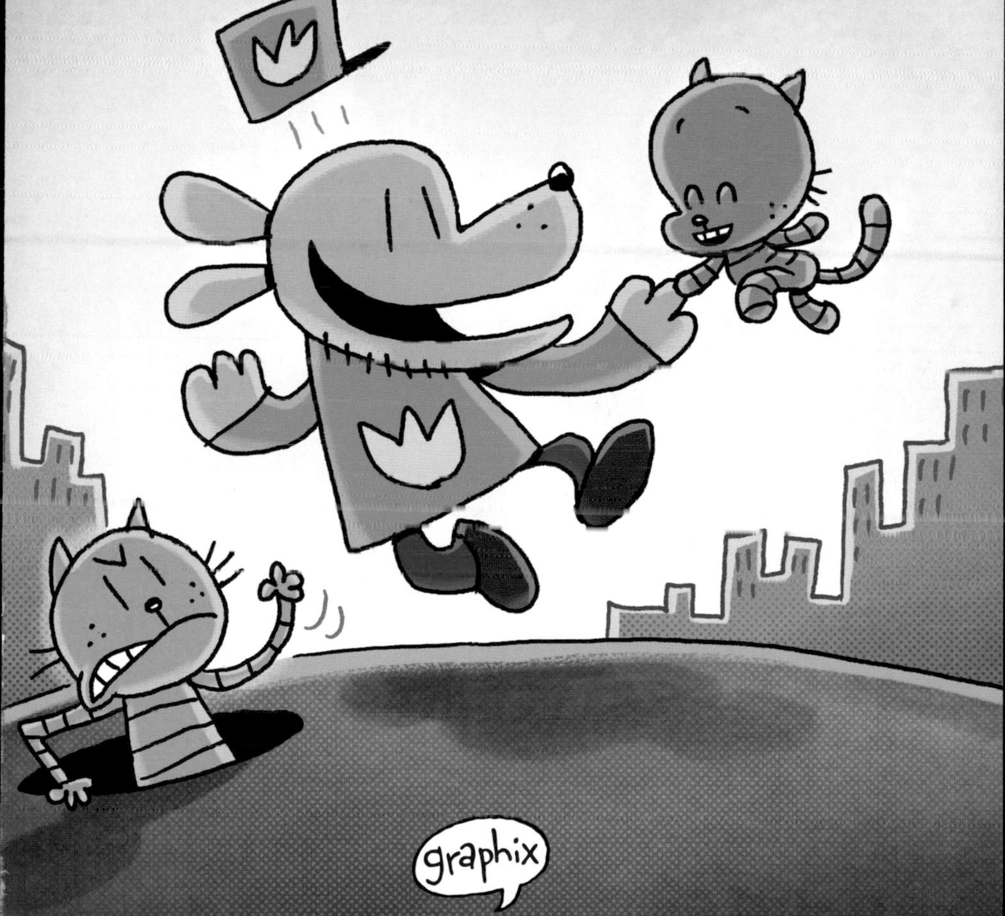

graphix

AN IMPRINT OF

SCHOLASTIC

HERE'S TO YOU, MR. ROBINSON!
(THANK YOU, DICK.)

With thanks to Charles Dickens, whose novels, particularly
A Tale of Two Cities, still resonate with readers today.

Library of Congress Control Number 2016961907

978-1-338-74105-6 (POB)
978-1-338-61199-1 (Library)

10 9 8 7 6 5 4 3 2 1   21 22 23 24 25

Printed in China   62
This edition first printing, August 2021

Edited by Anamika Bhatnagar
Book design by Dav Pilkey and Phil Falco
Color by Jose Garibaldi
Creative Director: Phil Falco
Publisher: David Saylor

Chapters

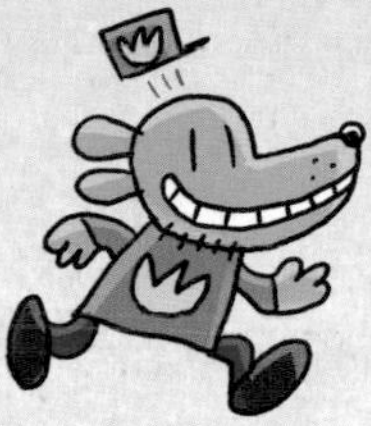

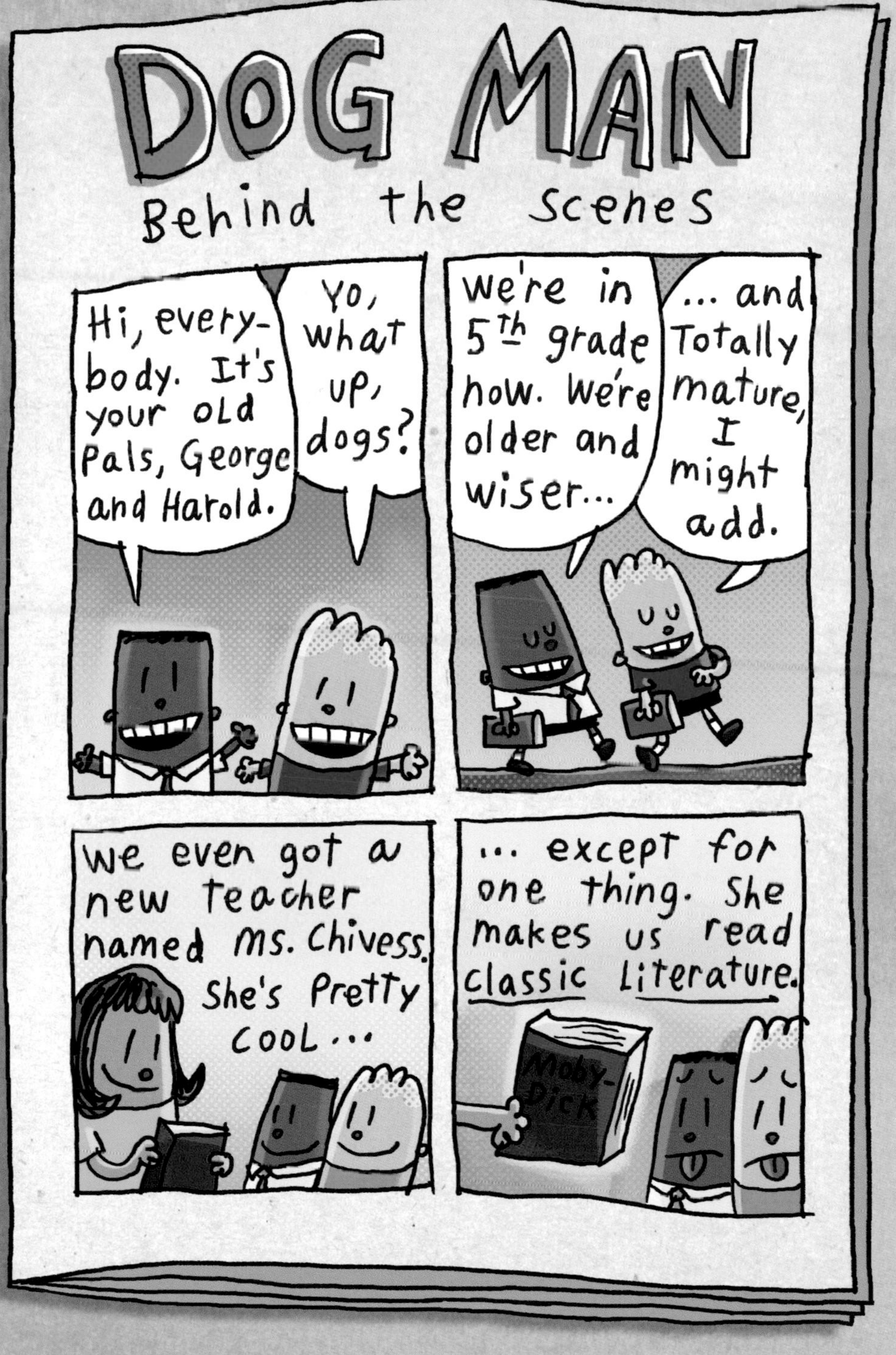
DOG MAN
Behind the Scenes
Hi, every-body. It's your old Pals, George and Harold.
Yo, what up, dogs?
We're in 5th grade now. We're older and wiser...
... and Totally mature, I might add.
We even got a new teacher named Ms. Chivess.
She's Pretty cool...
... except for one thing. She makes us read classic Literature.
Moby-Dick

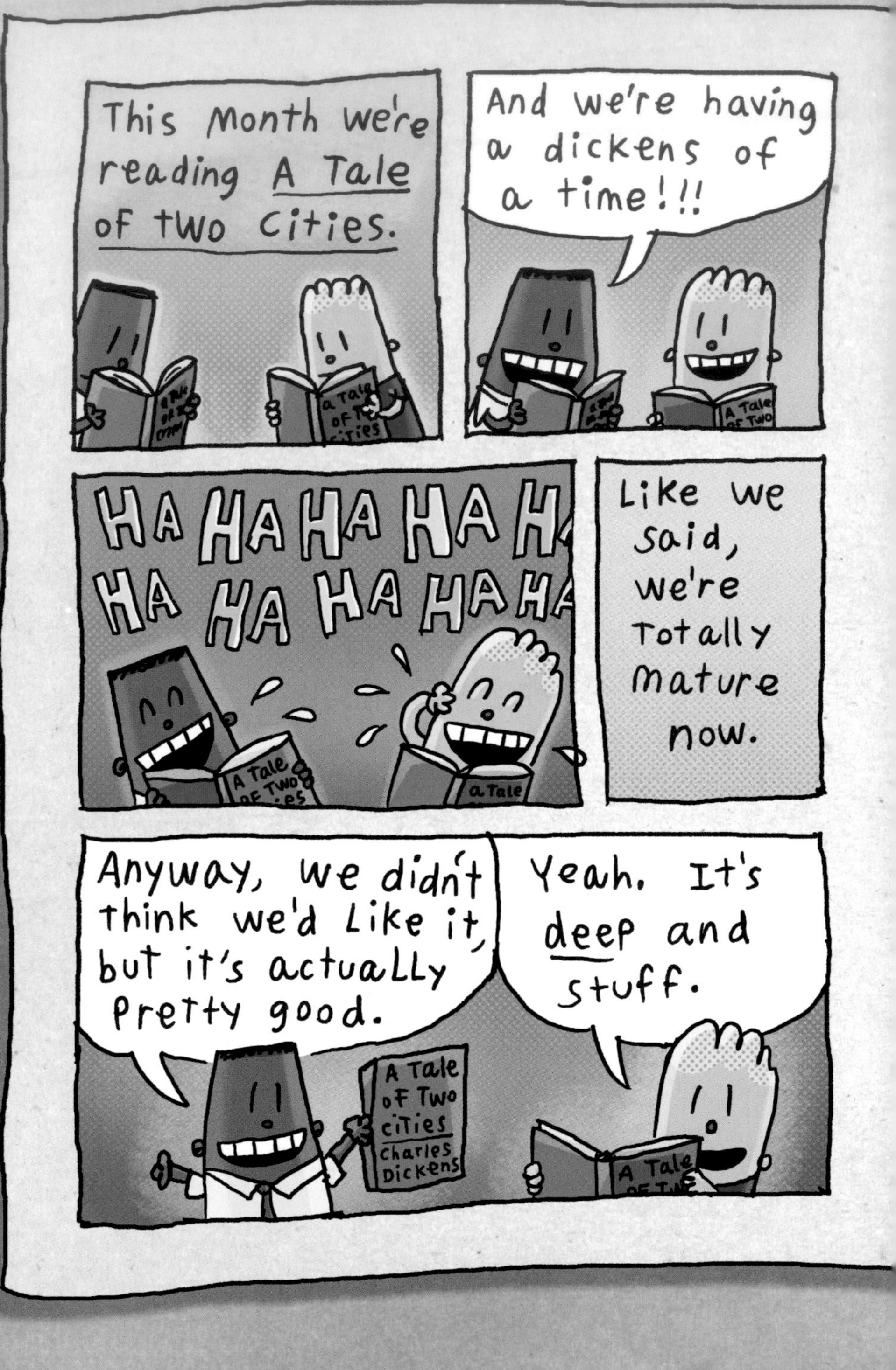
This Month we're reading A Tale of Two Cities.
And we're having a dickens of a time!!!
HA HA HA HA HA HA HA HA HA HA
Like we said, we're Totally mature now.
Anyway, we didn't think we'd Like it, but it's actuaLLy Pretty good.
A Tale of Two Cities Charles Dickens
Yeah. It's deep and stuff.

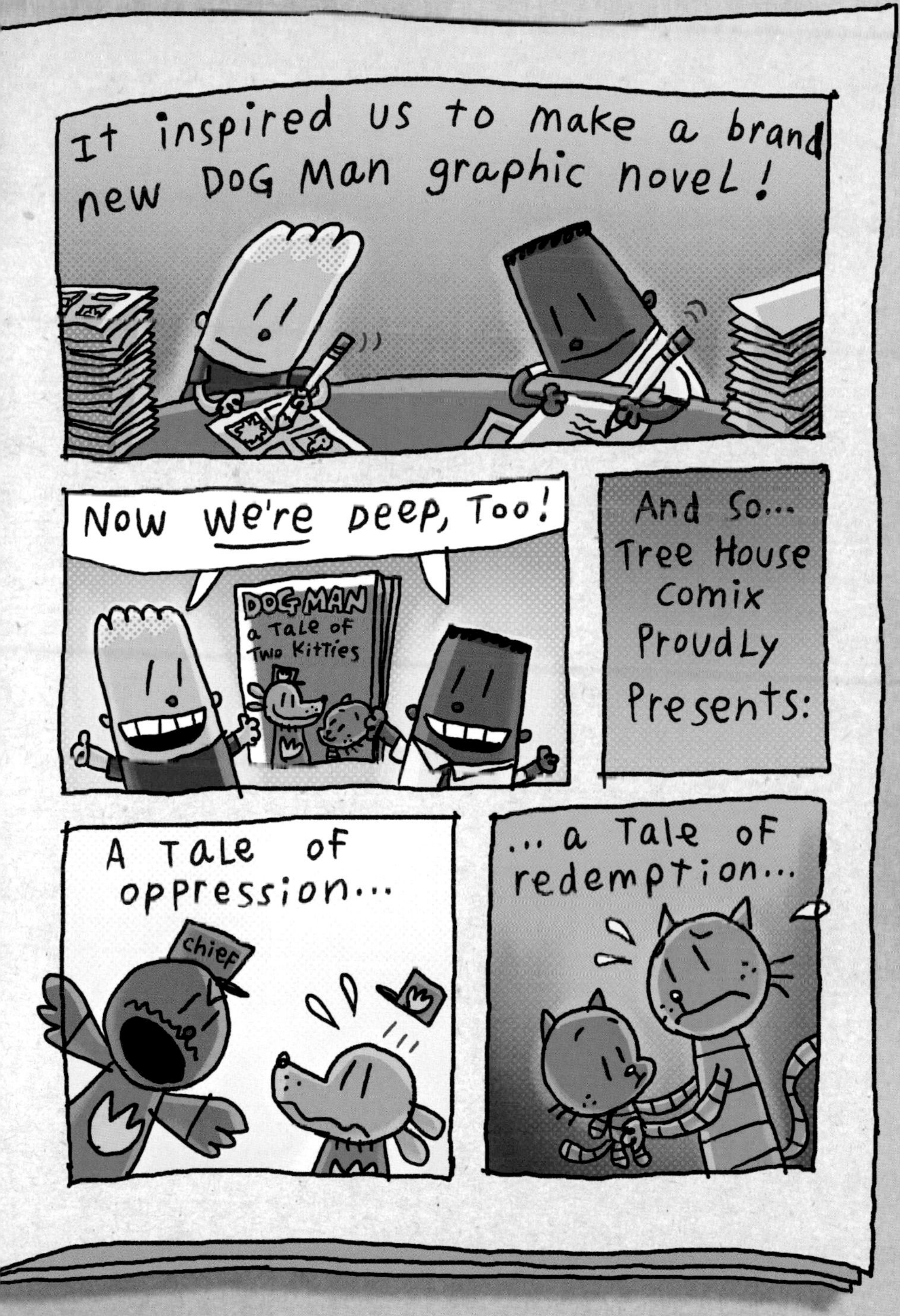
It inspired us to make a brand new DOG MAN graphic novel!
Now We're Deep, Too!
DOG MAN
a Tale of Two Kitties
And So... Tree House Comix Proudly Presents:
A Tale of oppression...
Chief
... a Tale of redemption...

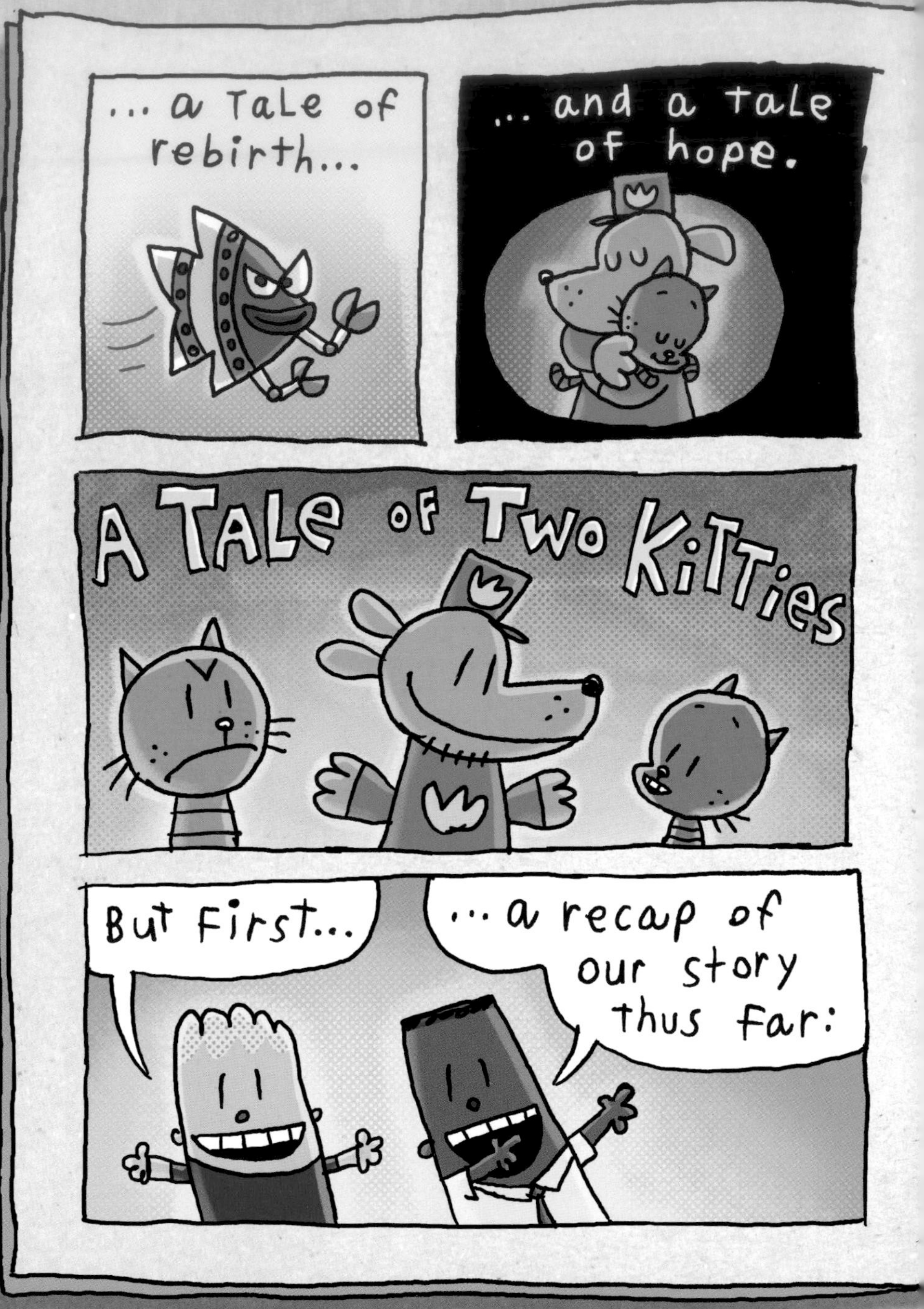

... a Tale of rebirth...
... and a tale of hope.
A Tale of Two Kitties
But First...
... a recap of our story thus far:

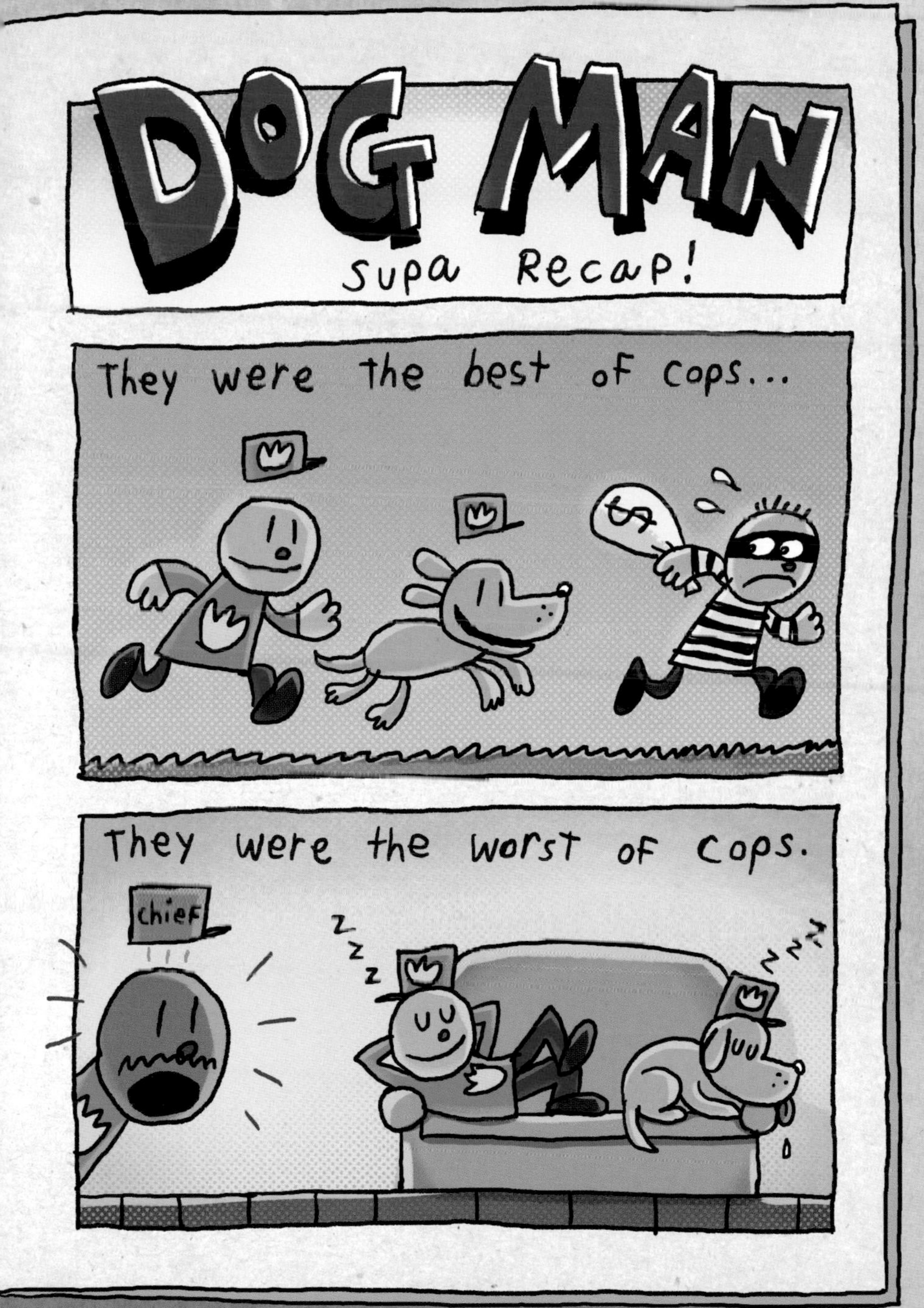
DOG MAN
Supa Recap!
They were the best of cops...
They were the worst of cops.
chief
Z
Z
Z
Z
Z
Z

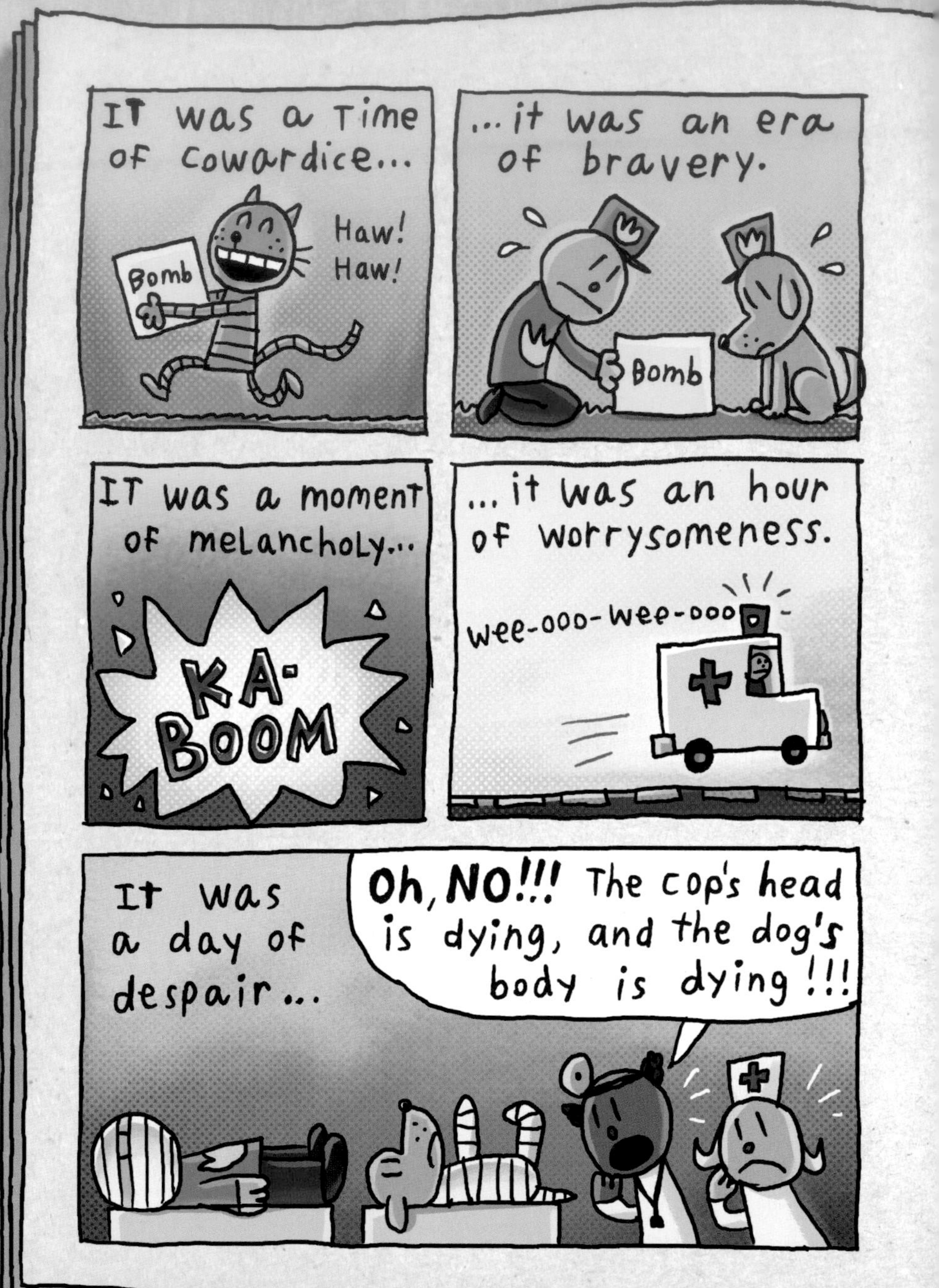
IT was a Time of cowardice...
Bomb
Haw! Haw!
...it was an era of bravery.
Bomb
IT was a moment of melancholy...
KA-BOOM
...it was an hour of worrysomeness.
wee-ooo-wee-ooo
It was a day of despair...
Oh, NO!!! The cop's head is dying, and the dog's body is dying!!!

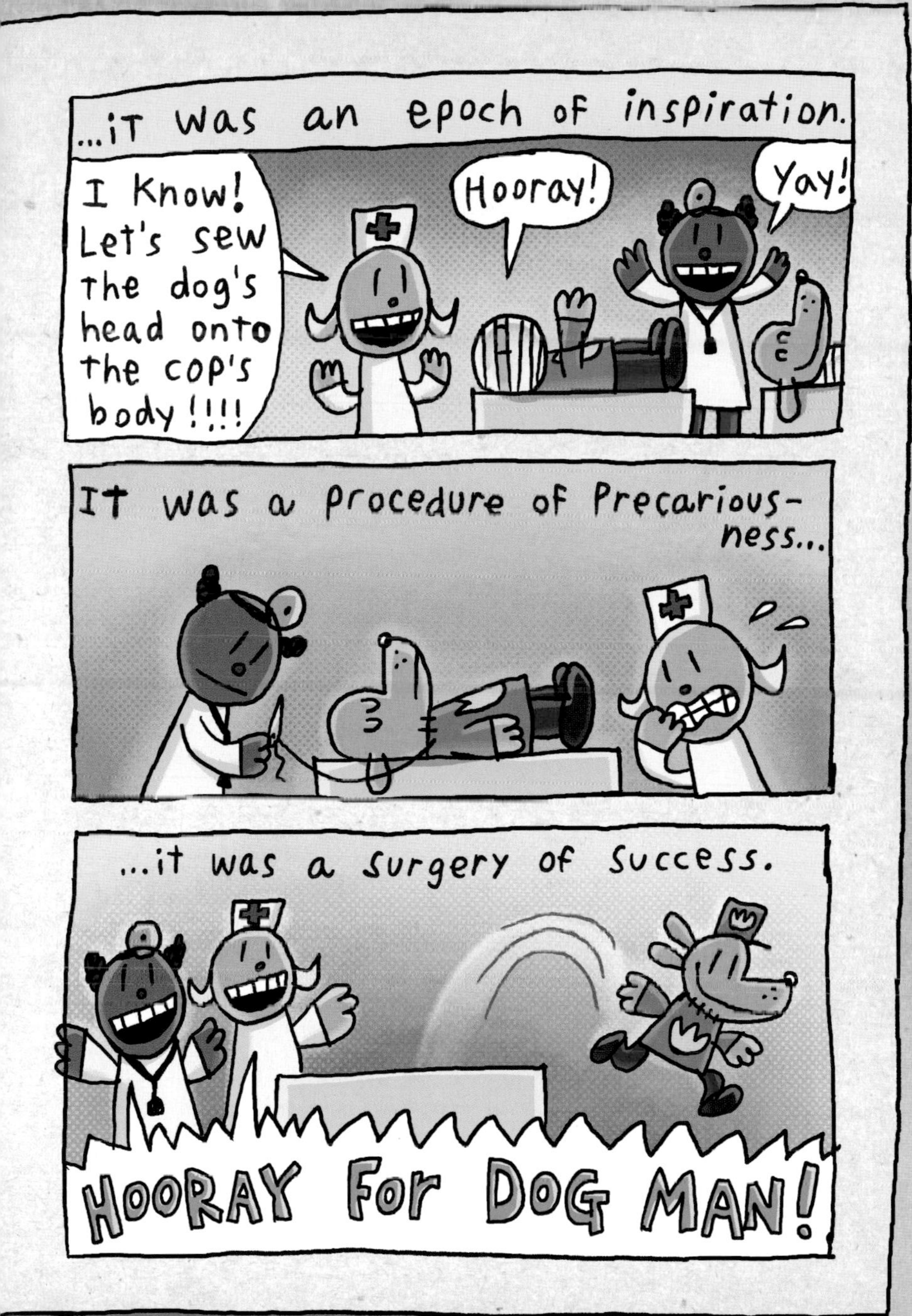
...iT was an epoch of inspiration.
I Know! Let's sew the dog's head onto the cop's body!!!!
Hooray!
Yay!
IT was a procedure of Precarious-ness...
...it was a surgery of success.
HOORAY For DOG MAN!

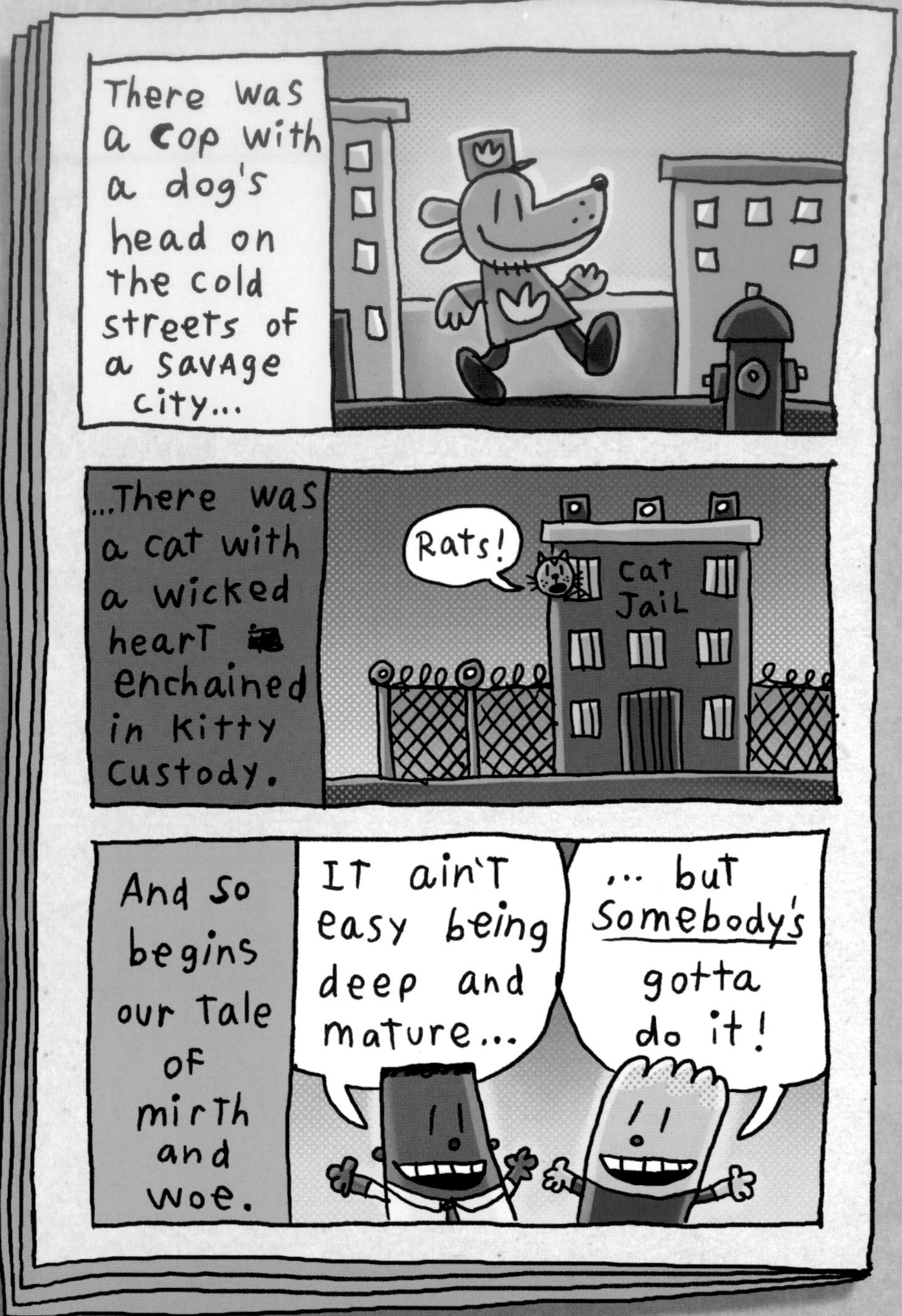
There was a cop with a dog's head on the cold streets of a savage city...
...There was a cat with a wicked hearT enchained in kitty custody.
Rats!
Cat Jail
And so begins our Tale of mirTh and woe.
IT ain'T easy being deep and mature...
... but Somebody's gotta do it!

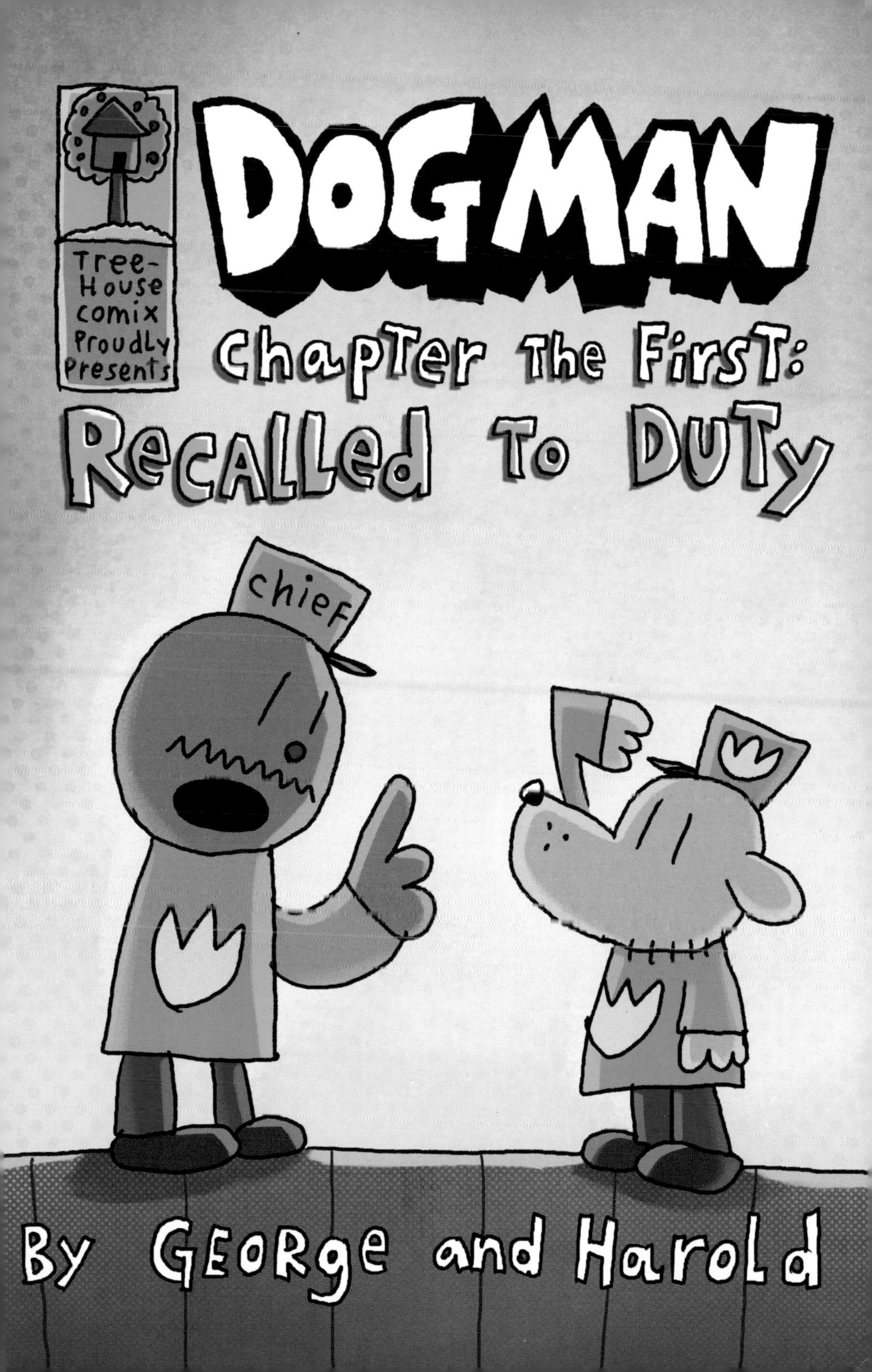
Tree-House comix Proudly Presents
DOG MAN
Chapter the First:
Recalled To Duty
chief
By George and Harold

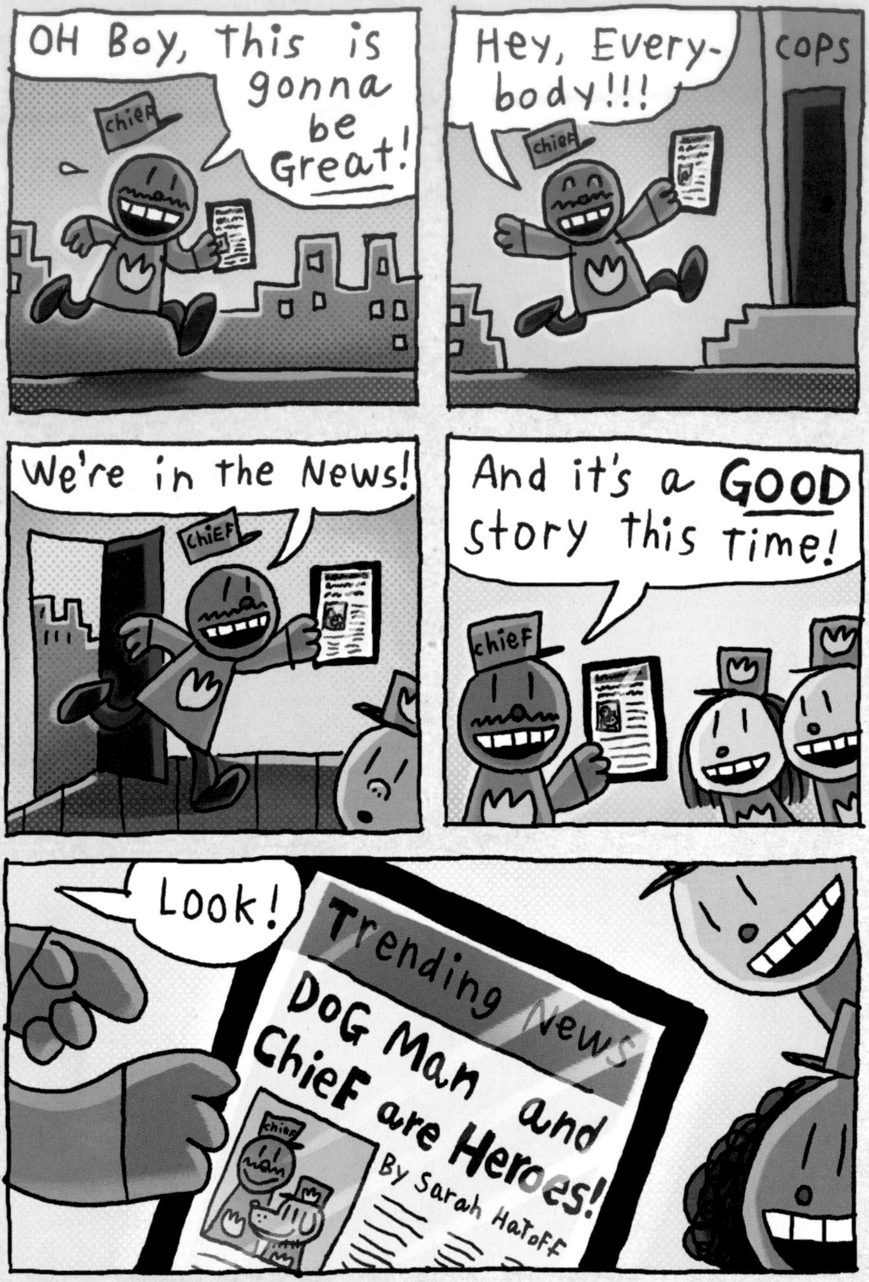
OH Boy, this is gonna be Great!
chief
Hey, Every-body!!!
COPS
chief
We're in the News!
chief
And it's a GOOD story this time!
chief
Look!
Trending News
DoG Man and ChieF are Heroes!
By Sarah HatoFF
chief

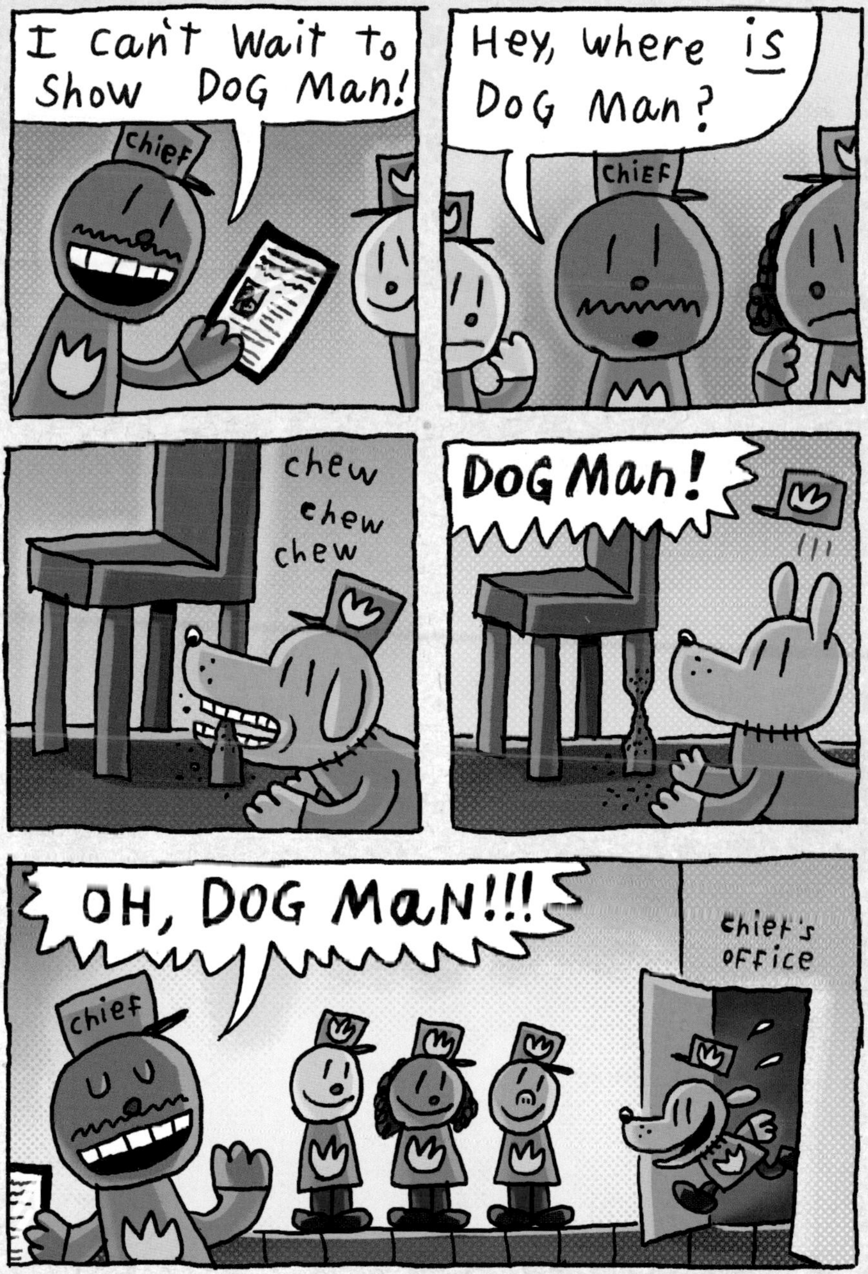
I can't wait to show DOG MAN!
chief
Hey, where is DOG Man?
chief
chew
chew
chew
DOG Man!
OH, DOG MaN!!!
chief
chief's office

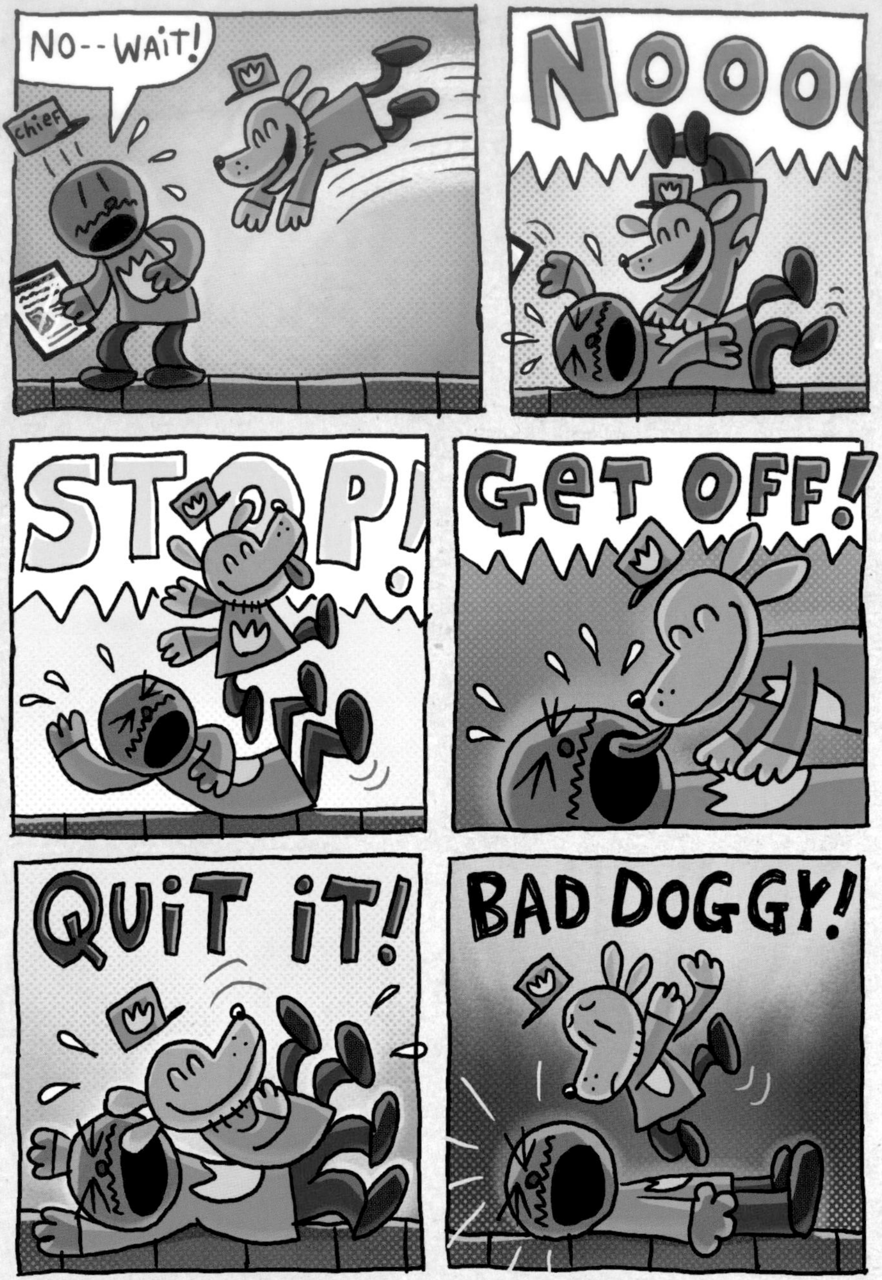
NO--WAIT!
chief
NOOOO
STOP!
GET OFF!
QUIT IT!
BAD DOGGY!

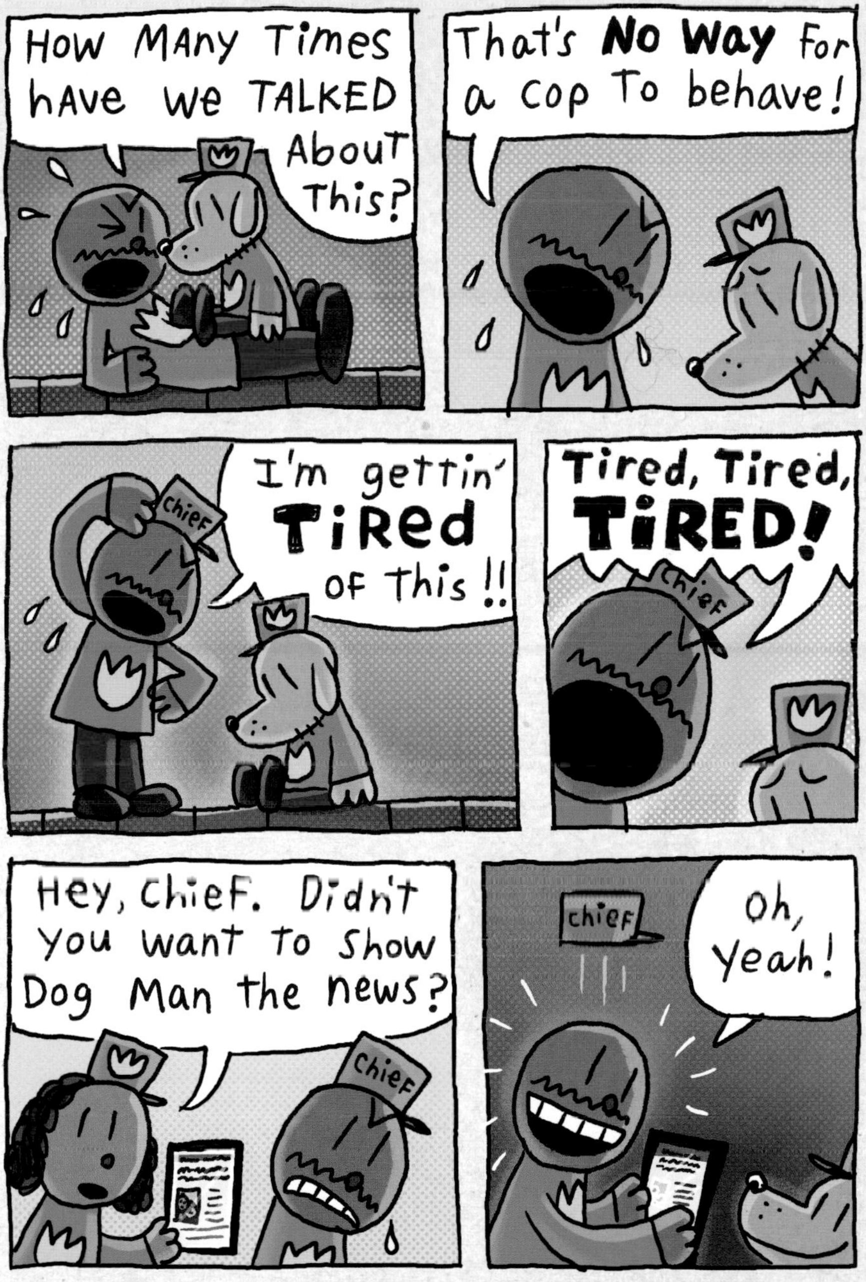
How Many Times have we TALKED About This?
That's **No Way** For a cop To behave!
I'm gettin' **TIRED** of This!!
Tired, Tired, **TIRED!**
Hey, Chief. Didn't you want to show Dog Man the news?
Oh, yeah!
Chief

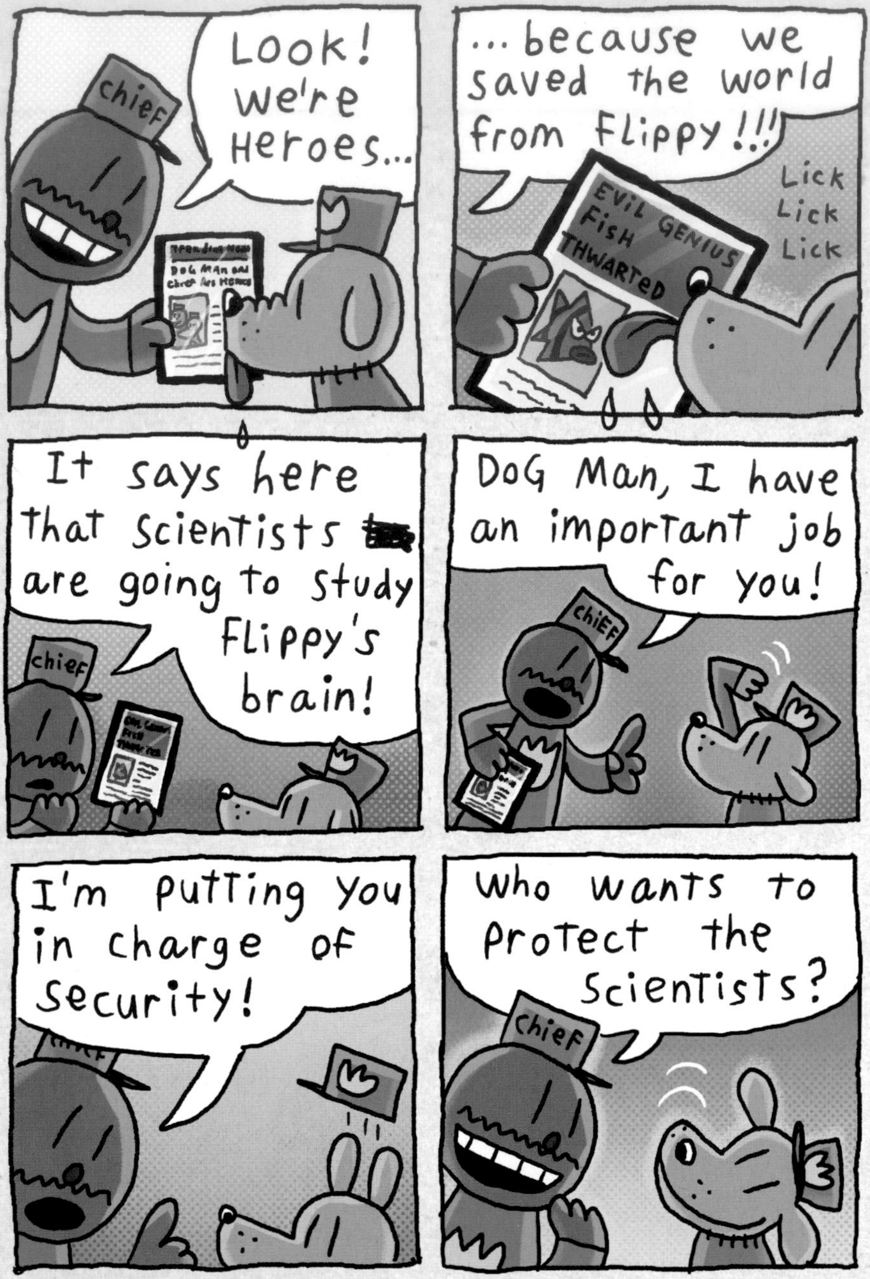
chief
Look! We're Heroes...
...because we saved the world from Flippy!!!
EVIL GENIUS FISH THWARTED
Lick Lick Lick
It says here that scientists are going to study Flippy's brain!
chief
Dog Man, I have an important job for you!
chief
I'm putting you in charge of security!
Who wants to protect the scientists?
chief

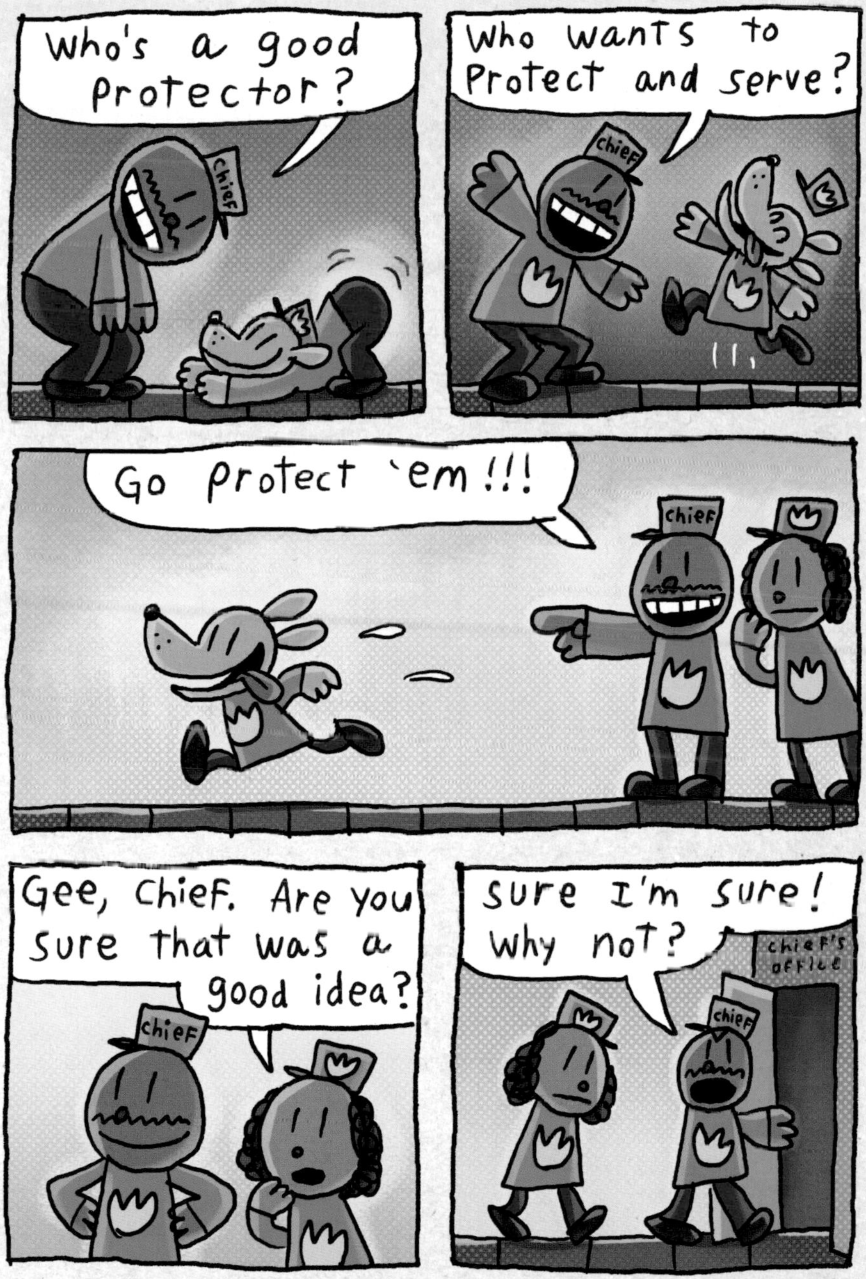
Who's a good protector?
Who wants to Protect and serve?
chief
Go protect 'em!!!
chief
Gee, Chief. Are you sure that was a good idea?
chief
Sure I'm sure! Why not?
chief's office
chief

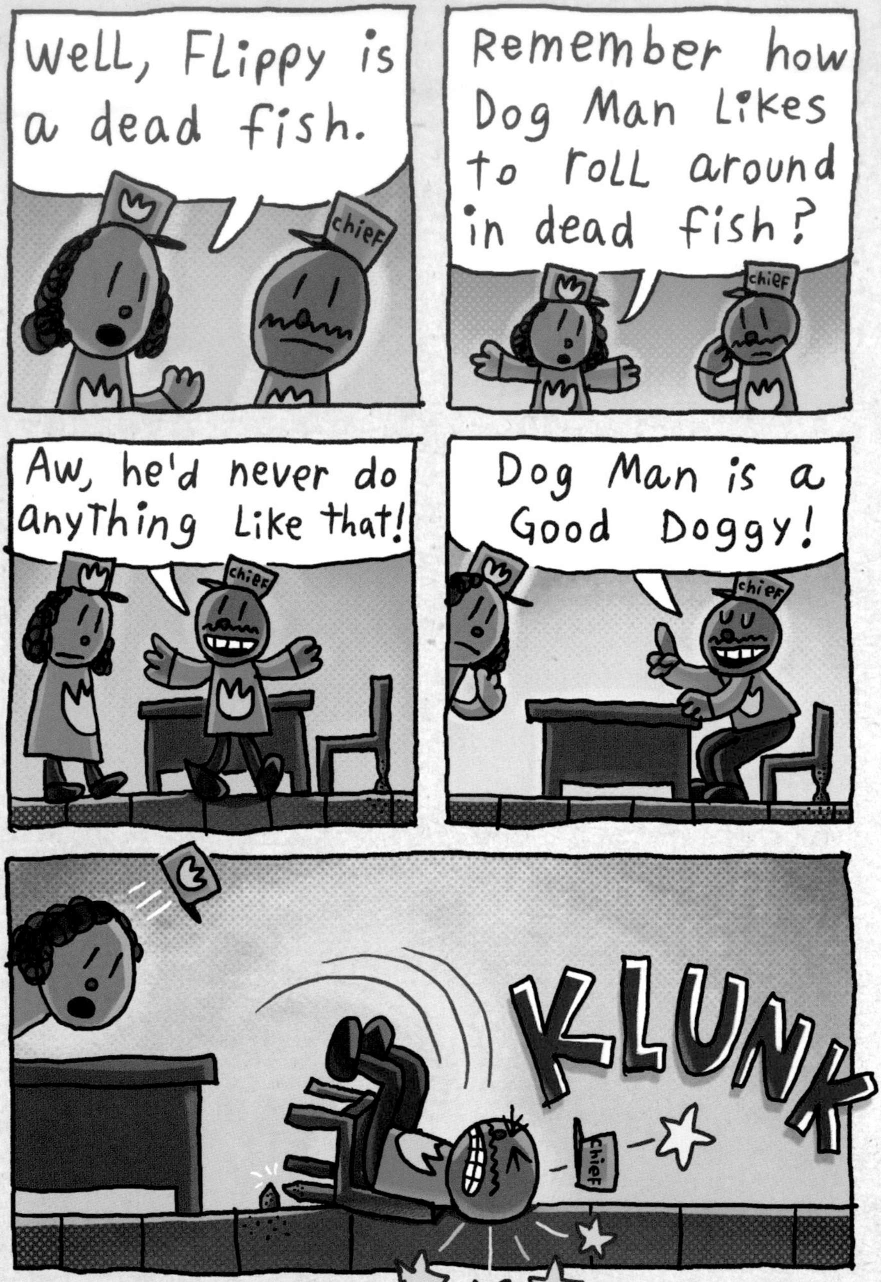
Well, Flippy is a dead fish.
Remember how Dog Man Likes to roll around in dead fish?
chief
Aw, he'd never do anything Like that!
Dog Man is a Good Doggy!
KLUNK
chief

Chapter the Second: You've Gotta Be Kitten Me!

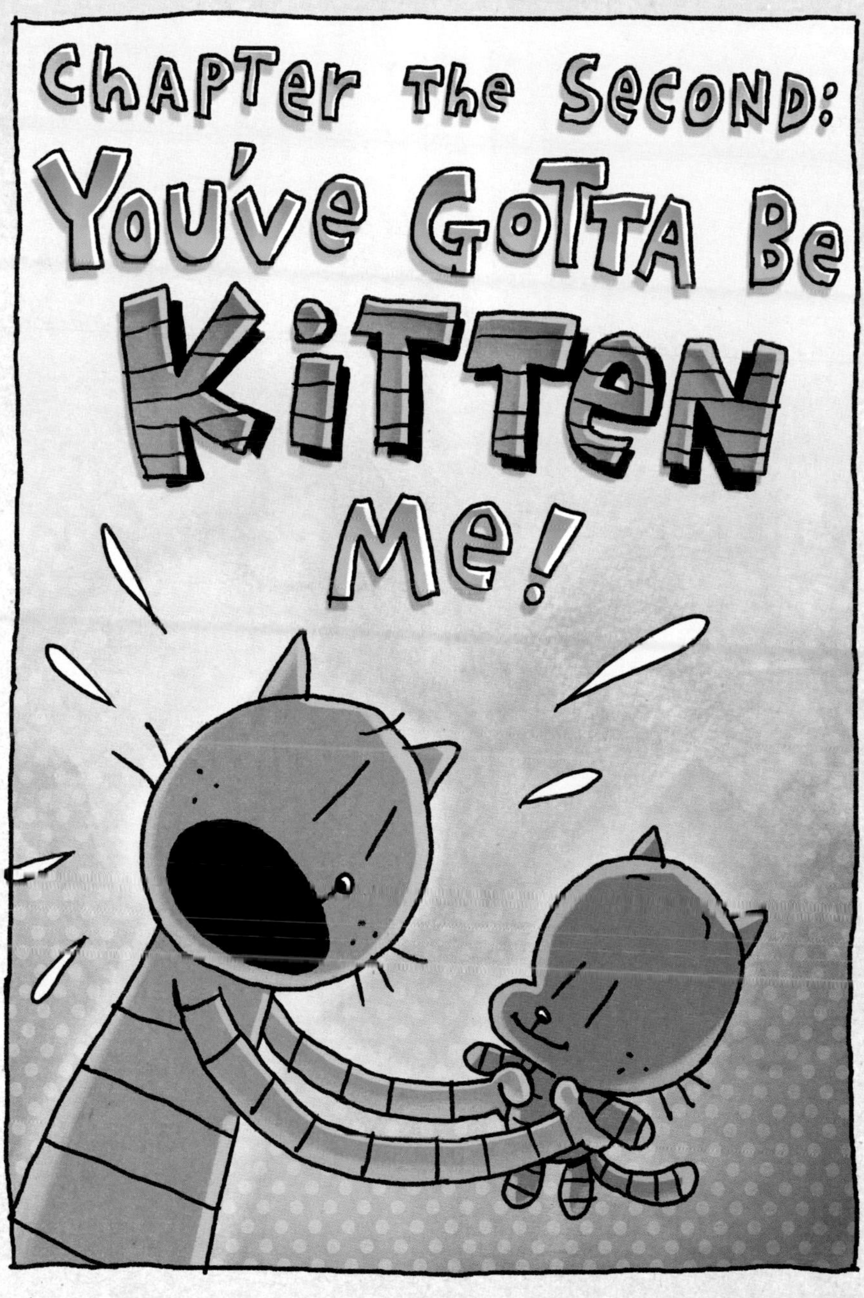

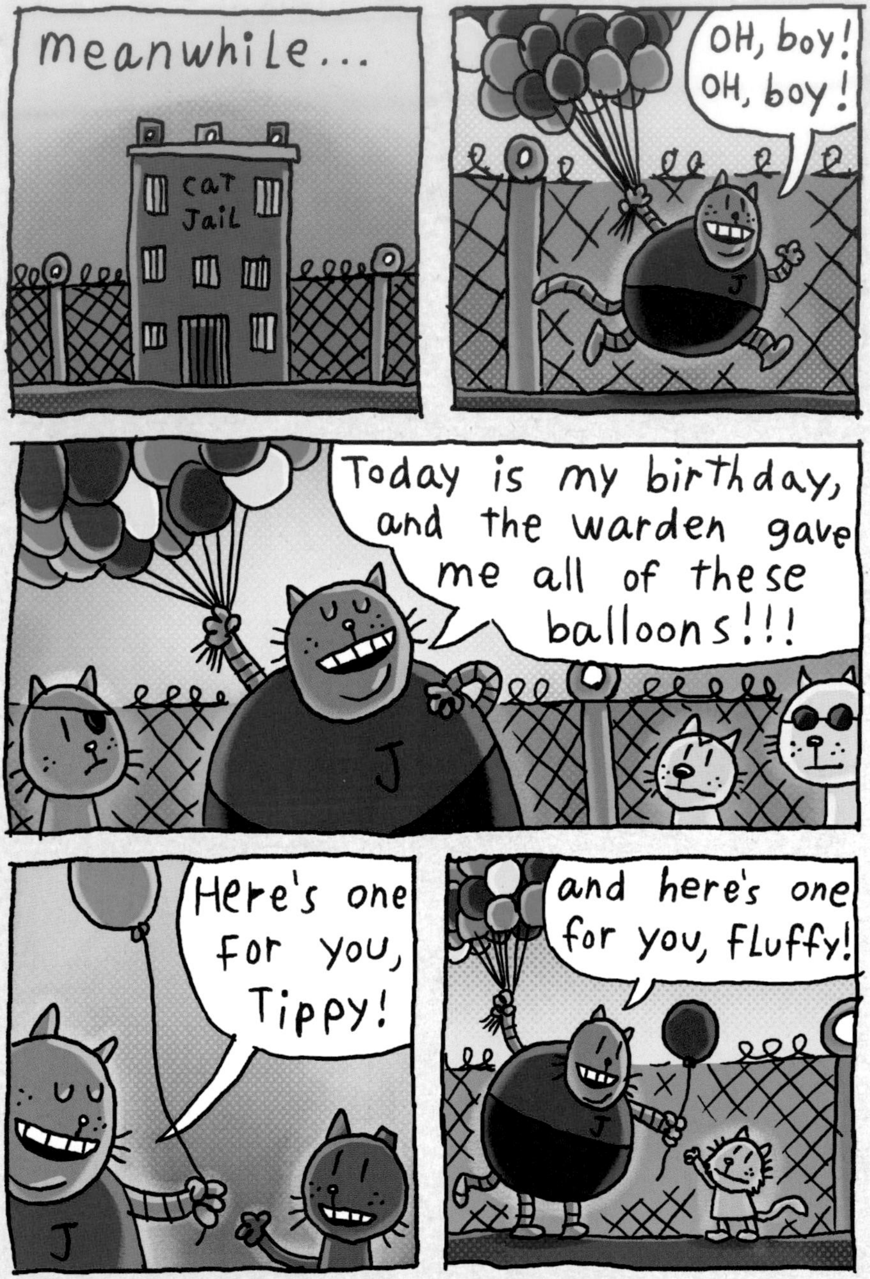
meanwhile...
Cat Jail
OH, boy! OH, boy!
Today is my birthday, and the warden gave me all of these balloons!!!
Here's one for you, Tippy!
and here's one for you, Fluffy!

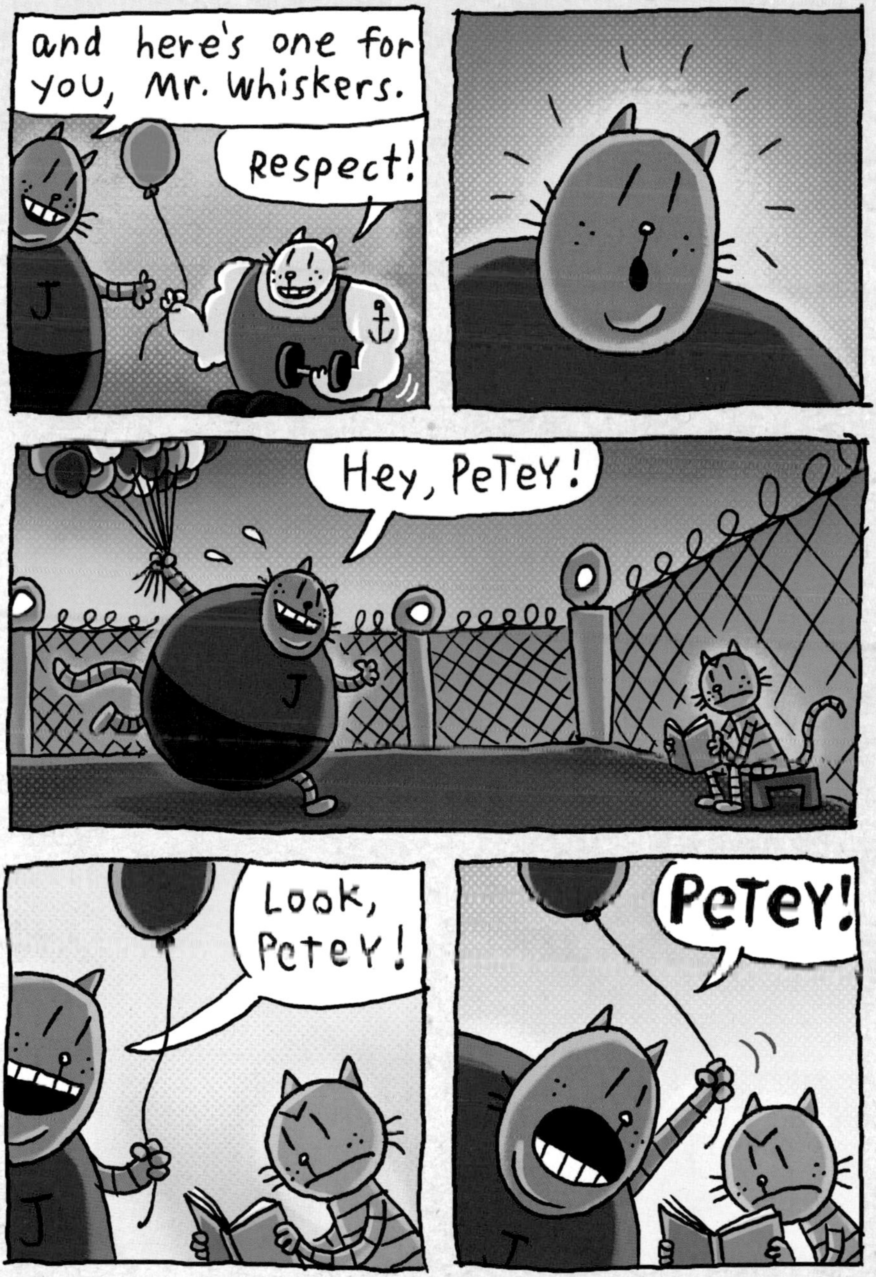
and here's one for you, Mr. Whiskers.
Respect!
Hey, PeTey!
Look, PeTeY!
PeTeY!

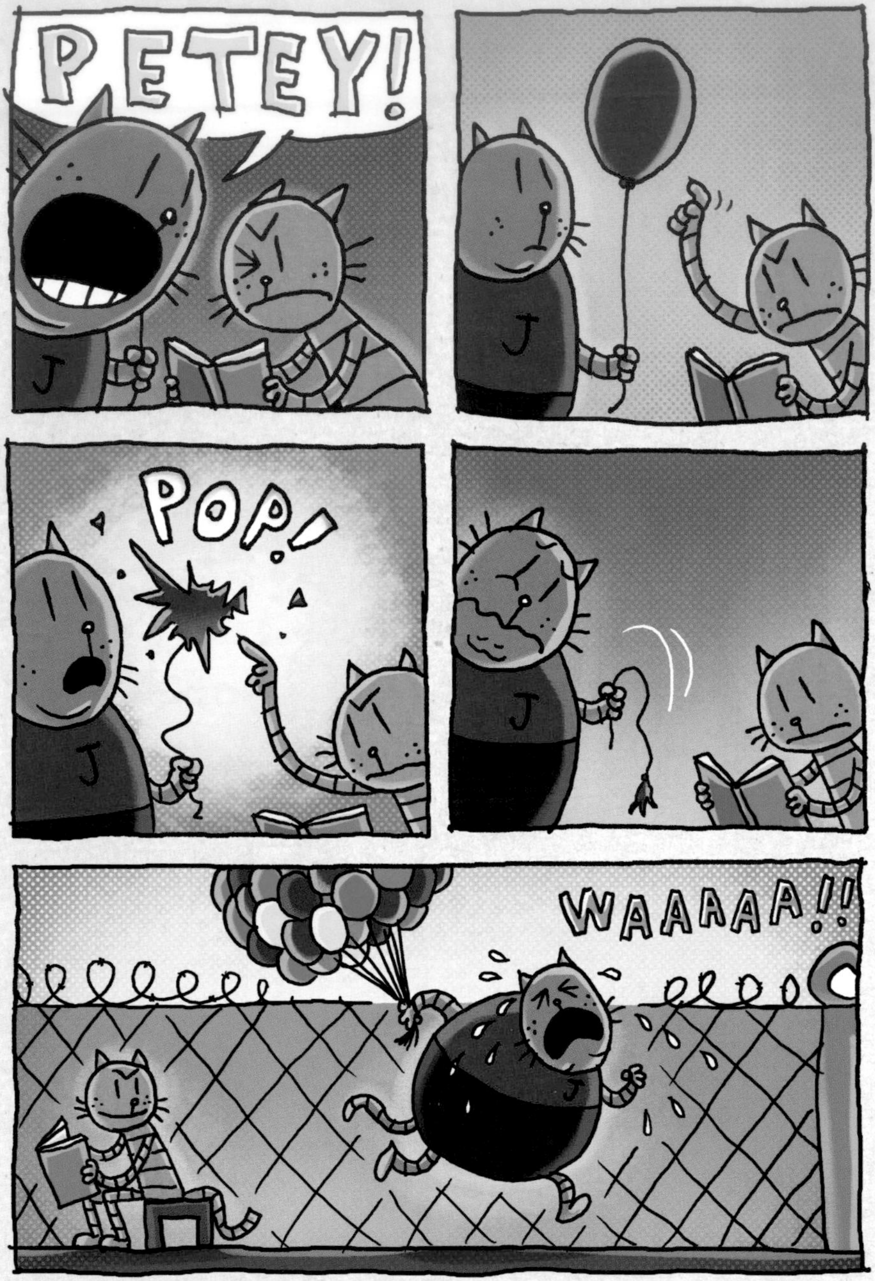
PETEY!
POP!
WAAAAA!!

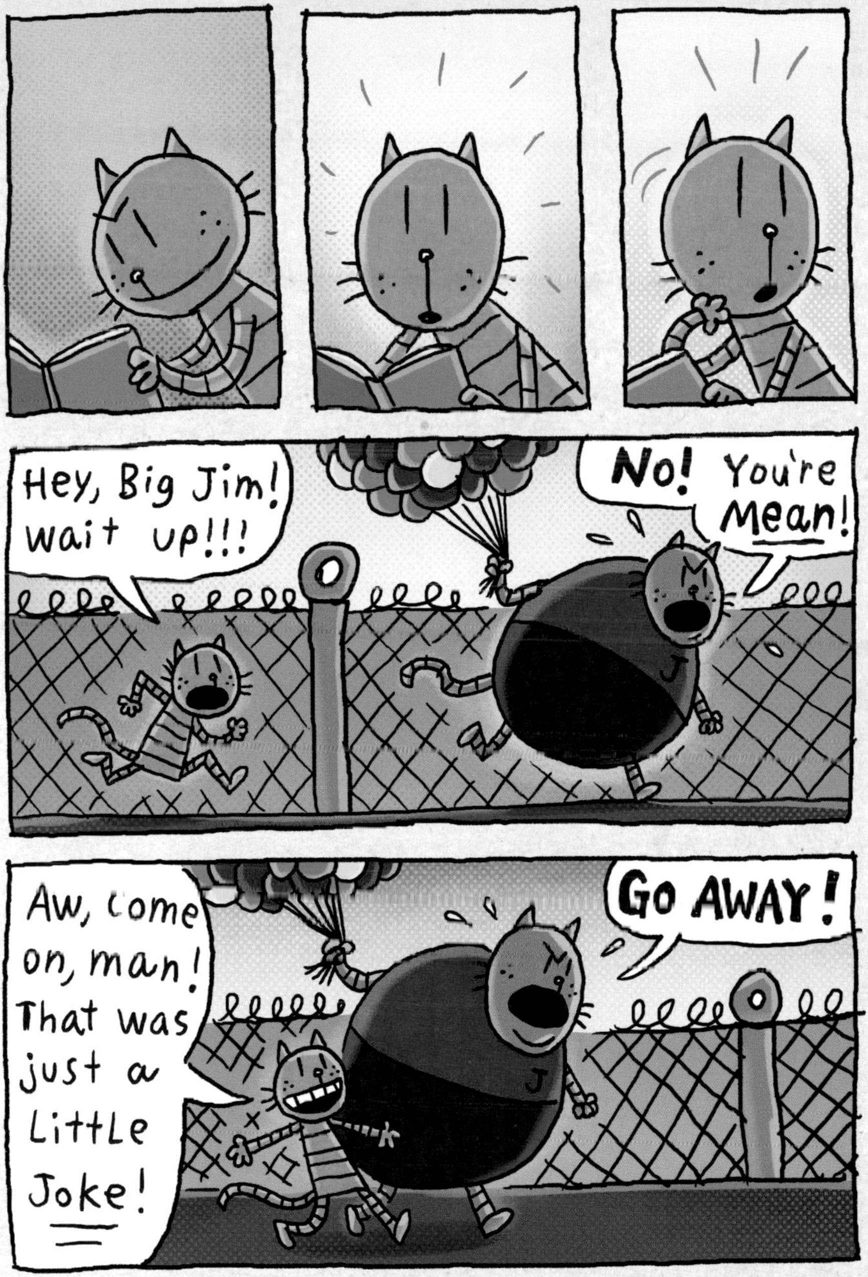
Hey, Big Jim! wait up!!!
No! You're Mean!
Aw, come on, man! That was just a Little Joke!
GO AWAY!

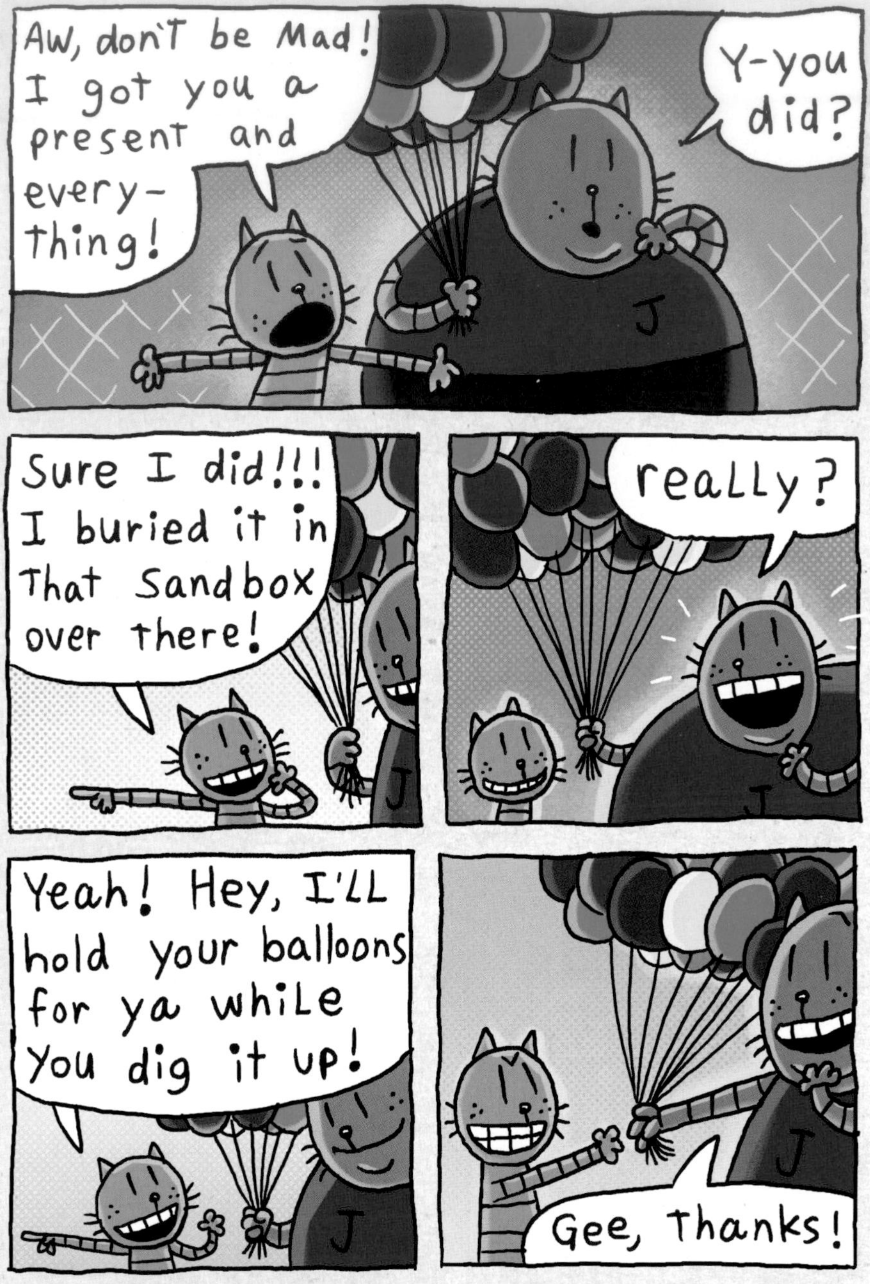
Aw, don't be Mad! I got you a present and every-thing!
Y-you did?
Sure I did!!! I buried it in That Sandbox over there!
really?
Yeah! Hey, I'LL hold your balloons for ya whiLe you dig it up!
Gee, Thanks!

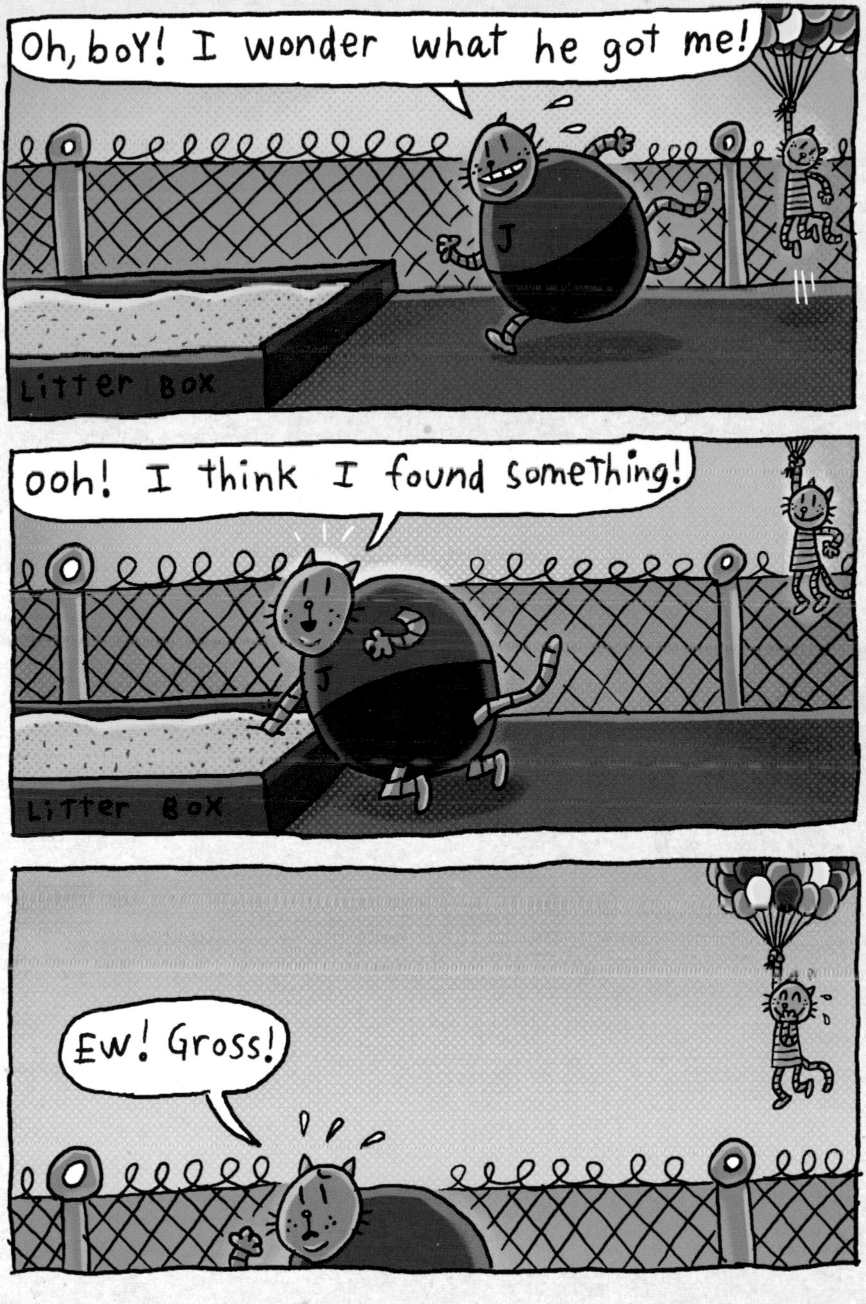
Oh, boY! I wonder what he got me!
LiTTer BOX
ooh! I think I found something!
LiTTer BOX
Ew! Gross!

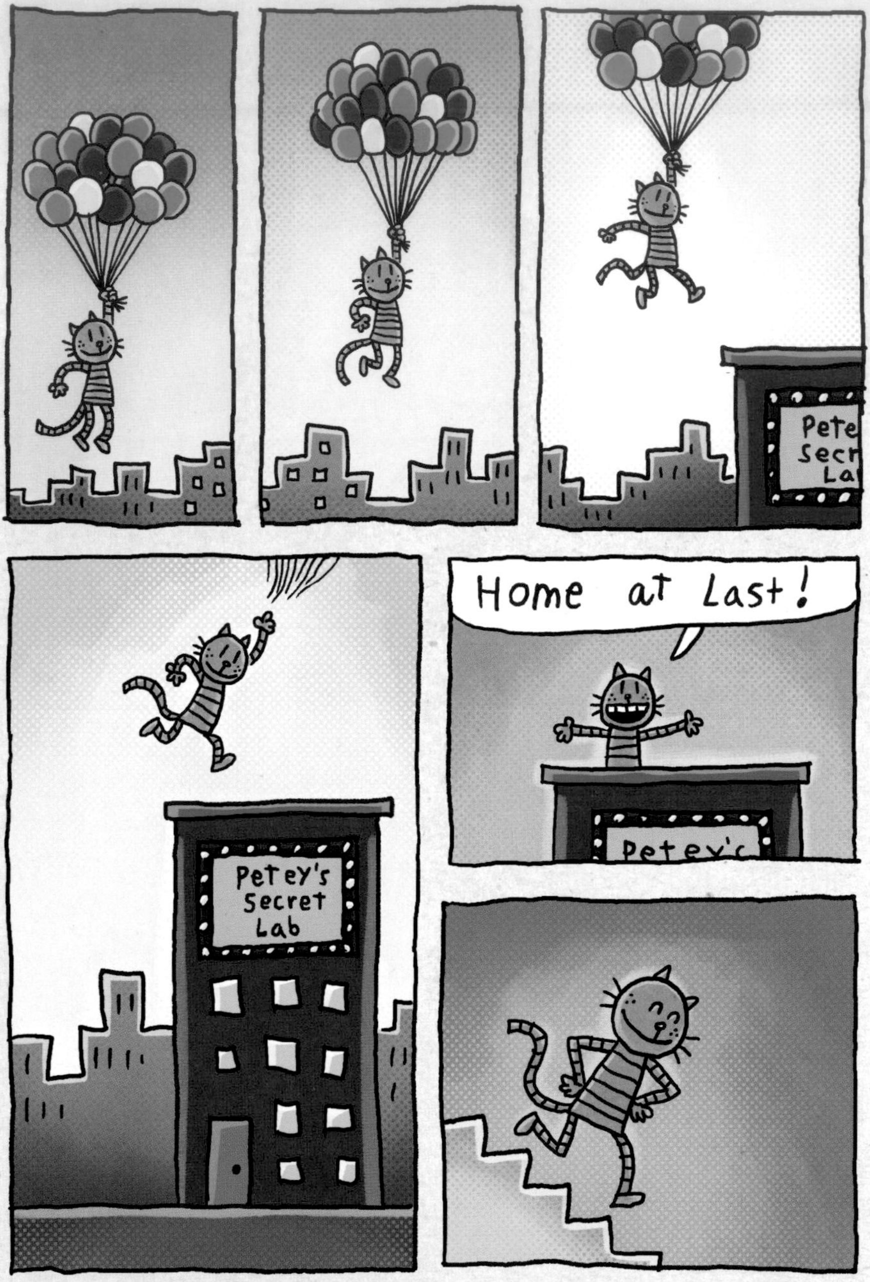
Pete
Secr
La
Petey's
Secret
Lab
Home at Last!
Petey's

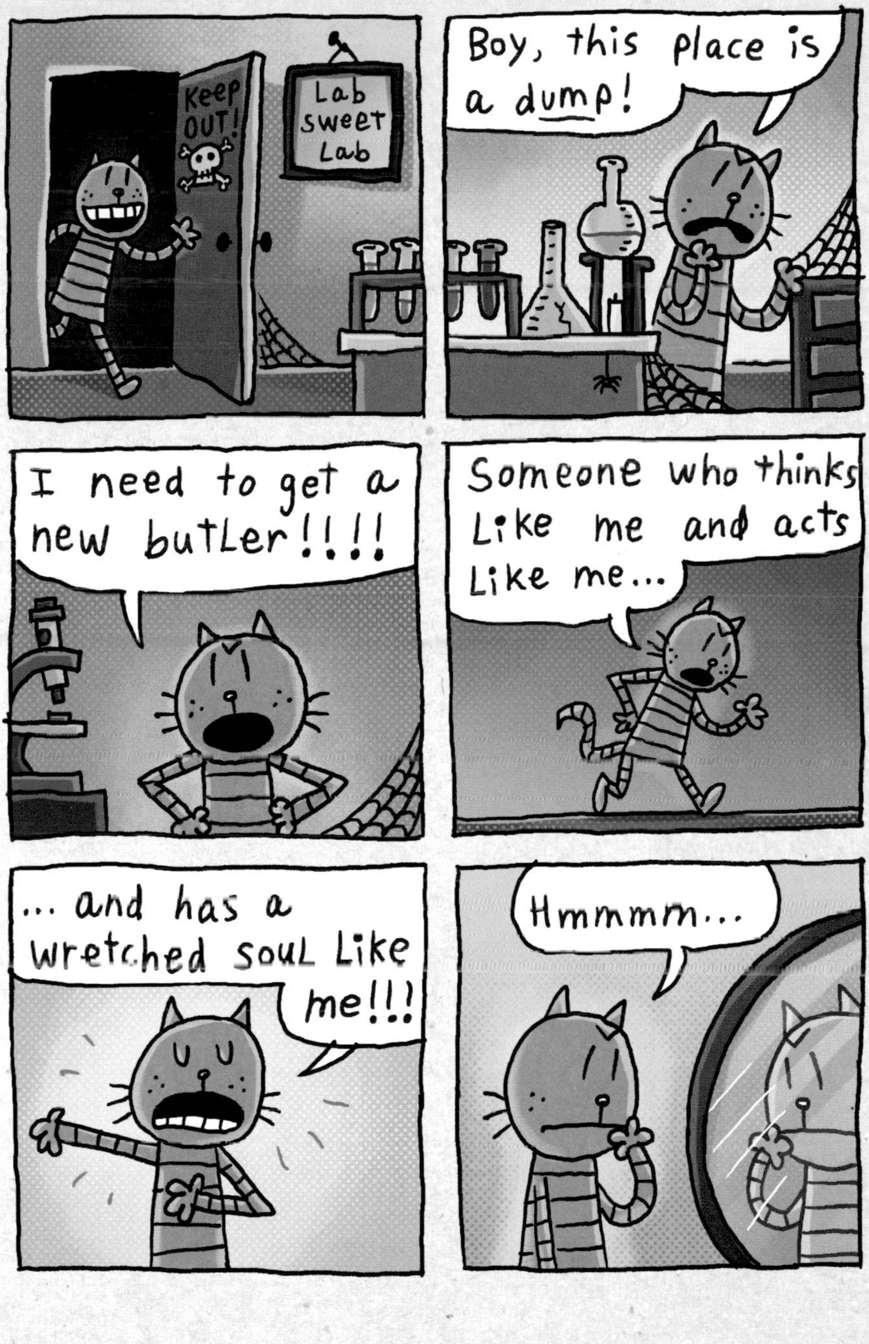
Keep OUT!
Lab Sweet Lab
Boy, this place is a dump!
I need to get a new butler!!!!
Someone who thinks like me and acts like me...
... and has a wretched soul like me!!!
Hmmmm...

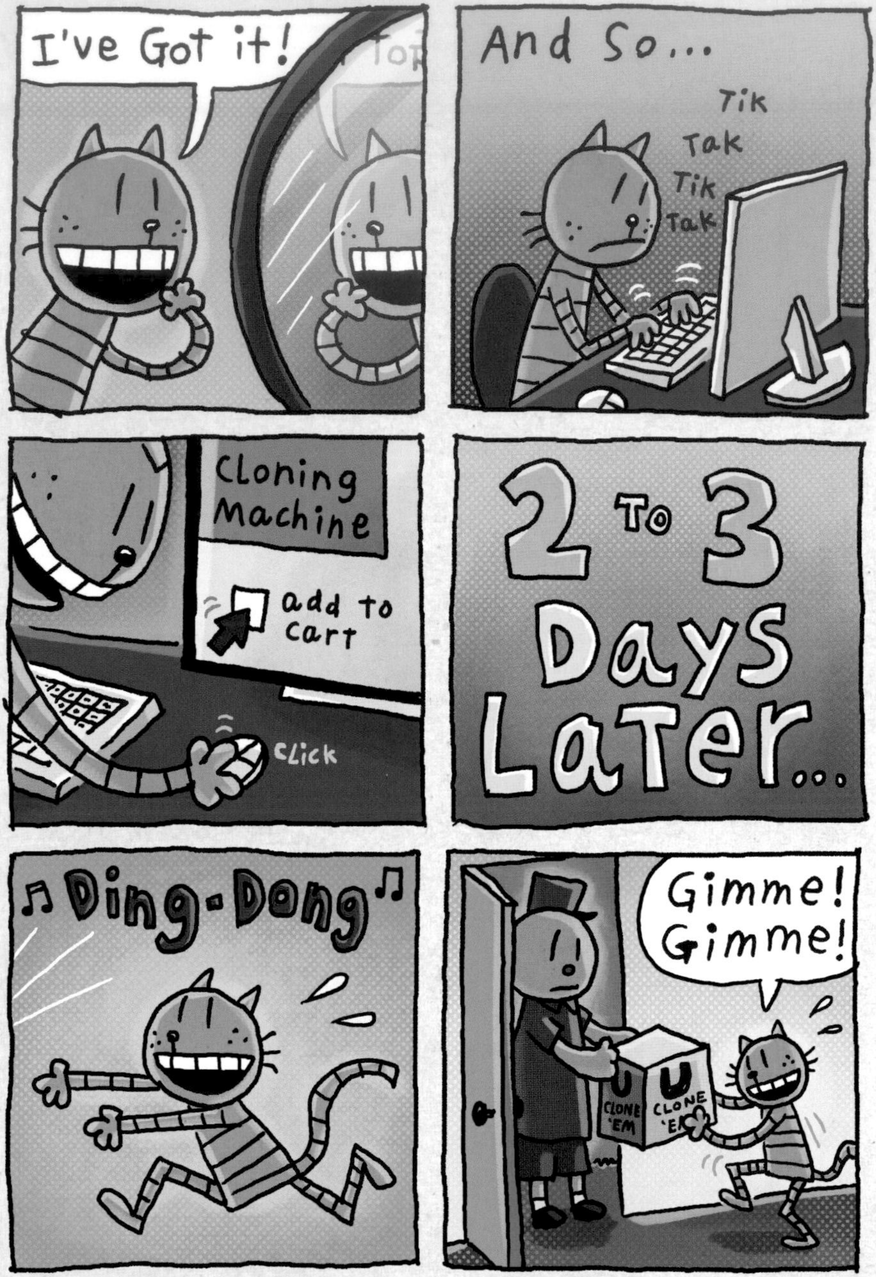
I've Got it!
And So...
Tik
Tak
Tik
Tak
Cloning Machine
add to cart
Click
2 To 3 Days Later...
Ding-Dong
Gimme! Gimme!
U CLONE 'EM

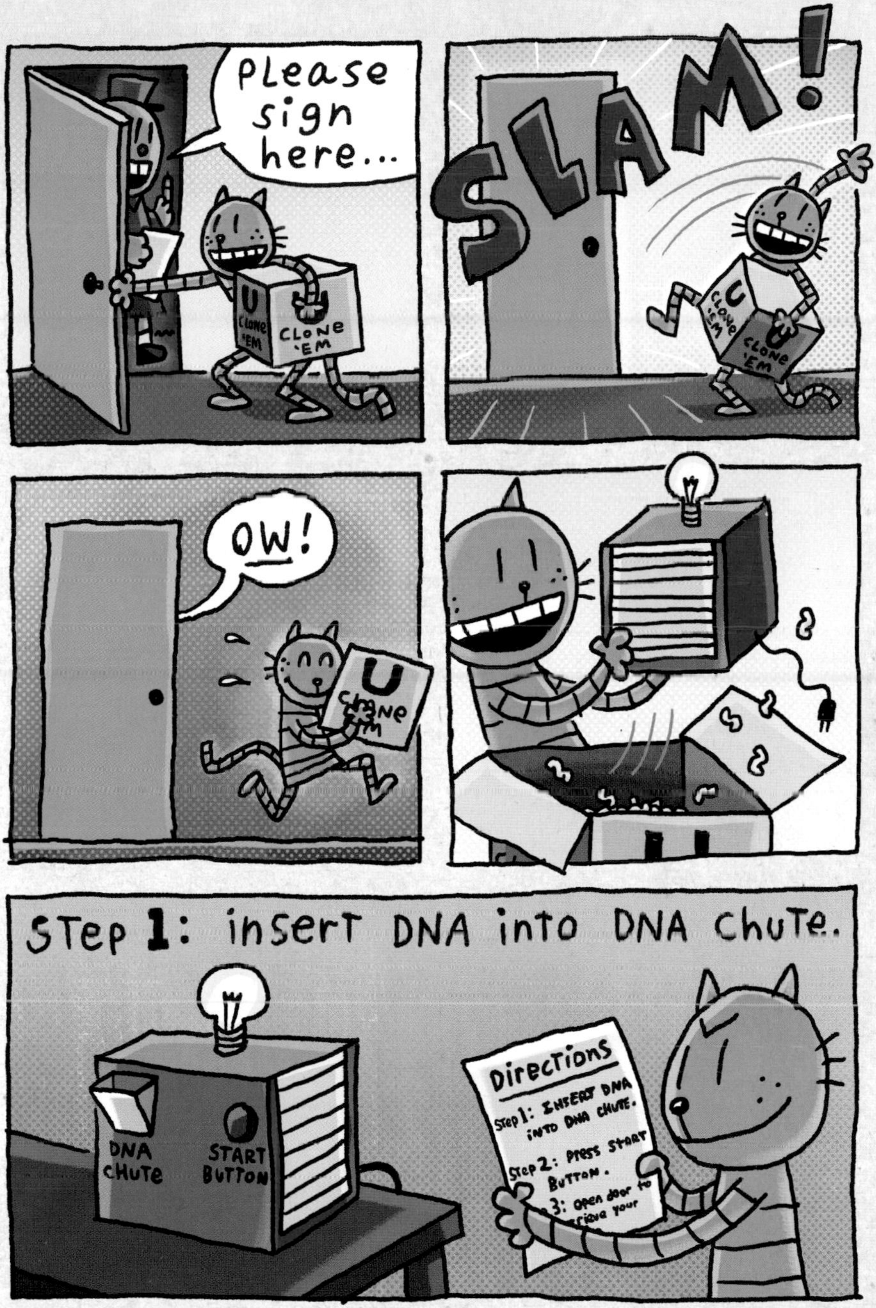
Please sign here...
U CLONE 'EM
U CLONE 'EM
SLAM!
U CLONE 'EM
U CLONE 'EM
OW!
U CLONE 'EM
STEP 1: insert DNA into DNA chute.
DNA CHUTE
START BUTTON
Directions
Step 1: INSERT DNA INTO DNA CHUTE.
Step 2: Press START BUTTON.

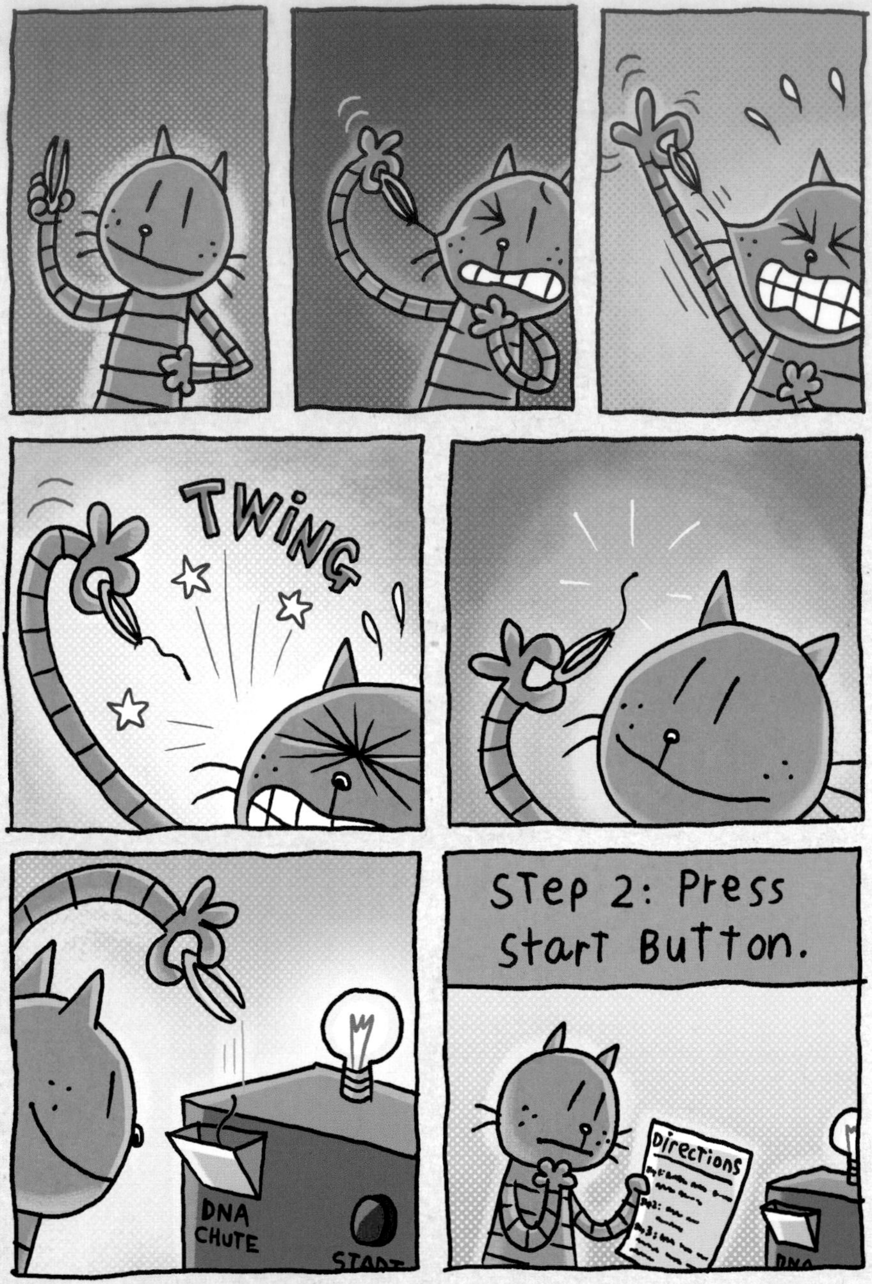
TWING
DNA CHUTE
STEP 2: Press start Button.
Directions

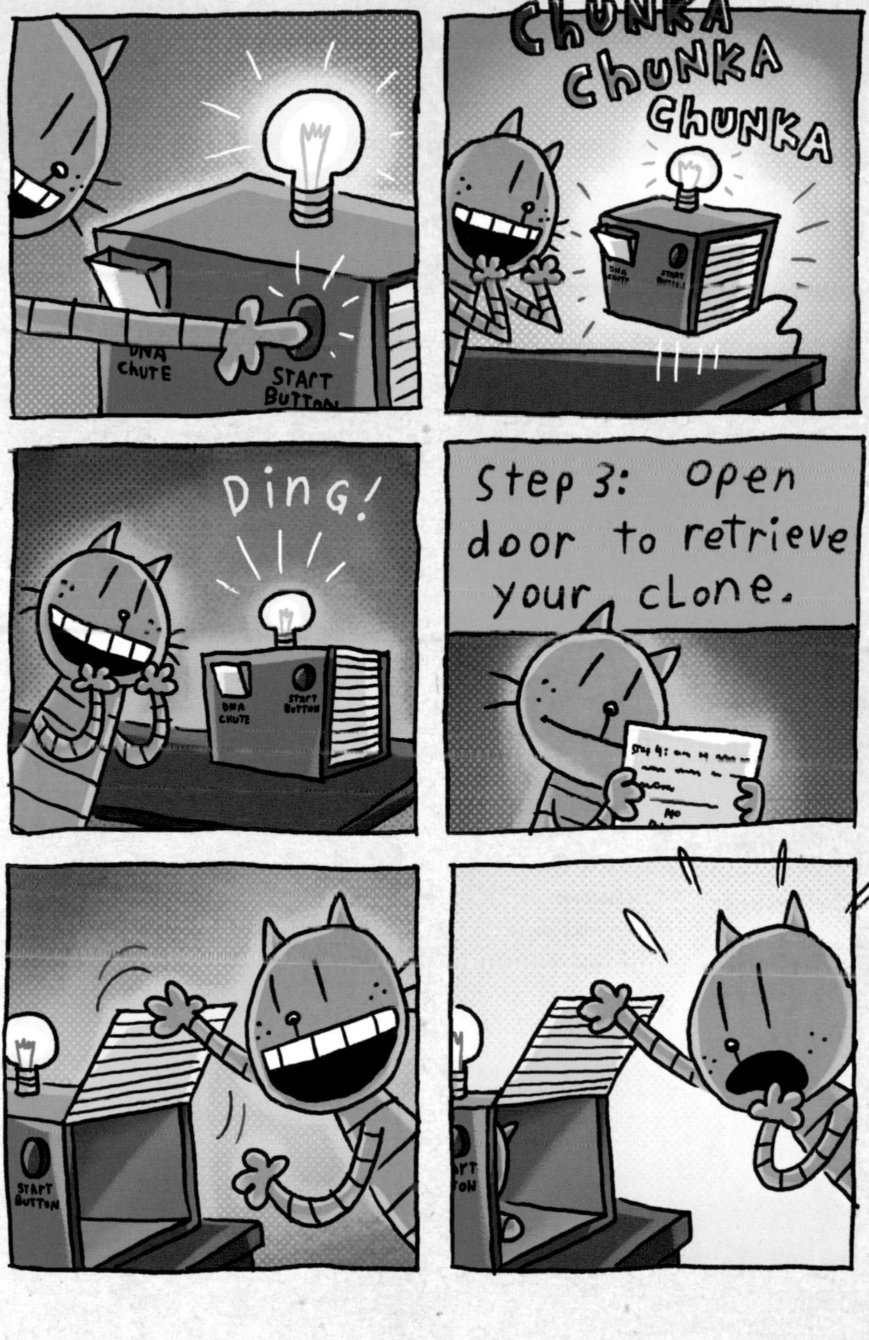
DNA CHUTE
START BUTTON
CHUNKA
CHUNKA
CHUNKA
DING!
Step 3: Open door to retrieve your clone.
START BUTTON

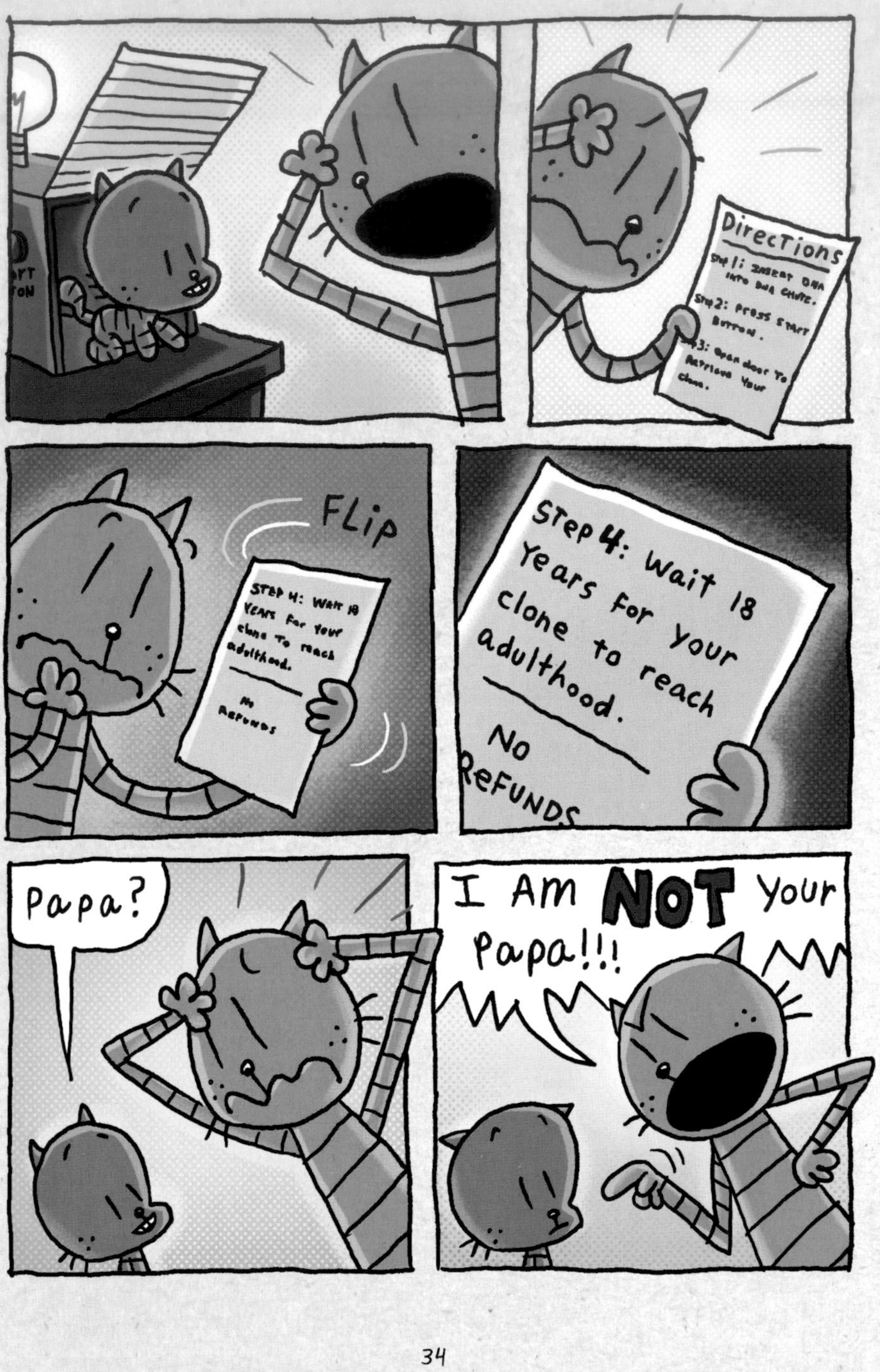

Directions
Step 1: Insert DNA into DNA chute.
Step 2: Press Start Button.
3: Open door To Retrieve Your clone.
FLip
Step 4: Wait 18 Years for your clone to reach adulthood.
No Refunds
Papa?
I Am NOT your Papa!!!

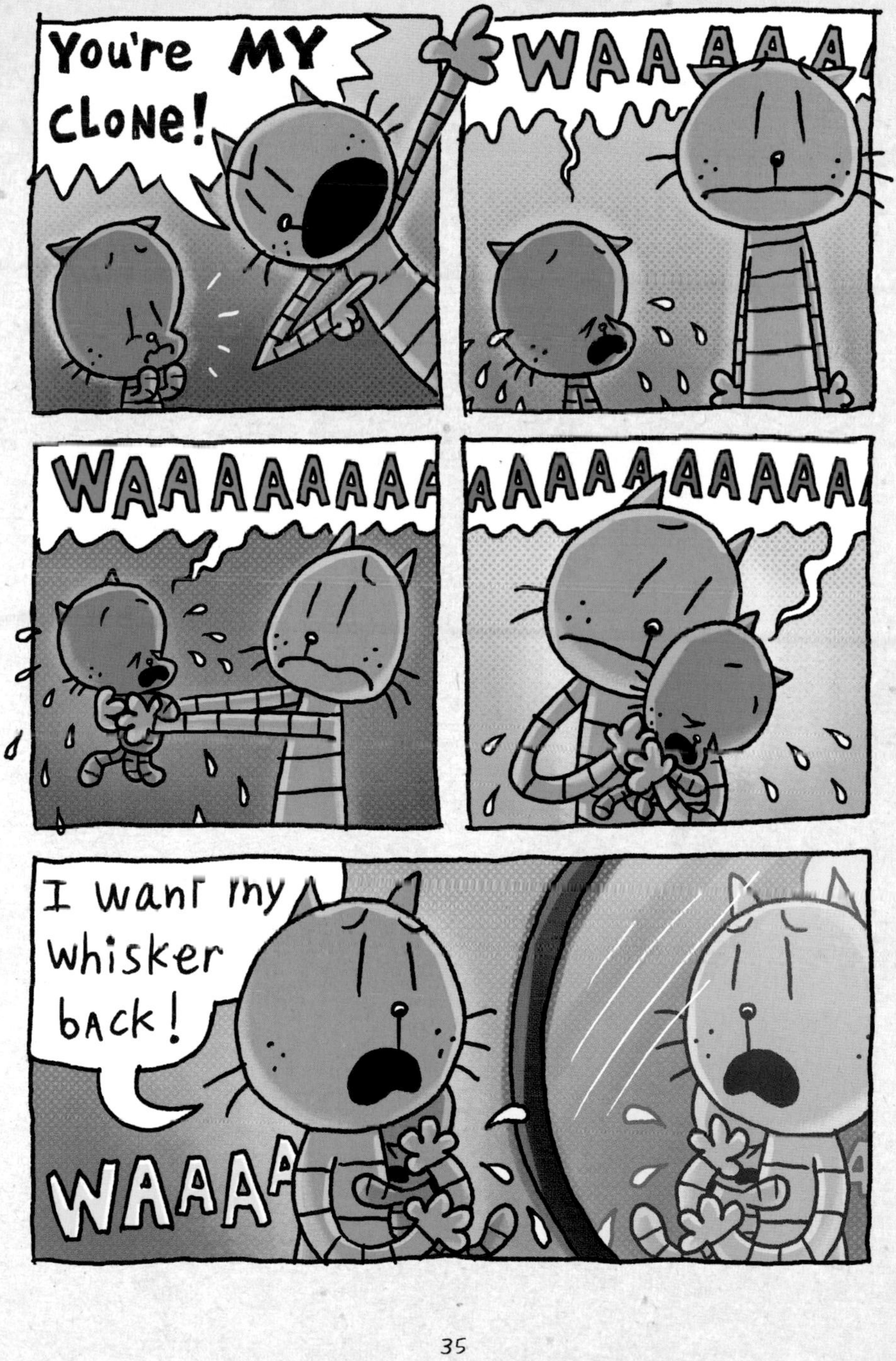
You're MY CLONE!
WAAAAAA
WAAAAAAAA
AAAAAAAAAA
I want my whisker back!
WAAAA

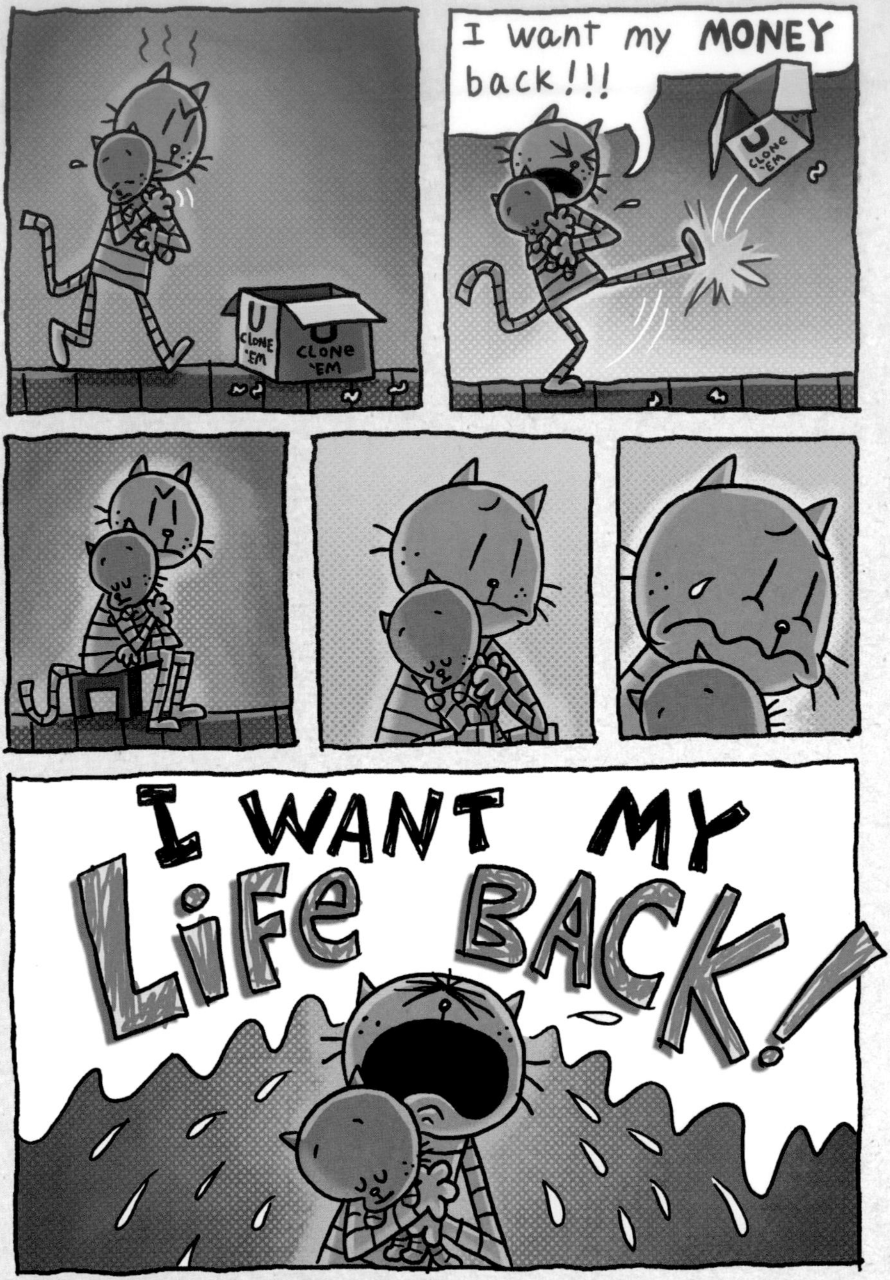
U CLONE 'EM
U CLONE 'EM
I want my MONEY back!!!
U CLONE 'EM
I WANT MY LIFE BACK!

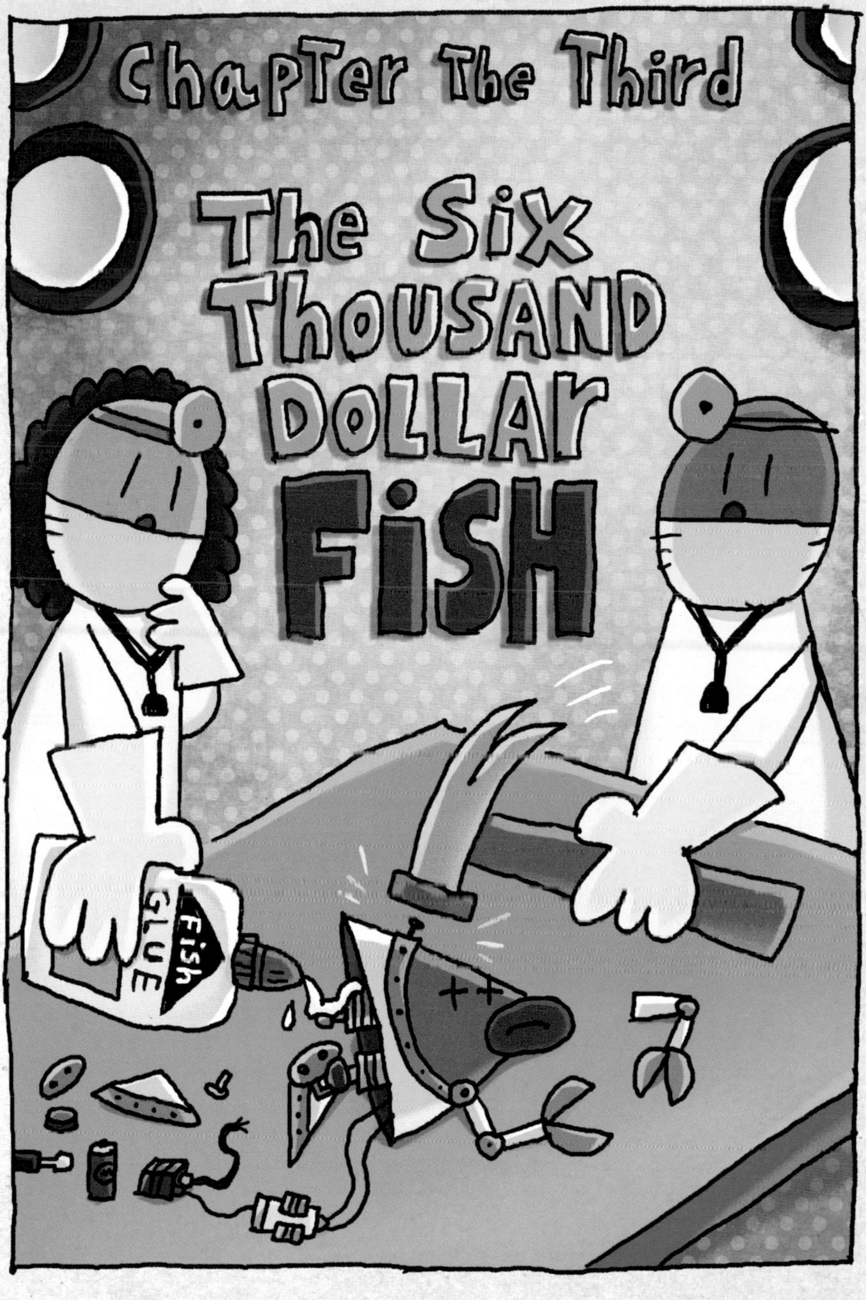
Chapter The Third
The Six Thousand Dollar Fish
Fish GLUE

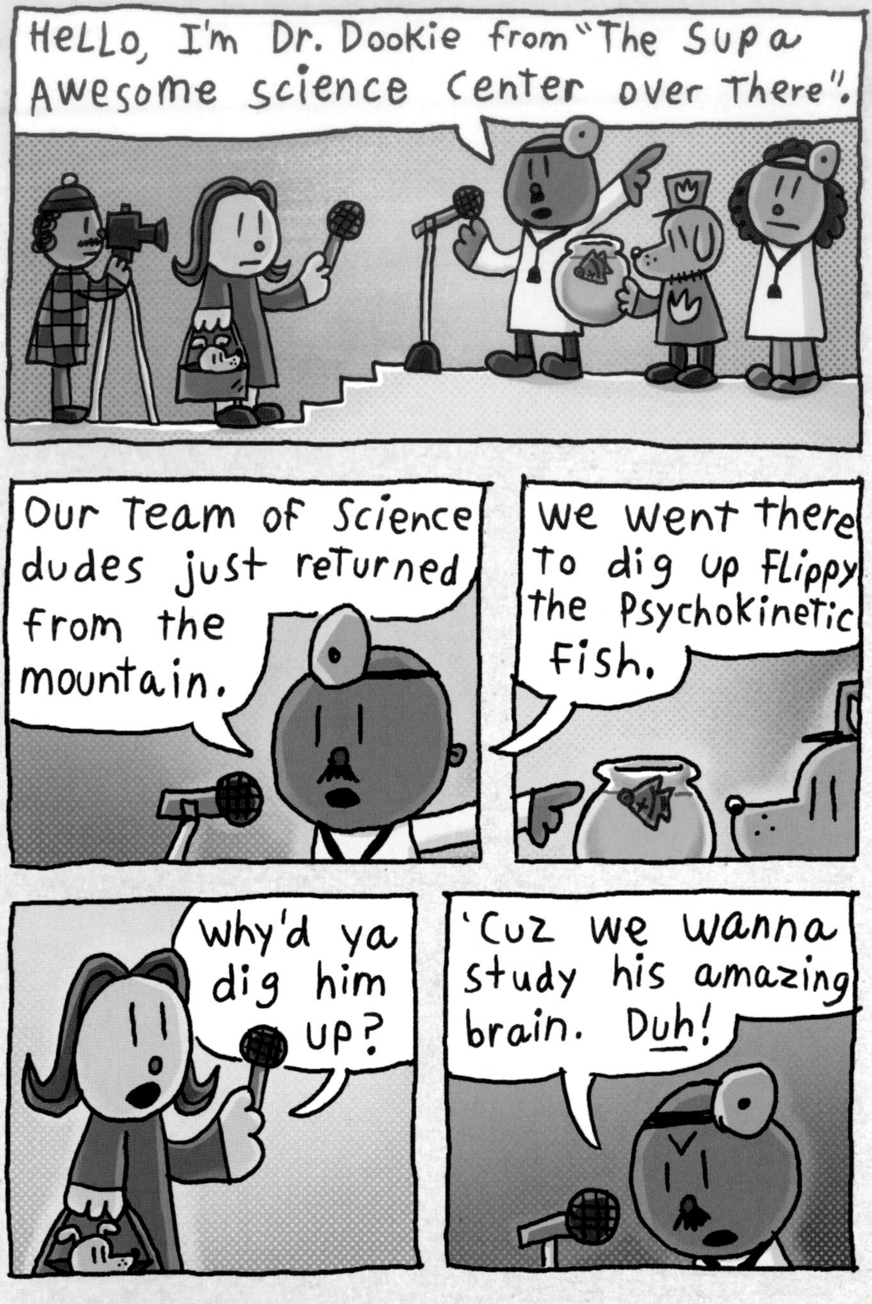
HeLLo, I'm Dr. Dookie from "The Supa Awesome science center over There".
Our Team of Science dudes just returned from the mountain.
We went there to dig up FLippy the Psychokinetic Fish.
Why'd ya dig him up?
'Cuz we wanna study his amazing brain. Duh!

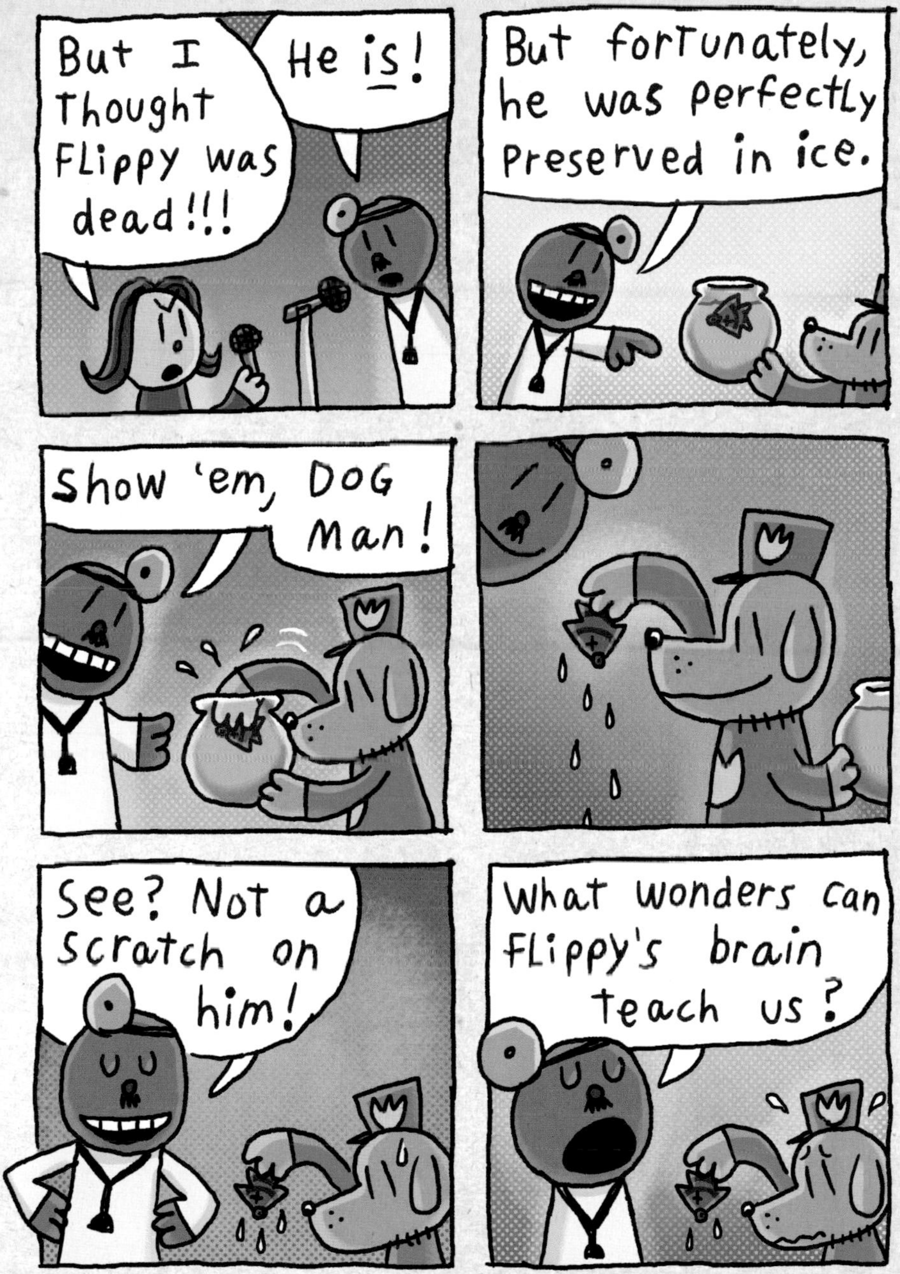
But I Thought Flippy was dead!!!
He is!
But fortunately, he was perfectly preserved in ice.
Show 'em, Dog Man!
See? Not a scratch on him!
What wonders can Flippy's brain teach us?

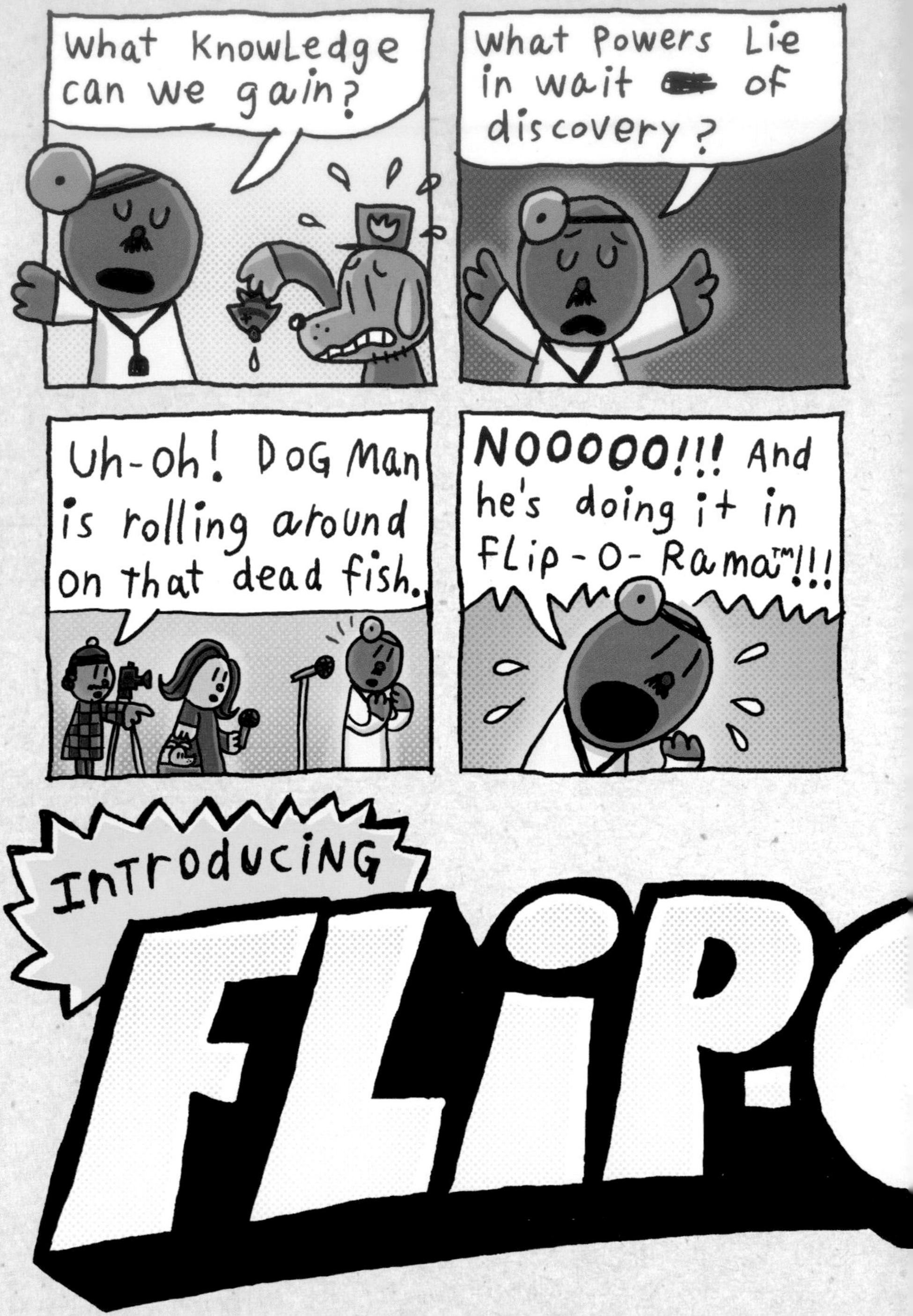
What Knowledge can we gain?
What Powers Lie in wait [redacted] of discovery?
Uh-Oh! DOG Man is rolling around on that dead fish.
NOOOOO!!! And he's doing it in FLip-O-Rama™!!!
INTRODUCING
FLIP

STEP 1.

First, place your left hand inside the dotted lines marked "Left hand here". Hold the book open FLAT!

STEP 2:

Grasp the right-hand page with your thumb and index finger (inside the dotted lines marked "Right Thumb Here").

STEP 3:

Now QUICKLY flip the right-hand page back and forth until the picture appears to be Animated.

(for extra fun, try adding your own sound-effects!)

O-RAMA

Remember,

while you are flipping,
be sure you can see
the image on page **43**
AND the image on page **45**.

If you flip quickly,
the two pictures will
start to look like
one **ANimated** cartoon!

Don't forget to
add your own
sound-effects!

Left
hand here.

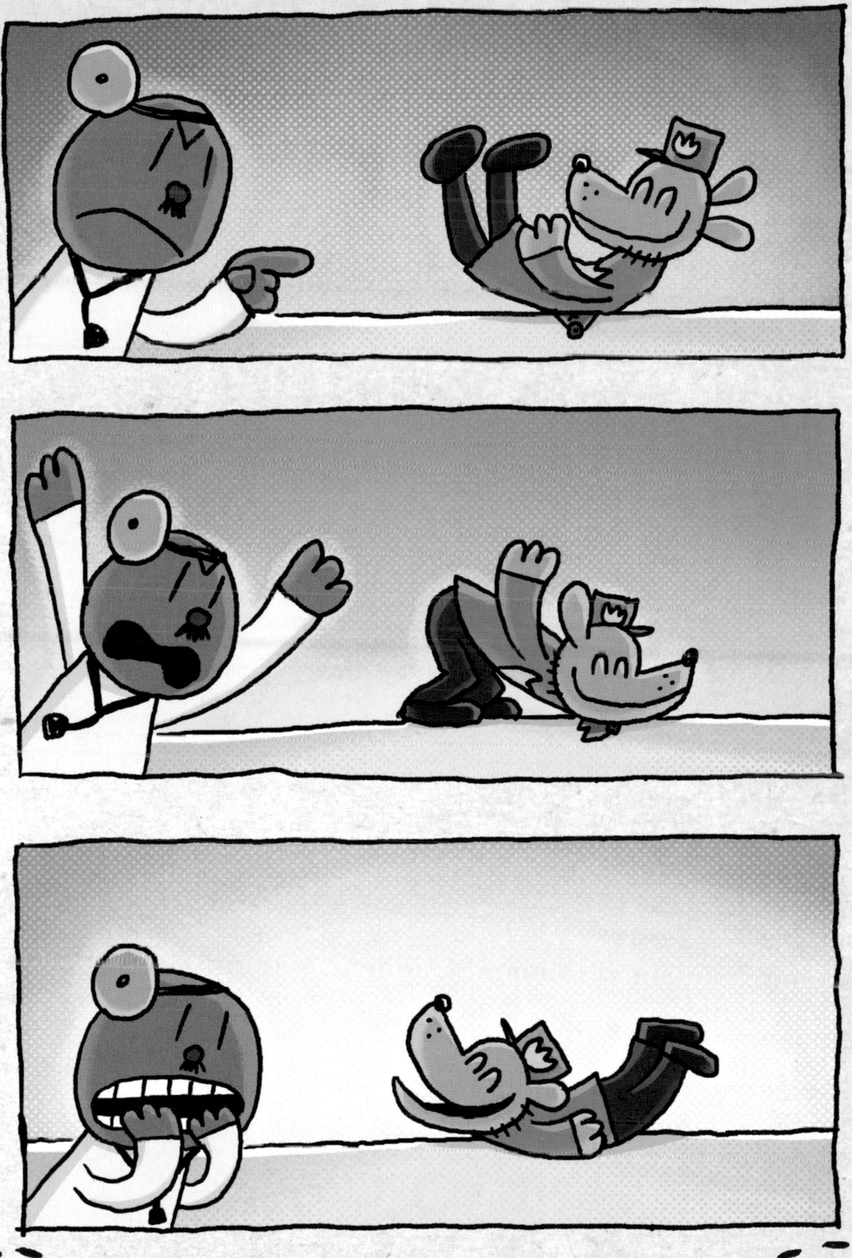

Right Thumb here.

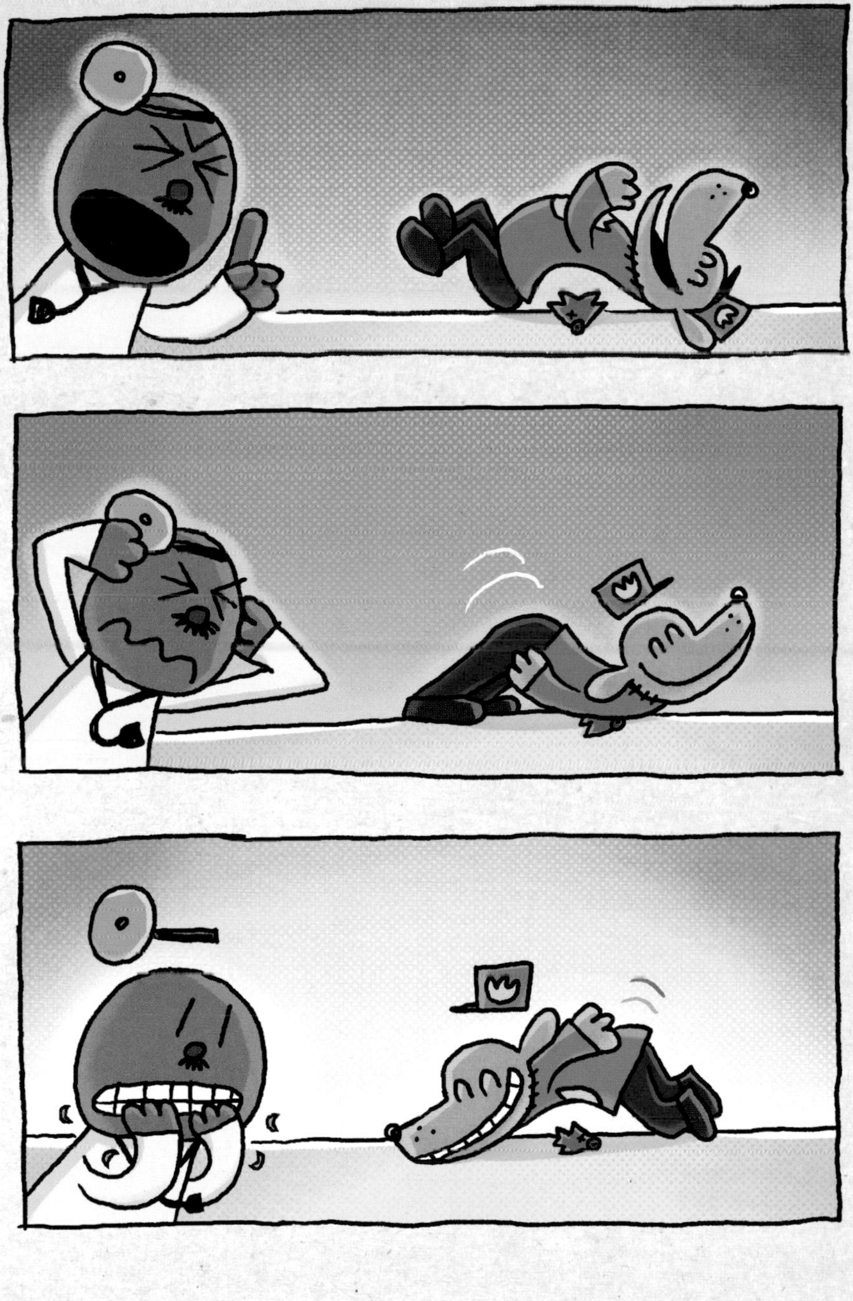

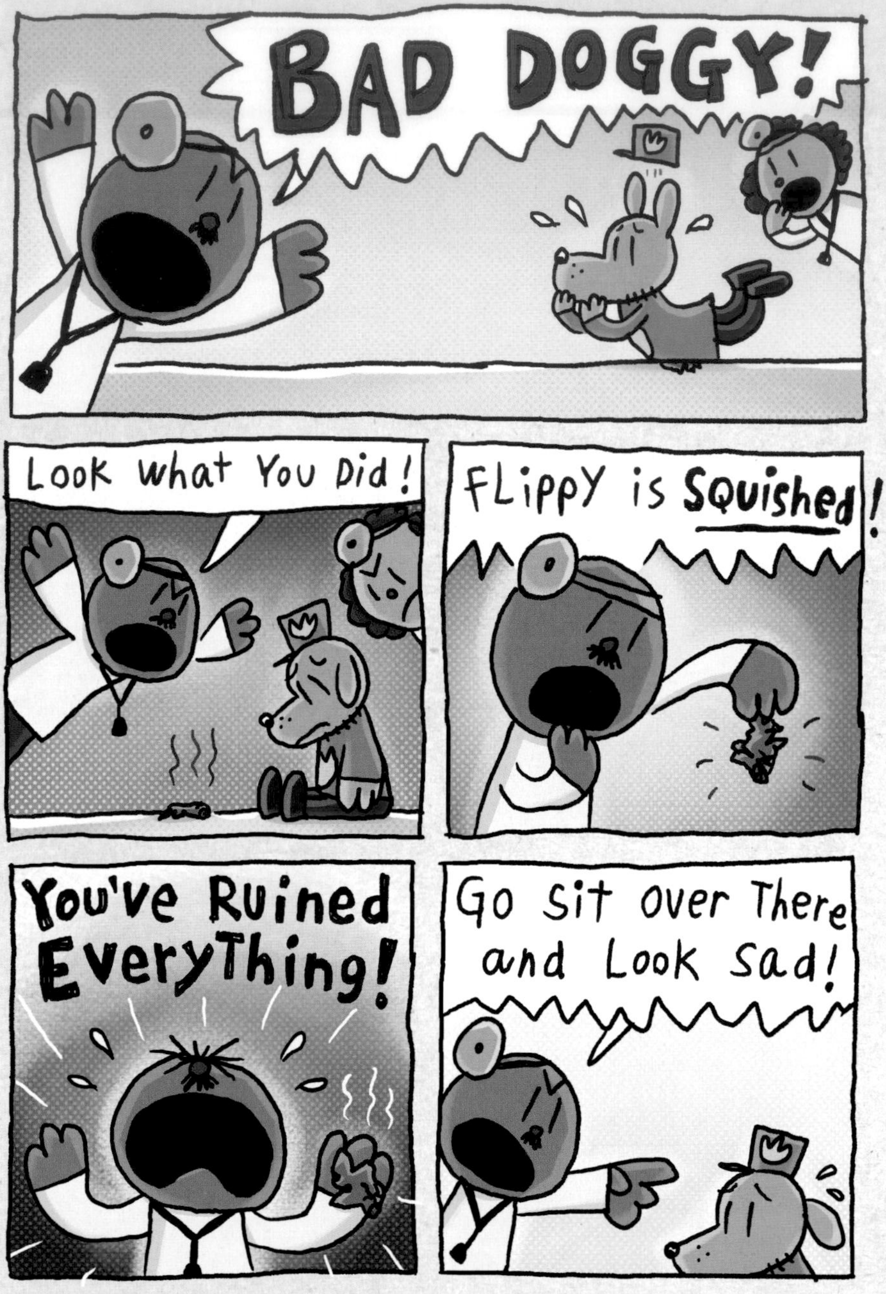
BAD DOGGY!
Look what You Did!
FLippY is Squished!
You've Ruined EveryThing!
Go sit over There and Look sad!

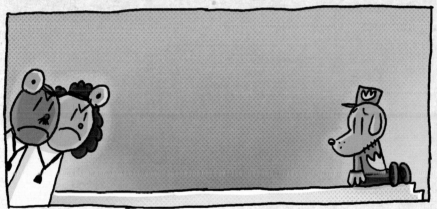

SADDER!!!

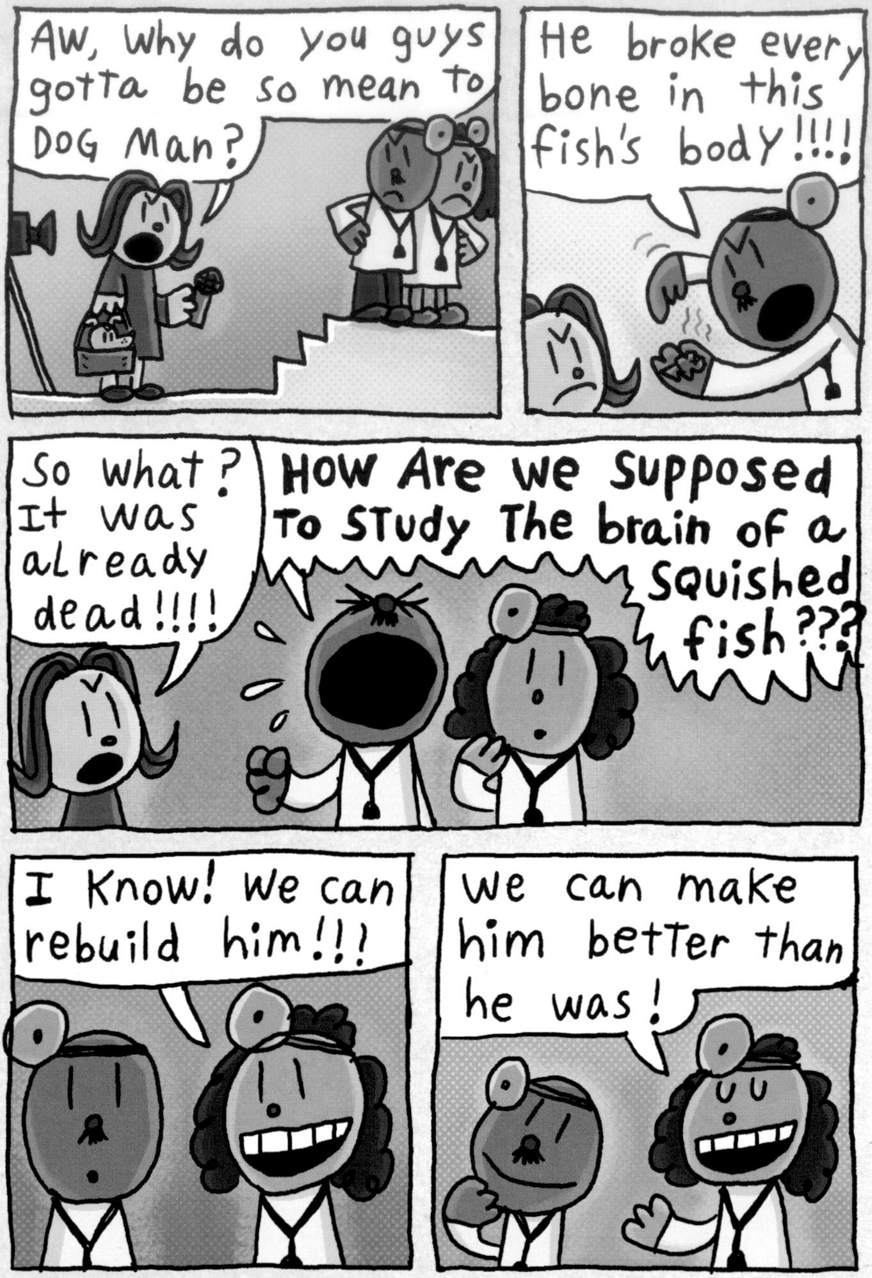

Aw, Why do you guys gotta be so mean to DOG Man?
He broke every bone in this fish's body!!!!
So what? It was already dead!!!!
HOW Are we Supposed To STudy The brain of a Squished fish???
I Know! We can rebuild him!!!
We can make him better than he was!

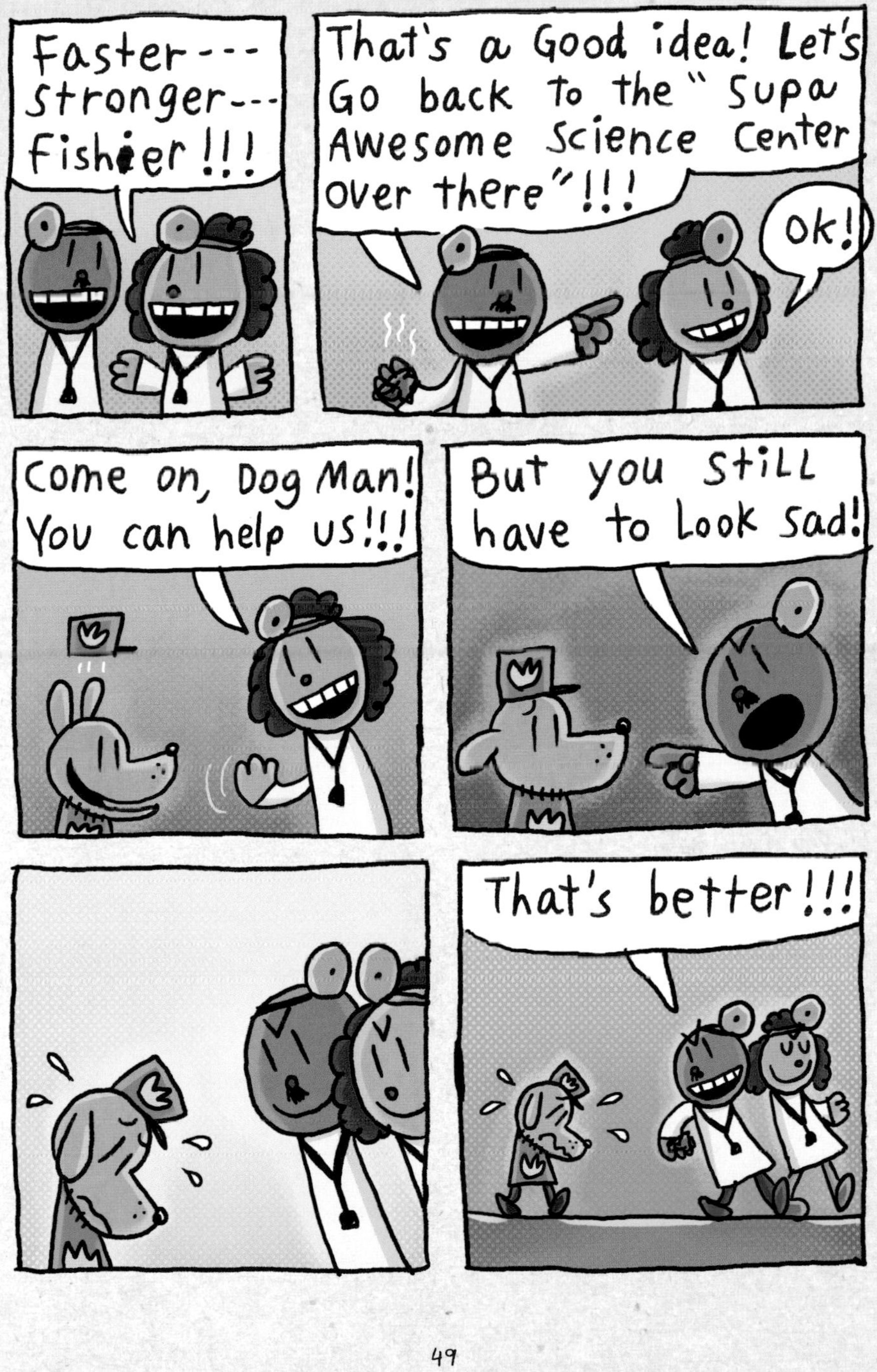

Faster--- Stronger--- Fishier!!!
That's a Good idea! Let's Go back to the "Supa Awesome Science Center over there"!!!
OK!
Come on, Dog Man! You can help us!!!
But you STiLL have to Look Sad!
That's better!!!

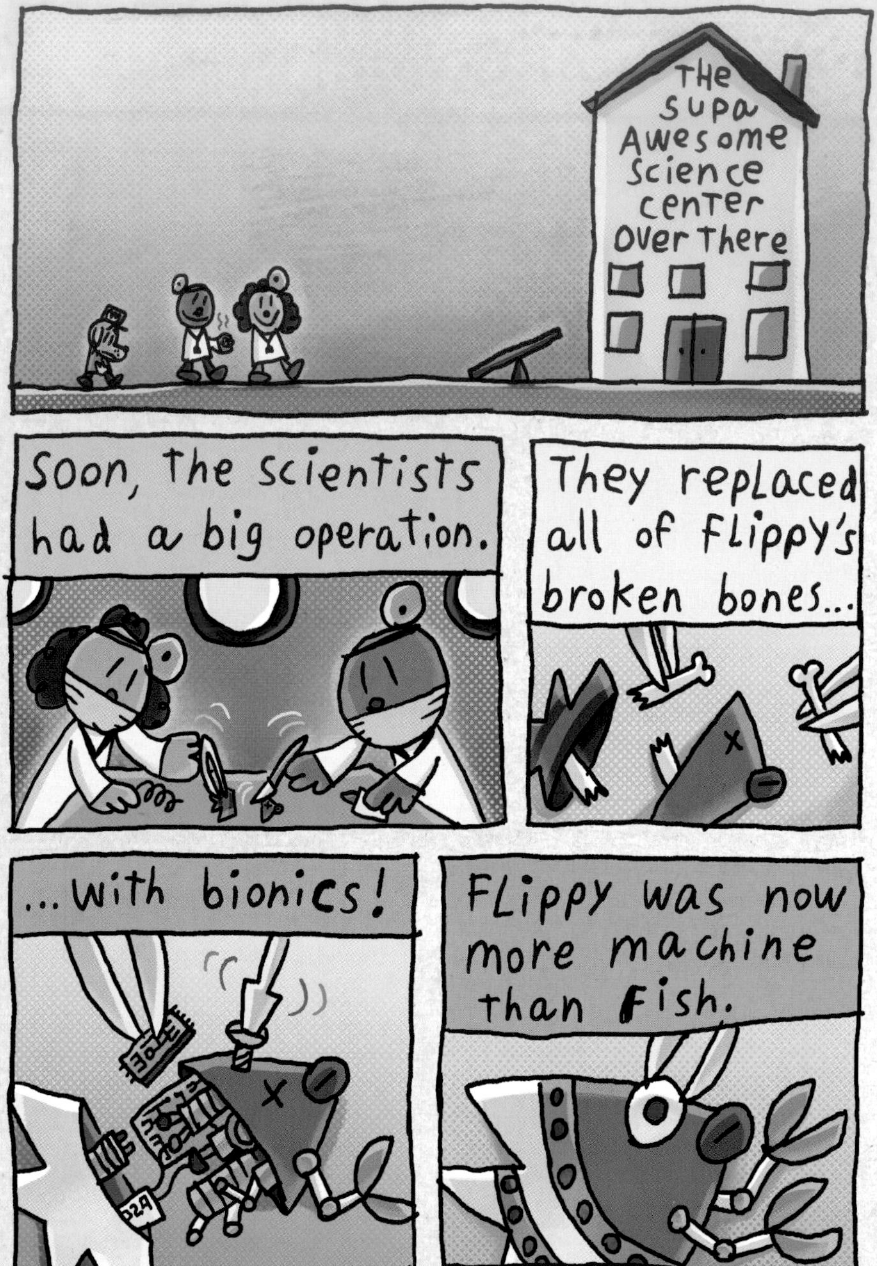
The Supa Awesome Science Center Over There
Soon, the scientists had a big operation.
They replaced all of Flippy's broken bones...
...with bionics!
Flippy was now more machine than fish.

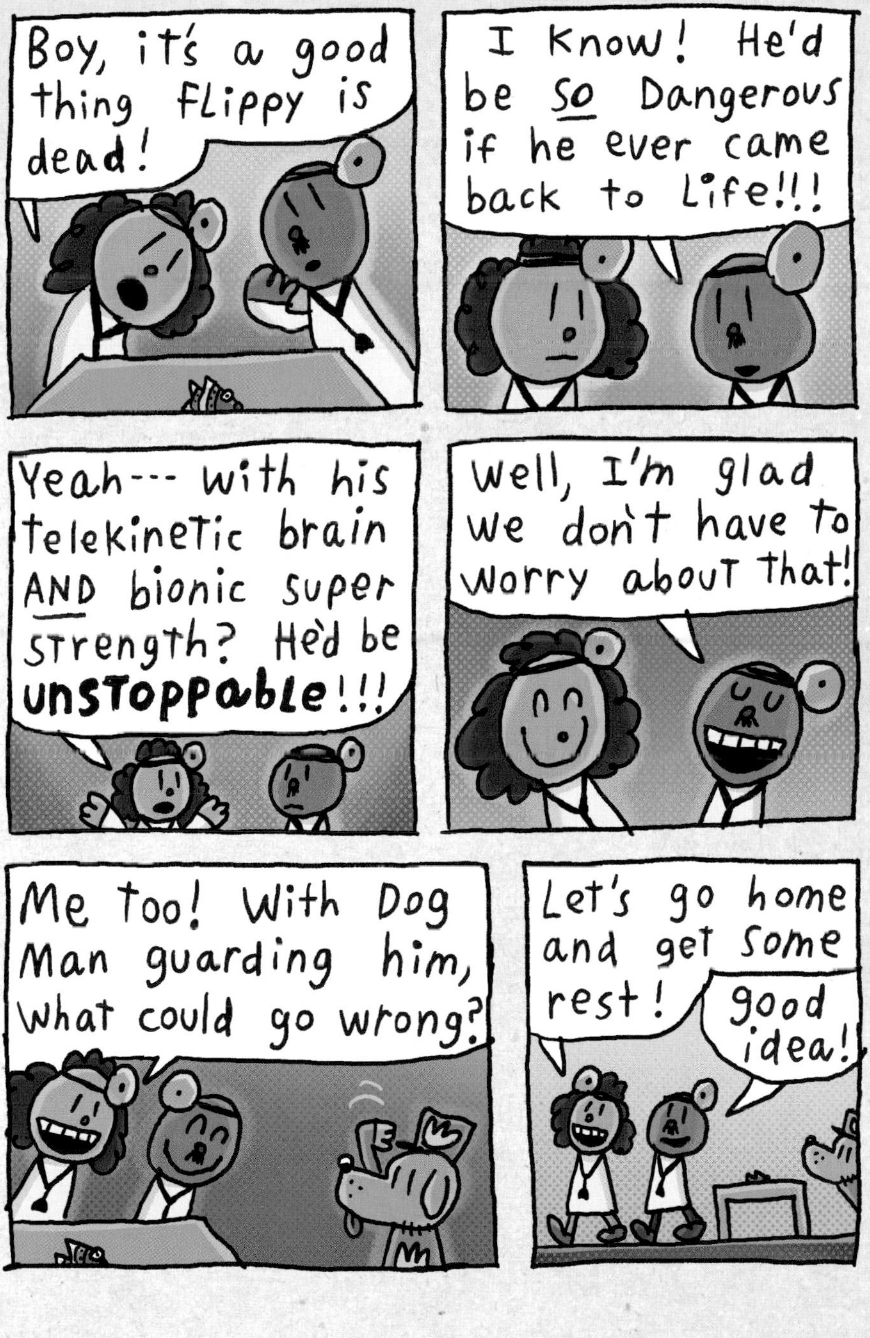
Boy, it's a good thing FLippy is dead!
I Know! He'd be SO Dangerous if he ever came back to Life!!!
Yeah--- with his telekinetic brain AND bionic super strength? He'd be UNSTOPPABLE!!!
Well, I'm glad we don't have to worry about that!
Me too! With Dog Man guarding him, what could go wrong?
Let's go home and get some rest!
good idea!

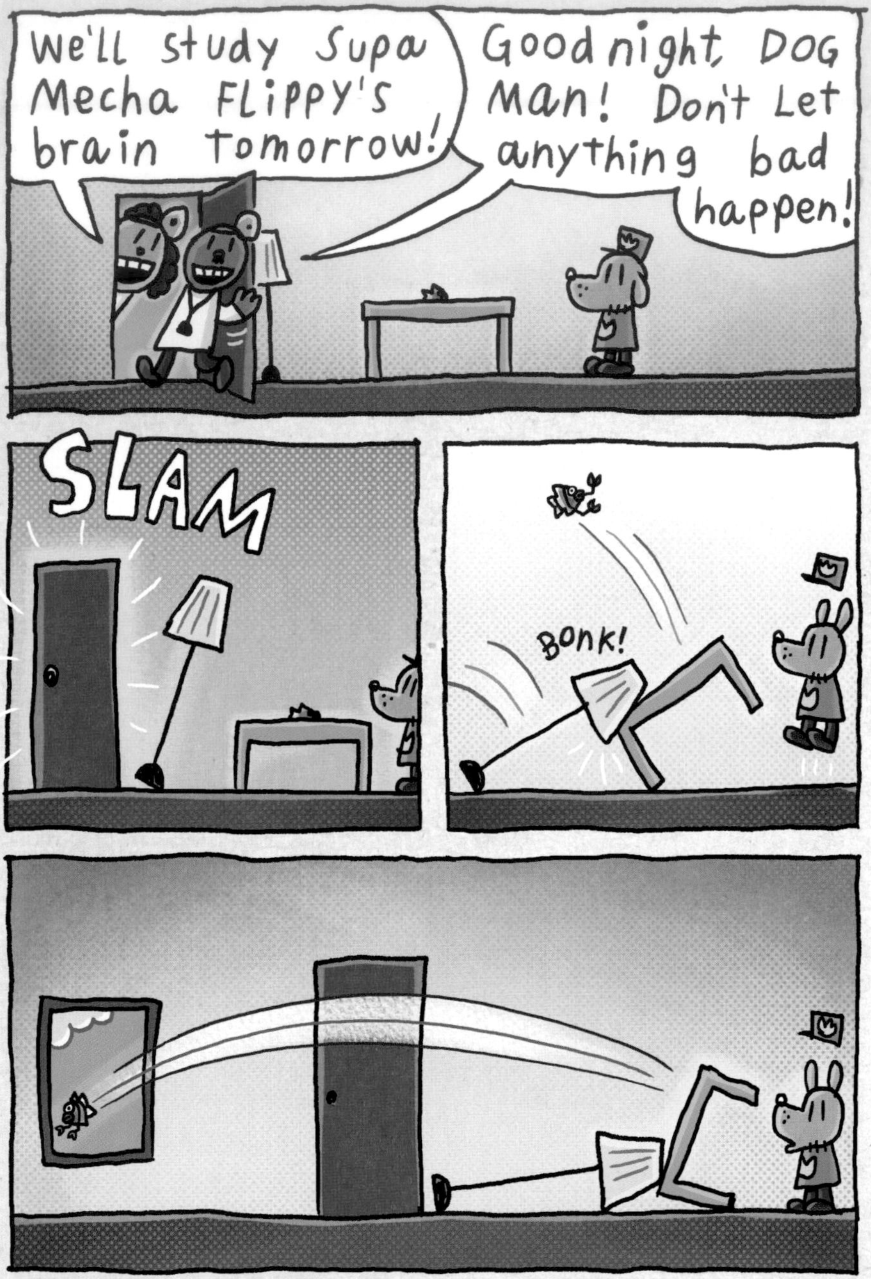
We'll study Supa Mecha FLiPPY's brain tomorrow!
Goodnight, DOG Man! Don't Let anything bad happen!
SLAM
BONK!

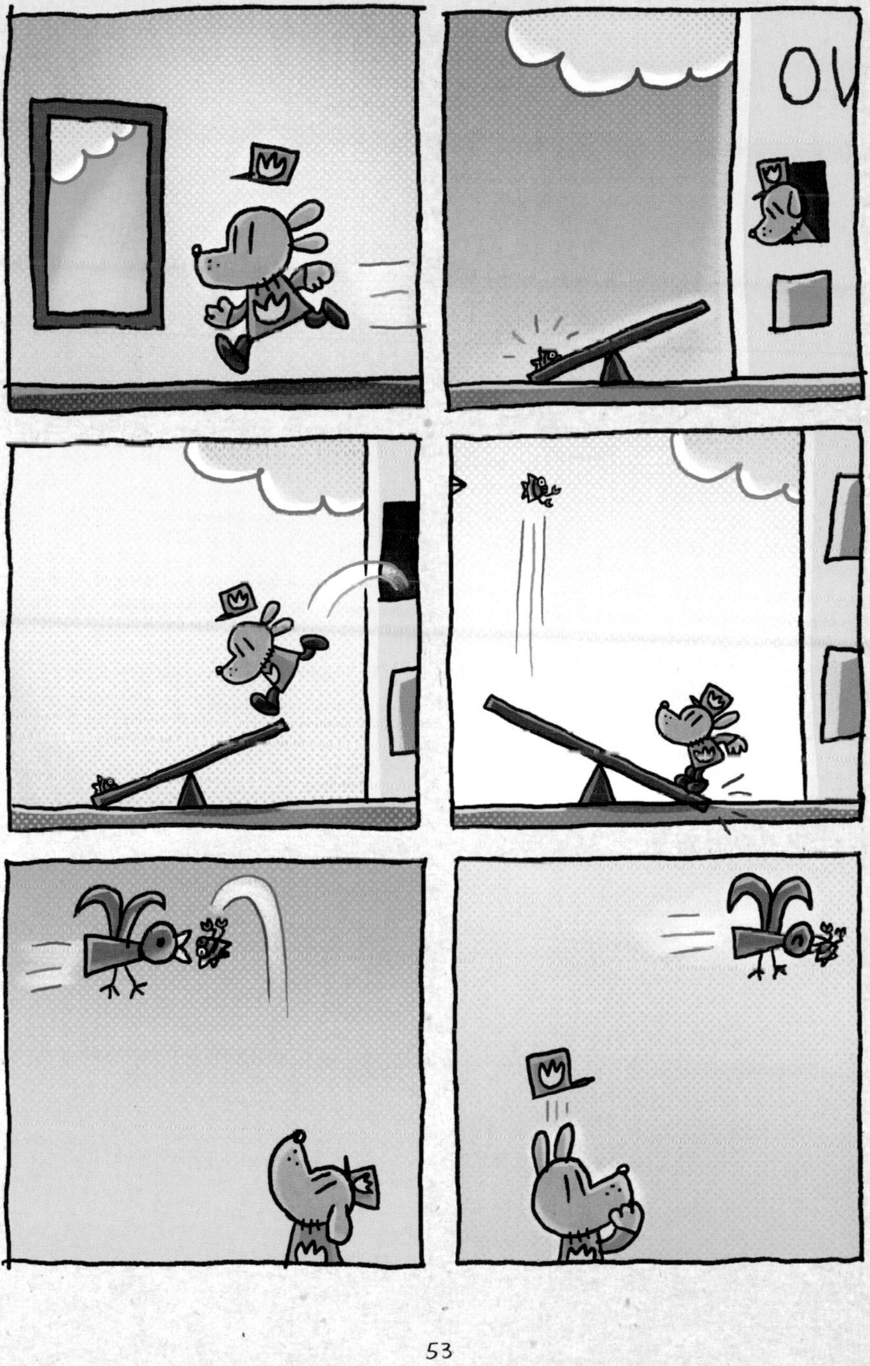

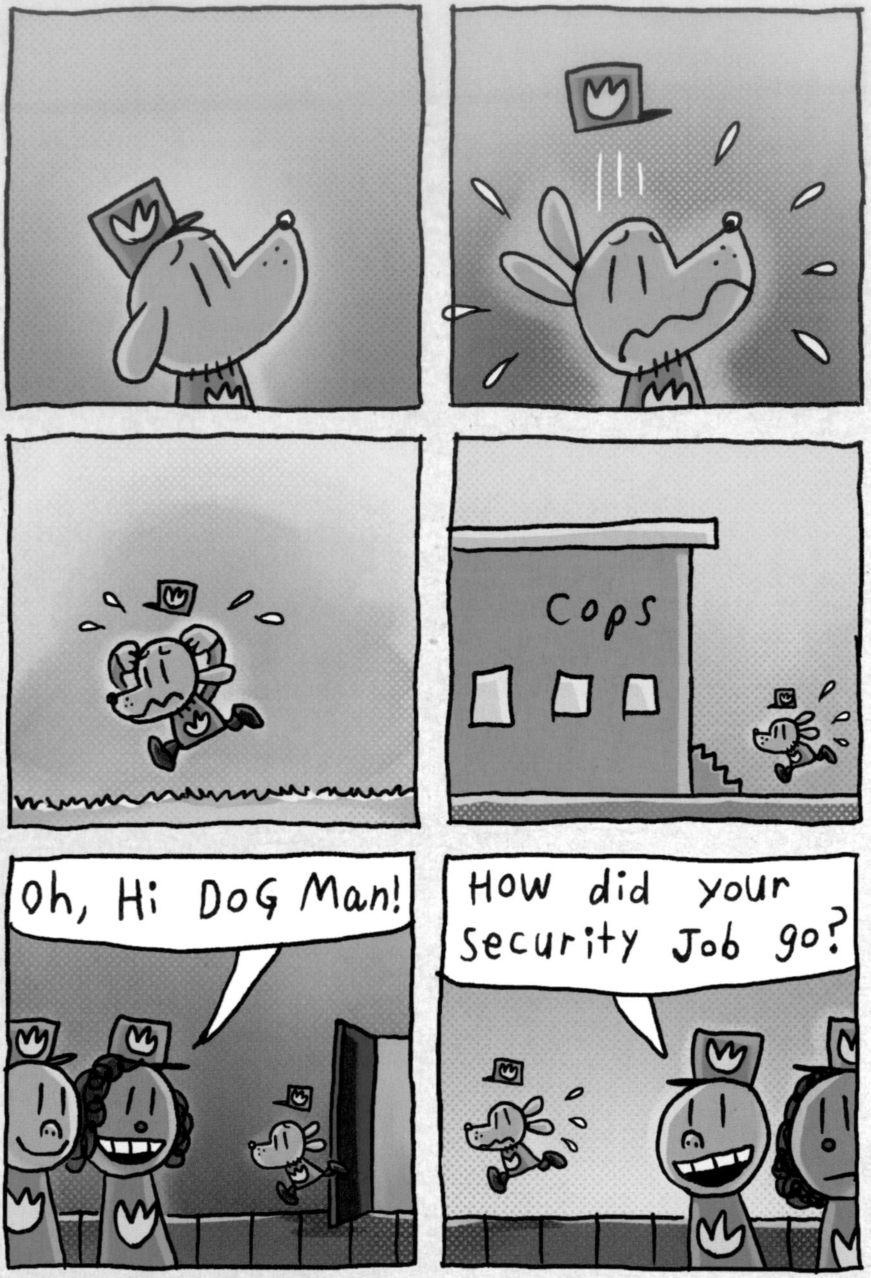
Cops
Oh, Hi DOG Man!
How did your security Job go?

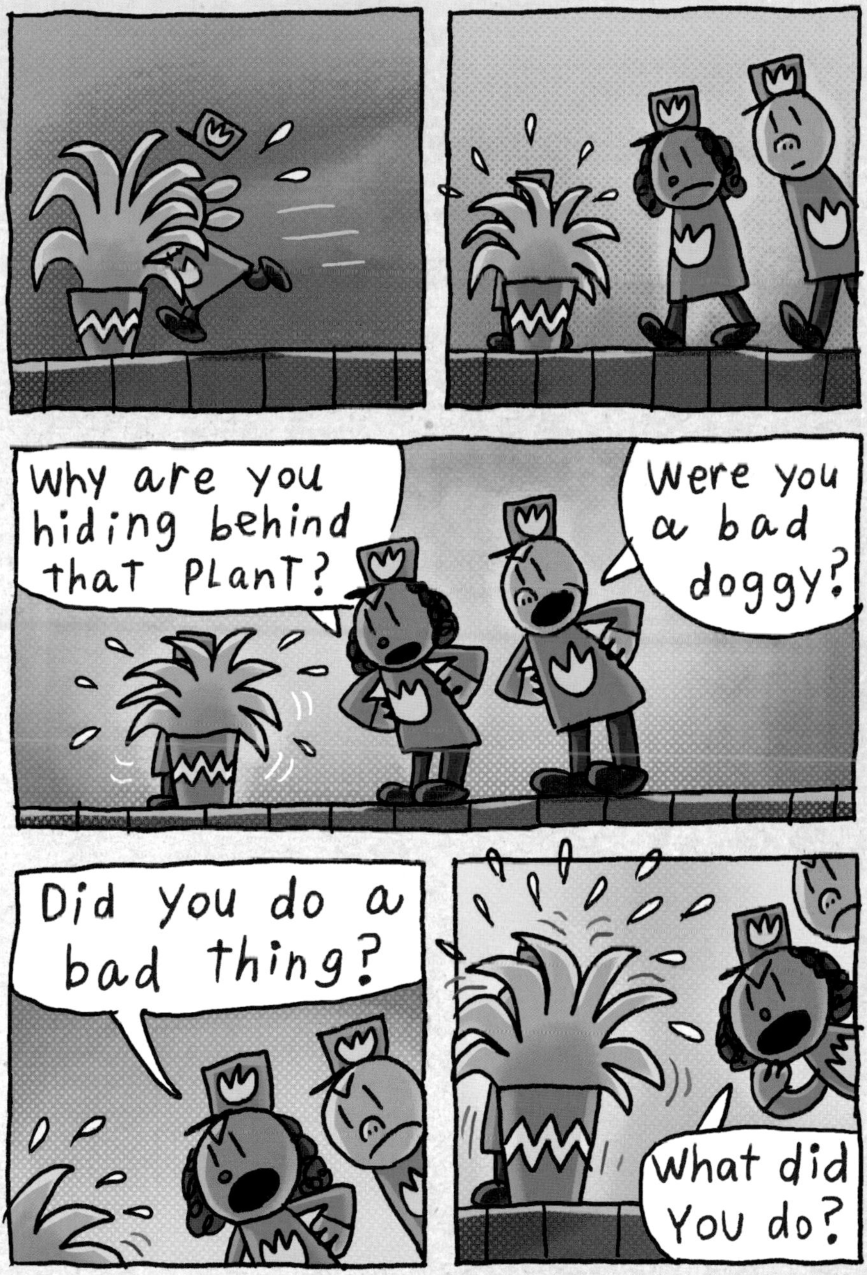
Why are you hiding behind that PLanT?
Were you a bad doggy?
Did you do a bad thing?
What did You do?

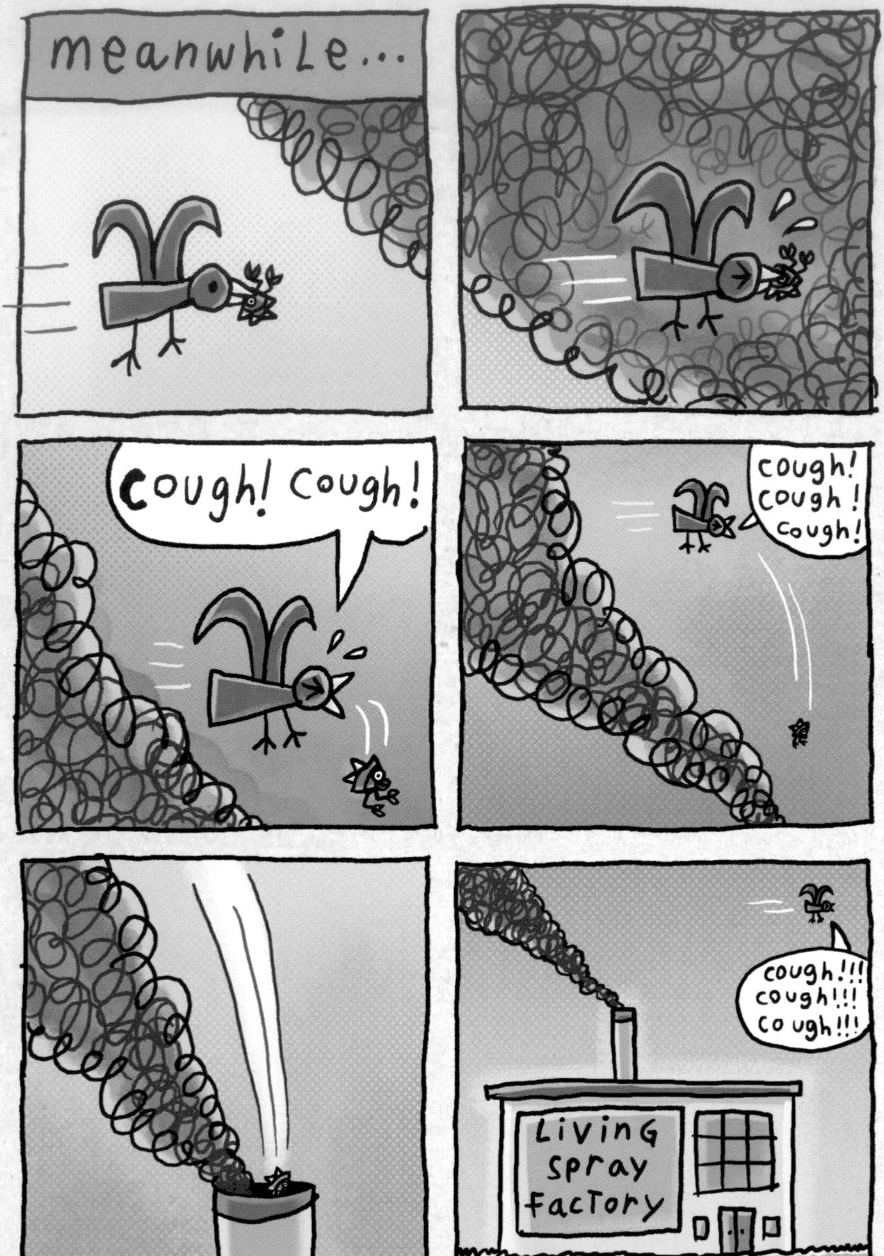
meanwhiLe...
Cough! Cough!
cough! cough! cough!
cough!!! cough!!! cough!!!
Living Spray Factory

Chapter The fourth
No More Kitten Around!

Free kitty

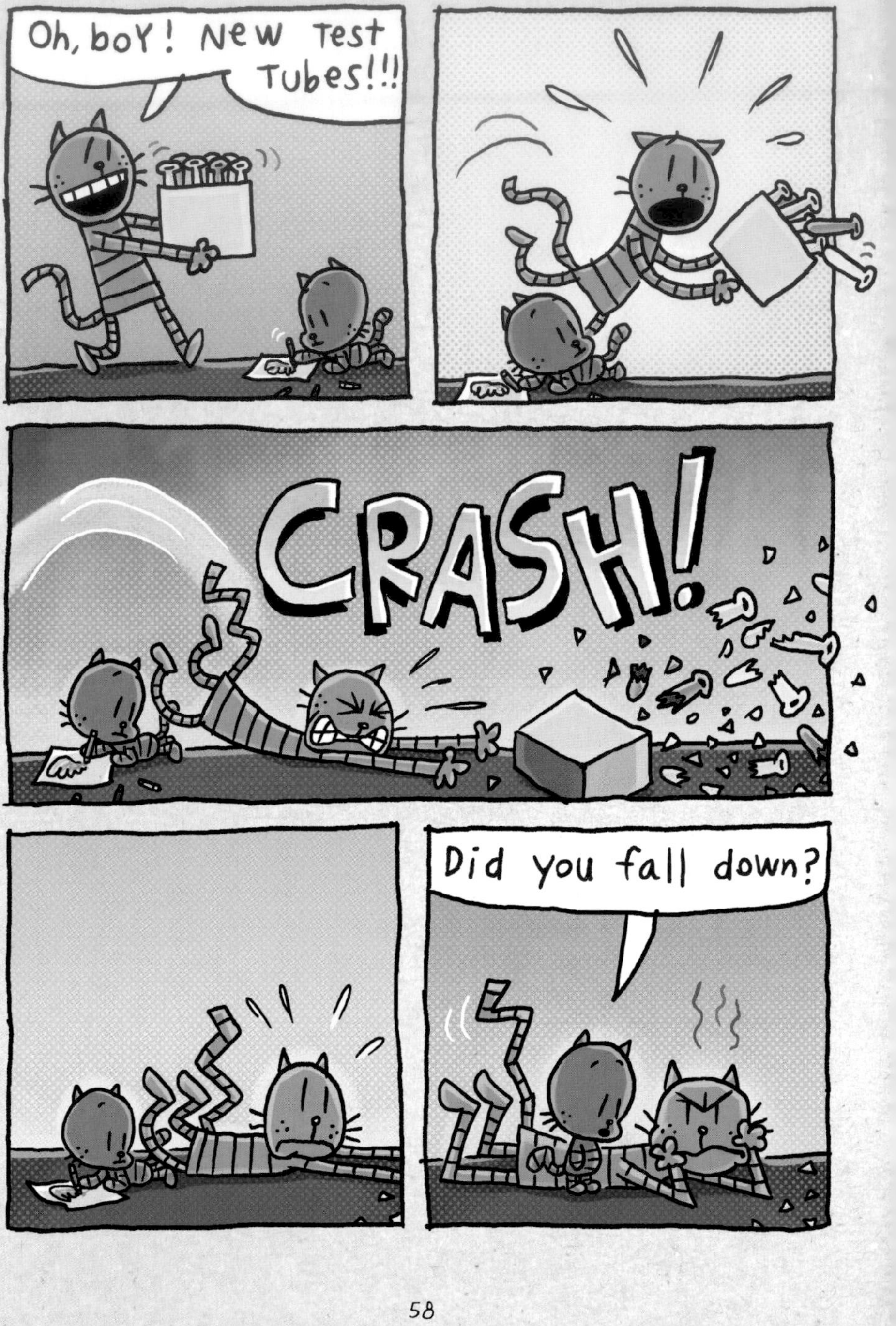
Oh, boy! New Test Tubes!!!
CRASH!
Did you fall down?

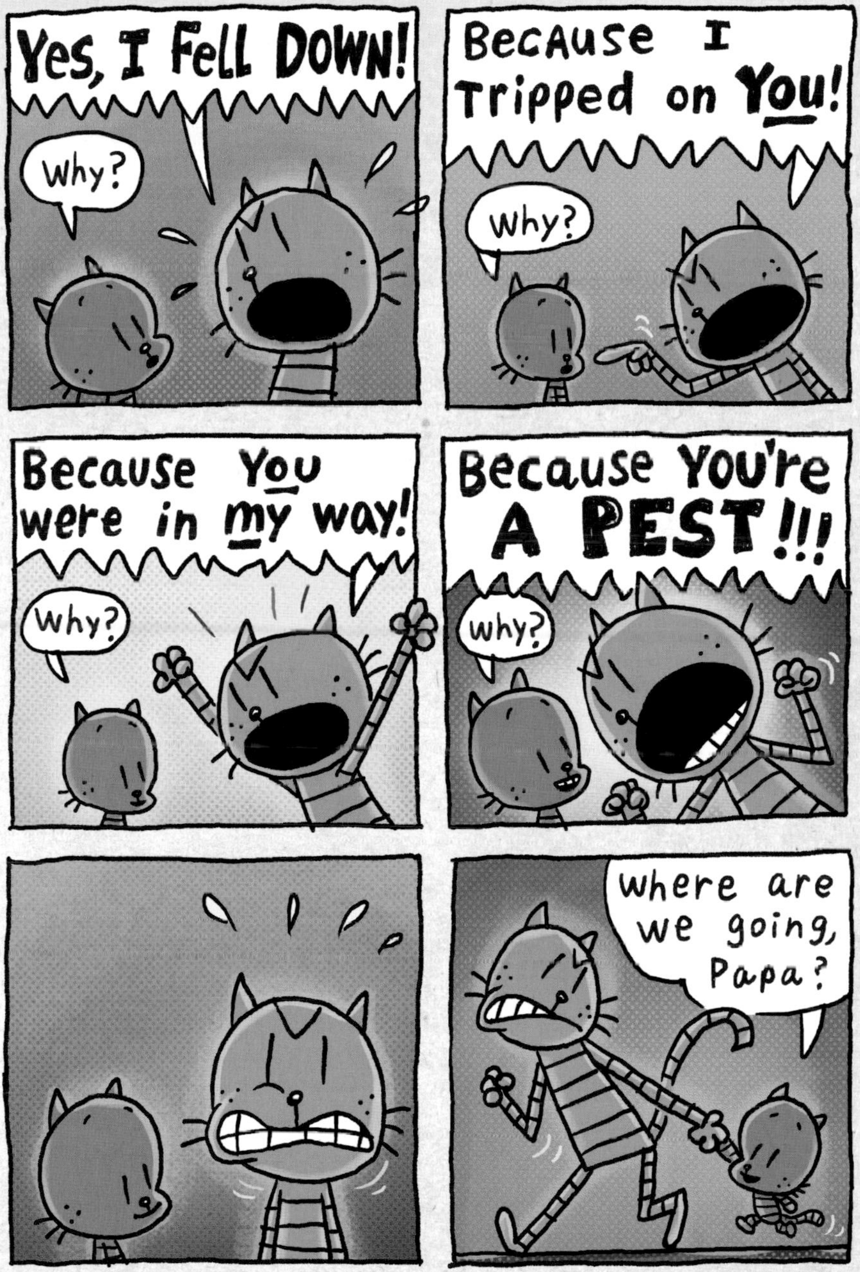
Yes, I Fell DOWN!
Why?
Because I Tripped on You!
Why?
Because You were in my way!
Why?
Because You're A PEST!!!
Why?
Where are we going, Papa?

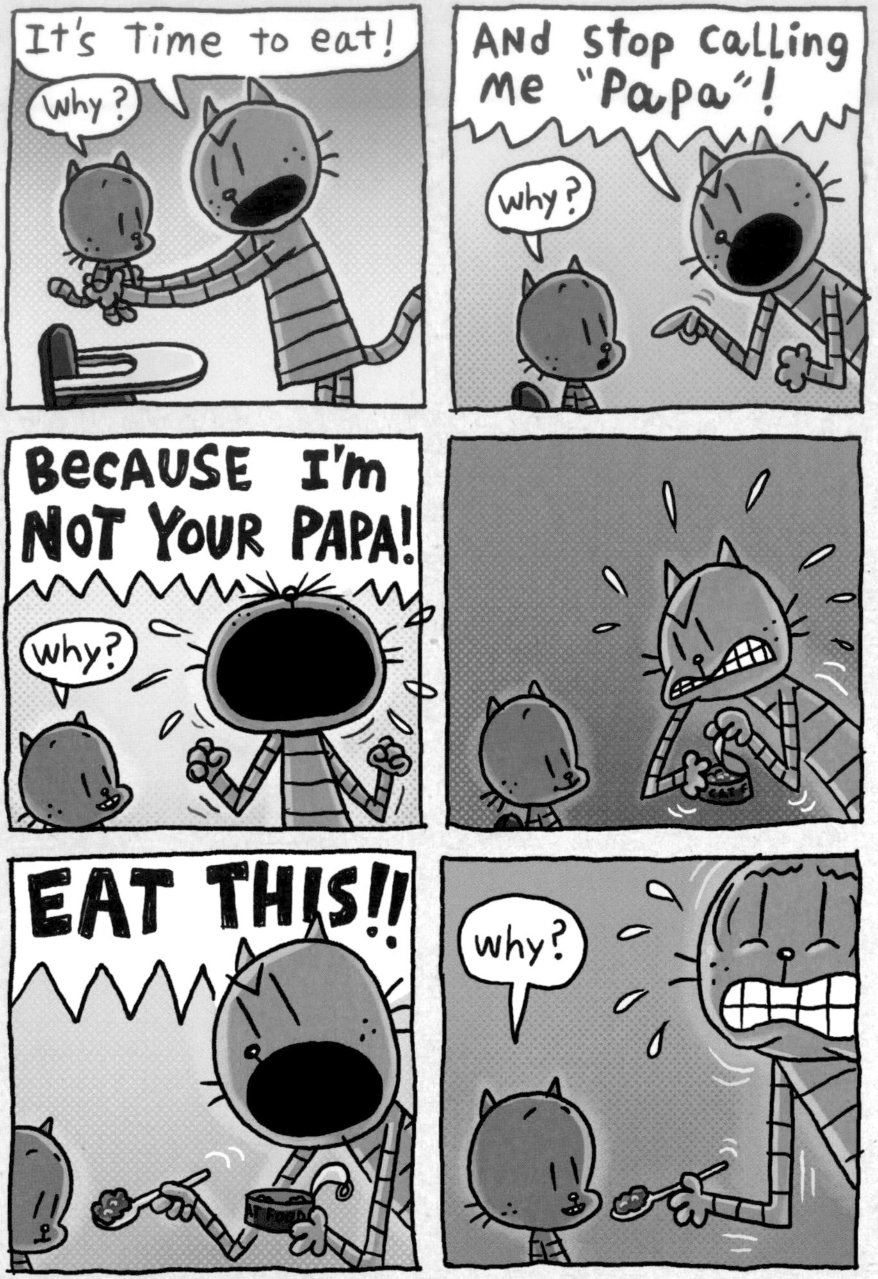
It's Time to eat!
Why?
ANd Stop calling me "Papa"!
why?
BECAUSE I'm NOT YOUR PAPA!
why?
EAT THIS!!
why?

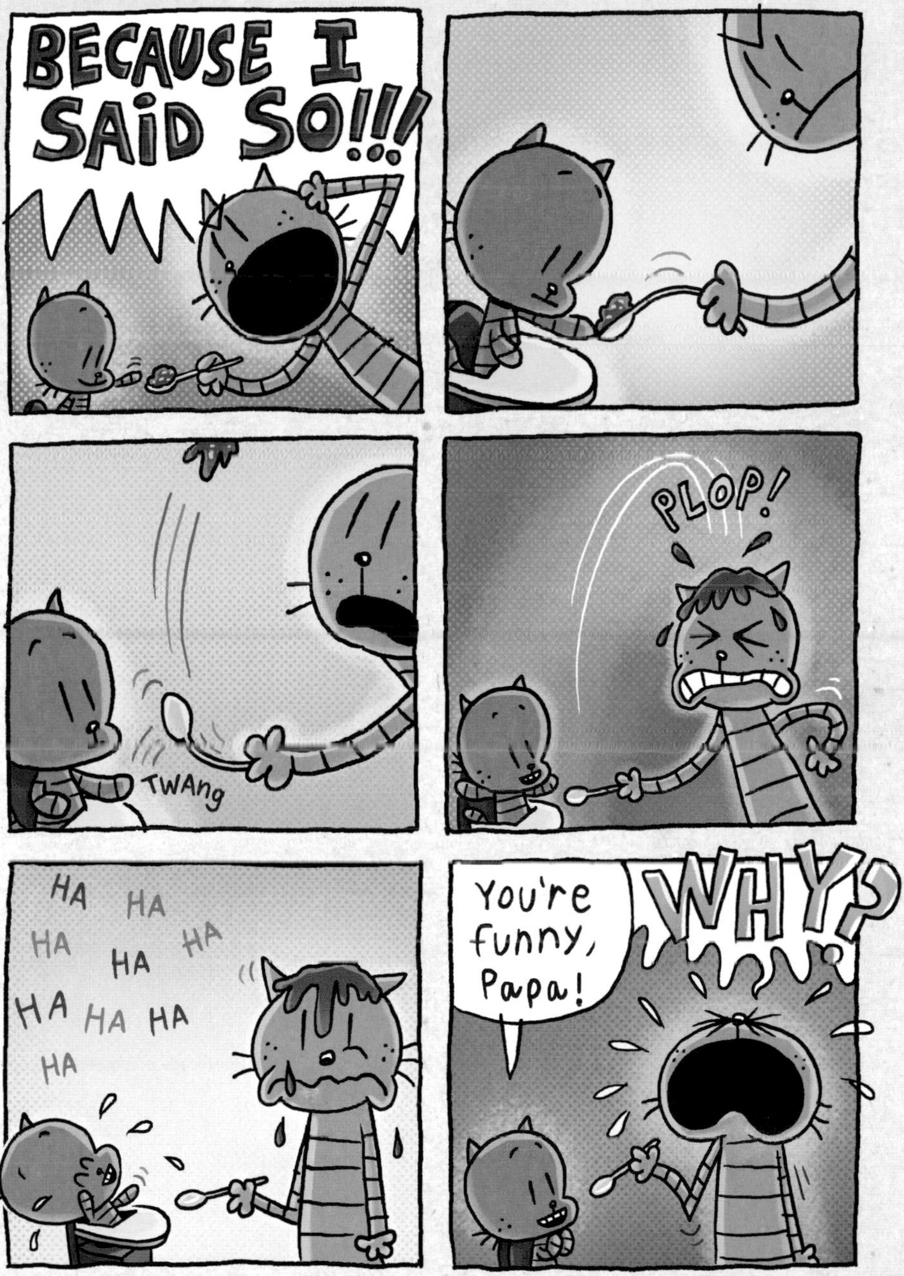
BECAUSE I SAID SO!!!
TWAng
PLOP!
HA HA HA HA HA HA HA HA HA
You're funny, Papa!
WHY?

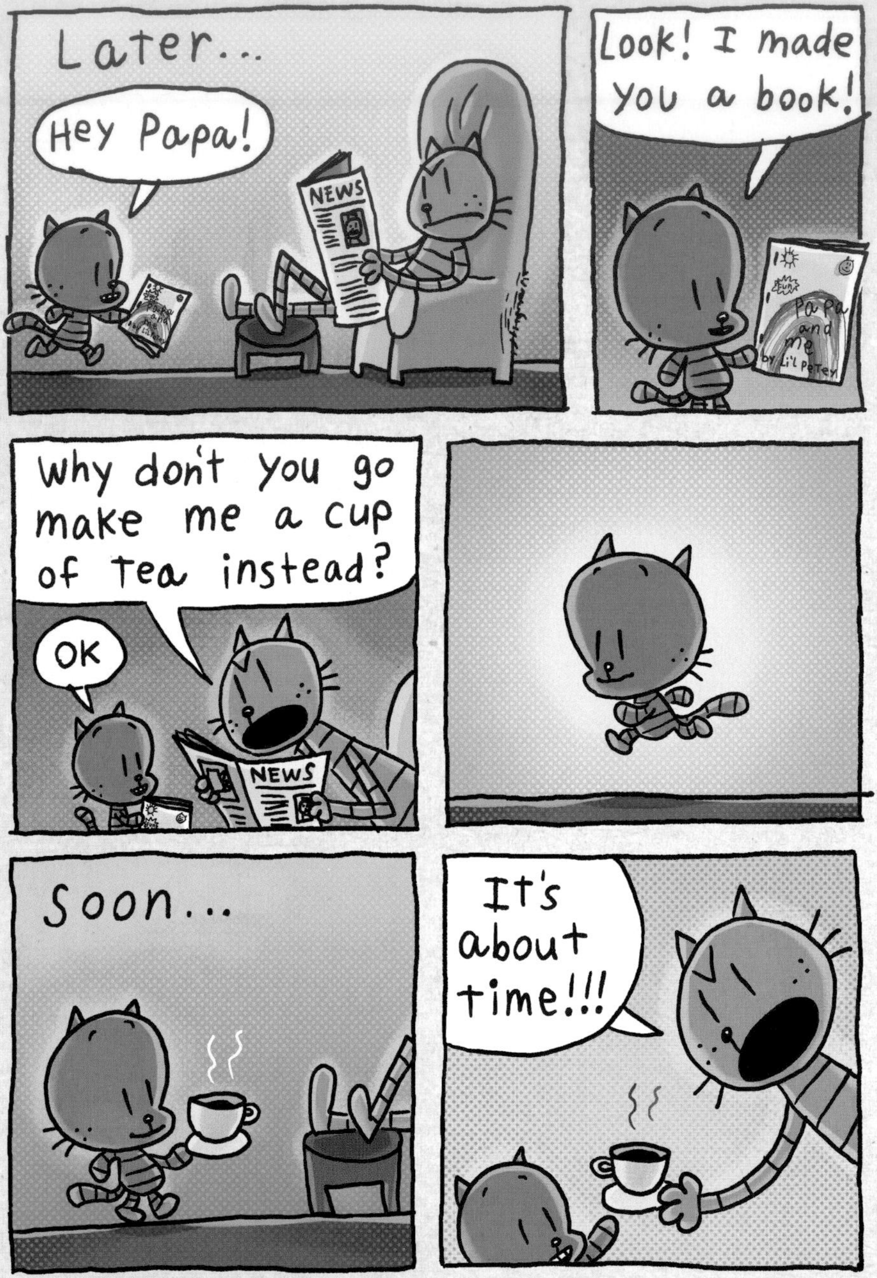
Later...
Hey Papa!
Look! I made you a book!
Papa and me by Li'l Petey
Why don't you go make me a cup of tea instead?
OK
Soon...
It's about time!!!

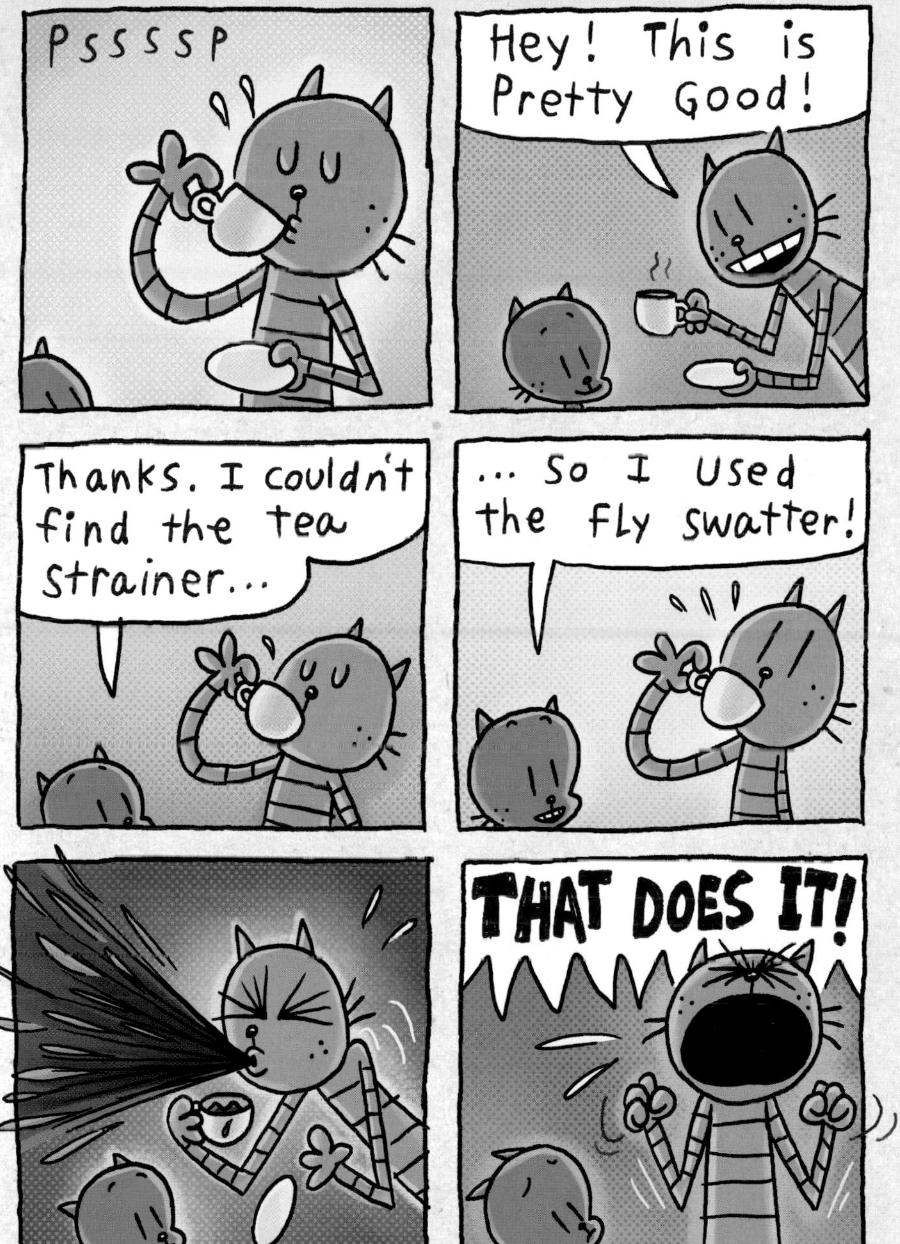
PSSSSP
Hey! This is Pretty Good!
Thanks. I couldn't find the tea strainer...
... So I Used the Fly swatter!
THAT DOES IT!

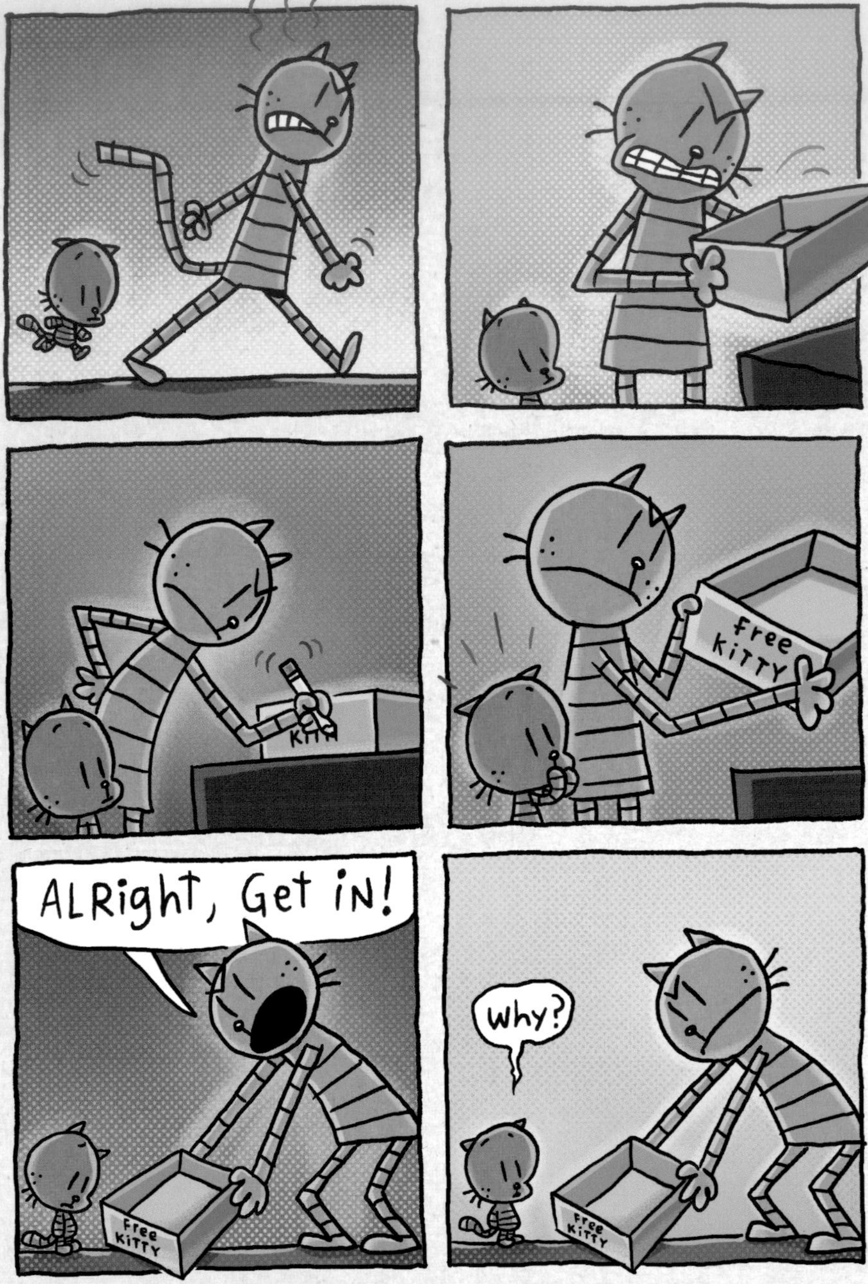
KITTY
Free KITTY
ALRight, Get iN!
Free KITTY
Why?
Free KITTY

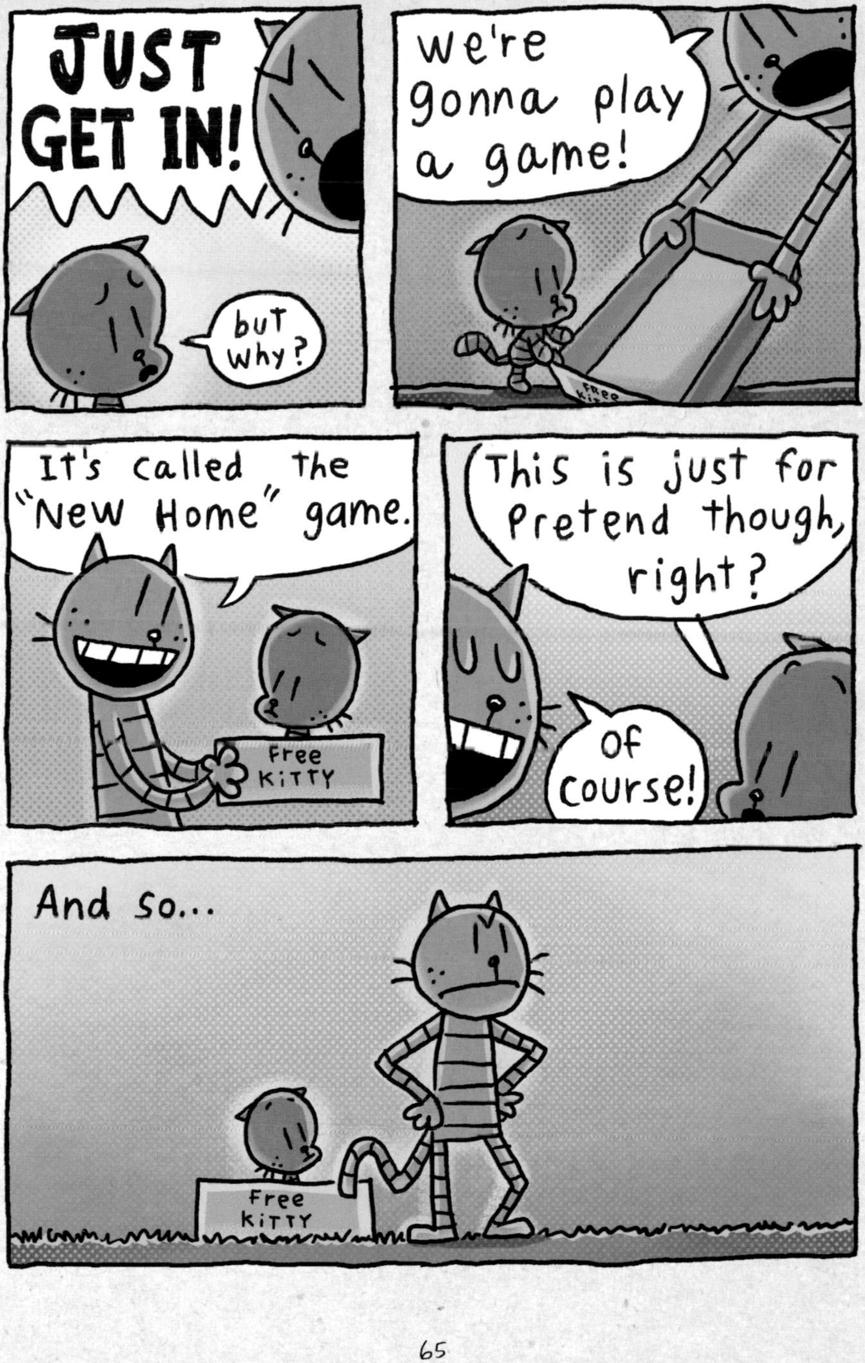
JUST GET IN!
but why?
we're gonna play a game!
FREE KITTY
It's called the "New Home" game.
Free KITTY
This is just for pretend though, right?
Of course!
And so...
Free KITTY

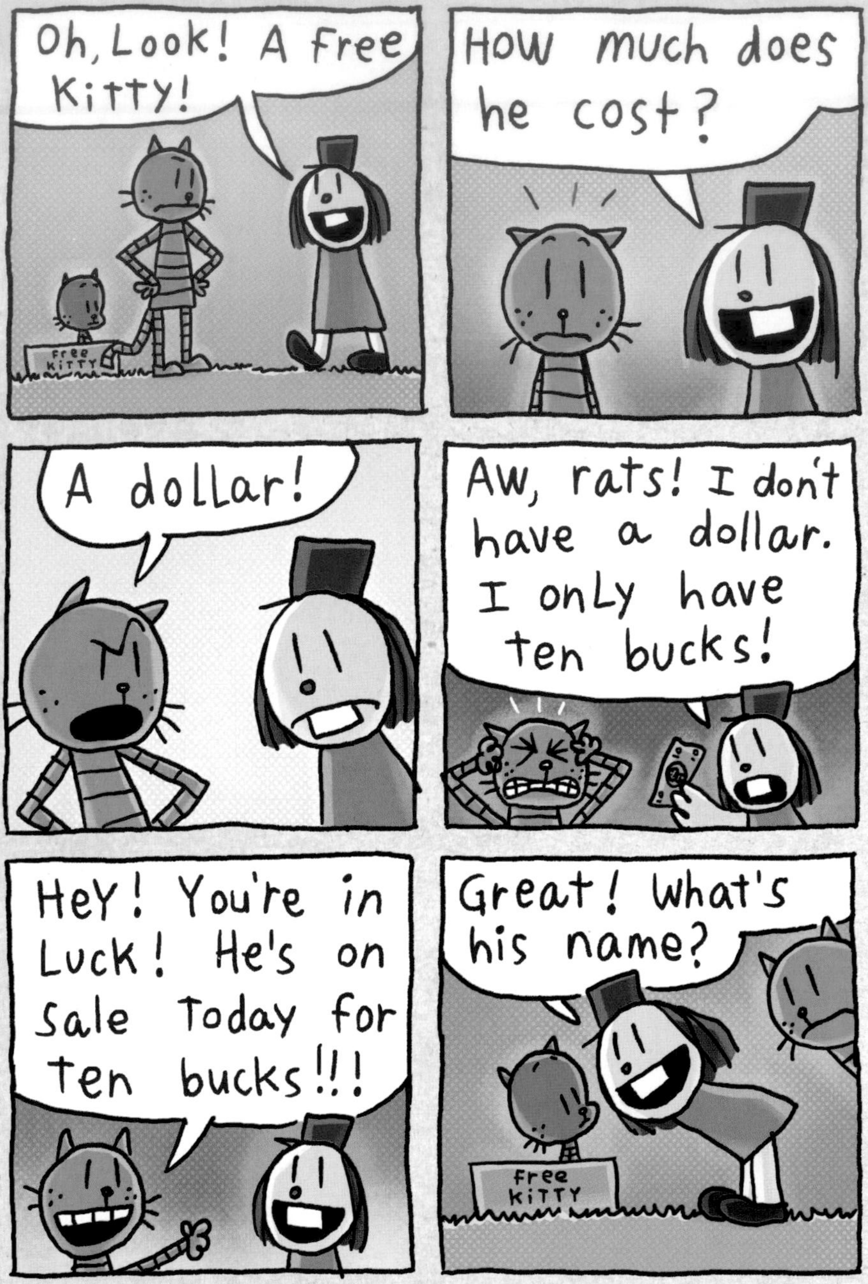
Oh, Look! A Free Kitty!
Free KiTTY
How much does he cost?
A dollar!
Aw, rats! I don't have a dollar. I onLy have ten bucks!
HeY! You're in Luck! He's on Sale Today for ten bucks!!!
Great! What's his name?
Free KiTTY

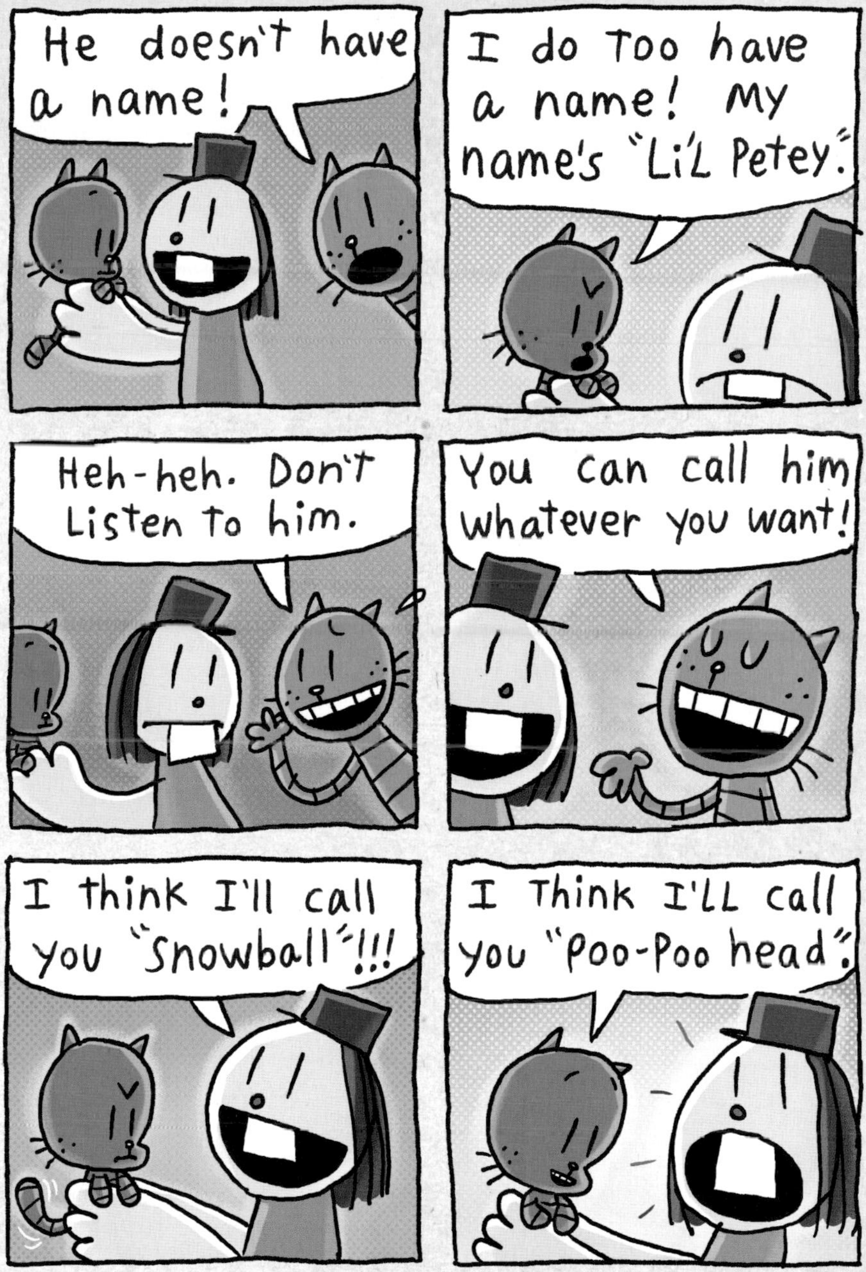
He doesn't have a name!
I do Too have a name! My name's "Li'L Petey."
Heh-heh. Don't Listen to him.
You can call him whatever you want!
I think I'll call you "Snowball"!!!
I Think I'LL call you "Poo-Poo head".

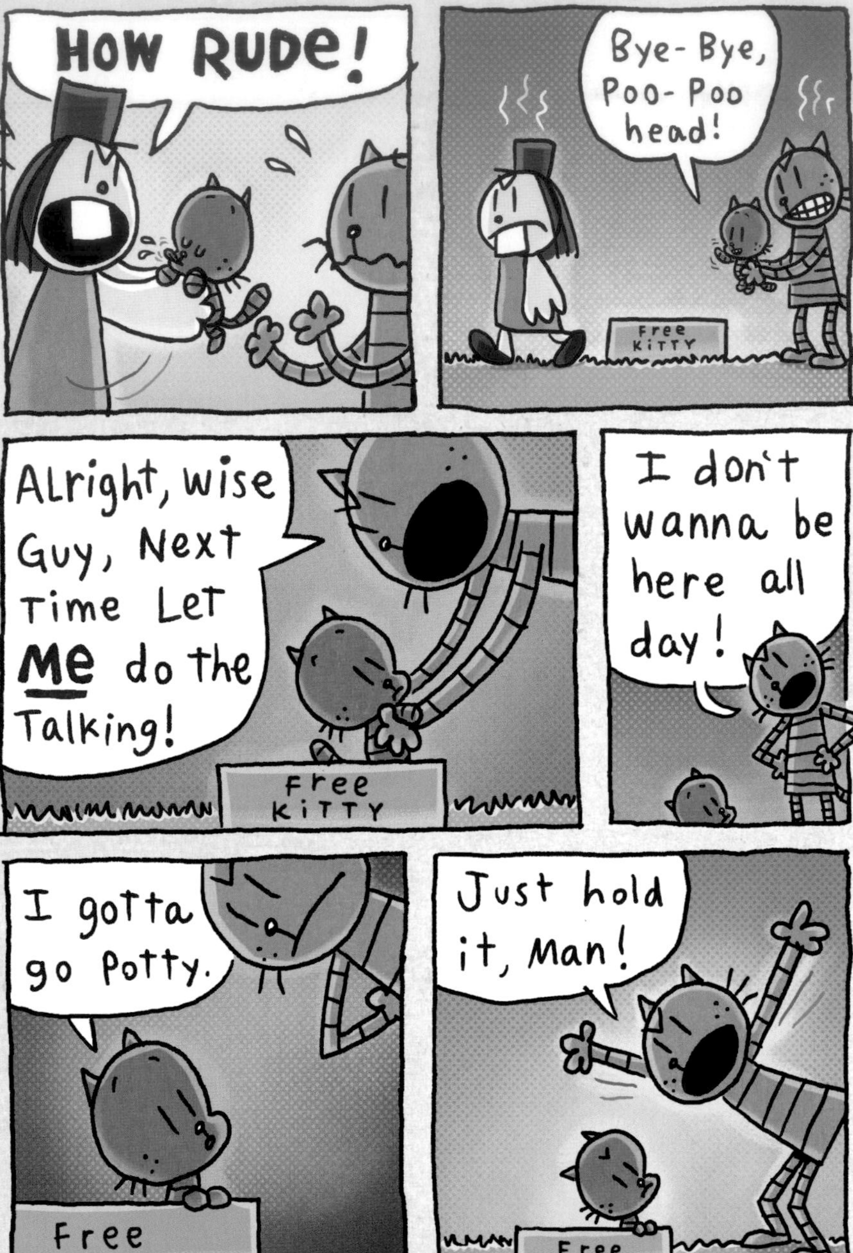
HOW RUDE!
Bye-Bye, Poo-Poo head!
Free KiTTY
Alright, wise Guy, Next Time Let ME do the Talking!
Free KiTTY
I don't wanna be here all day!
I gotta go Potty.
Free
Just hold it, Man!
Free

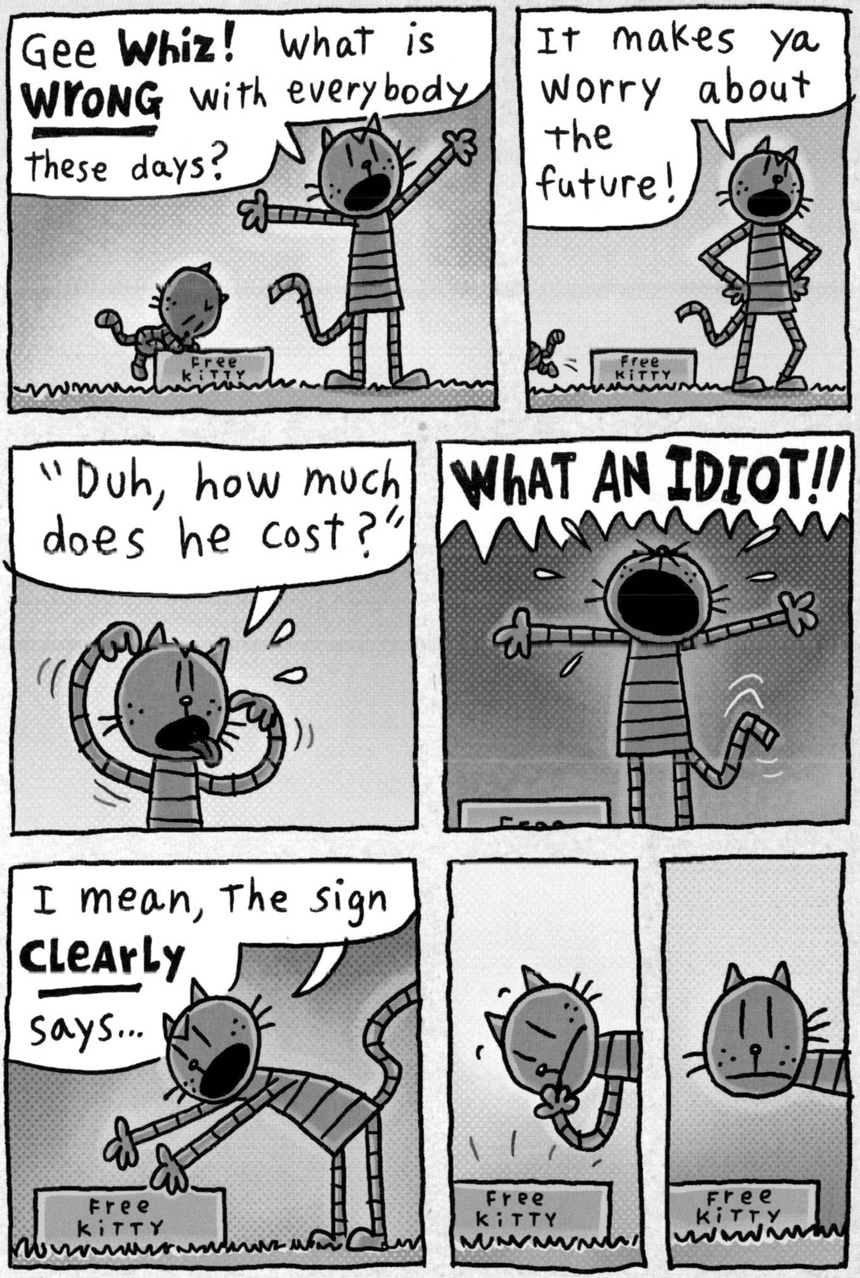
Gee **Whiz!** What is **WRONG** with everybody these days?
Free KiTTY
It makes ya worry about the future!
Free KiTTY
"Duh, how much does he cost?"
WHAT AN IDIOT!!
I mean, The sign **CLEARLY** says...
Free KiTTY
Free KiTTY
Free KiTTY

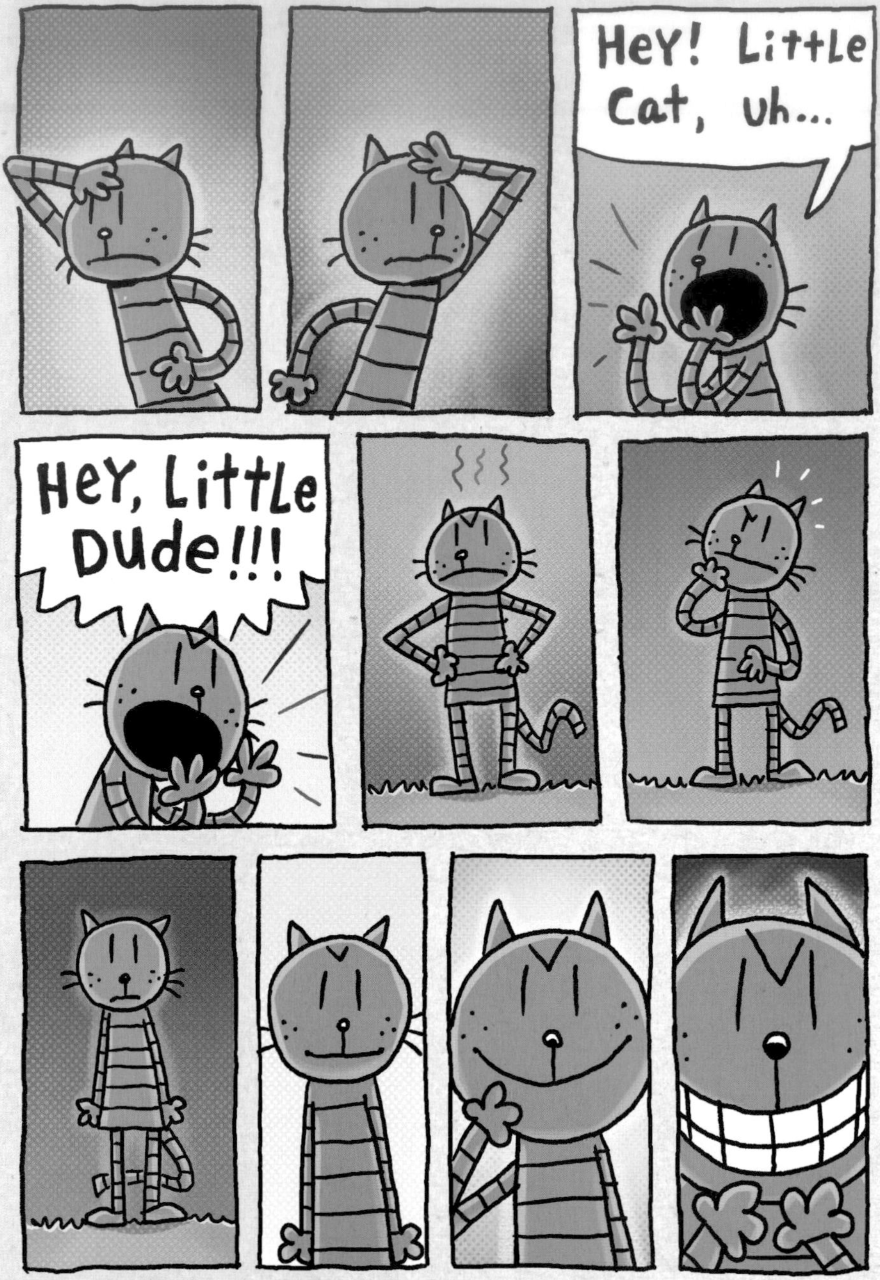
HEY! Little Cat, uh...
HEY, Little Dude!!!

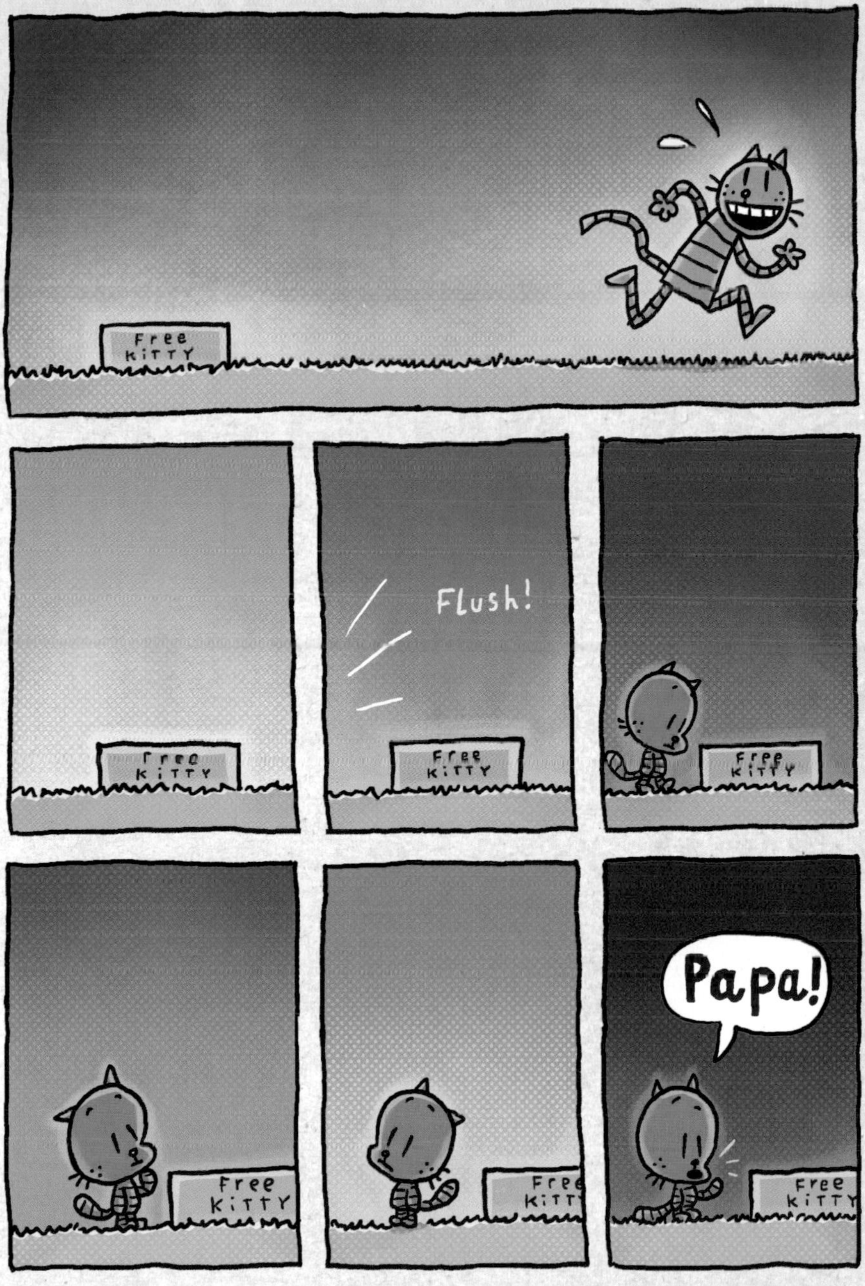
Free KiTTY
Free KiTTY
Flush!
Free KiTTY
Free KiTTY
Free KiTTY
Free KiTTY
Papa!
Free KiTTY

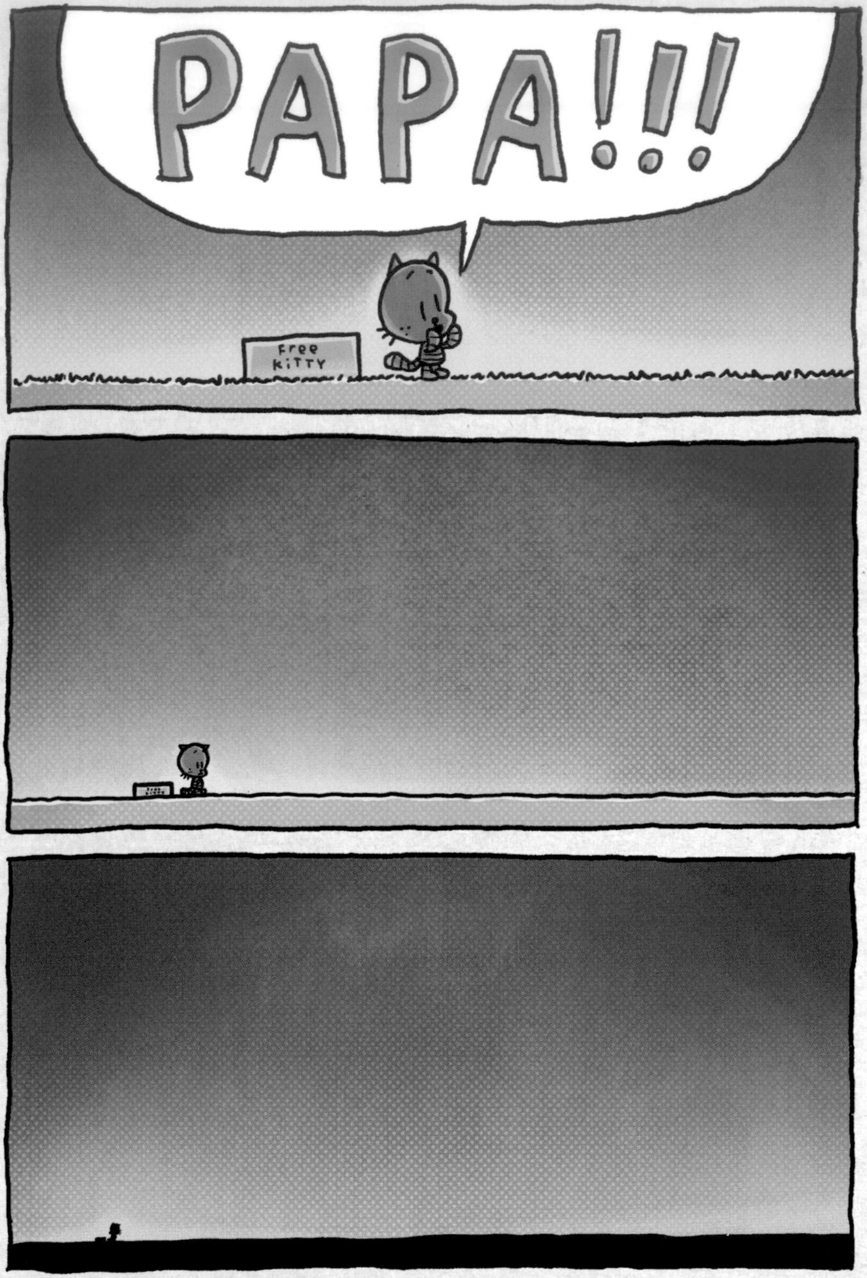
PAPA!!!
Free
KiTTY

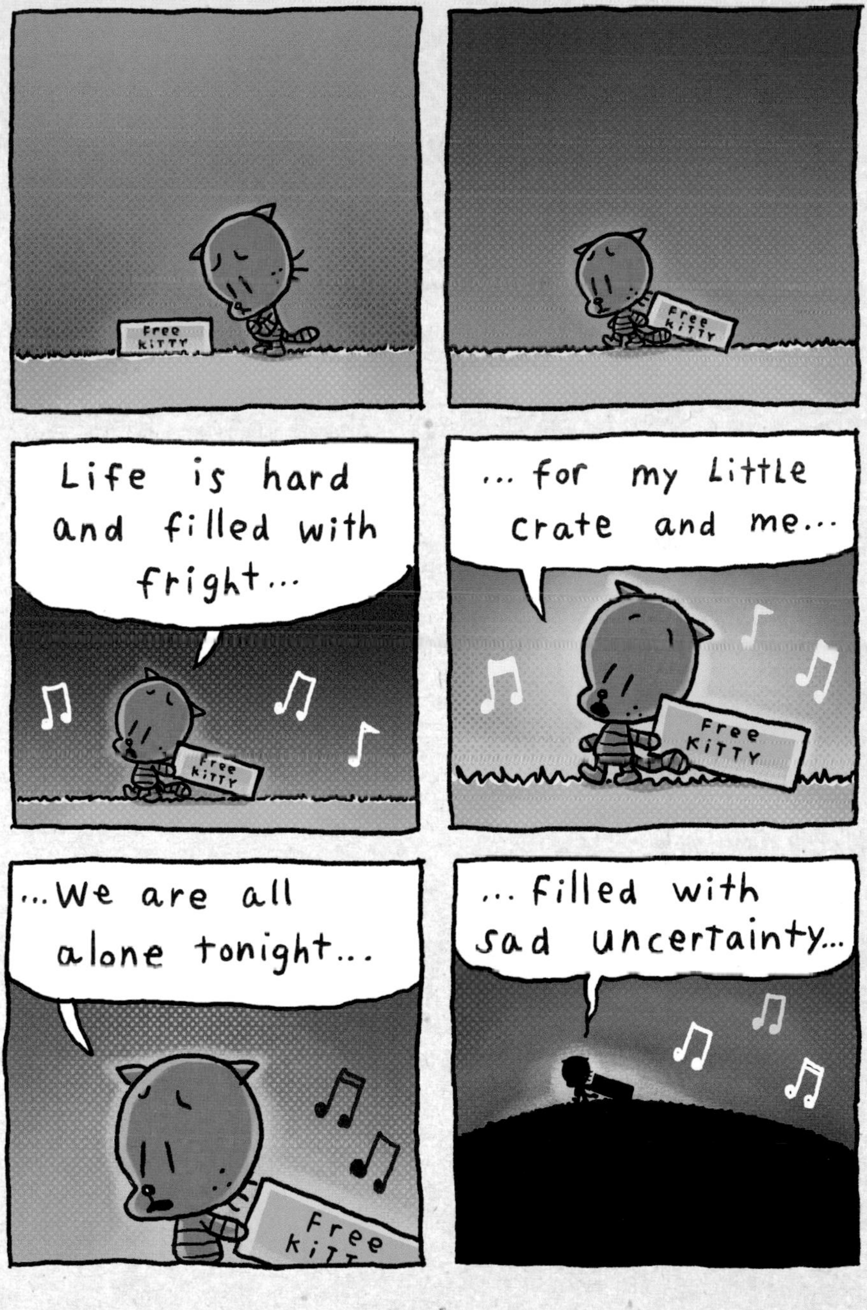
Free KiTTY
Free KiTTY
Life is hard and filled with fright...
Free KiTTY
... for my Little crate and me...
Free KiTTY
...We are all alone tonight...
... Filled with sad uncertainty...

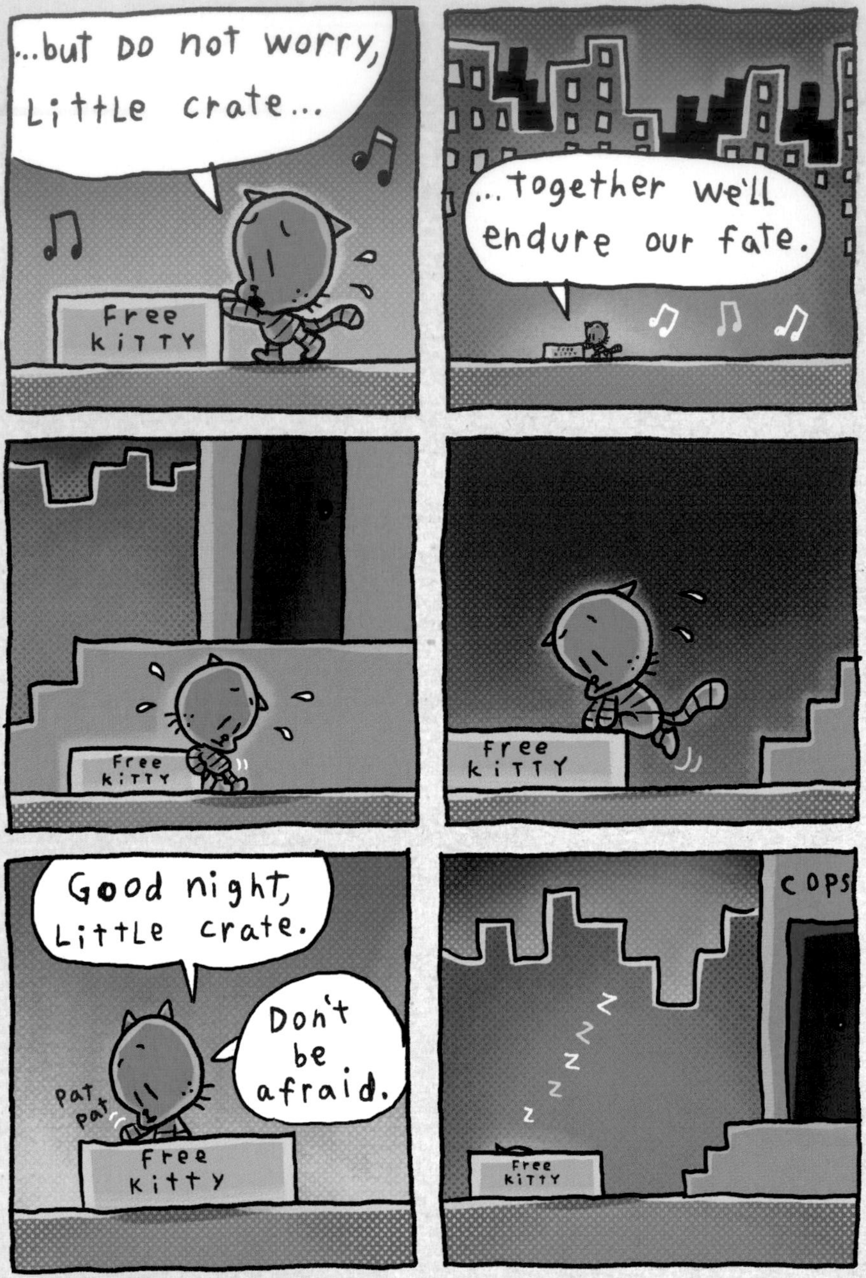
...but DO not worry, Little crate...
Free KiTTY
...together we'll endure our fate.
Free KiTTY
Free KiTTY
Good night, Little crate.
Don't be afraid.
pat pat
Free Kitty
COPS
Z Z Z Z Z
Free KiTTY

Chapter the Fifth

CRATE EXPECTATIONS

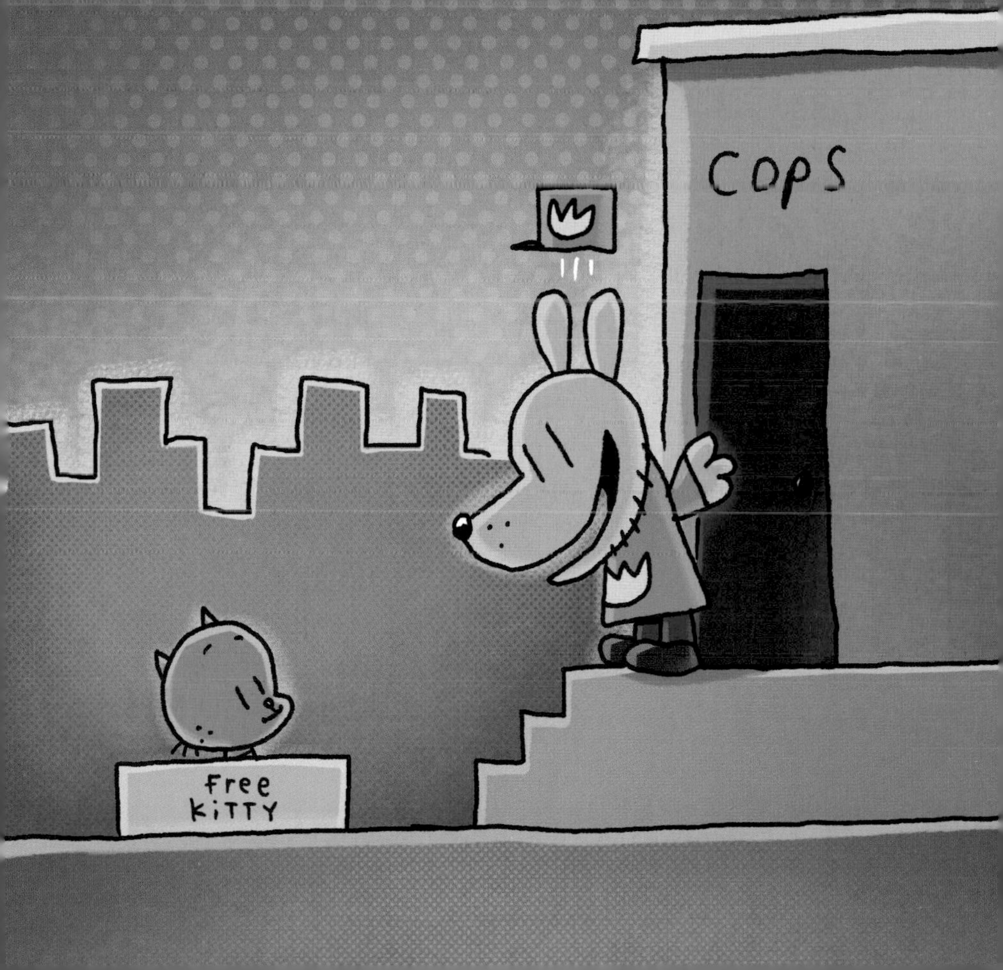
COPS
Free KITTY

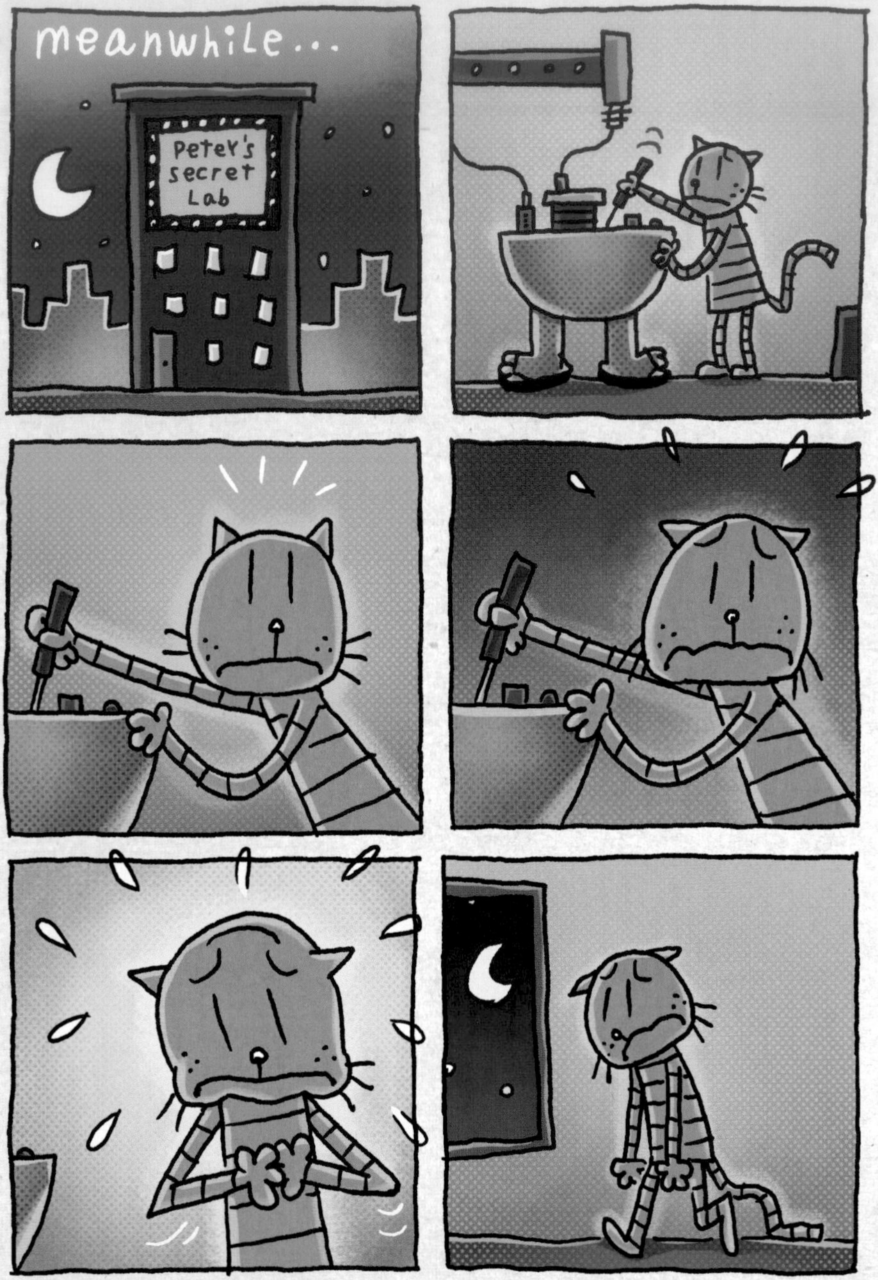
meanwhile...
Peter's secret Lab

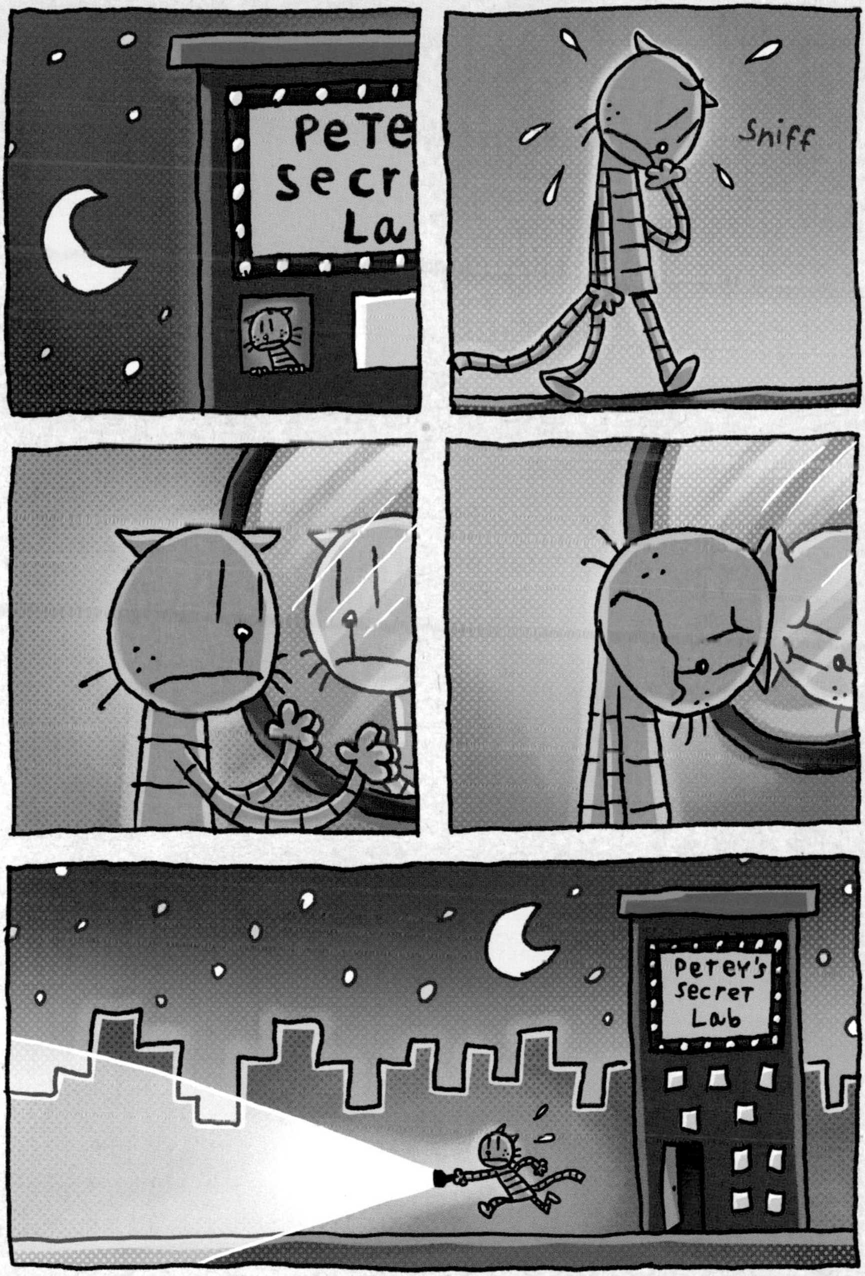
PeTe
Secr
La
Sniff
PeTey's
SecreT
Lab

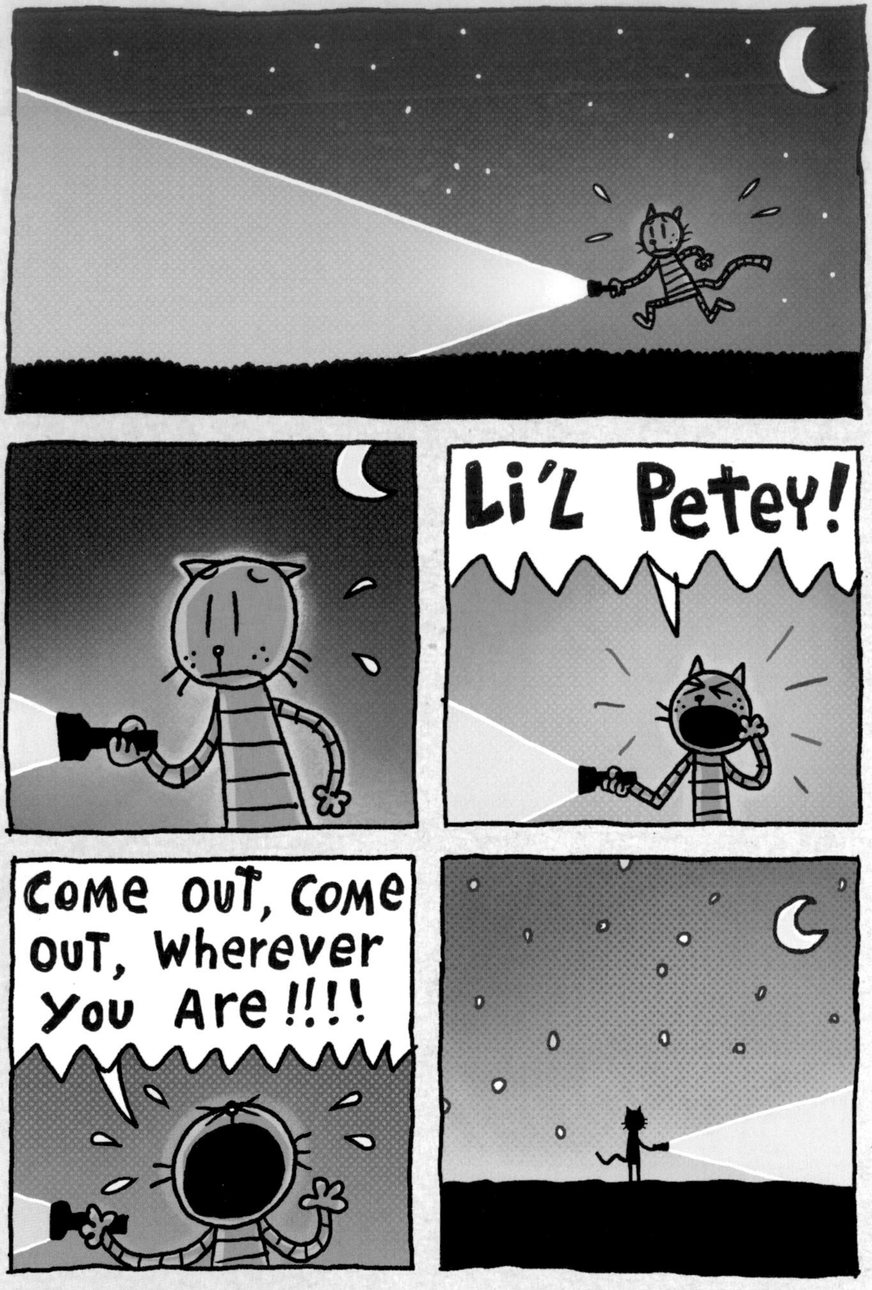
Li'L Petey!
Come out, come out, wherever you Are!!!!

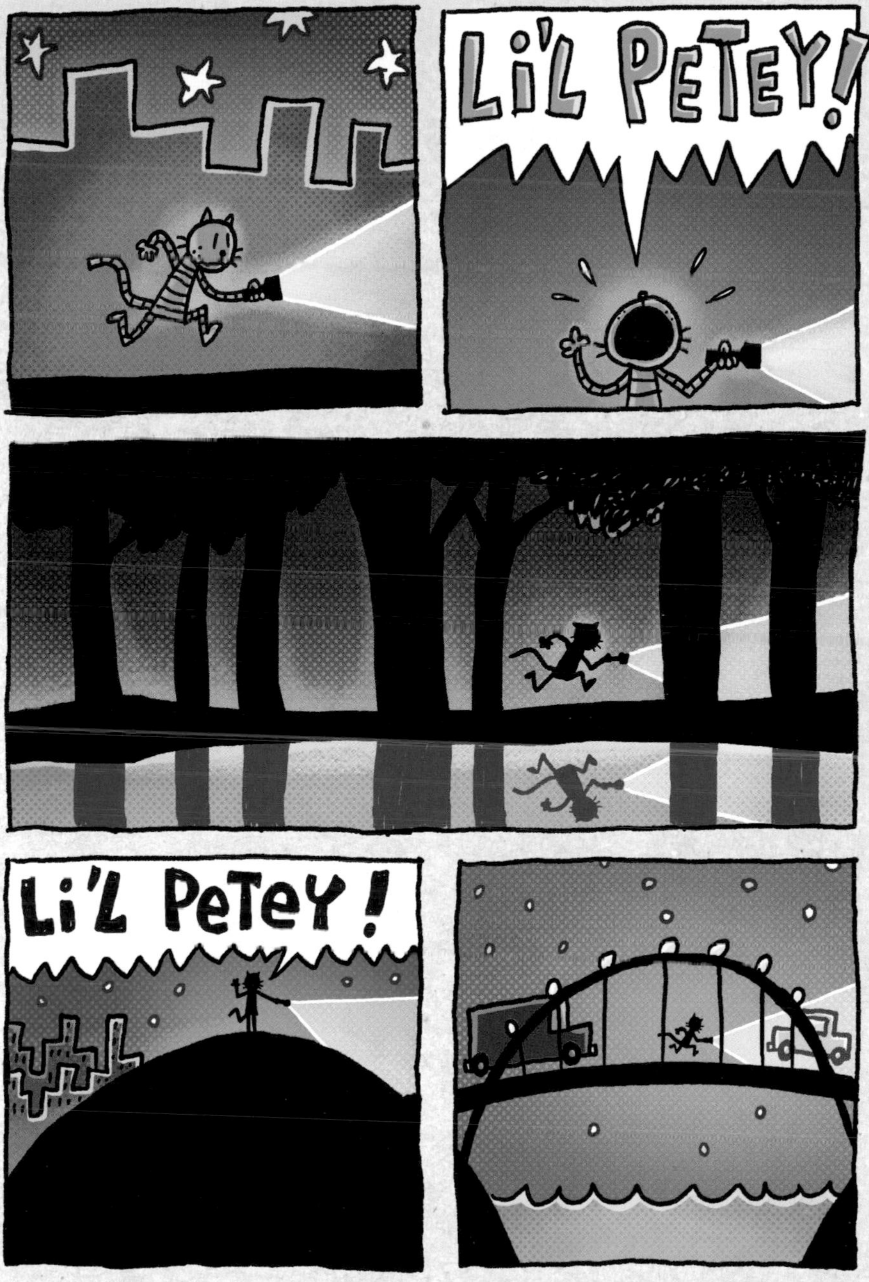
LI'L PETEY!
LI'L PETEY!

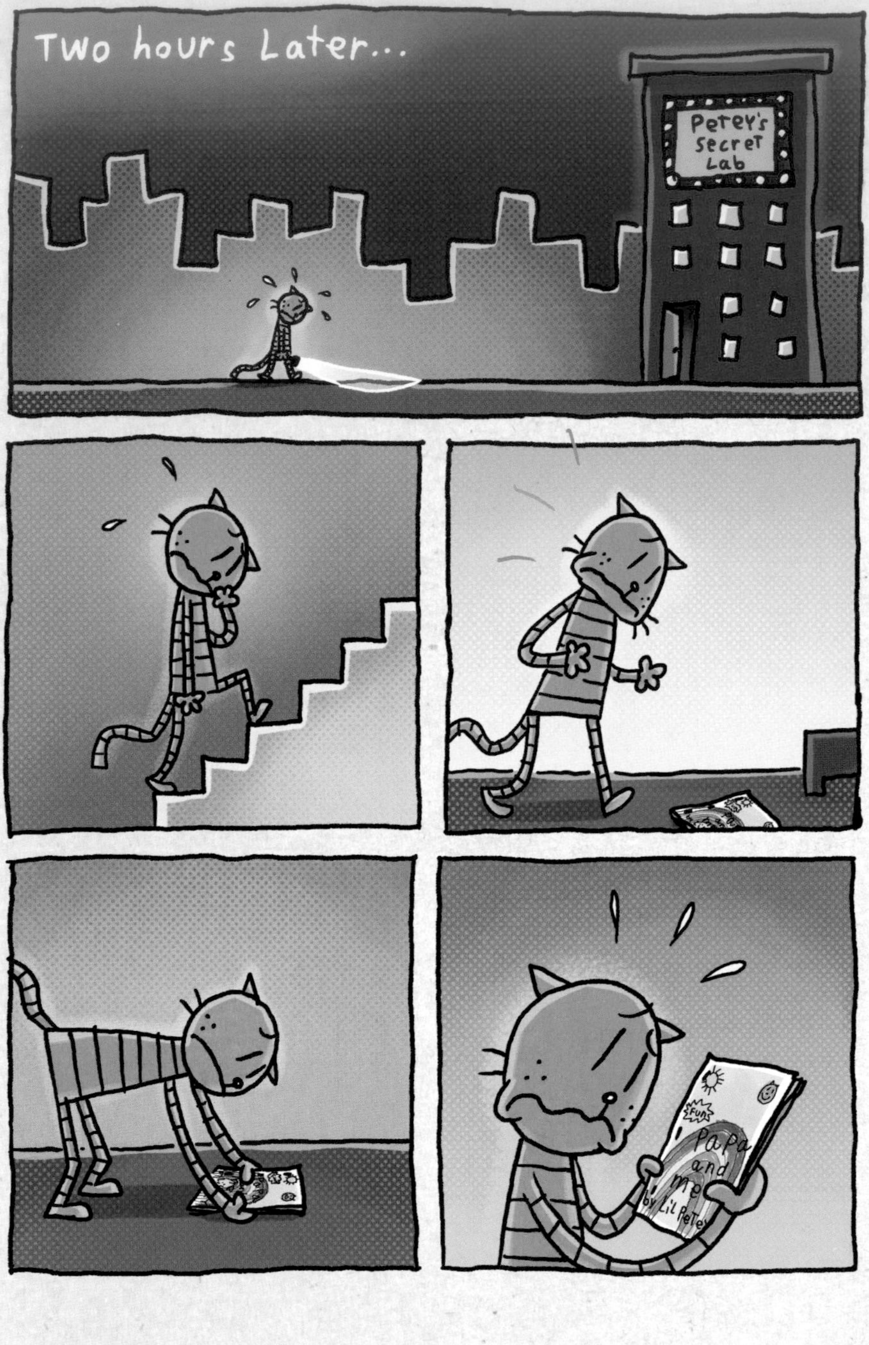
Two hours Later...
Petey's Secret Lab
FUN
Papa and me by Li'l Petey

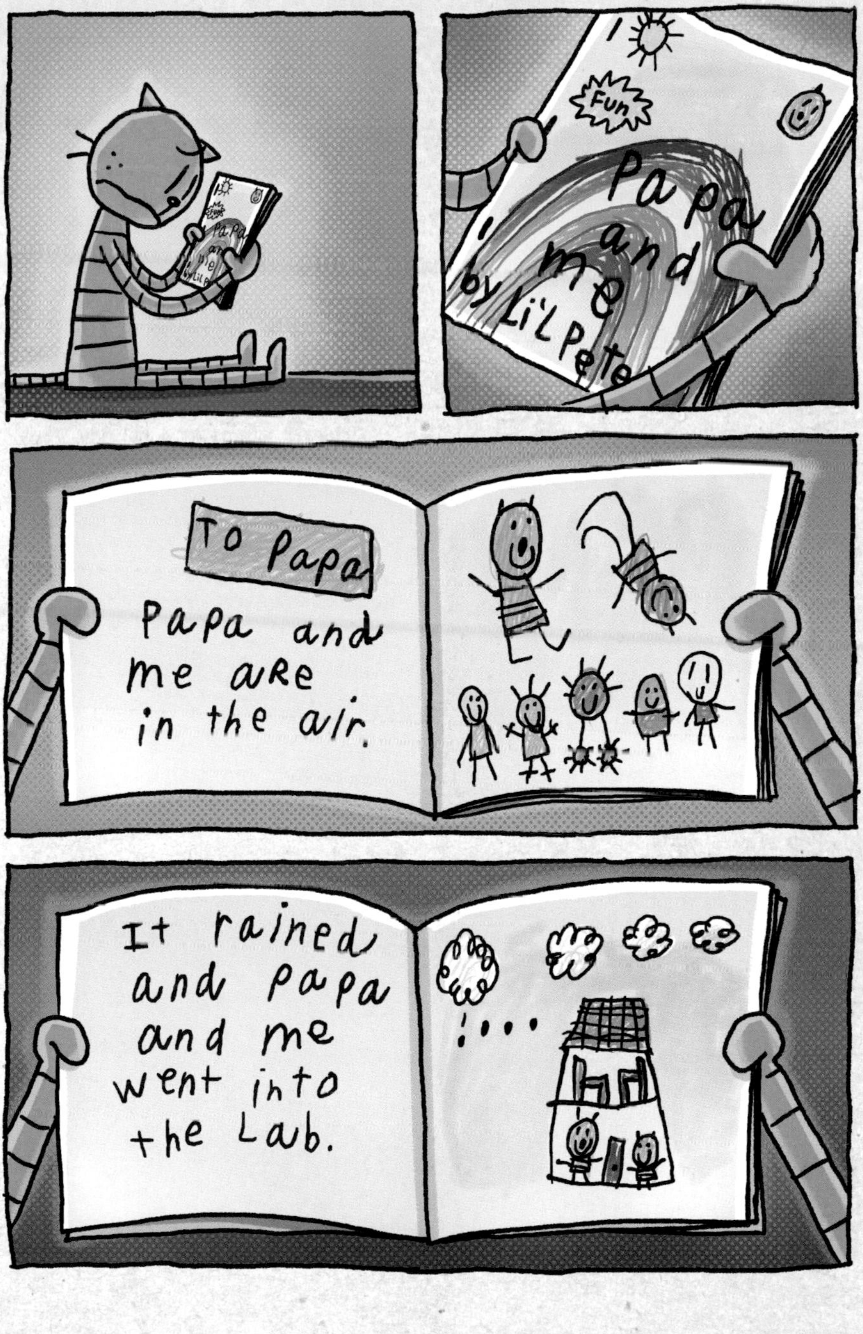
Fun
Papa and me
by Li'L Pete
To Papa
Papa and me aRe in the air.
It rained and papa and me went into the Lab.

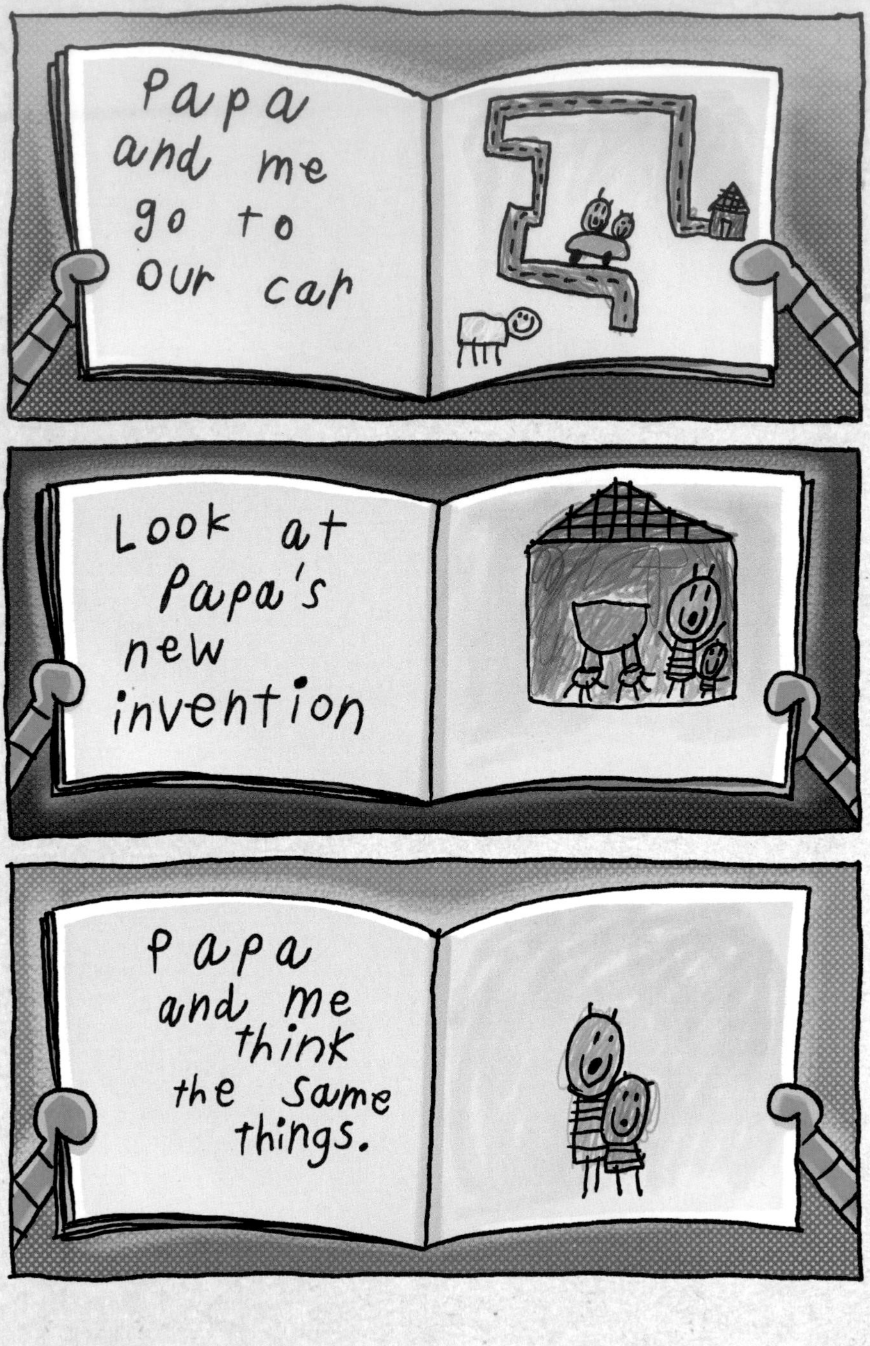
Papa and me go to our car
Look at Papa's new invention
Papa and me think the same things.

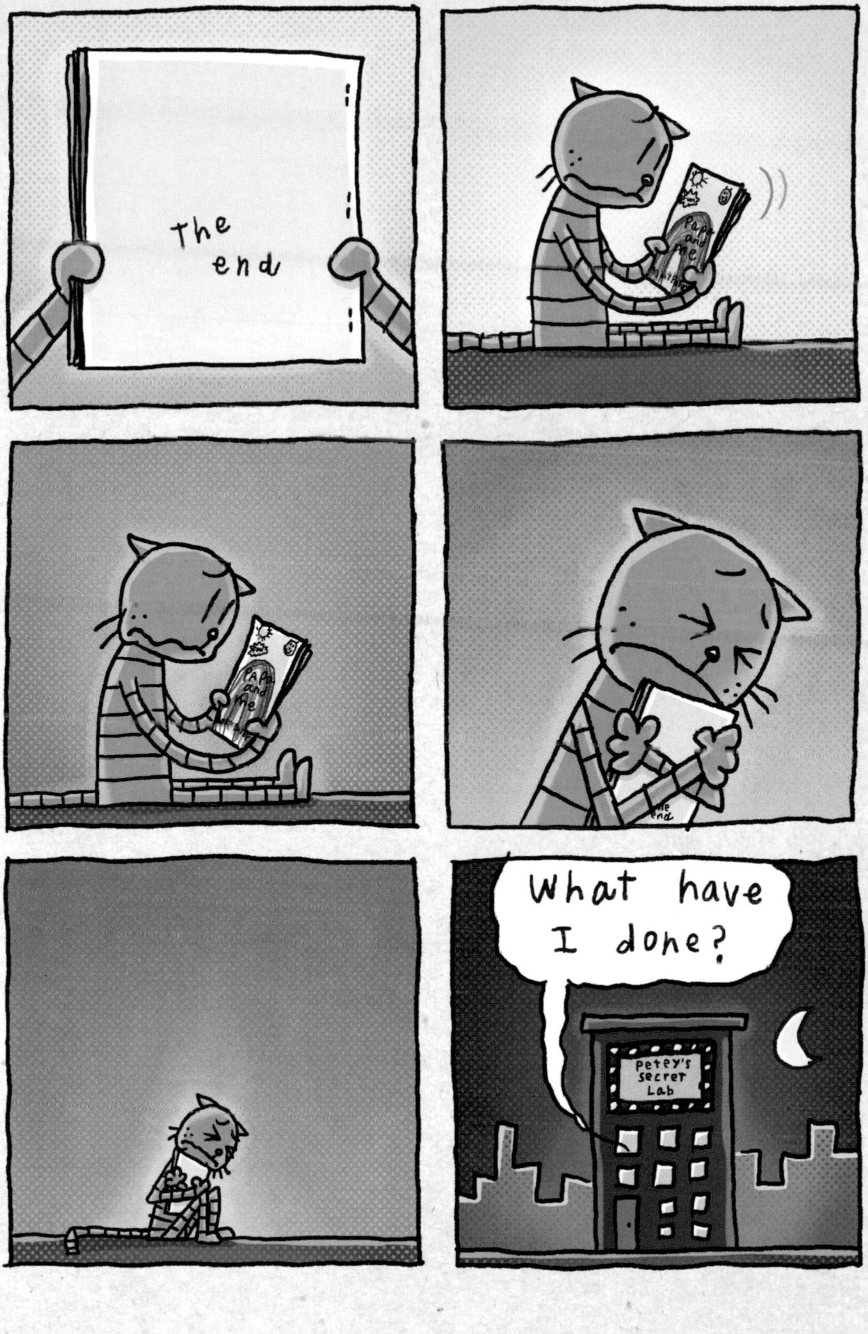
The end
Papa and me
PAPa and me
What have I done?
Petey's Secret Lab

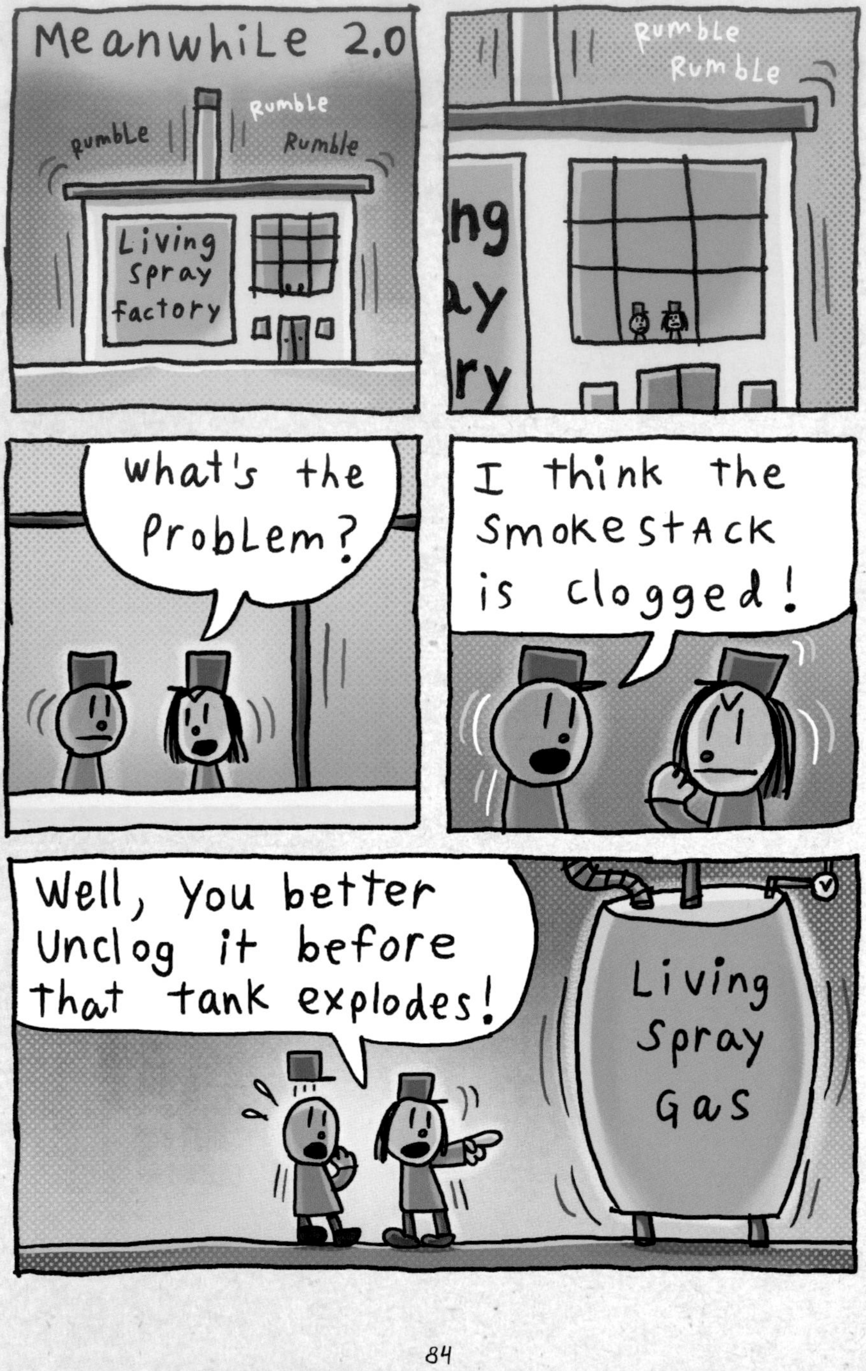
Meanwhile 2.0
Rumble
Rumble
Rumble
Living Spray Factory
Rumble
Rumble
What's the Problem?
I think the Smokestack is clogged!
Well, you better Unclog it before that tank explodes!
Living Spray Gas

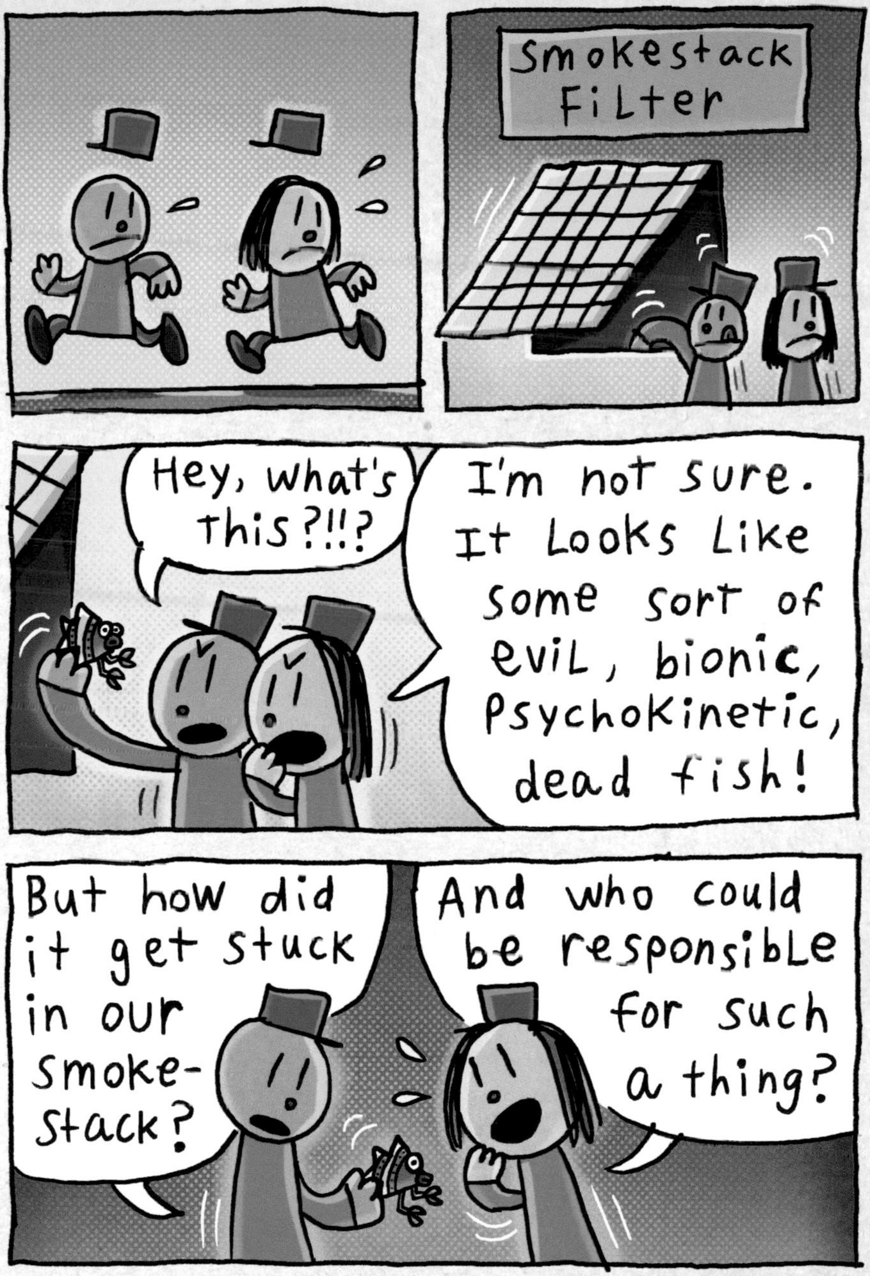
Smokestack Filter
Hey, what's this?!!?
I'm not sure. It looks like some sort of evil, bionic, psychokinetic, dead fish!
But how did it get stuck in our smoke-stack?
And who could be responsible for such a thing?

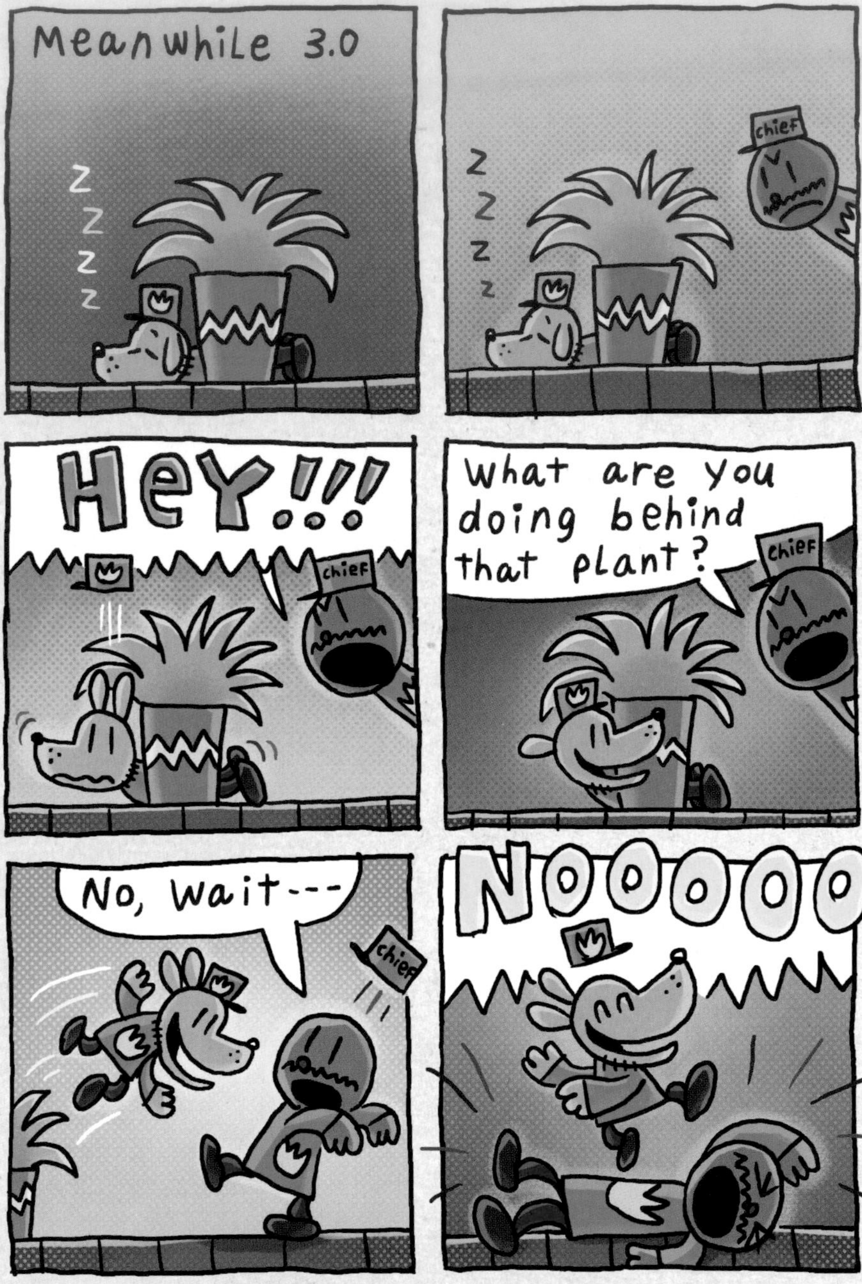
Meanwhile 3.0
Z Z Z Z
chief
Z Z Z Z
HEY!!!
chief
What are you doing behind that plant?
chief
No, wait---
chief
NOOOOO

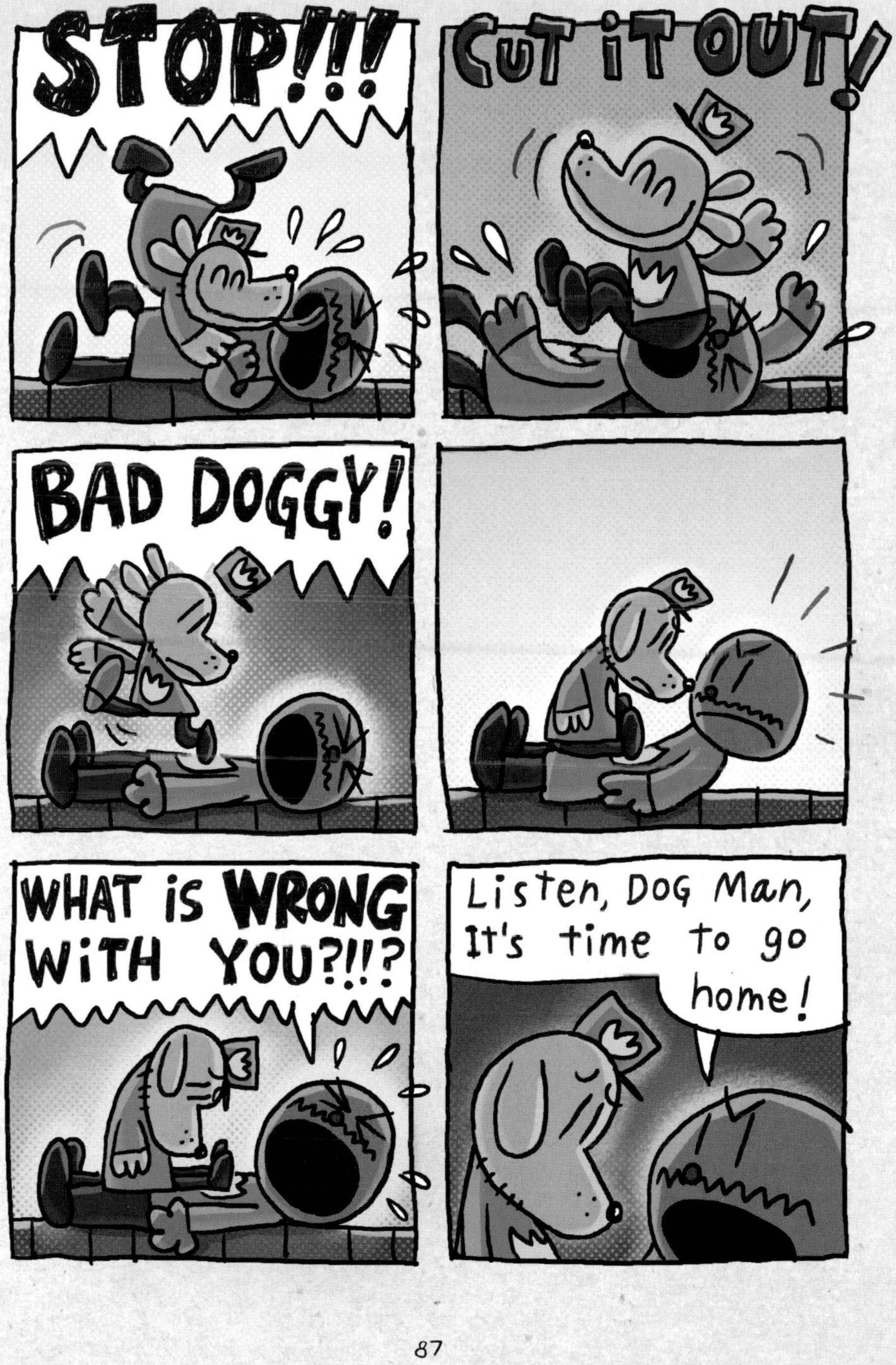
STOP!!!
CUT IT OUT!
BAD DOGGY!
WHAT is WRONG WiTH YOU?!!?
Listen, DOG Man, It's time to go home!

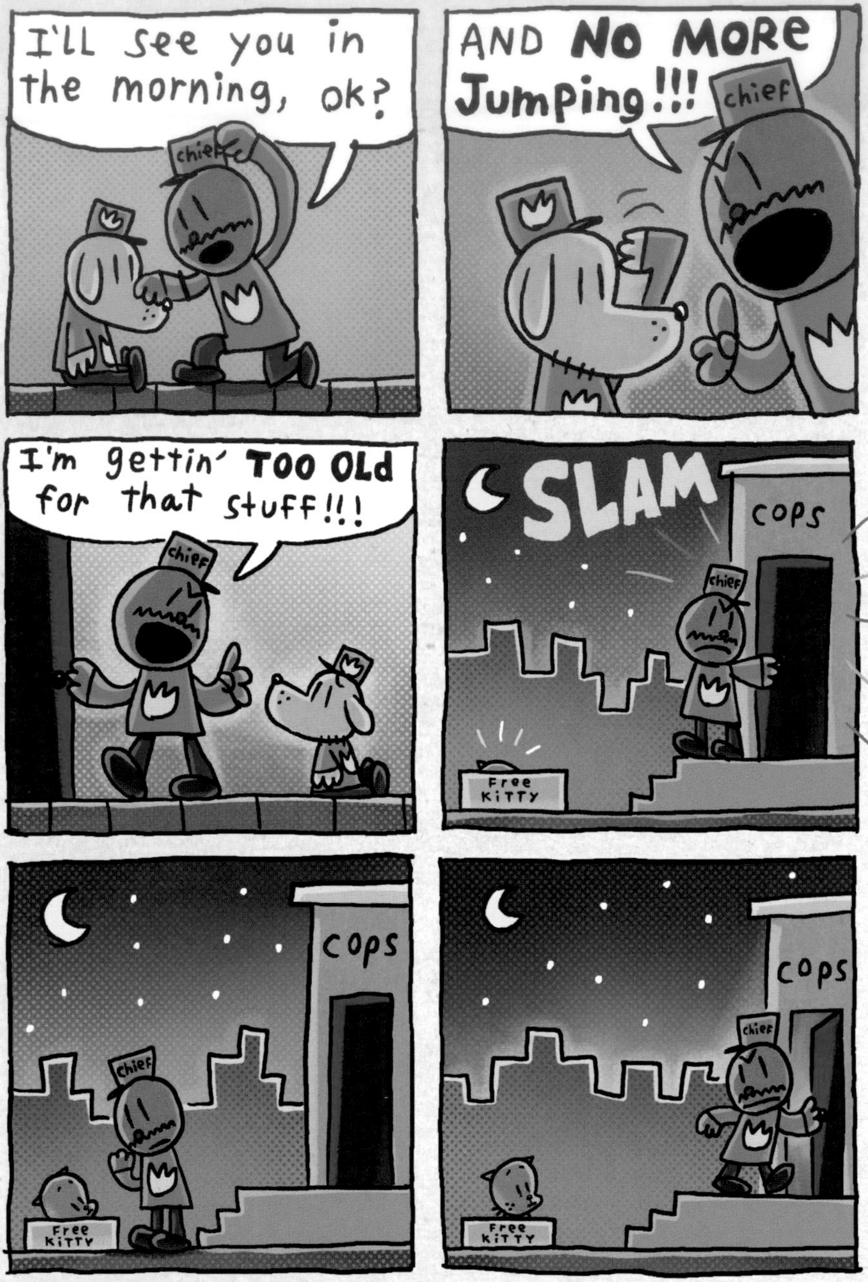
I'LL see you in the morning, ok?
chief
AND NO MORE Jumping!!!
chief
I'm gettin' TOO OLd for that stuff!!!
chief
SLAM
cops
chief
Free KiTTY
cops
chief
Free KiTTY
cops
chief
Free KiTTY

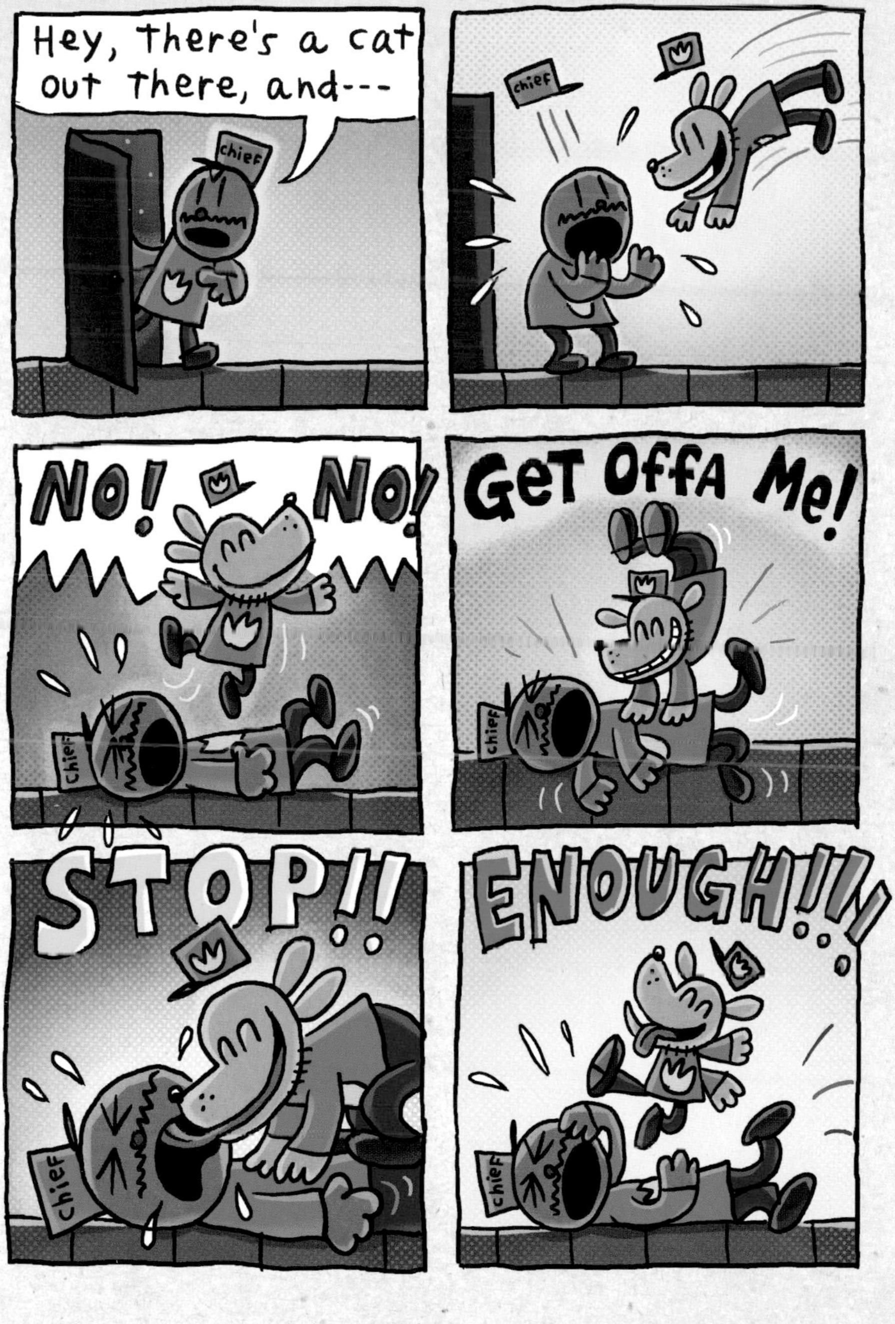
Hey, there's a cat out there, and---
chief
chief
NO! NO!
chief
GET OFFA ME!
chief
STOP!!
chief
ENOUGH!!!
chief

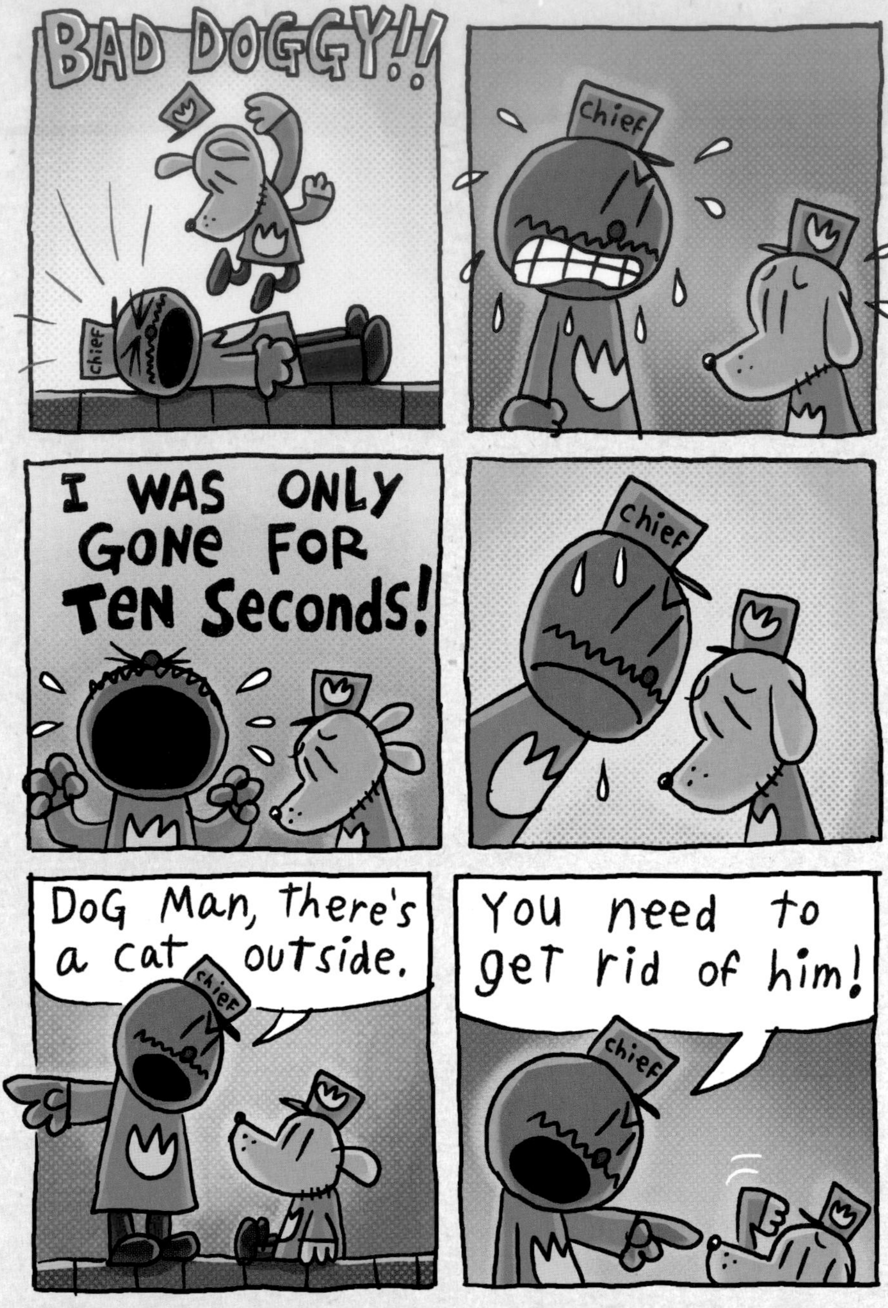
BAD DOGGY!!!
chief
chief
I WAS ONLY GONE FOR TEN Seconds!
chief
DoG Man, there's a cat outside.
chief
You need to get rid of him!
chief

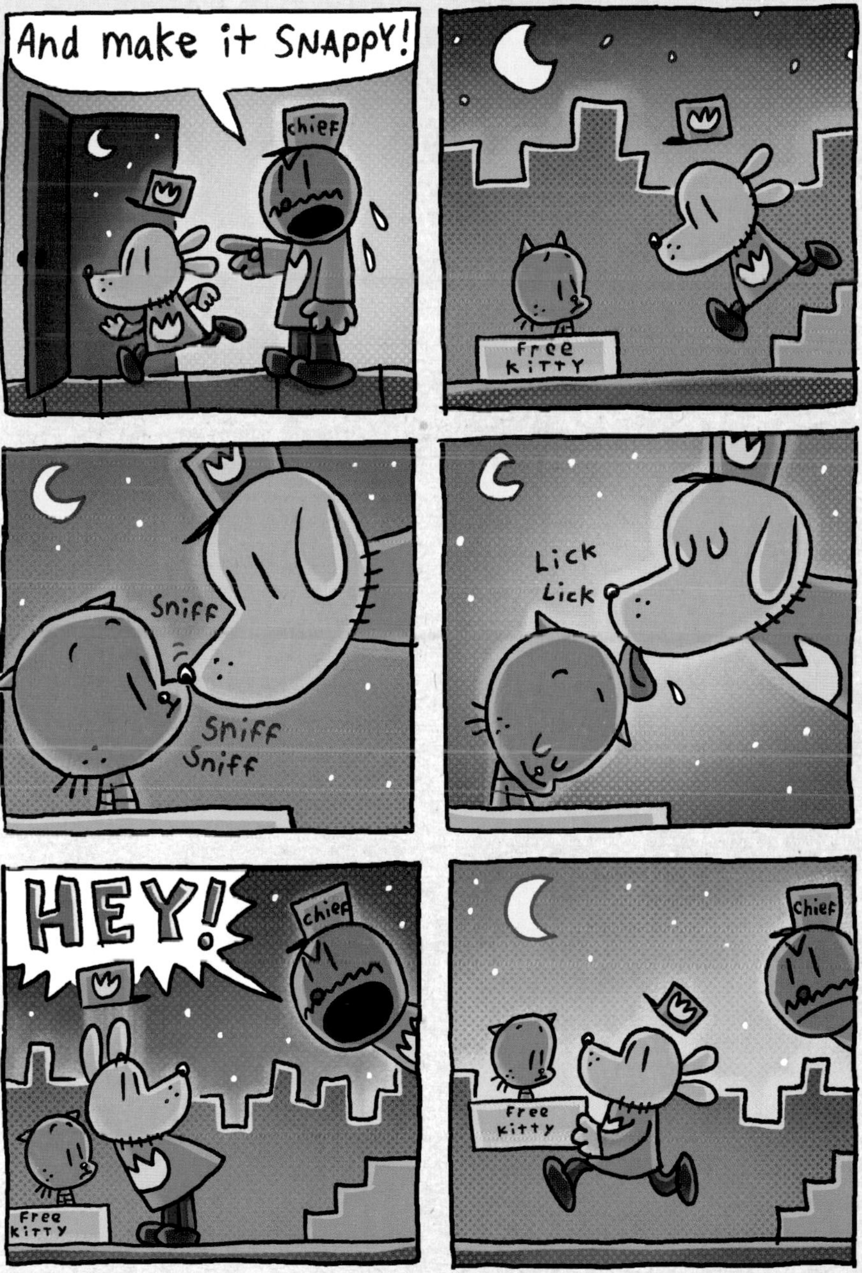

And make it SNAPPY!
chief
Free kitty
Sniff
Sniff
Sniff
Lick
Lick
HEY!
chief
Free kitty
Chief
Free kitty

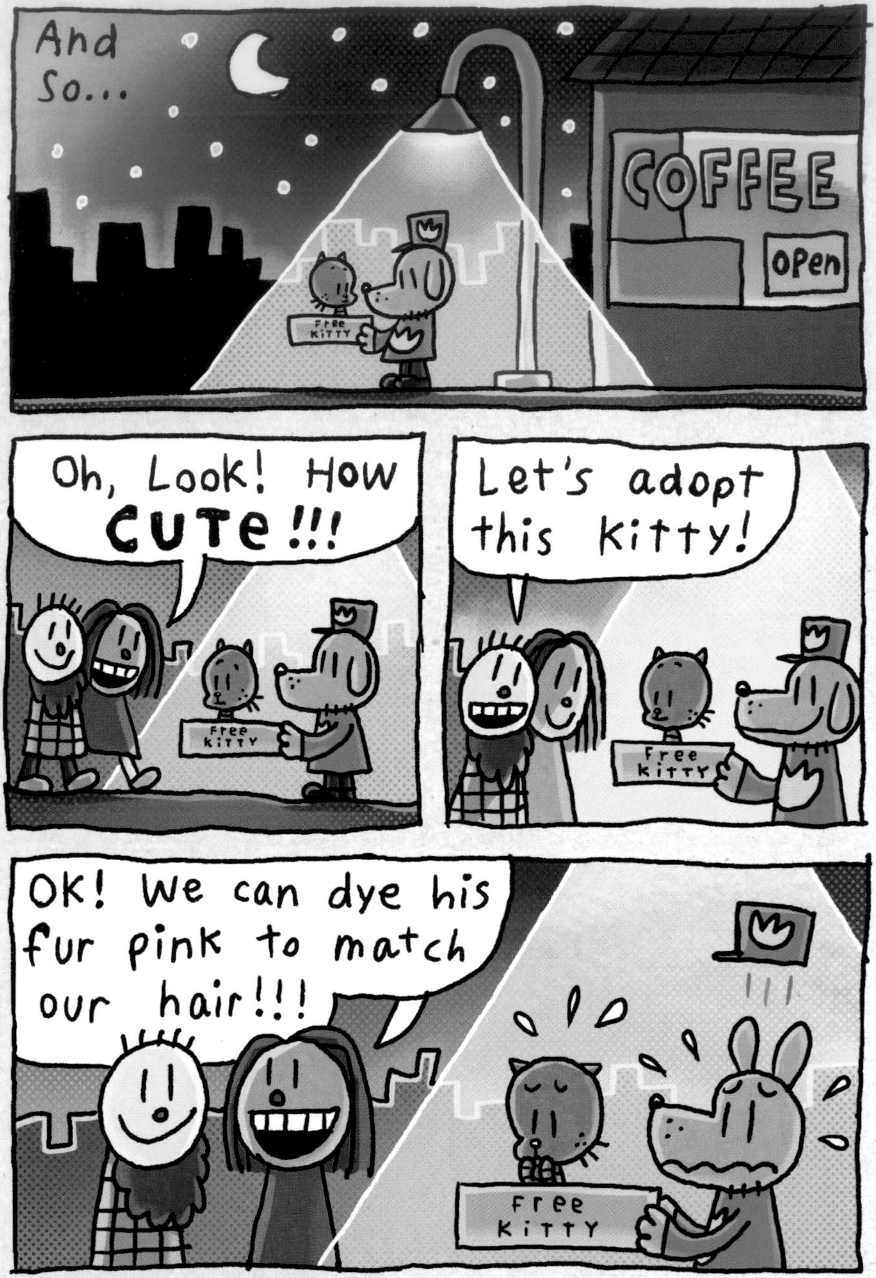
And So...
COFFEE
Open
Free KITTY
Oh, Look! How CUTE!!!
Free KITTY
Let's adopt this kitty!
Free KITTY
OK! We can dye his fur pink to match our hair!!!
Free KITTY

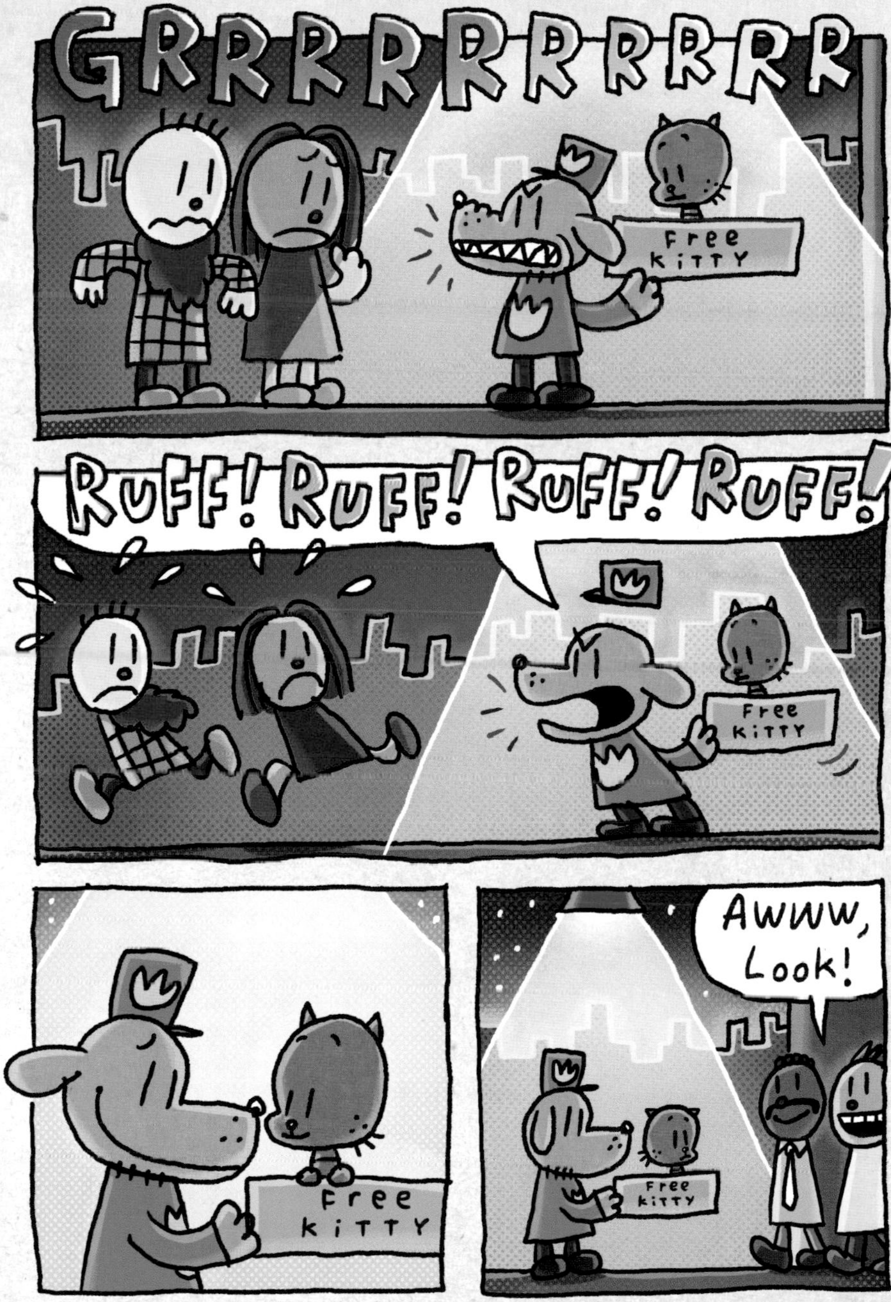
GRRRRRRRRRR
Free kitty
RUFF! RUFF! RUFF! RUFF!
Free kitty
Free kitty
AWWW, Look!
Free kitty

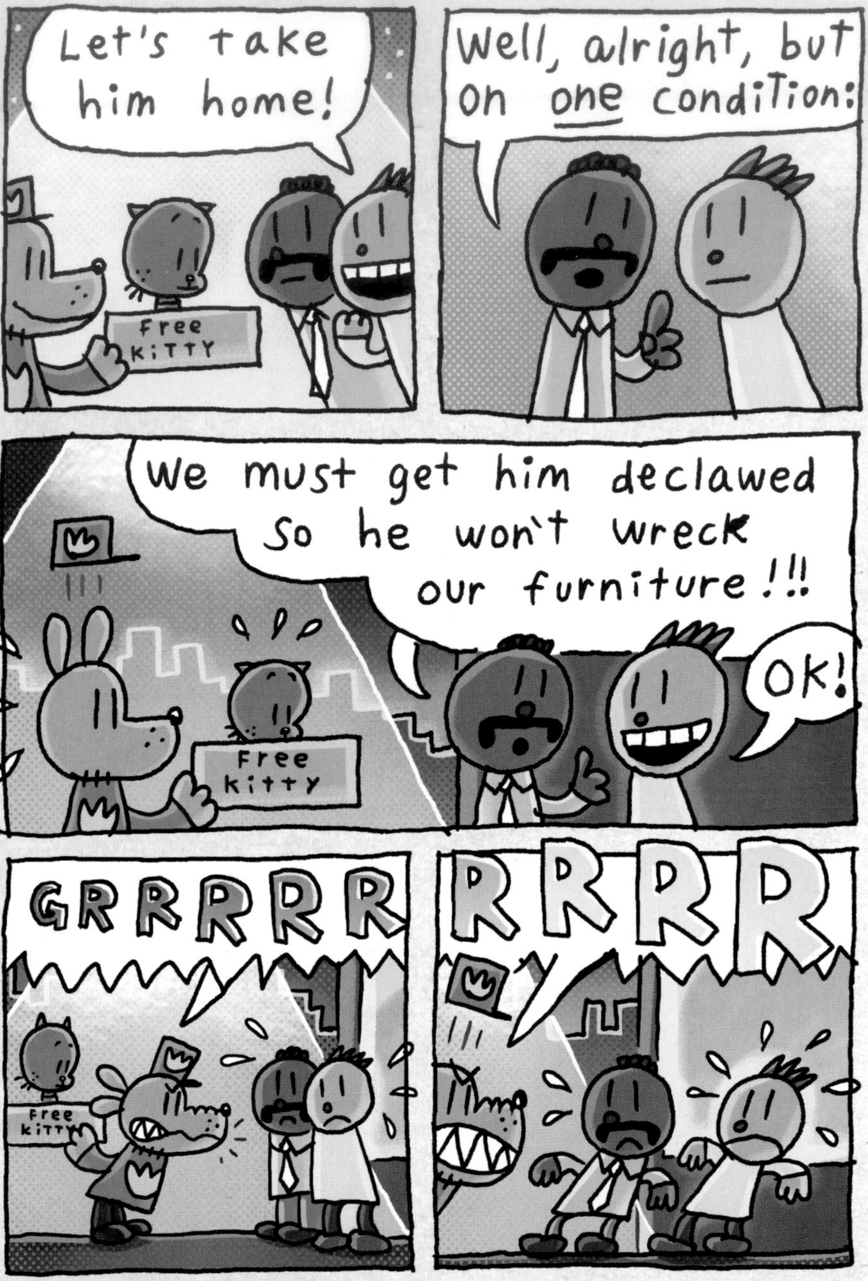
Let's take him home!
Free KiTTY
Well, alright, but on one condition:
We must get him declawed so he won't wreck our furniture!!!
OK!
Free kitty
GRRRRR RRRR
Free kiTT

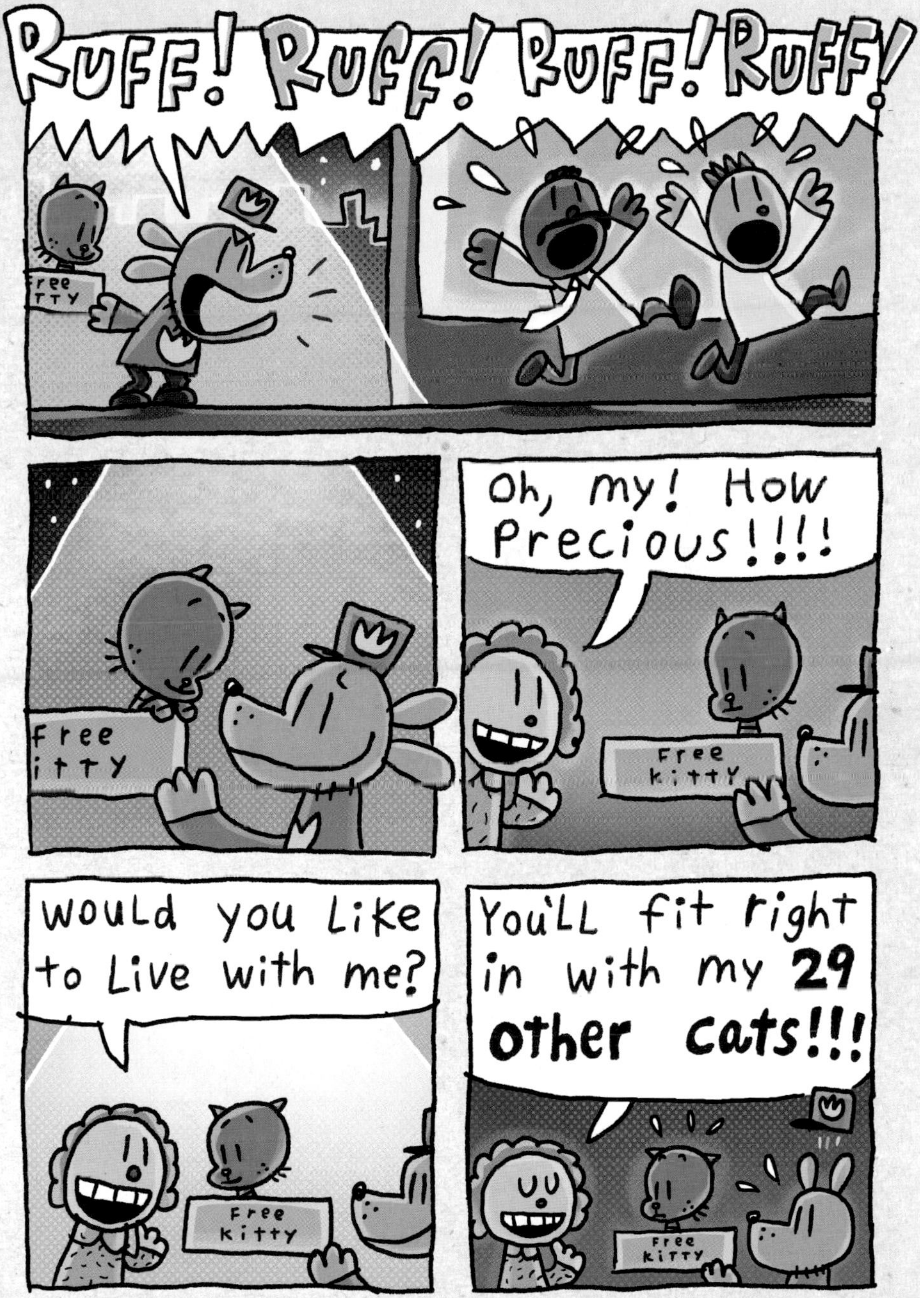
RUFF! RUFF! RUFF! RUFF!
Free KITTY
Free kitty
Oh, my! How Precious!!!!
Free kitty
Would you like to live with me?
Free kitty
You'll fit right in with my 29 other cats!!!
Free kitty

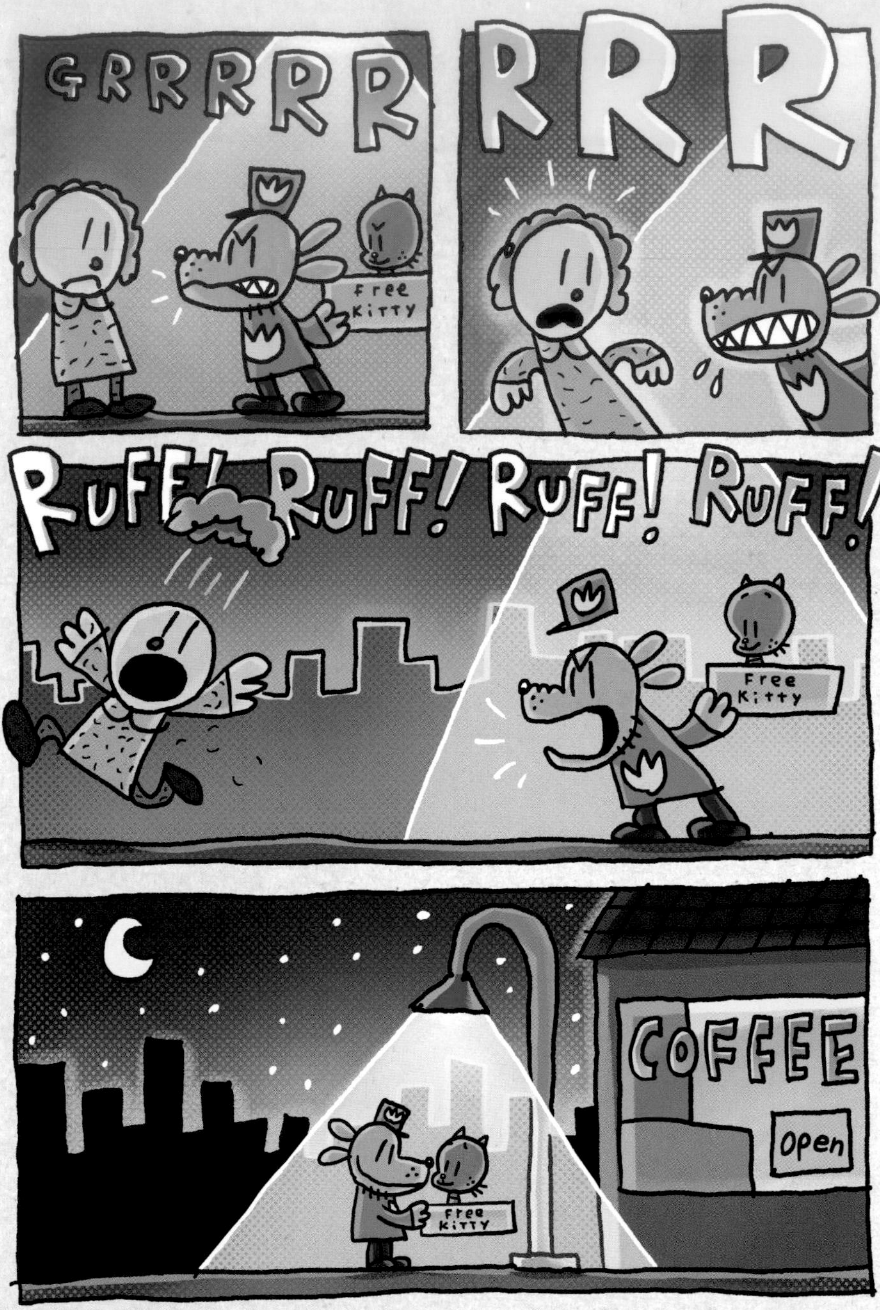
GRRRRR
Free Kitty
RRR
RUFF! RUFF! RUFF! RUFF!
Free Kitty
Free Kitty
COFFEE
Open

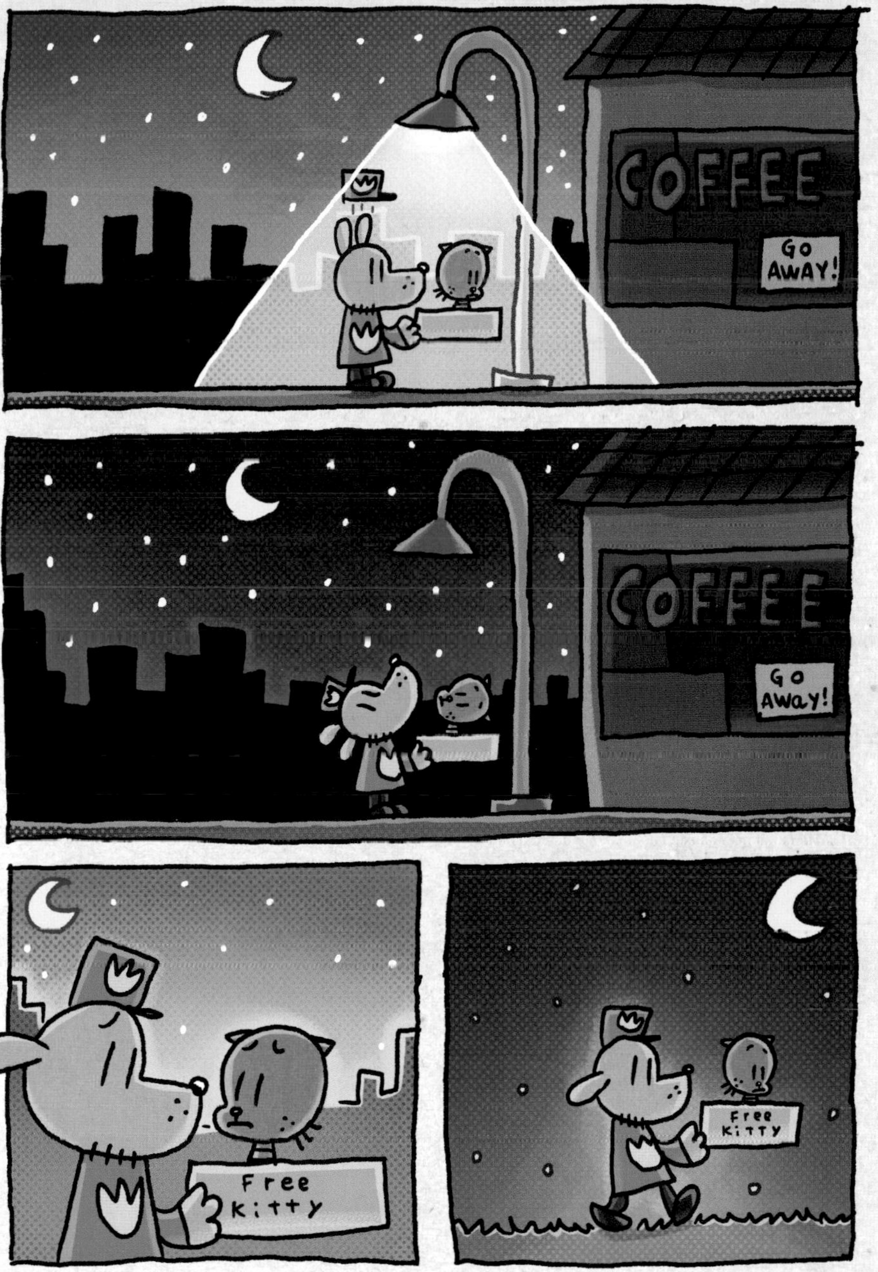
COFFEE
GO AWAY!
COFFEE
GO AWAY!
Free Kitty
Free Kitty

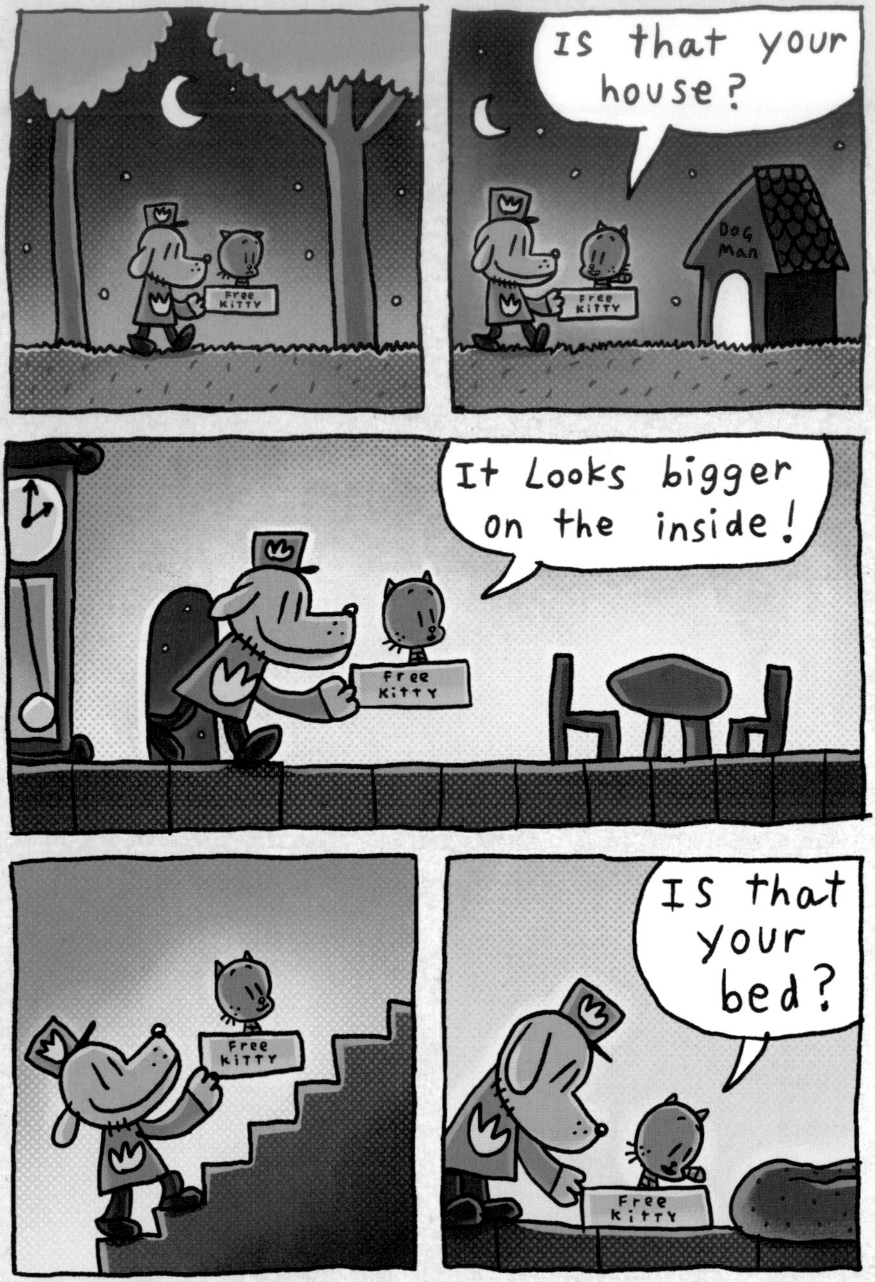
Free Kitty
Is that your house?
Dog Man
Free Kitty
It Looks bigger on the inside!
Free Kitty
Free Kitty
Is that your bed?
Free Kitty

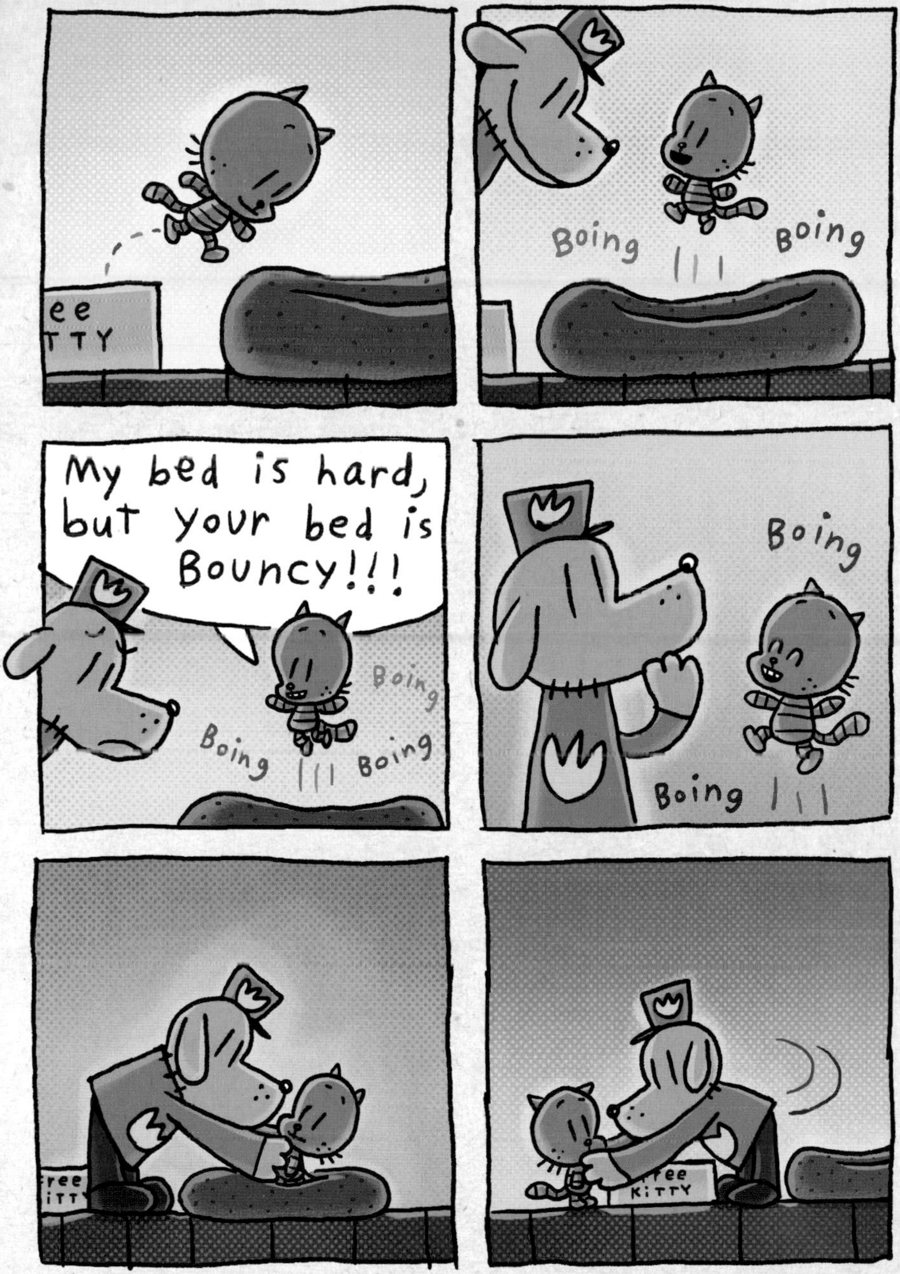
ee
TTY
Boing
Boing
My bed is hard, but your bed is Bouncy!!!
Boing
Boing
Boing
Boing
Boing
Free
KiTTY

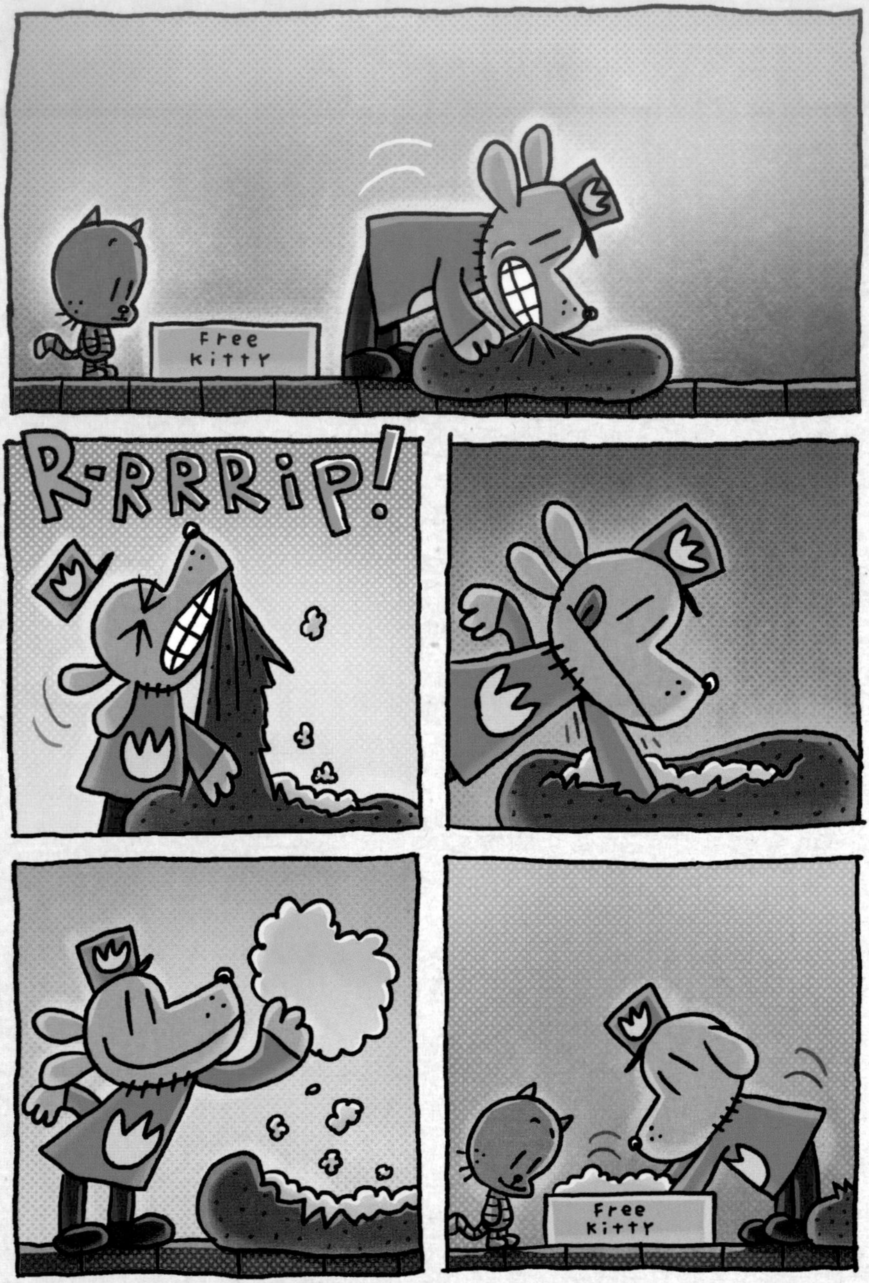
Free
Kitty
R-RRRIP!
Free
Kitty

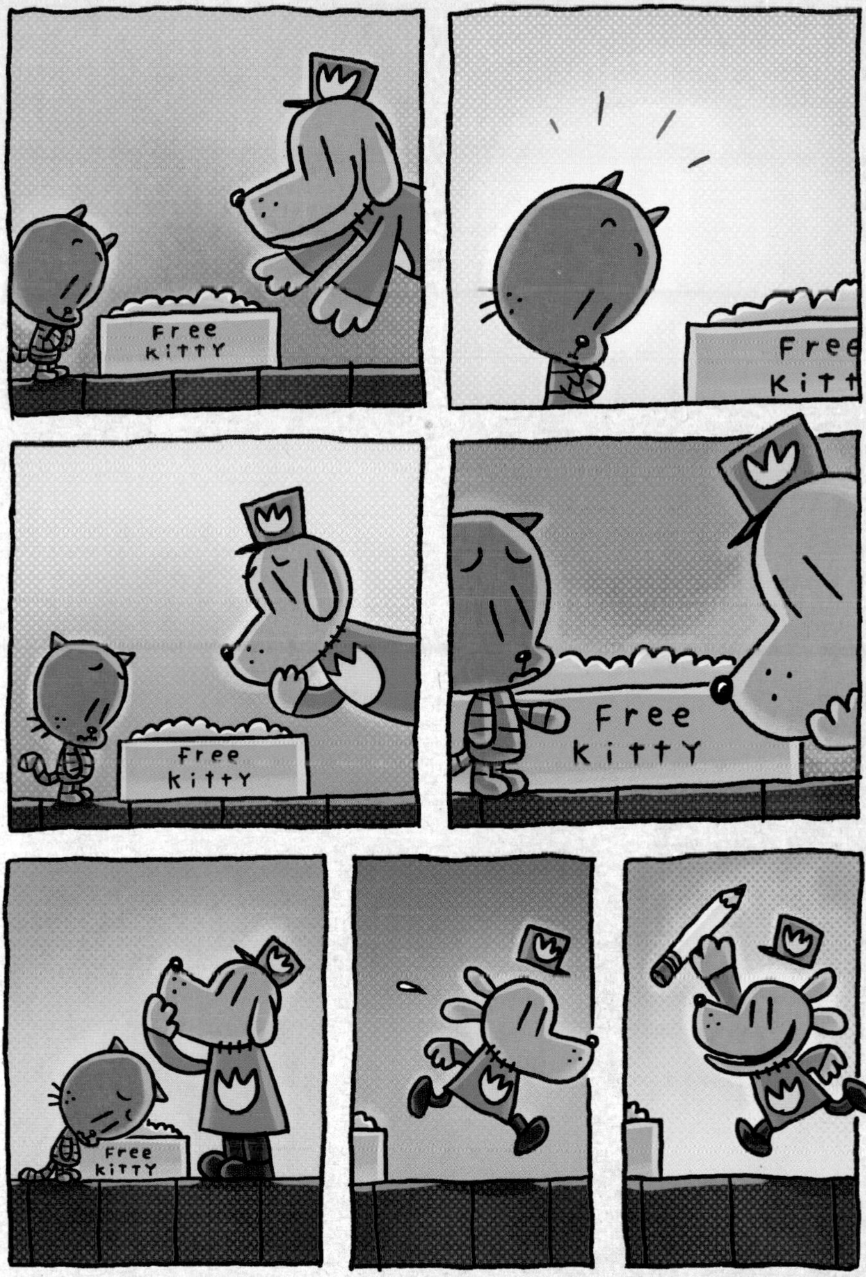
Free kitty
Free kitt
Free kitty
Free kitty
Free kitty

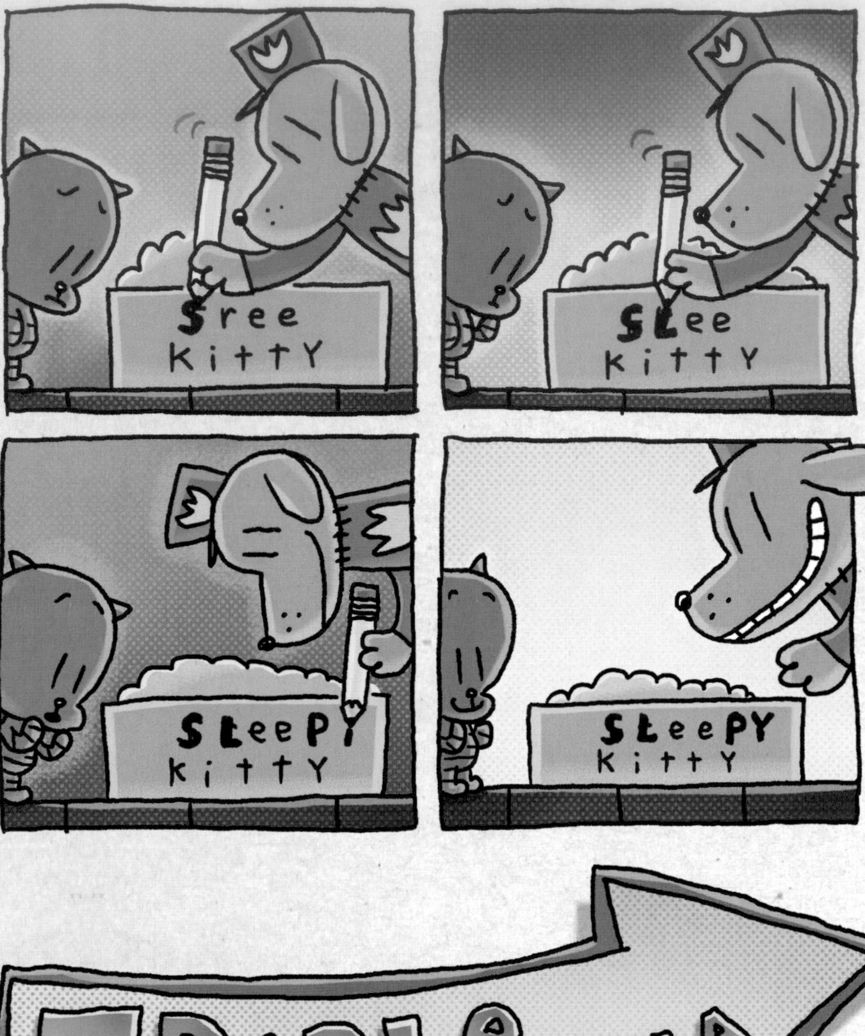
Sree
Kitty
SLee
Kitty
SLeeP
Kitty
SLeePY
Kitty

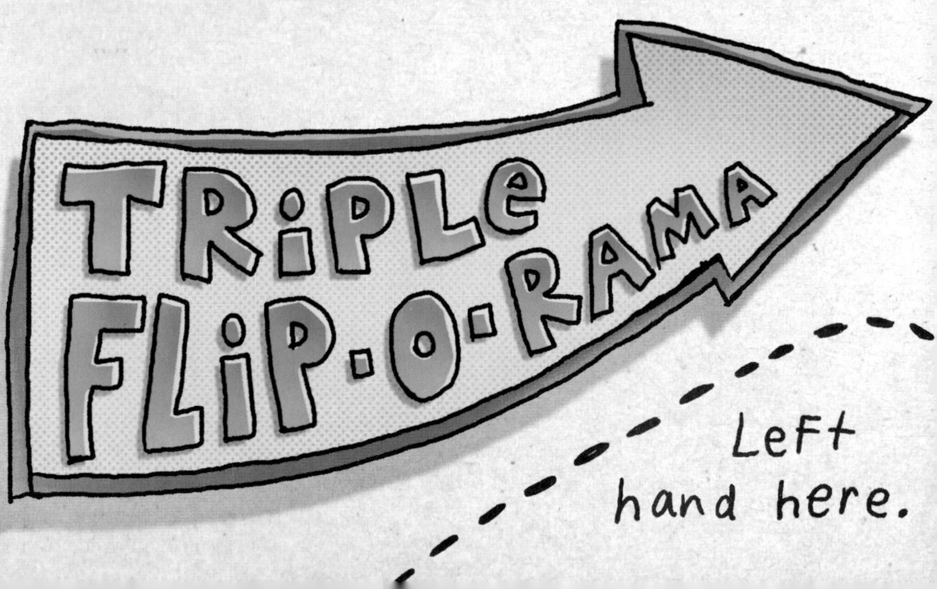
TRiPLE
FLiP-O-RAMA

Left
hand here.

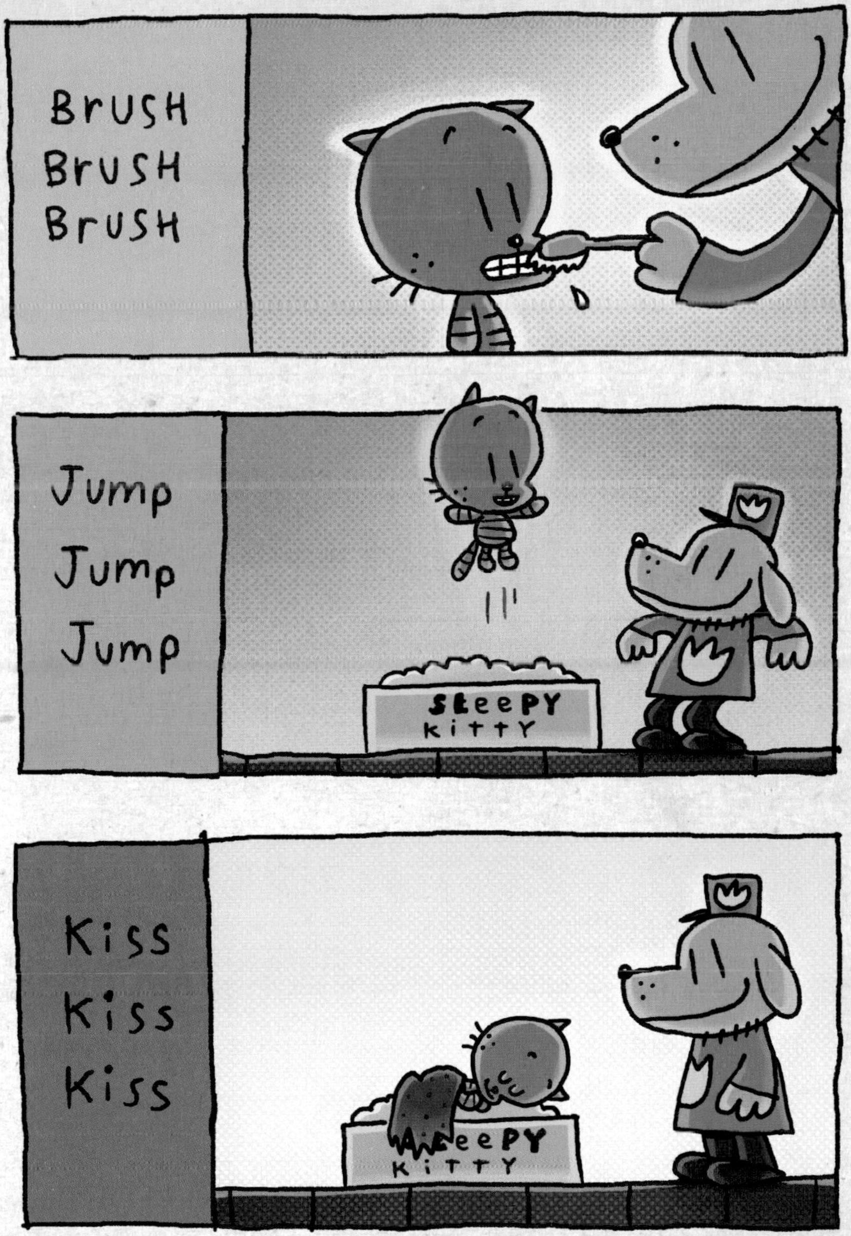
BrUSH
BrUSH
BrUSH
Jump
Jump
Jump
SLEEPY
KiTTY
Kiss
Kiss
Kiss

Right Thumb here.

BRUSH
BRUSH
BRUSH

Jump
Jump
Jump

Kiss
Kiss
Kiss

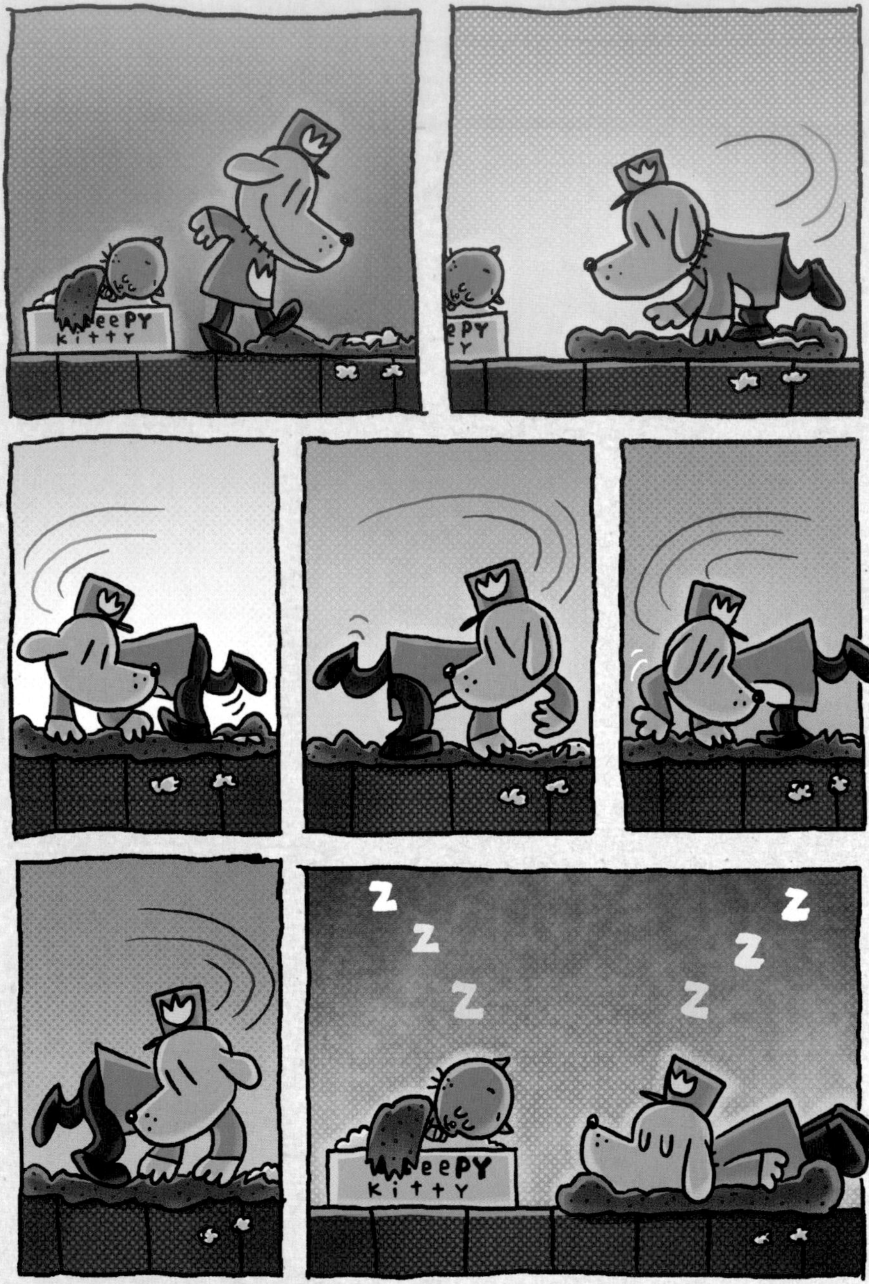
eePY
KiTTY
eePY
KiTTY
Z Z Z
Z Z Z

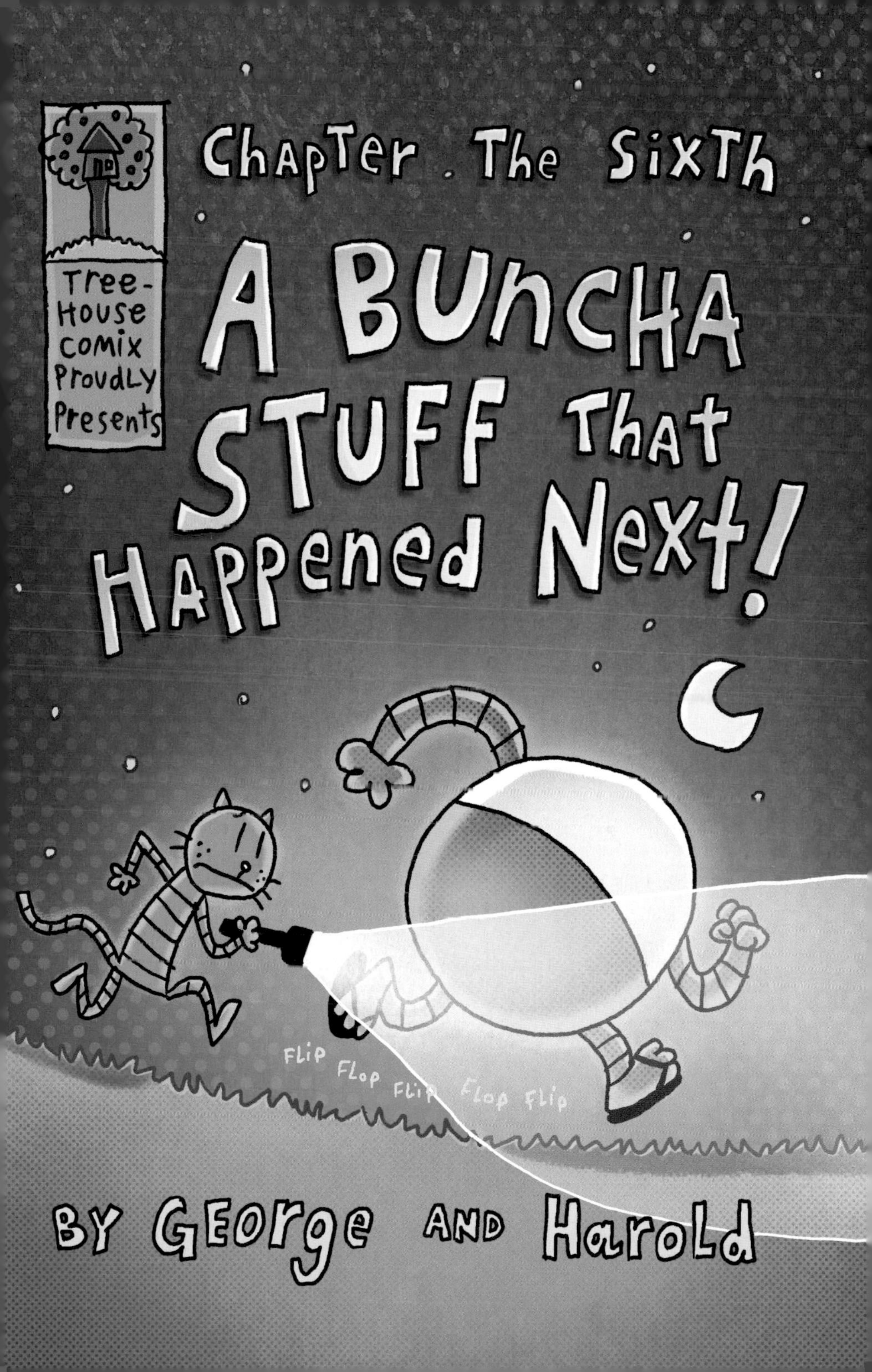
Tree-House Comix Proudly Presents
Chapter The Sixth
A BUNCHA STUFF That Happened Next!
FLIP
FLop
FLIP
FLop
FLIP
BY GEORge AND HaroLd

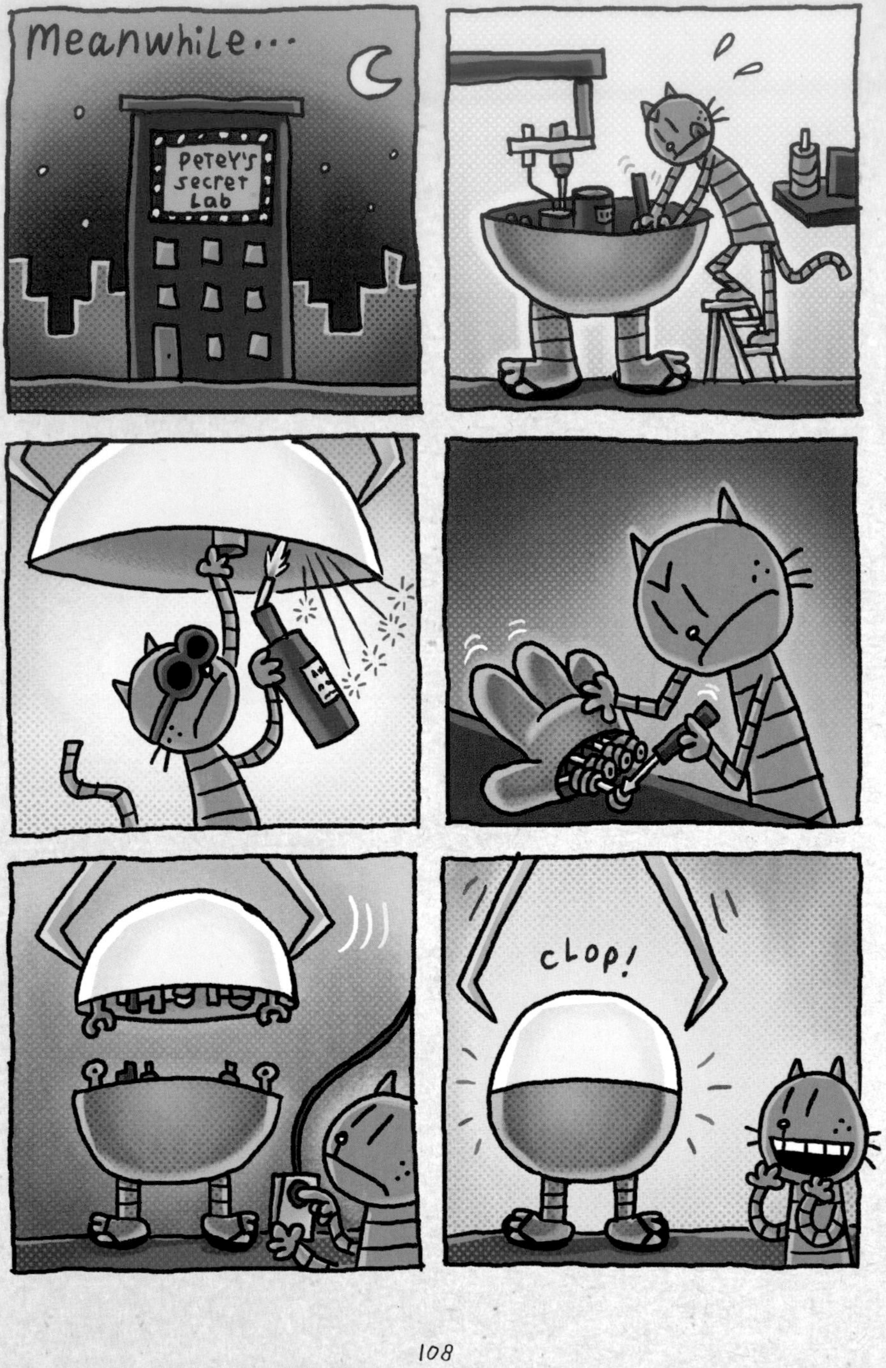
Meanwhile...
Petey's Secret Lab
CLOP!

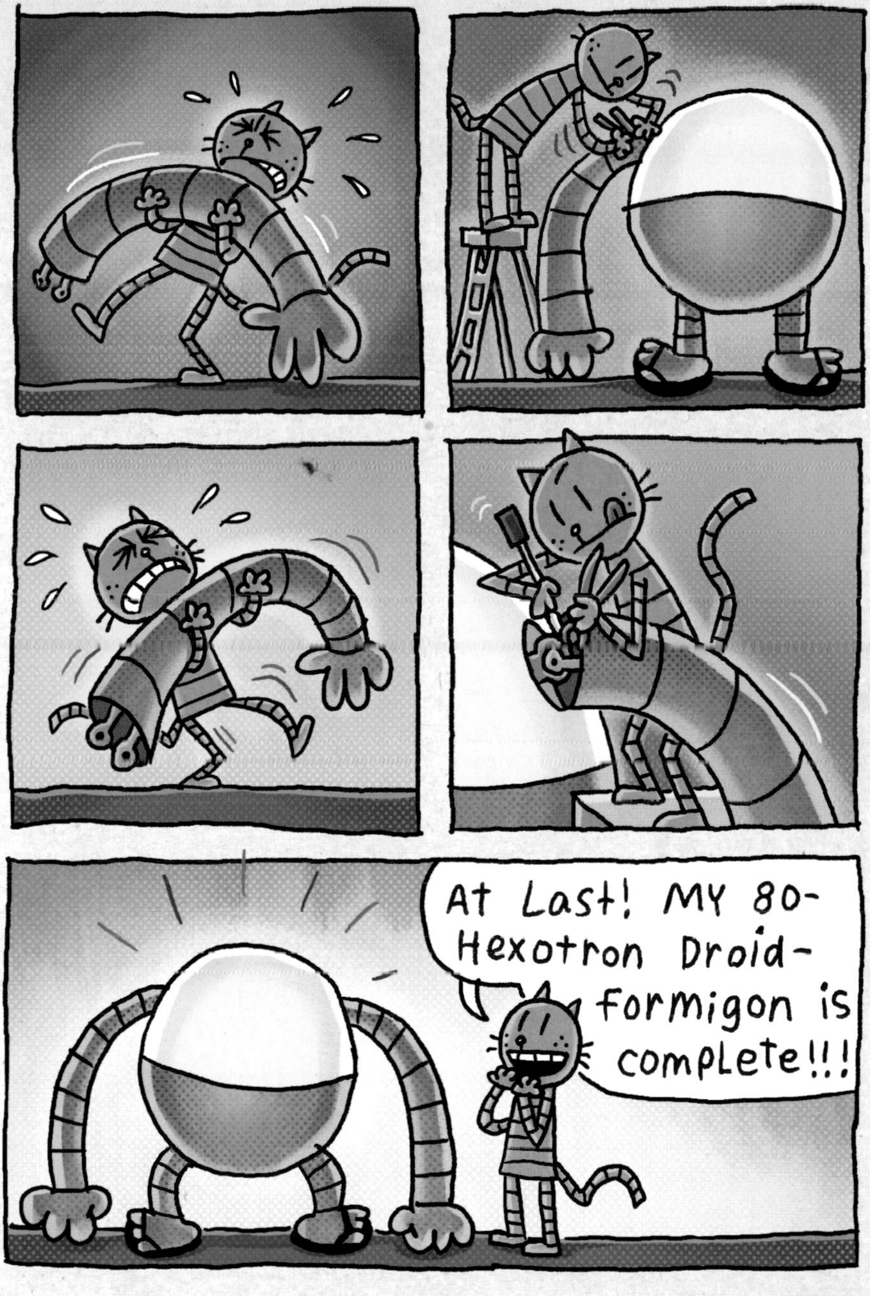
At Last! MY 80-Hexotron Droid-Formigon is complete!!!

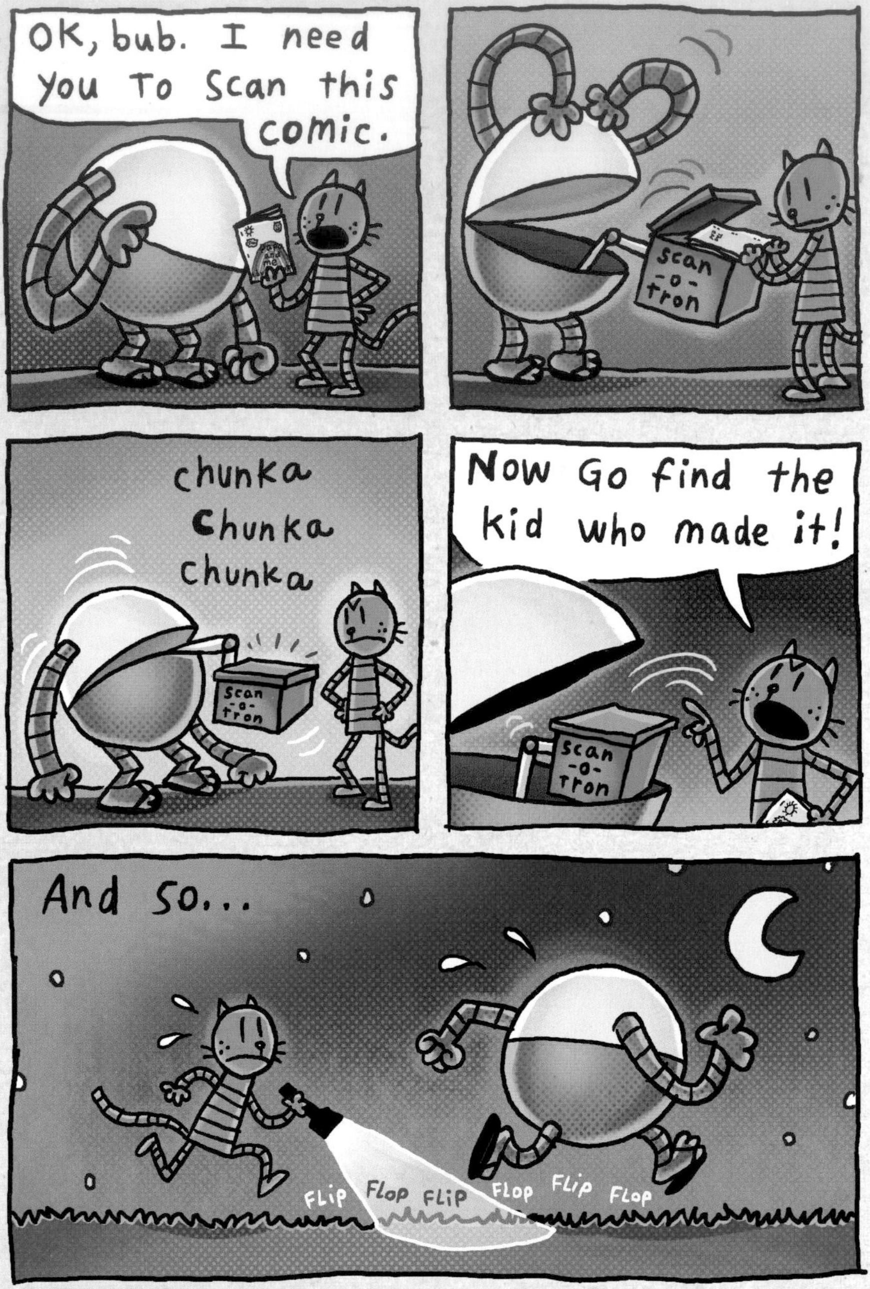
OK, bub. I need you To Scan this comic.
Scan -o- Tron
chunka Chunka chunka
Scan -o- Tron
Now Go find the kid who made it!
Scan -o- Tron
And so...
FLiP FLoP FLiP FLoP FLiP FLoP

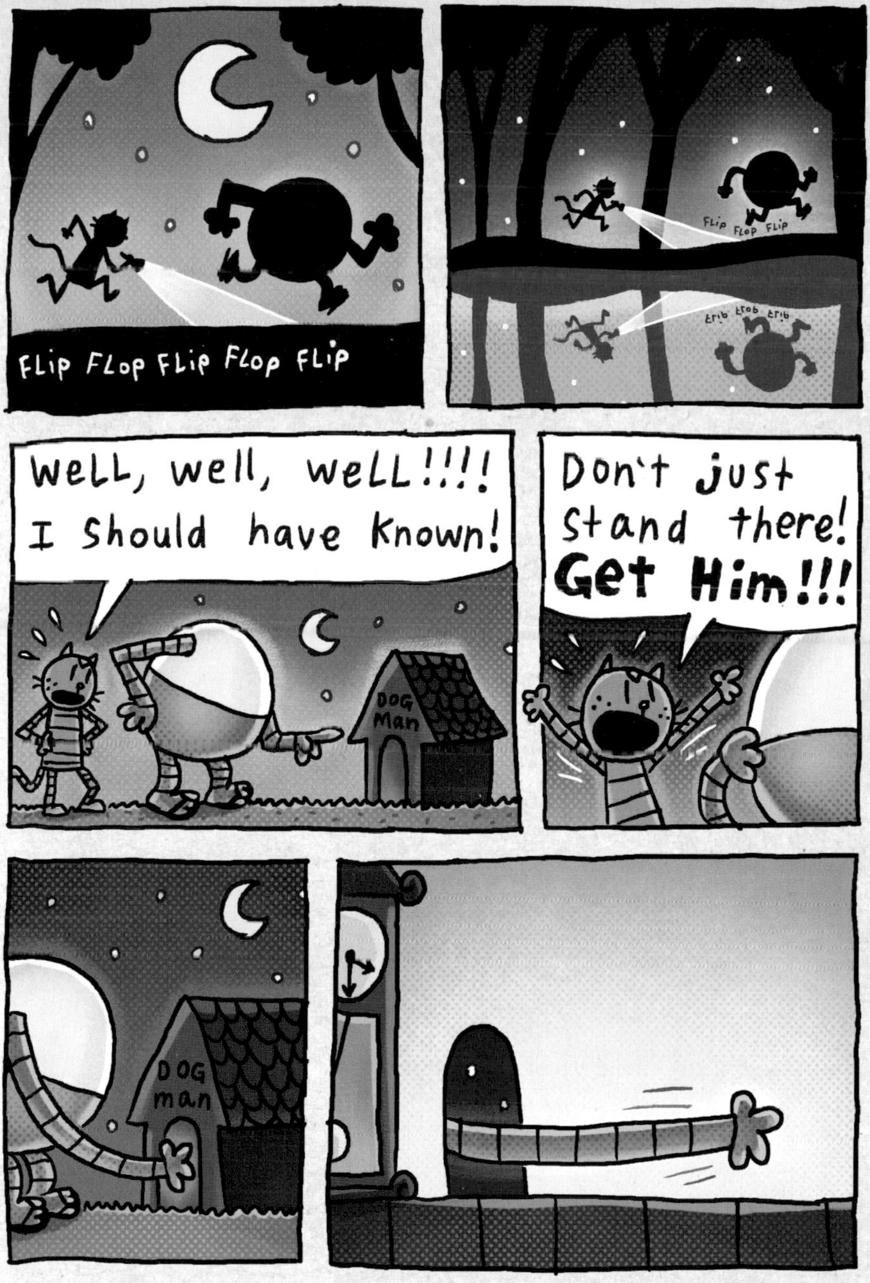
FLIP FLOP FLIP FLOP FLIP
FLIP FLOP FLIP
WELL, well, wELL!!!! I Should have Known!
DOG man
Don't just Stand there! Get Him!!!
DOG man

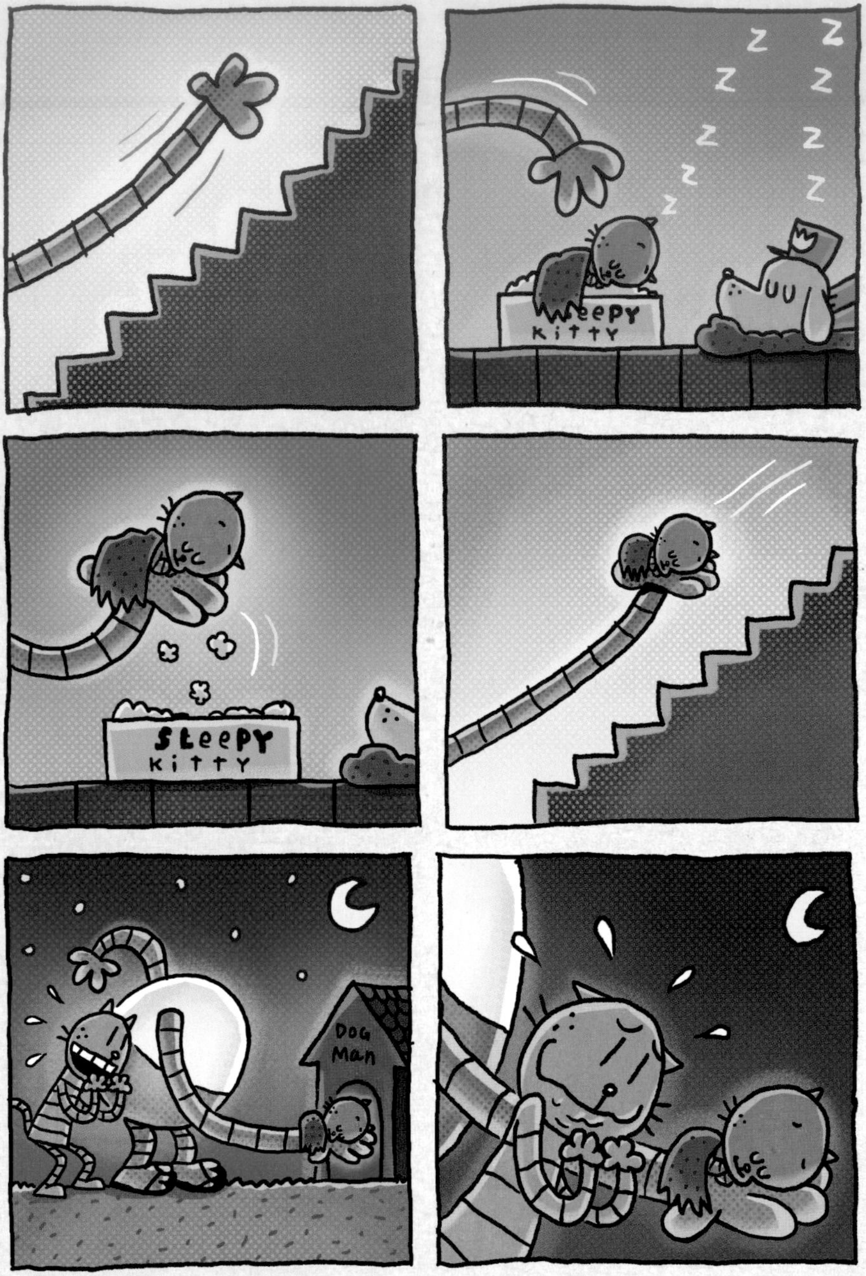
Z Z Z Z Z Z Z Z Z Z
SLEEPY KITTY
SLEEPY KITTY
DOG MAN

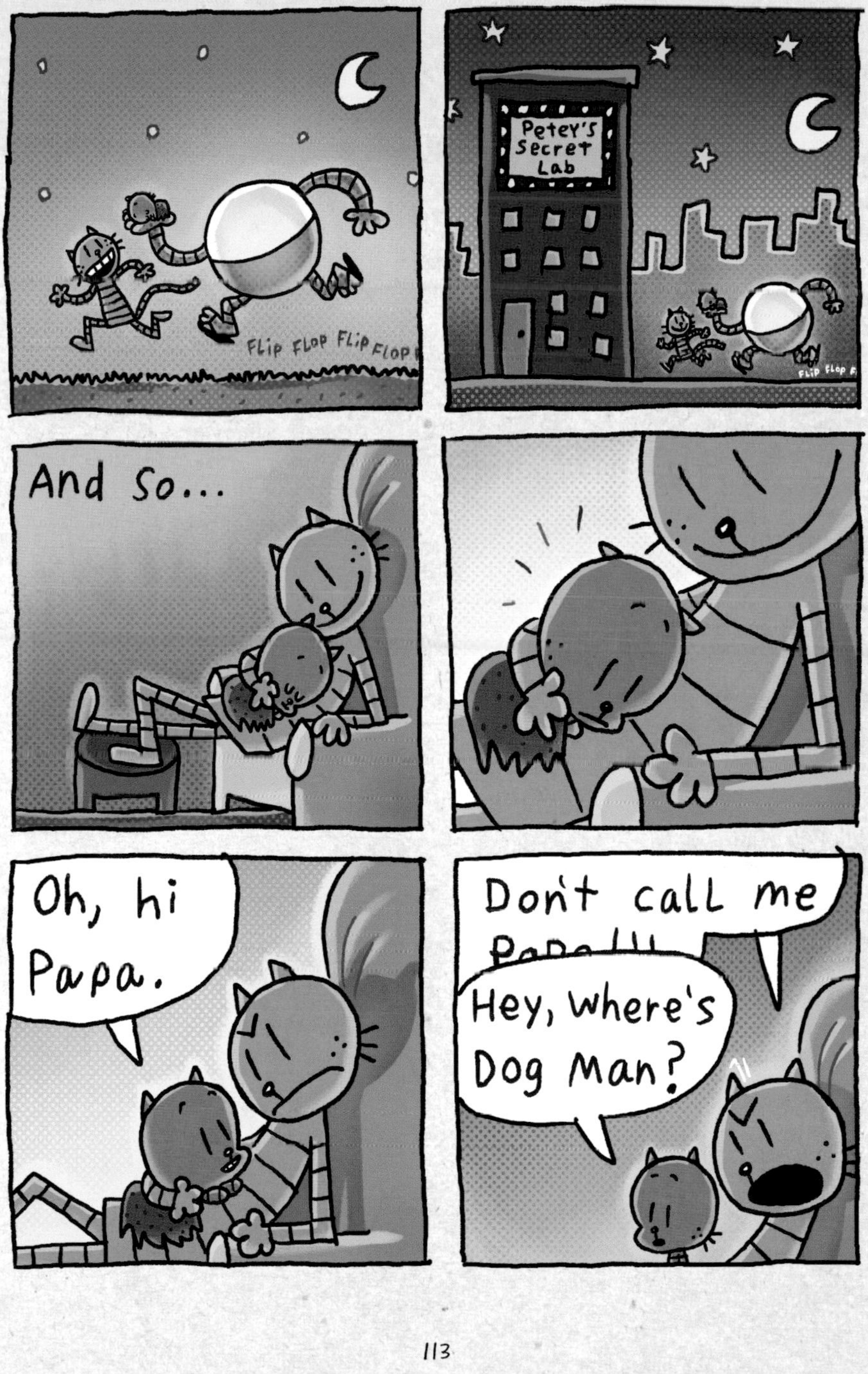
FLIP FLOP FLIP FLOP
Petey's Secret Lab
FLIP FLOP
And so...
Oh, hi Papa.
Don't call me Papa!!!
Hey, where's Dog Man?

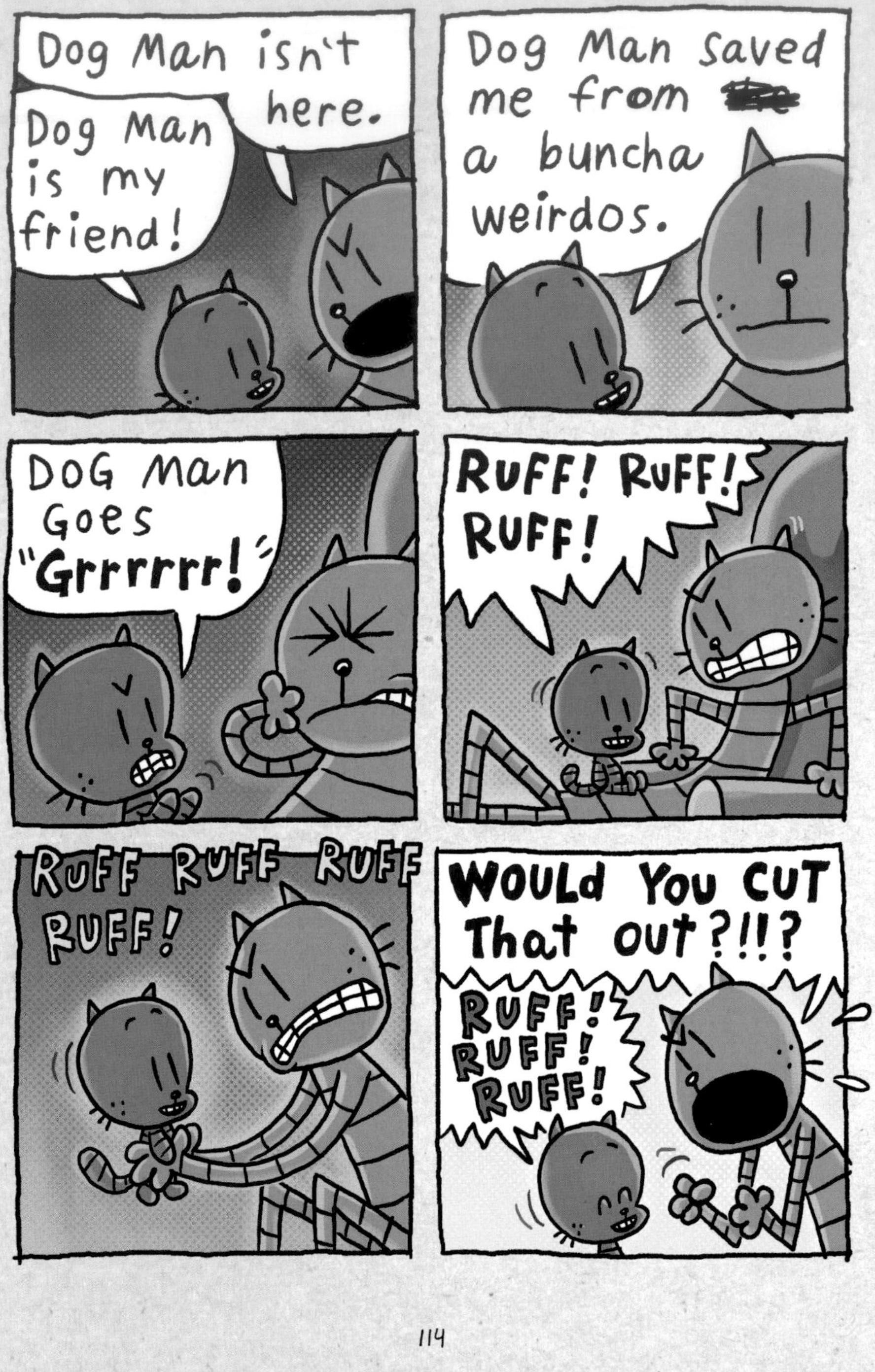
Dog Man isn't here.
Dog Man is my friend!
Dog Man saved me from [redacted] a buncha weirdos.
DOG Man Goes "Grrrrrr!"
RUFF! RUFF! RUFF!
RUFF RUFF RUFF RUFF!
WOULd You CUT That out?!!?
RUFF! RUFF! RUFF!

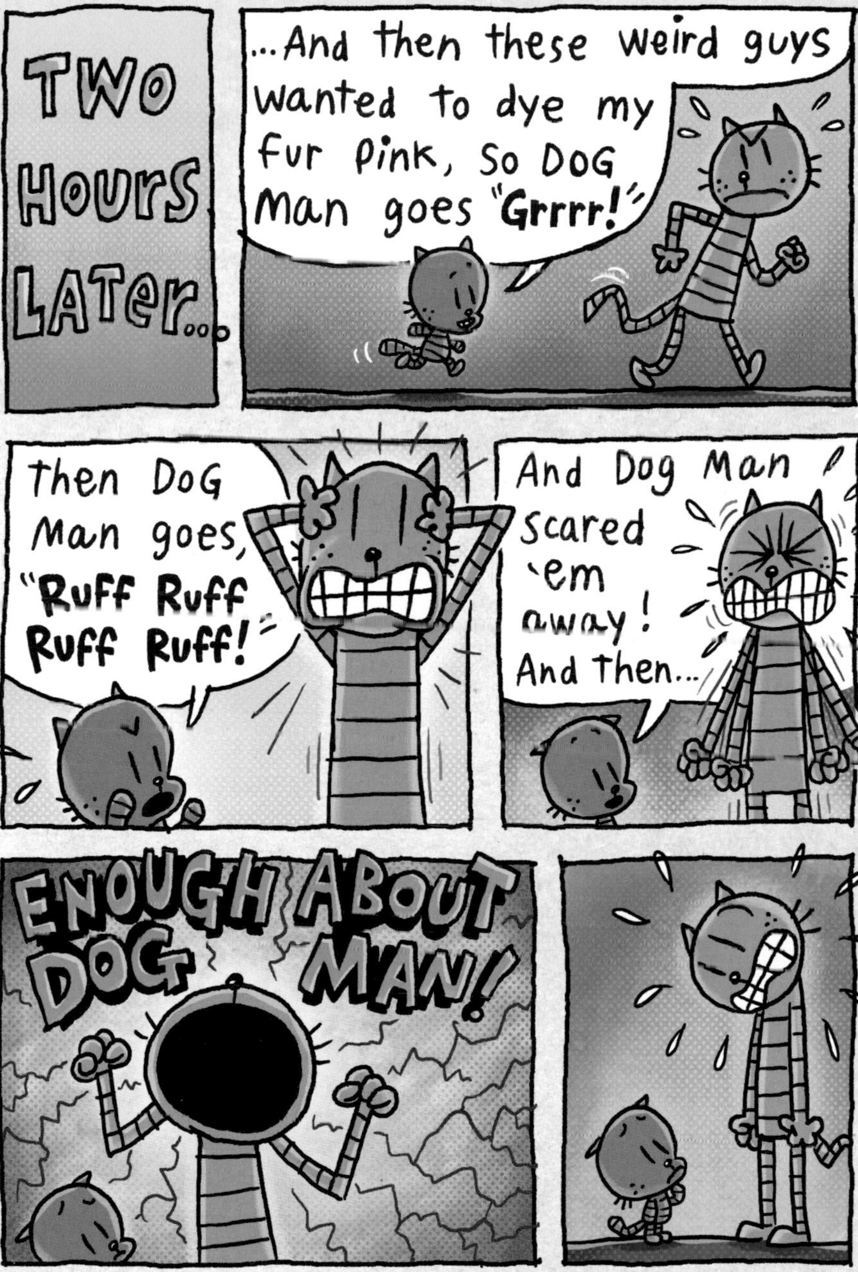
TWO HOURS LATER...
...And then these weird guys wanted to dye my fur pink, so DOG Man goes "Grrrr!"
then DOG Man goes, "Ruff Ruff Ruff Ruff!"
And Dog Man scared 'em away! And then...
ENOUGH ABOUT DOG MAN!

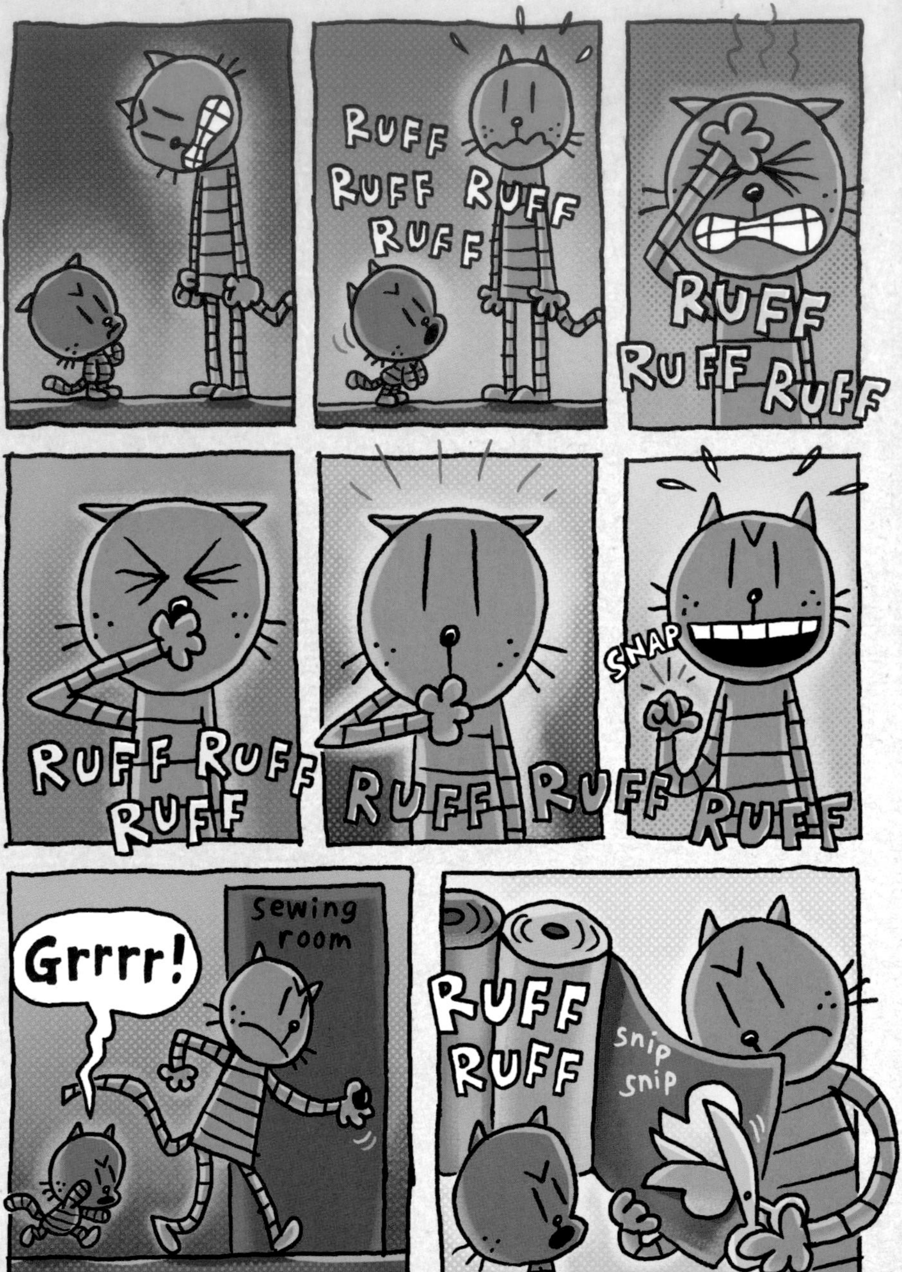
RUFF
RUFF RUFF
RUFF
RUFF
RUFF RUFF
RUFF RUFF
RUFF
RUFF RUFF
SNAP
RUFF
Grrrr!
sewing room
RUFF
RUFF
snip
snip

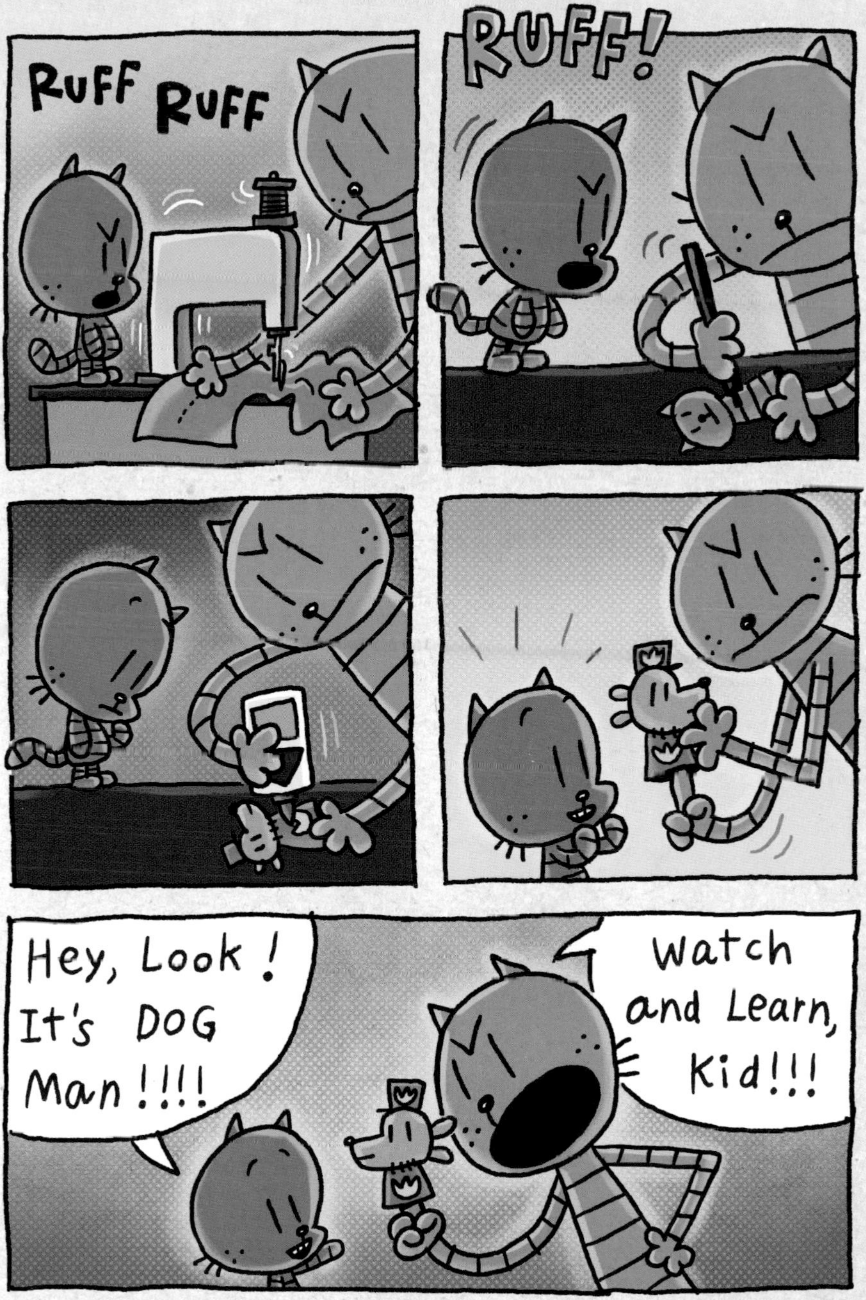
RUFF RUFF
RUFF!
Hey, Look! It's DOG Man!!!!
Watch and Learn, Kid!!!

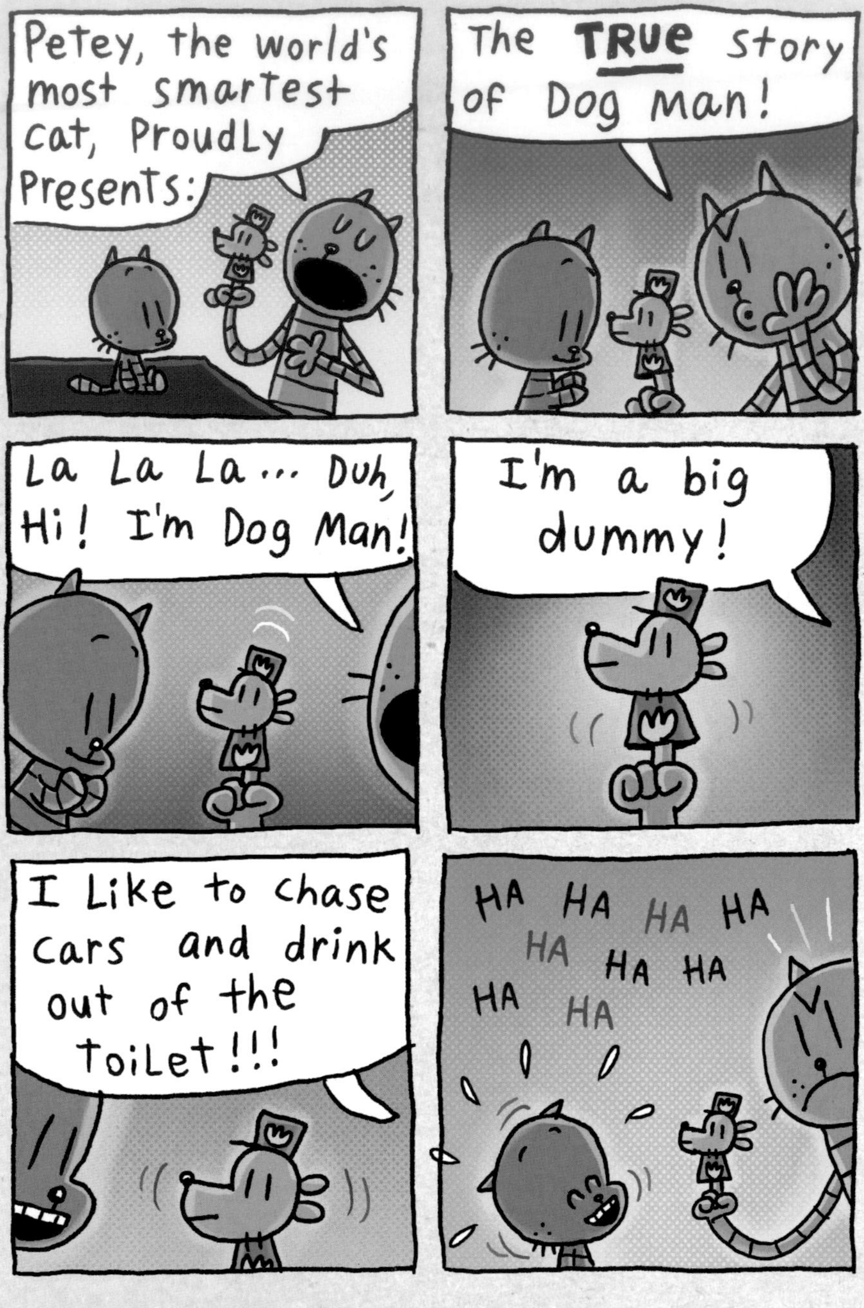
Petey, the world's most smartest cat, Proudly Presents:
The TRUE story of Dog Man!
La La La... Duh, Hi! I'm Dog Man!
I'm a big dummy!
I Like to chase cars and drink out of the toiLet!!!
HA HA HA HA HA HA HA HA HA

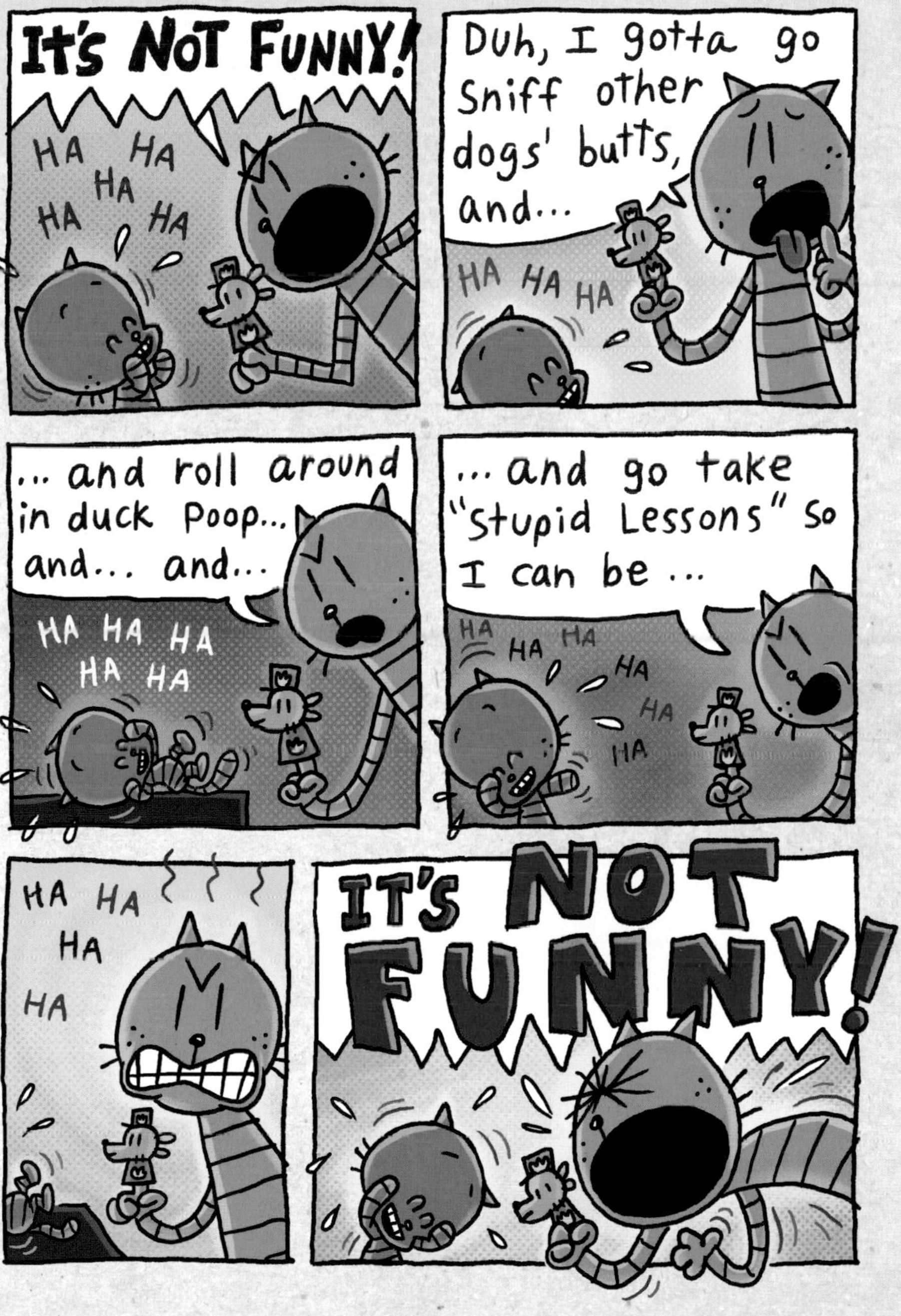
IT'S NOT FUNNY!
HA HA HA HA HA
Duh, I gotta go sniff other dogs' butts, and...
HA HA HA
... and roll around in duck poop... and... and...
HA HA HA HA HA
... and go take "Stupid Lessons" so I can be ...
HA HA HA HA HA HA
HA HA HA HA
IT'S NOT FUNNY!

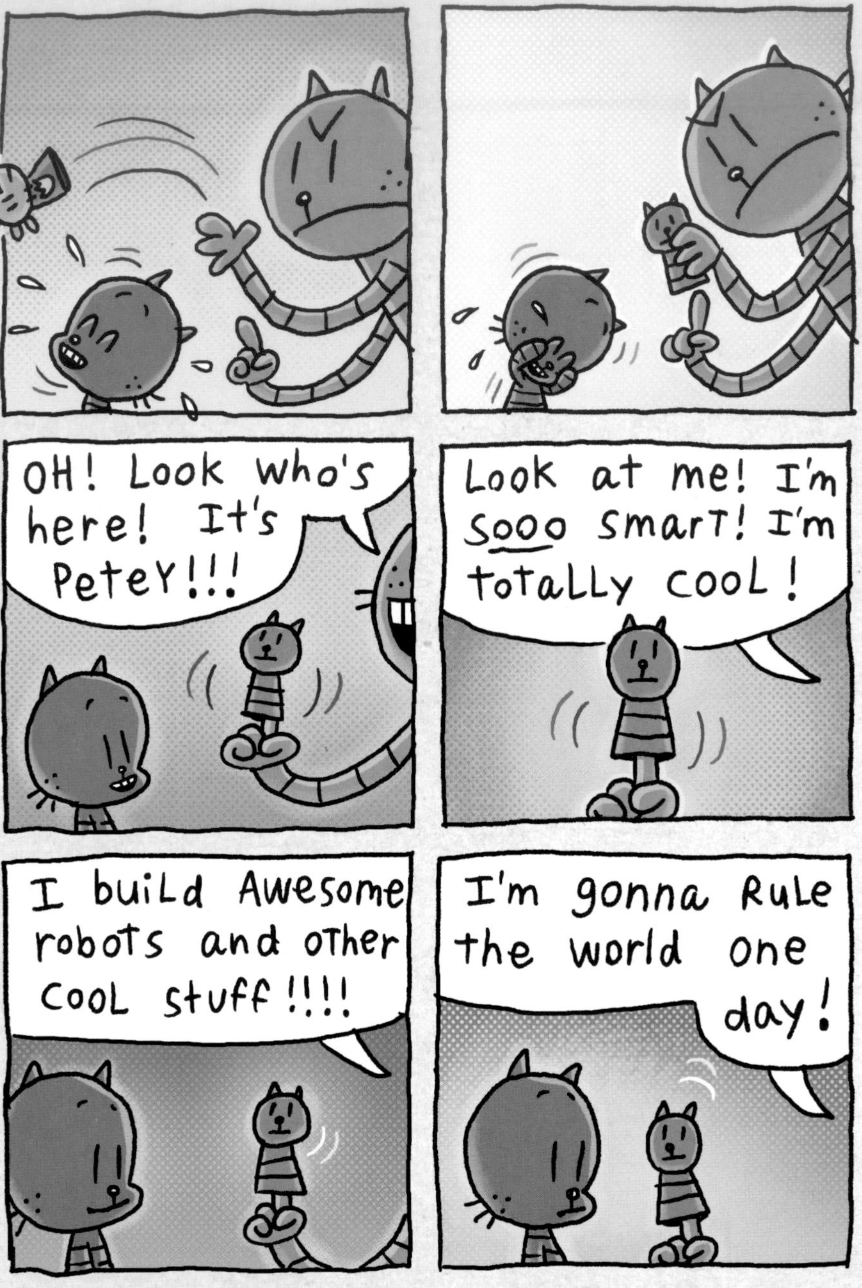
OH! Look who's here! It's Petey!!!
Look at me! I'm sooo smart! I'm totally cool!
I build Awesome robots and other cool stuff!!!!
I'm gonna Rule the world one day!

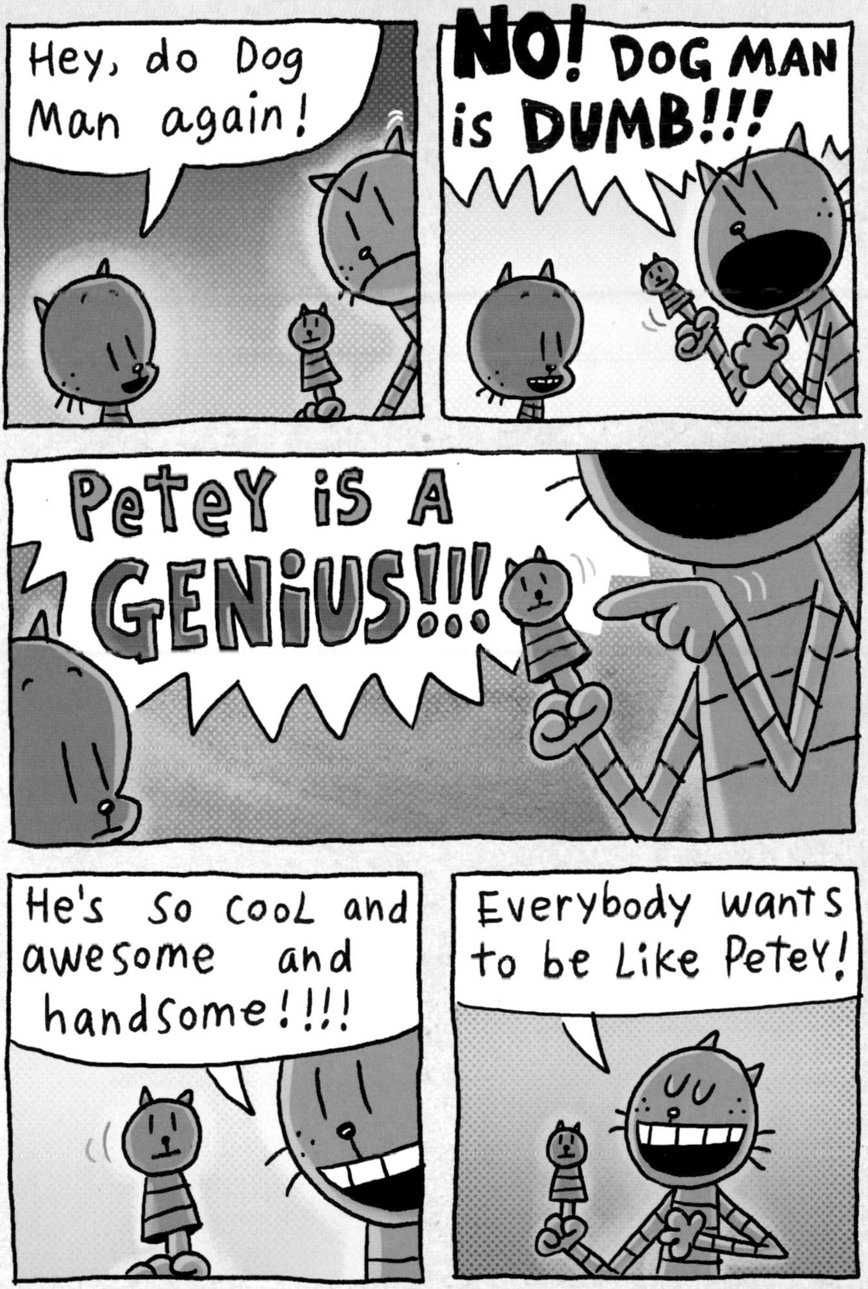
Hey, do Dog Man again!
NO! DOG MAN is DUMB!!!
PeteY iS A GENiUS!!!
He's so cool and awesome and handsome!!!!
Everybody wants to be Like Petey!

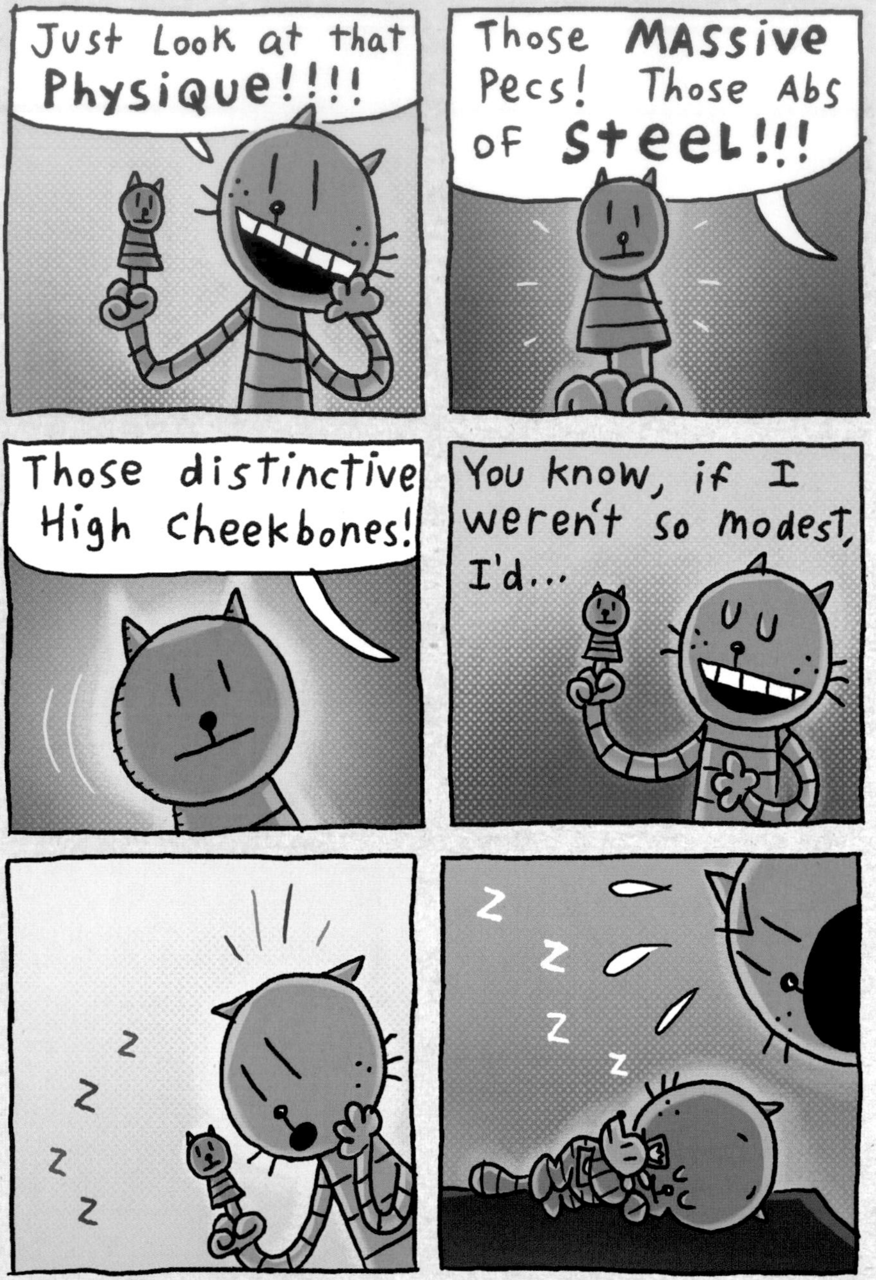
Just Look at that Physique!!!!
Those MASSive Pecs! Those Abs of Steel!!!
Those distinctive High cheekbones!
You know, if I weren't so modest, I'd...
Z
Z
Z
Z
Z
Z
Z
Z

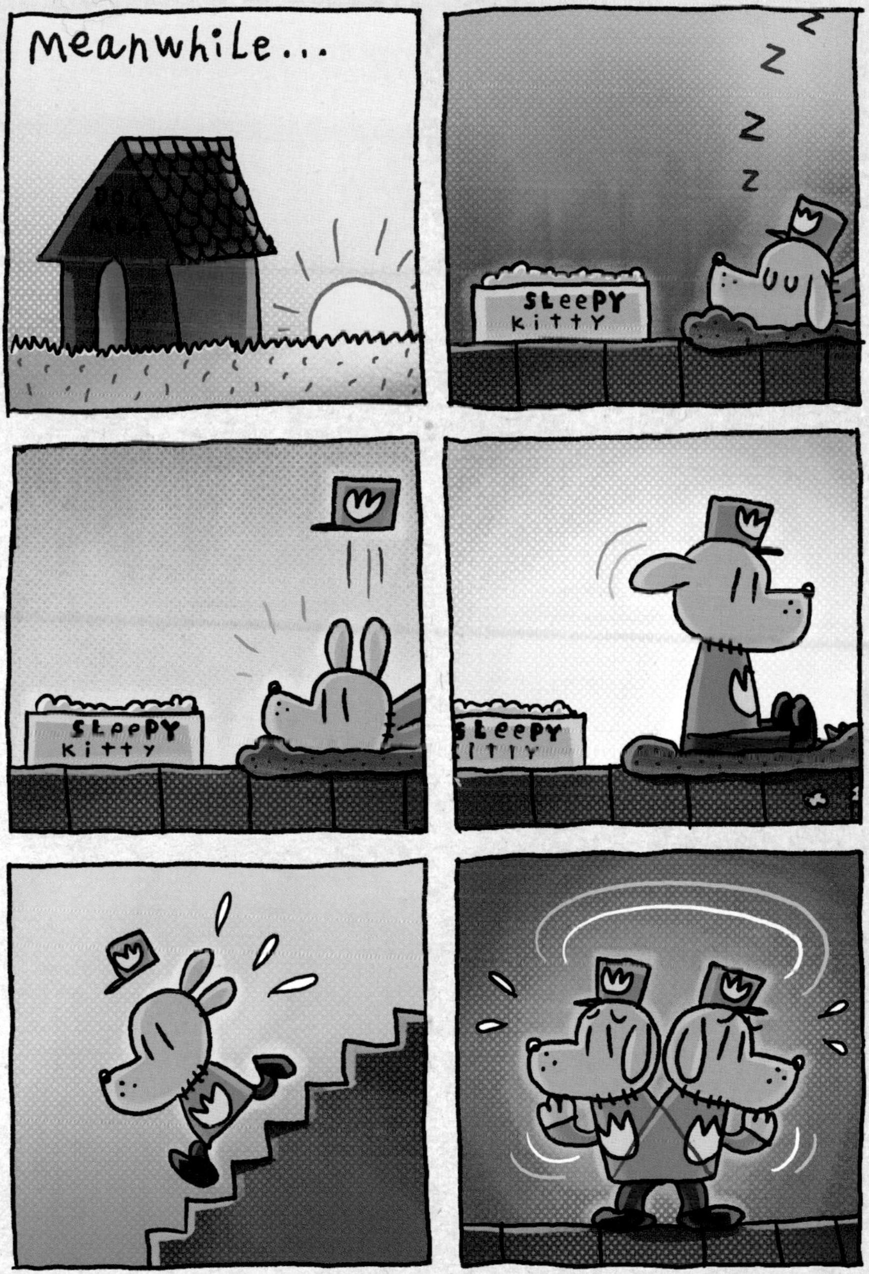
Meanwhile...
Z
Z
Z
Z
SLEEPY KITTY
SLEEPY KITTY
SLEEPY

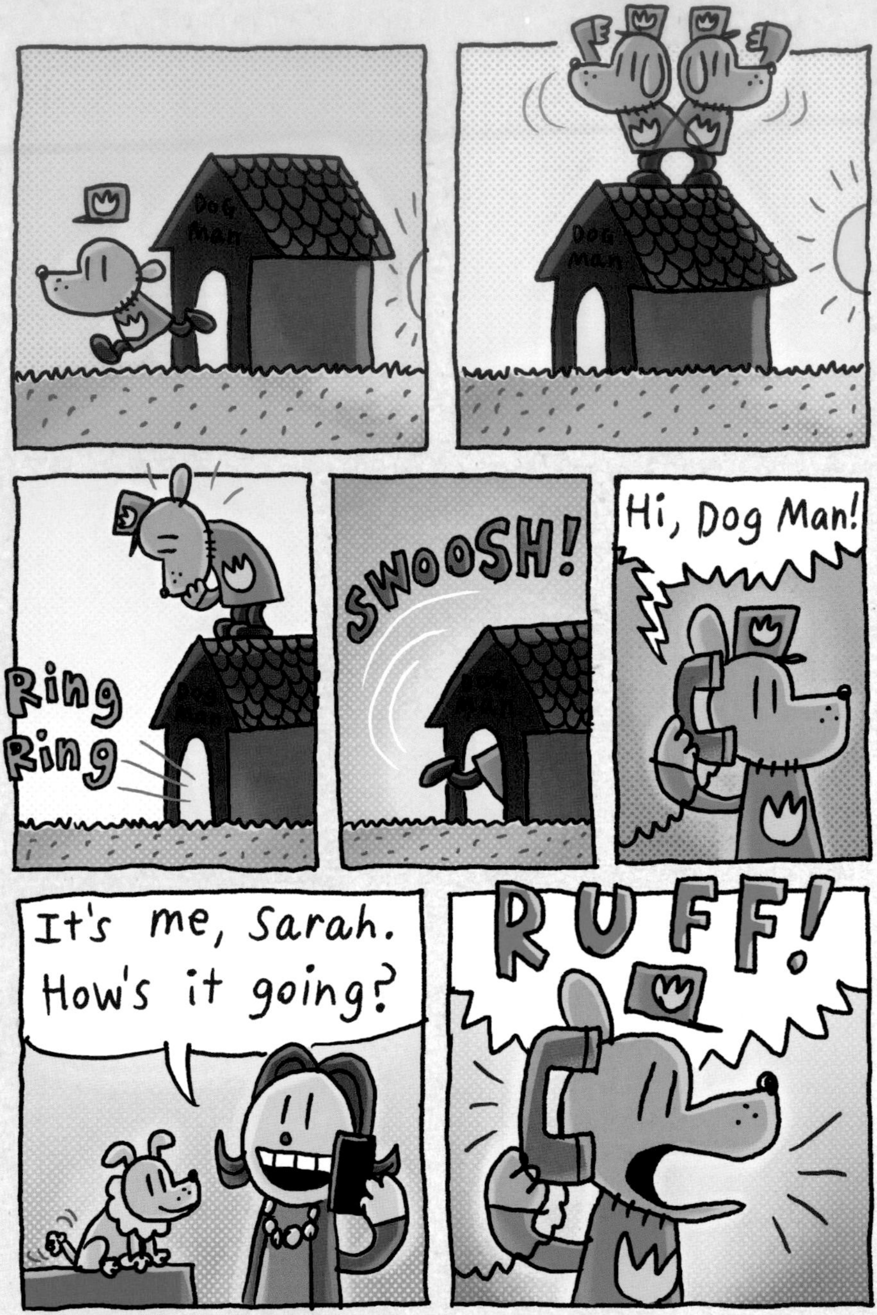
Ring
Ring
SWOOSH!
Hi, Dog Man!
It's me, Sarah. How's it going?
RUFF!

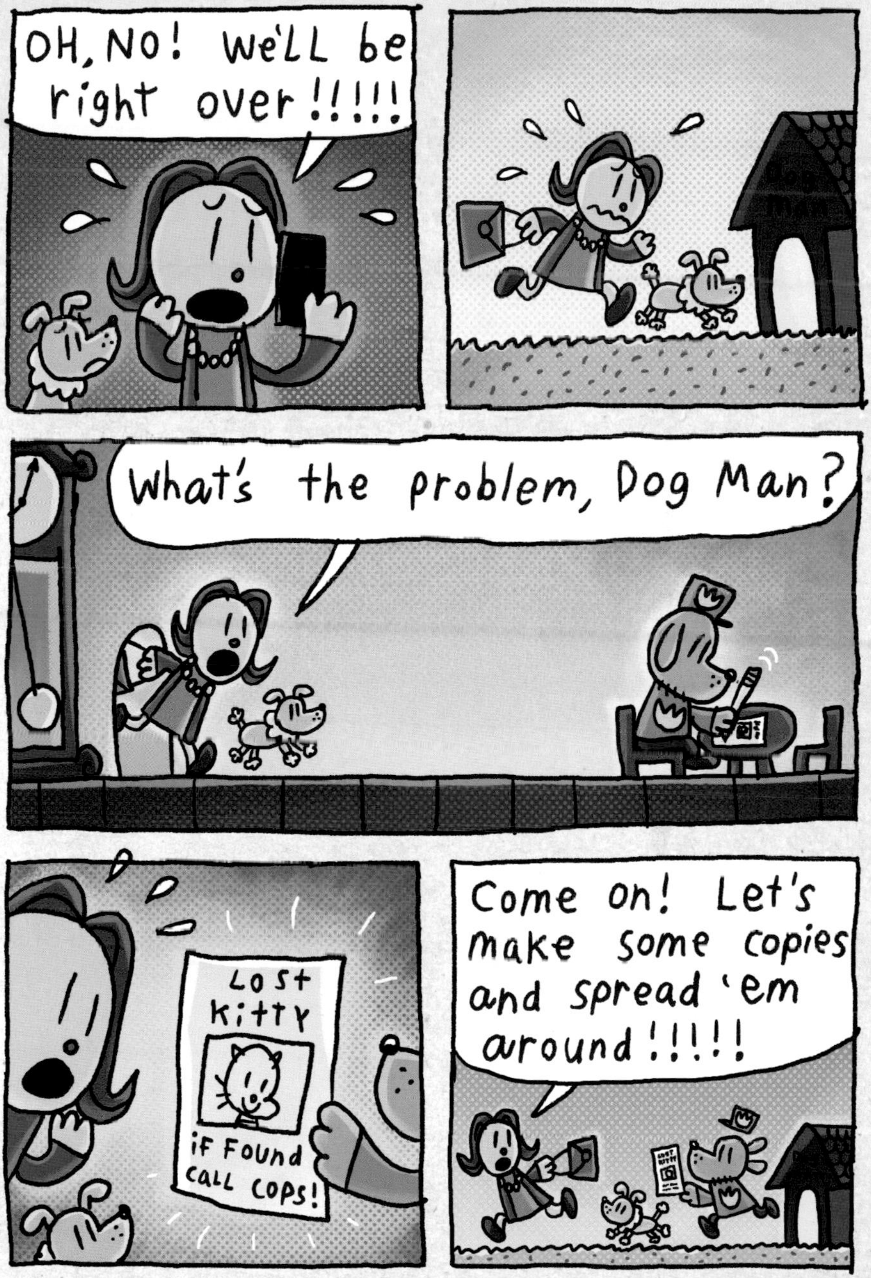
OH, NO! We'LL be right over!!!!!
What's the problem, Dog Man?
LoSt kitty
iF Found CALL COPS!
Come on! Let's make some copies and spread 'em around!!!!!

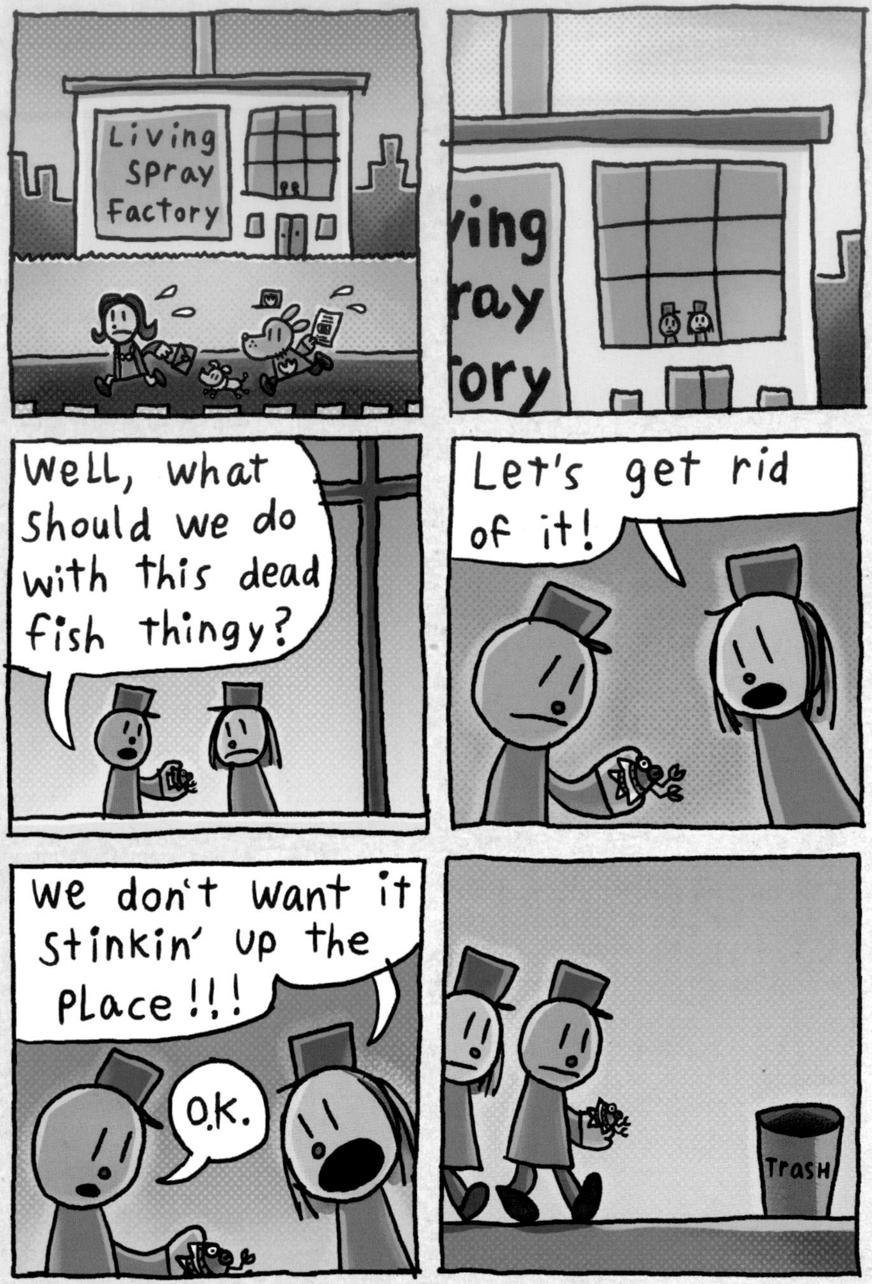
Living Spray Factory
ving
ray
tory
Well, what should we do with this dead fish thingy?
Let's get rid of it!
We don't want it stinkin' up the place!!!
O.K.
TRASH

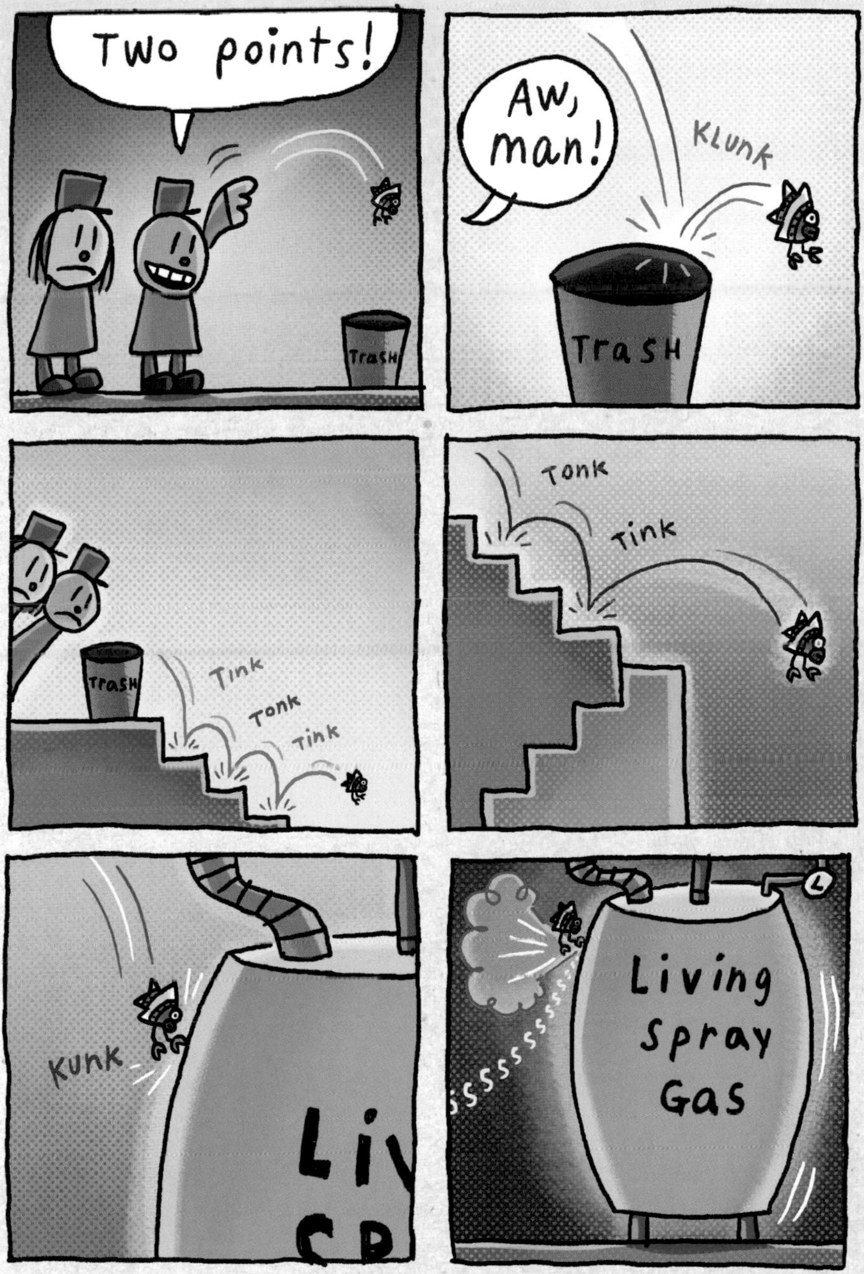
Two points!
Aw, man!
KLUNK
Tink
Tonk
Tink
TONK
Tink
KUNK
Living Spray Gas
SSSSSSSSSS

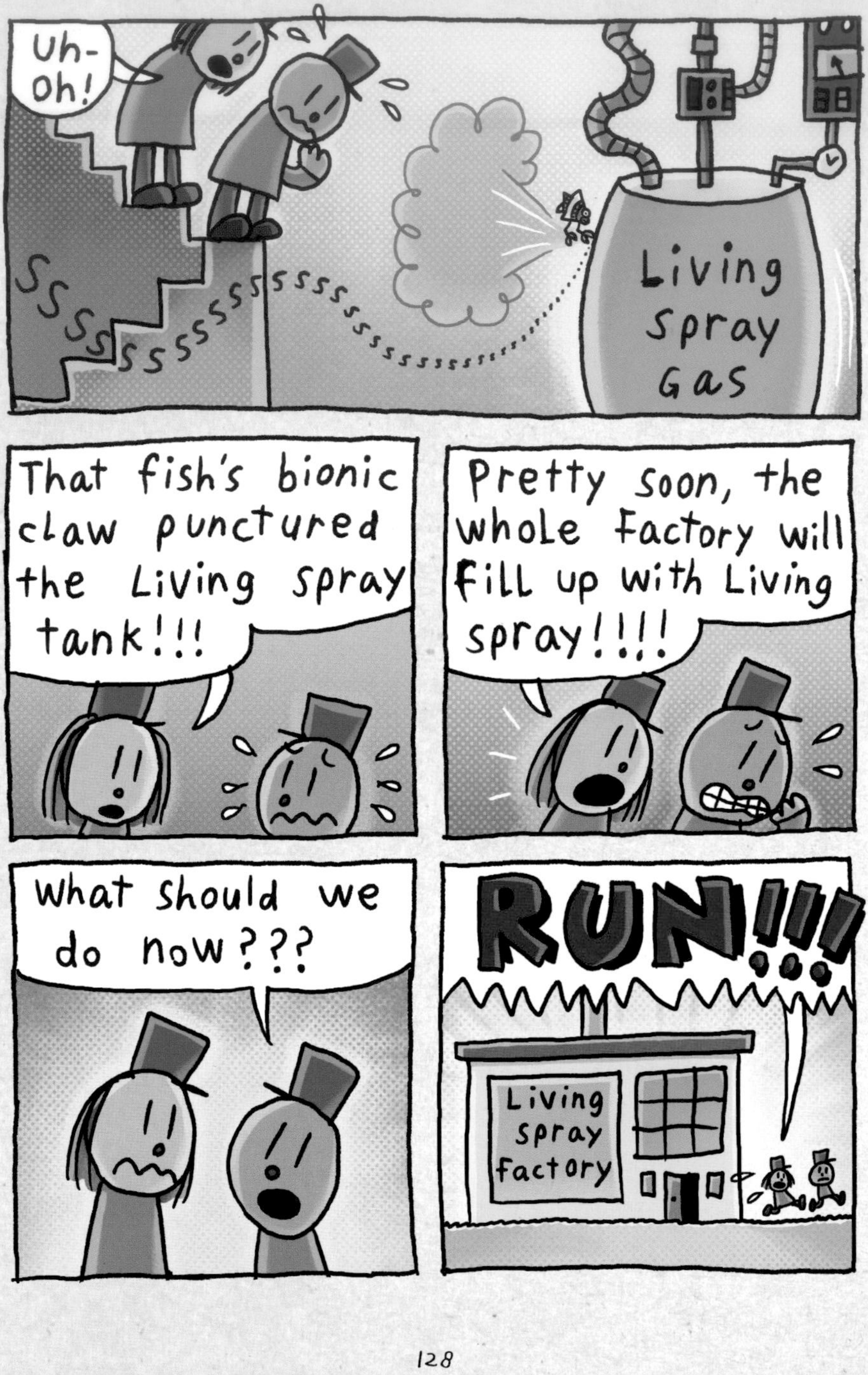
Uh-Oh!
SSSSSSSSSSSSSSSSSSSSSSSSSSSSSSSS
Living Spray Gas
That fish's bionic claw punctured the Living spray tank!!!
Pretty soon, the whole factory will fill up with Living spray!!!!
What should we do now???
RUN!!!!
Living spray factory

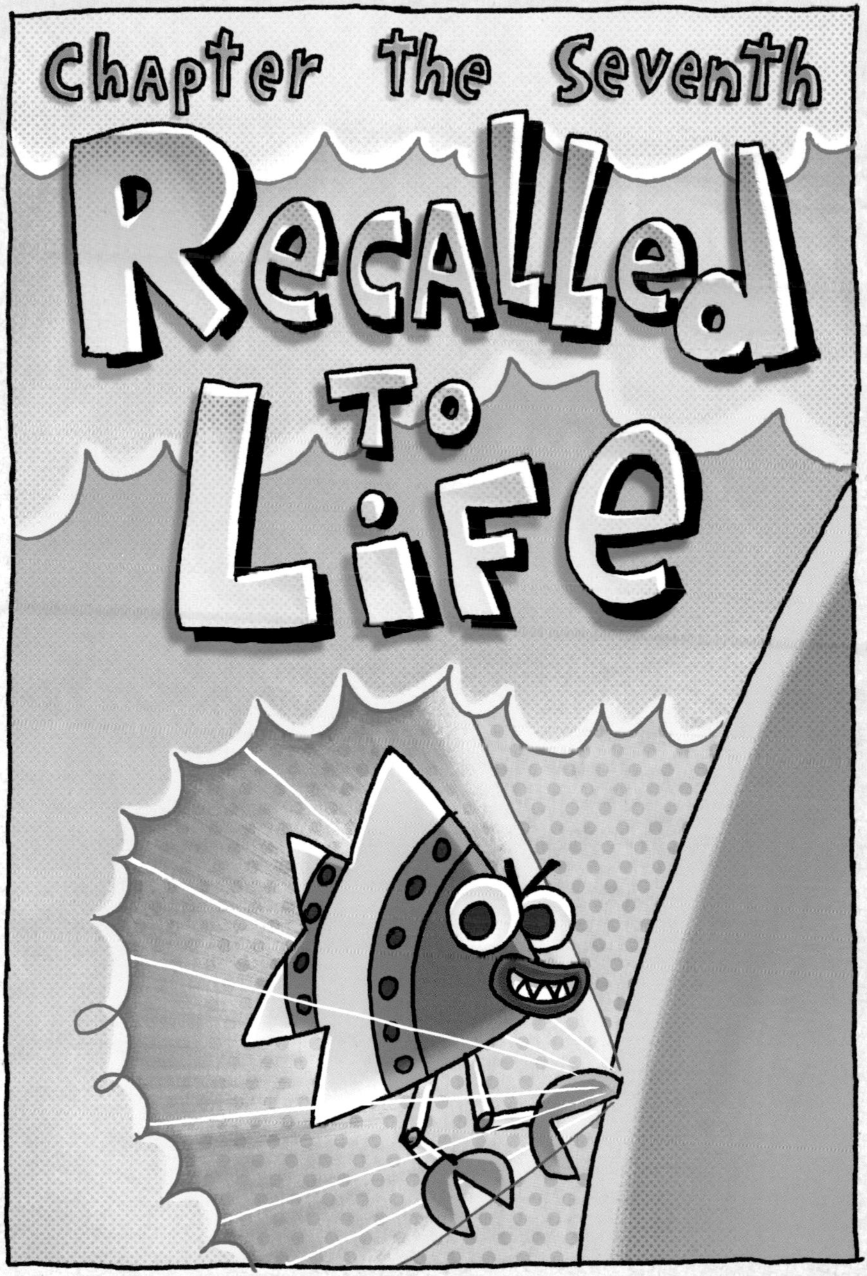
Chapter the Seventh
Recalled to Life

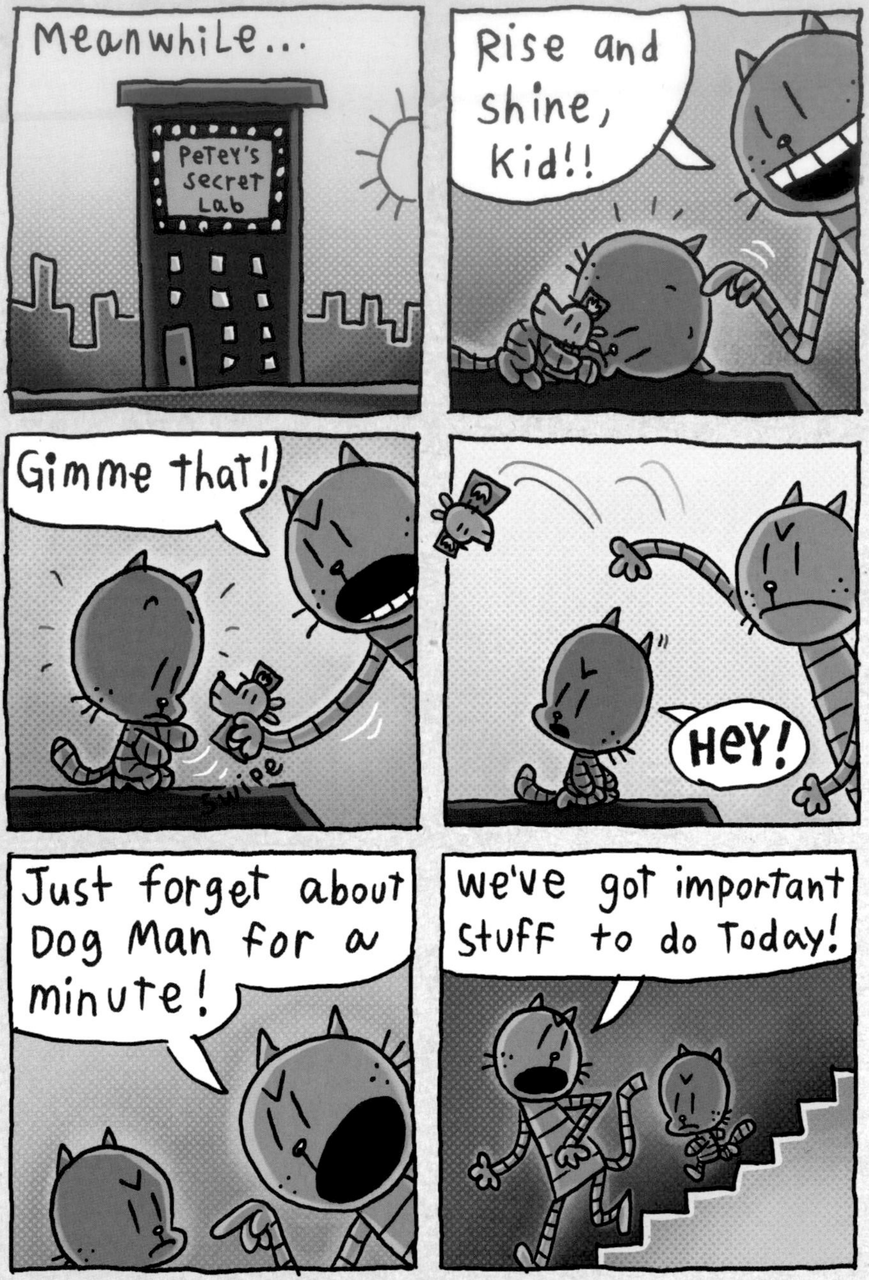
Meanwhile...
Petey's Secret Lab
Rise and shine, Kid!!
Gimme that!
Swipe
HEY!
Just forget about Dog Man for a minute!
We've got important stuff to do Today!

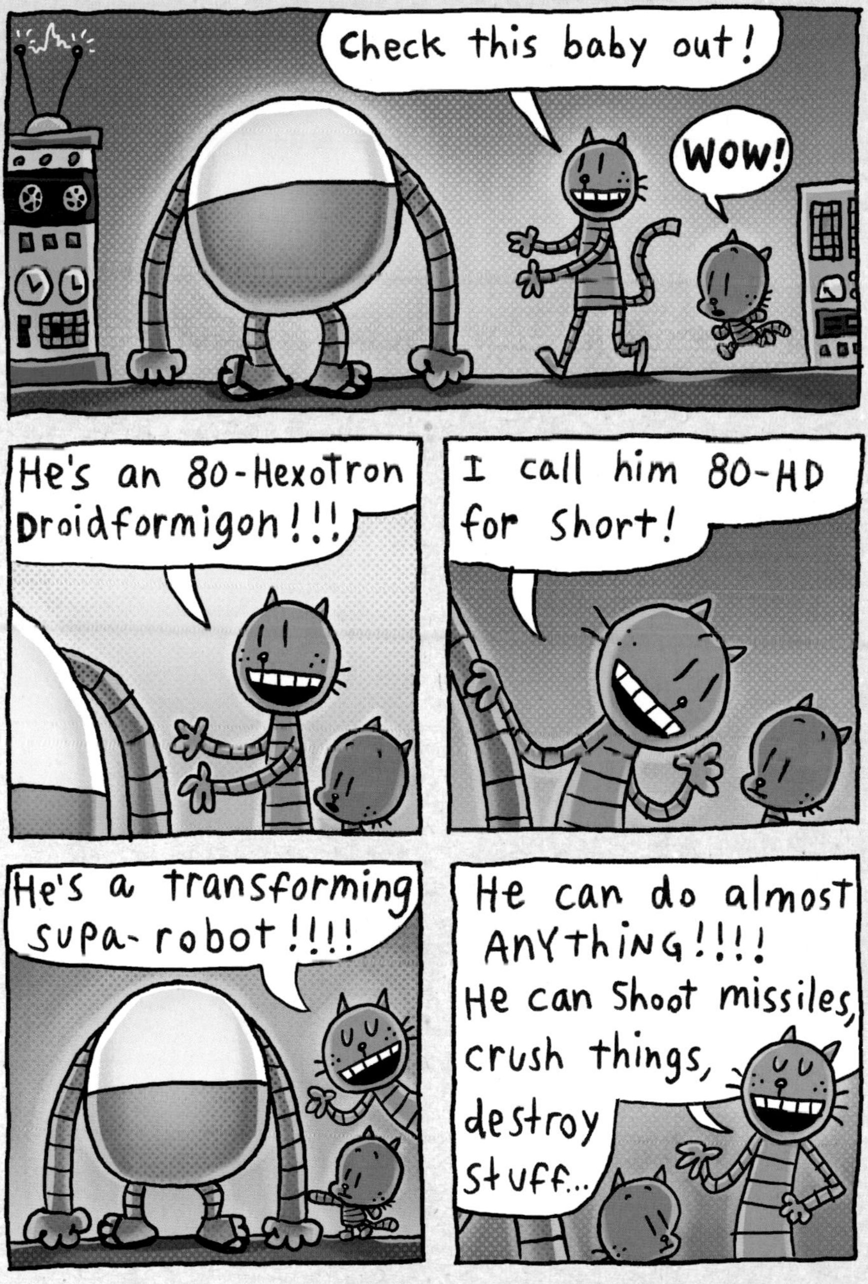
Check this baby out!
WOW!
He's an 80-Hexotron Droidformigon!!!
I call him 80-HD for Short!
He's a transforming supa-robot!!!!
He can do almost ANYTHING!!!!
He can Shoot missiles, crush things, destroy stuff...

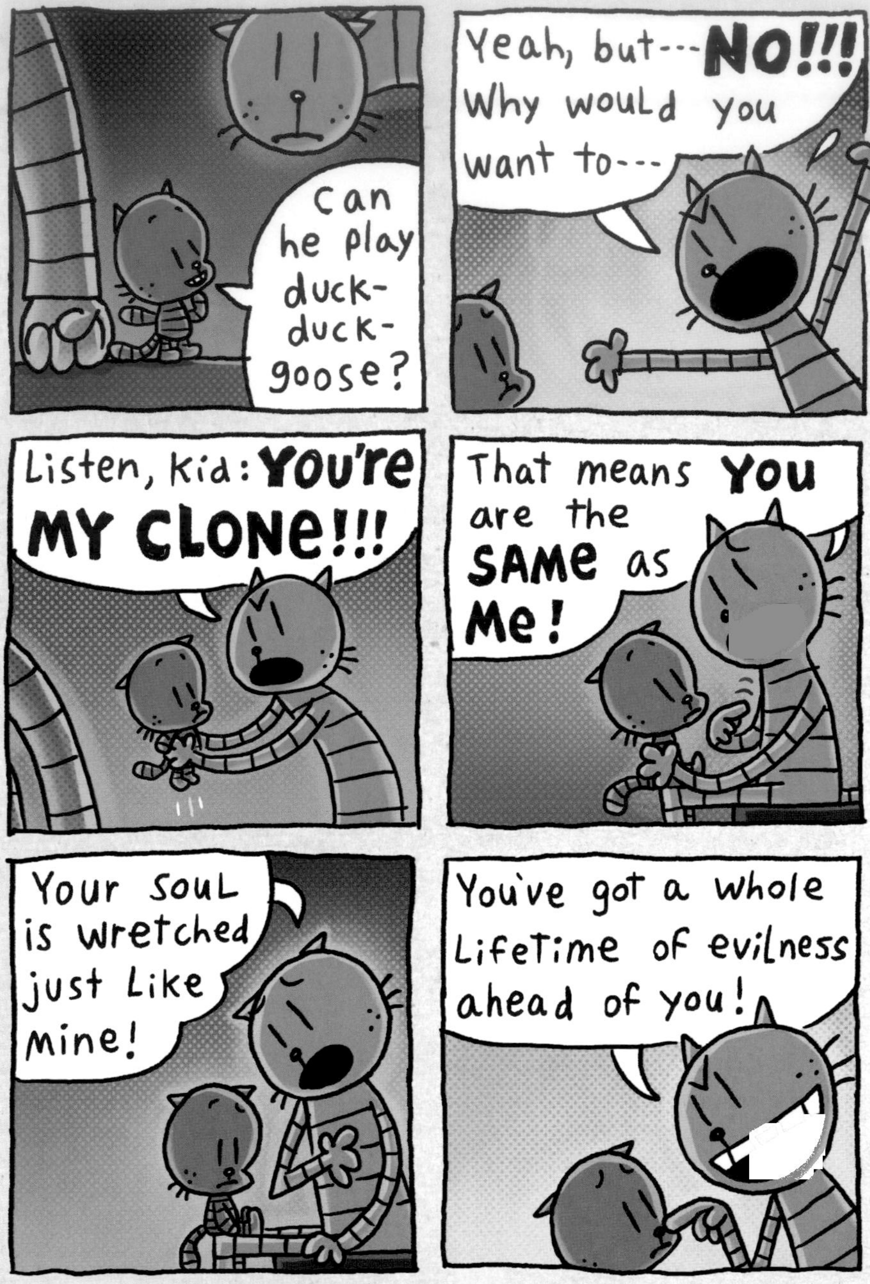
Can he play duck-duck-goose?
Yeah, but---NO!!! Why would you want to---
Listen, kid: YOU'RE MY CLONE!!!
That means YOU are the SAME as ME!
Your soul is wretched just like mine!
You've got a whole lifetime of evilness ahead of you!

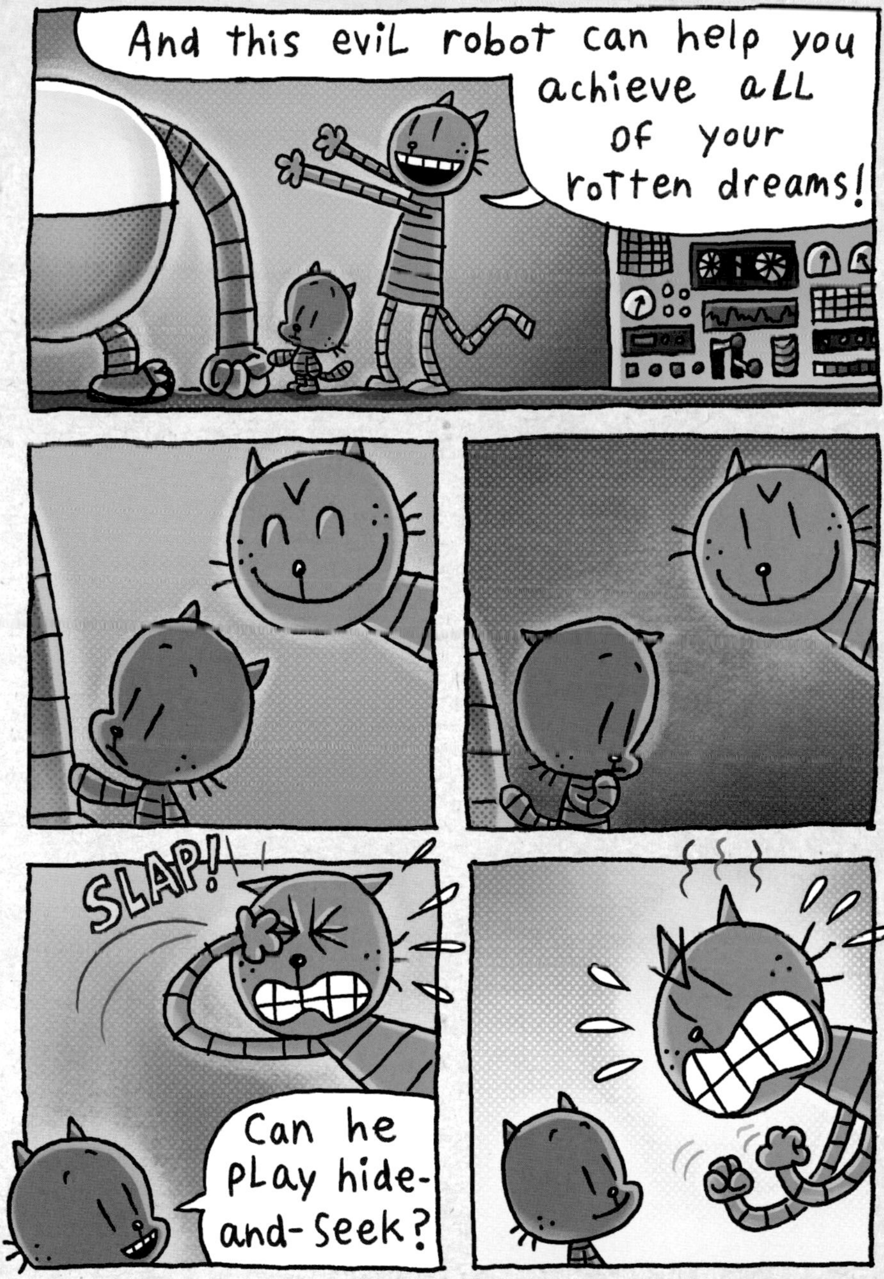
And this eviL robot can help you achieve aLL of your rotten dreams!
SLAP!
Can he pLay hide-and-seek?

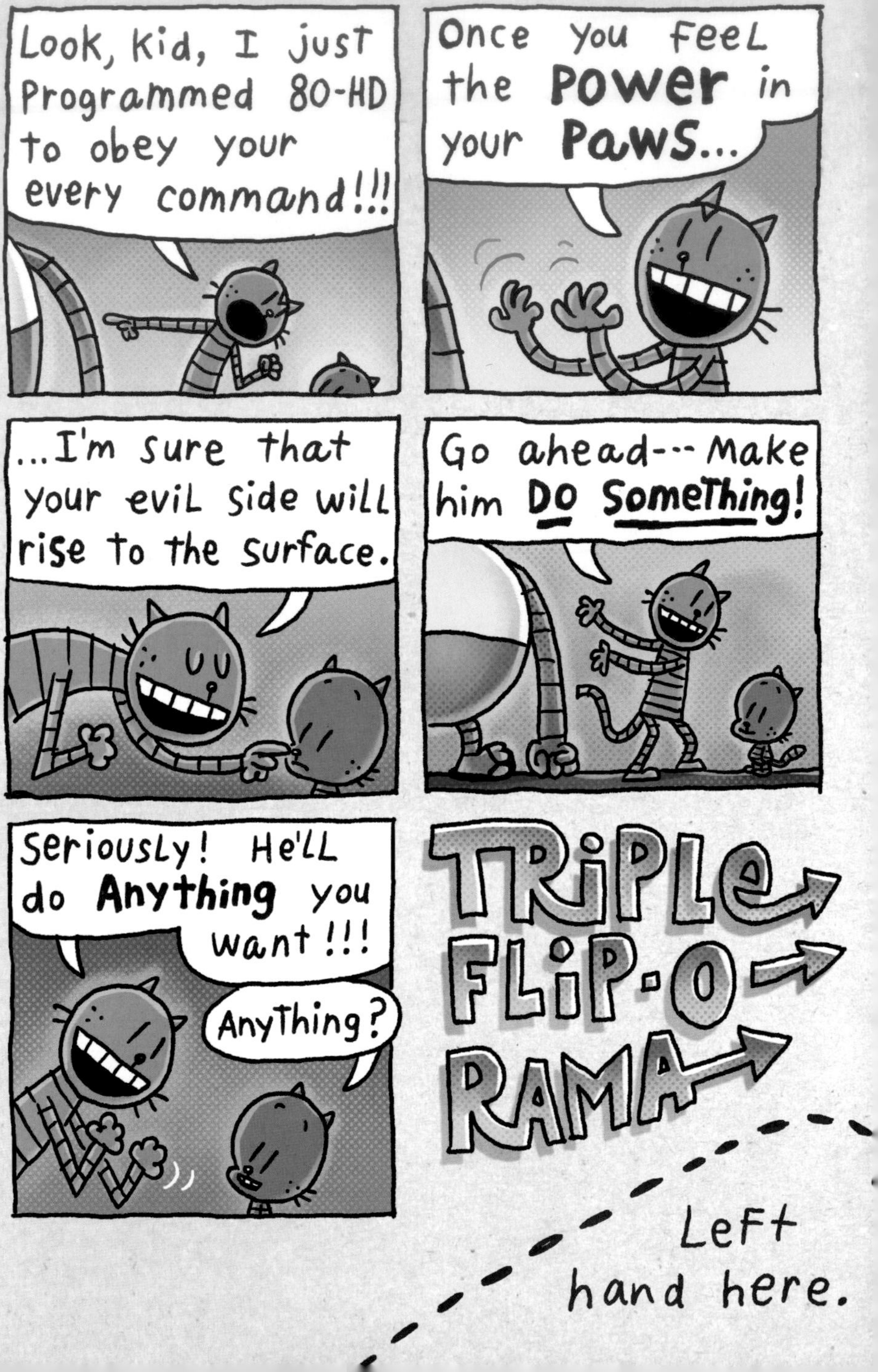
Look, Kid, I just Programmed 80-HD to obey your every command!!!
Once you feel the POWER in your PAWS...
...I'm sure that your evil side will rise to the surface.
Go ahead--- Make him DO SOMETHING!
Seriously! He'll do Anything you want!!!
Anything?
TRIPLE FLIP-O-RAMA
Left hand here.

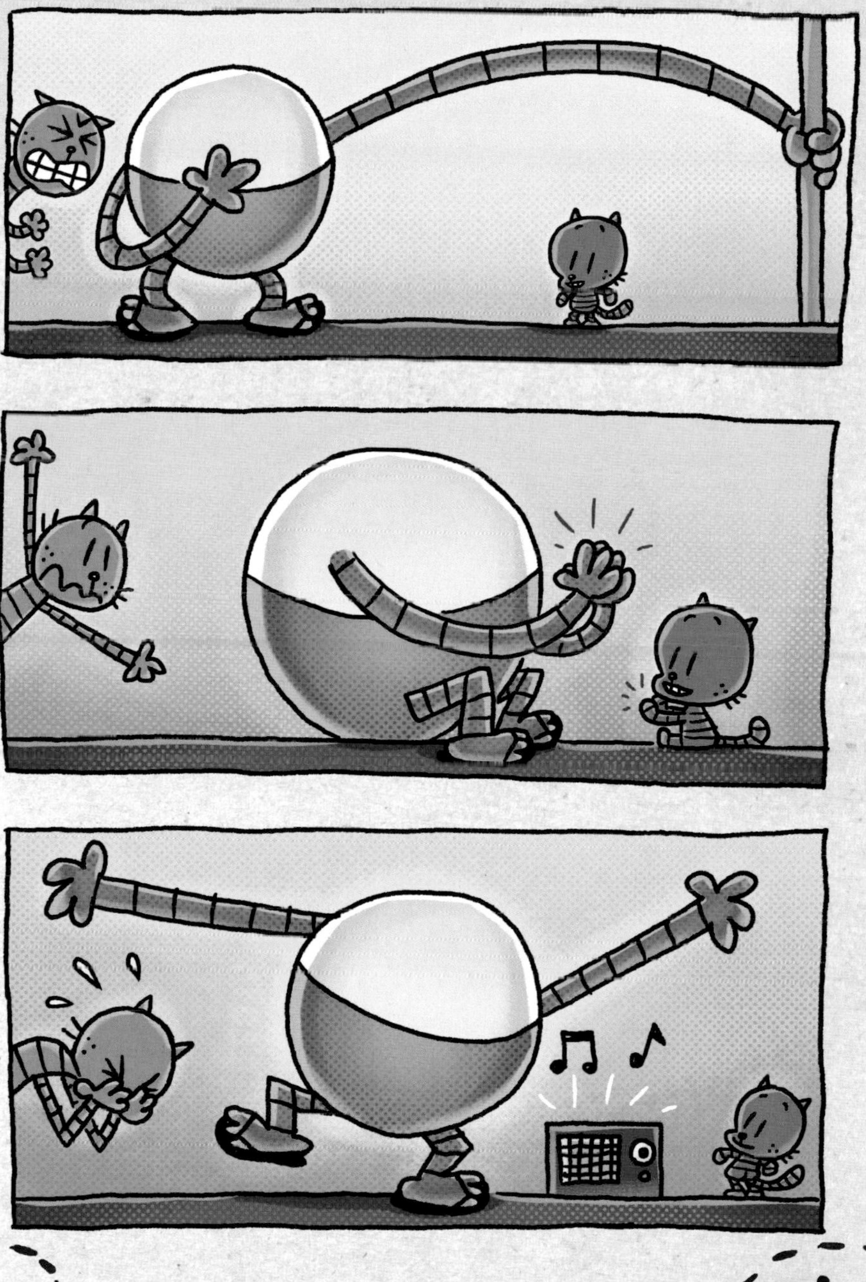

Right Thumb here.

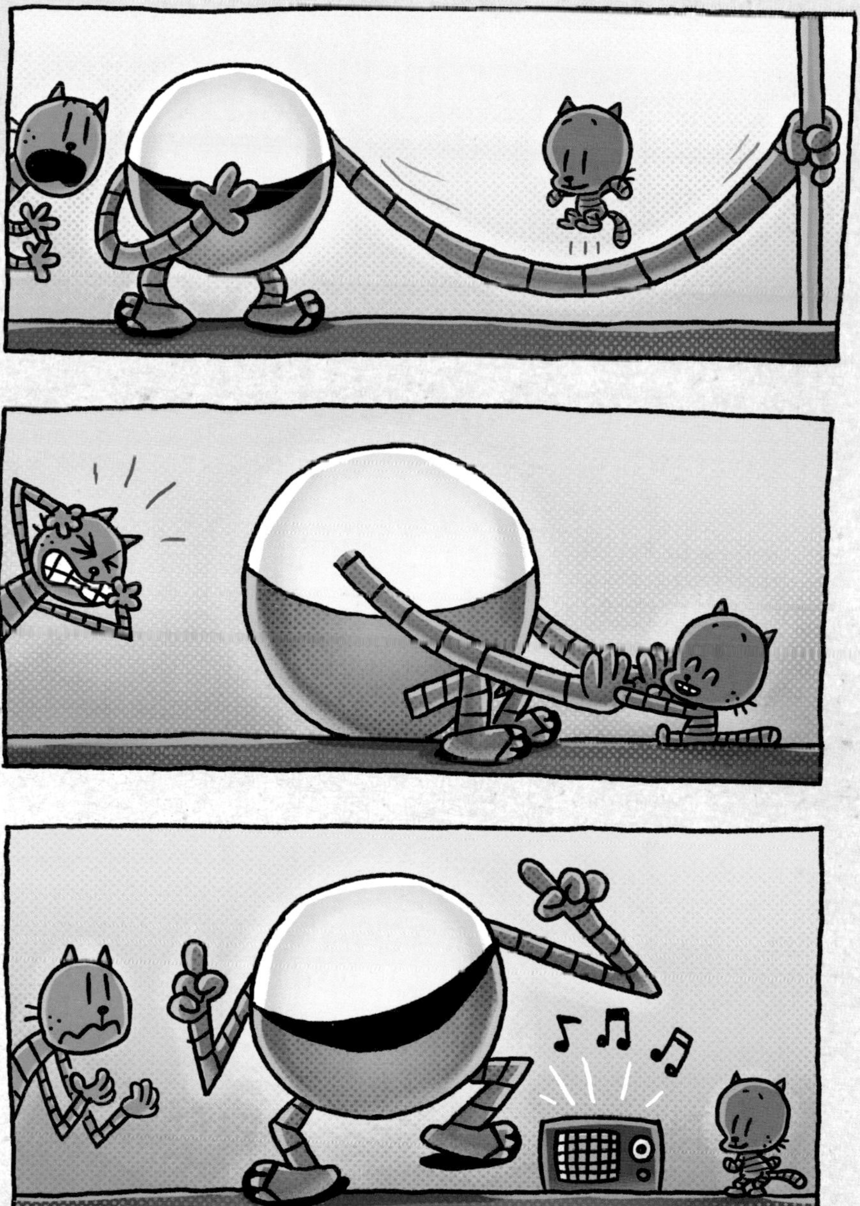

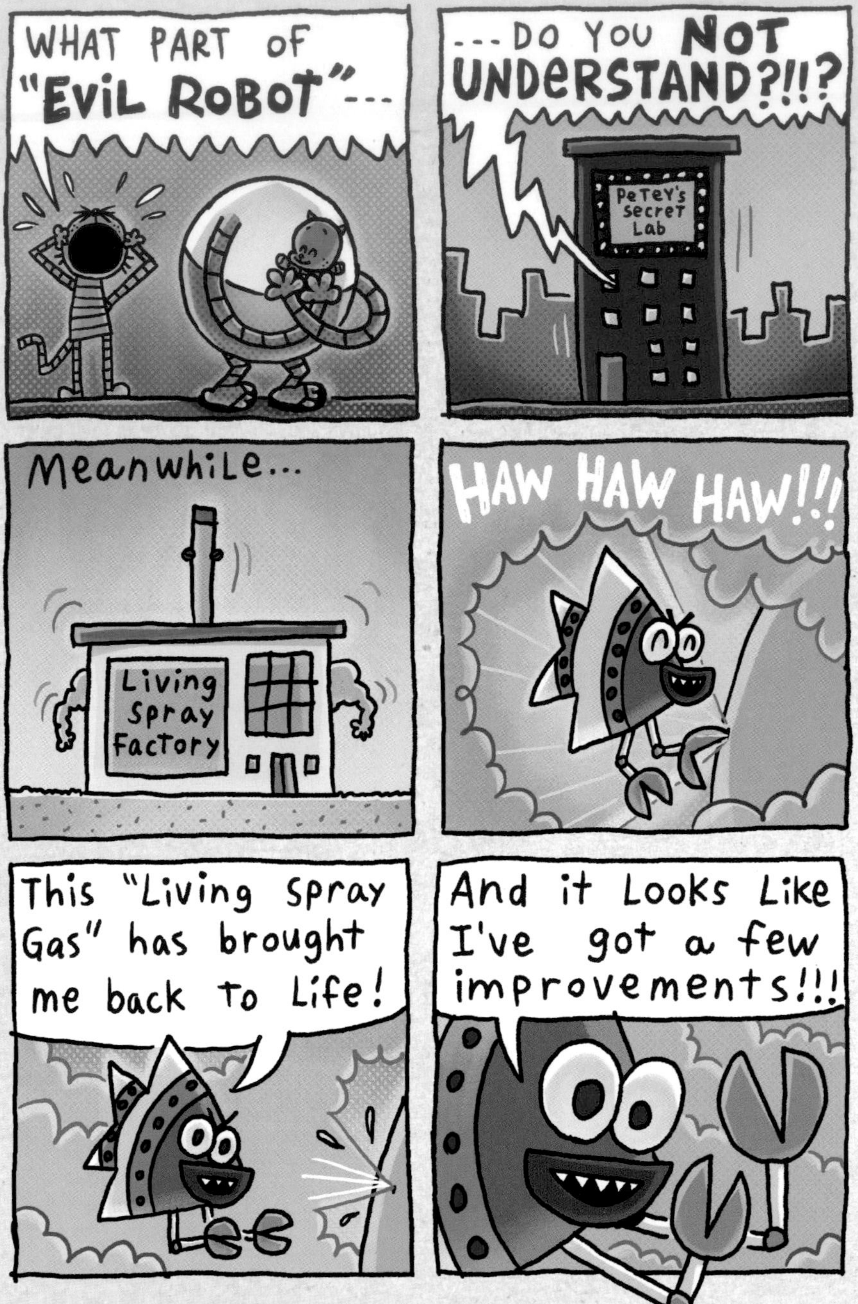
WHAT PART OF "EVIL ROBOT"---
---DO YOU NOT UNDERSTAND?!!?
PeTey's Secret Lab
Meanwhile...
Living Spray Factory
HAW HAW HAW!!!
This "Living Spray Gas" has brought me back to Life!
And it Looks Like I've got a few improvements!!!

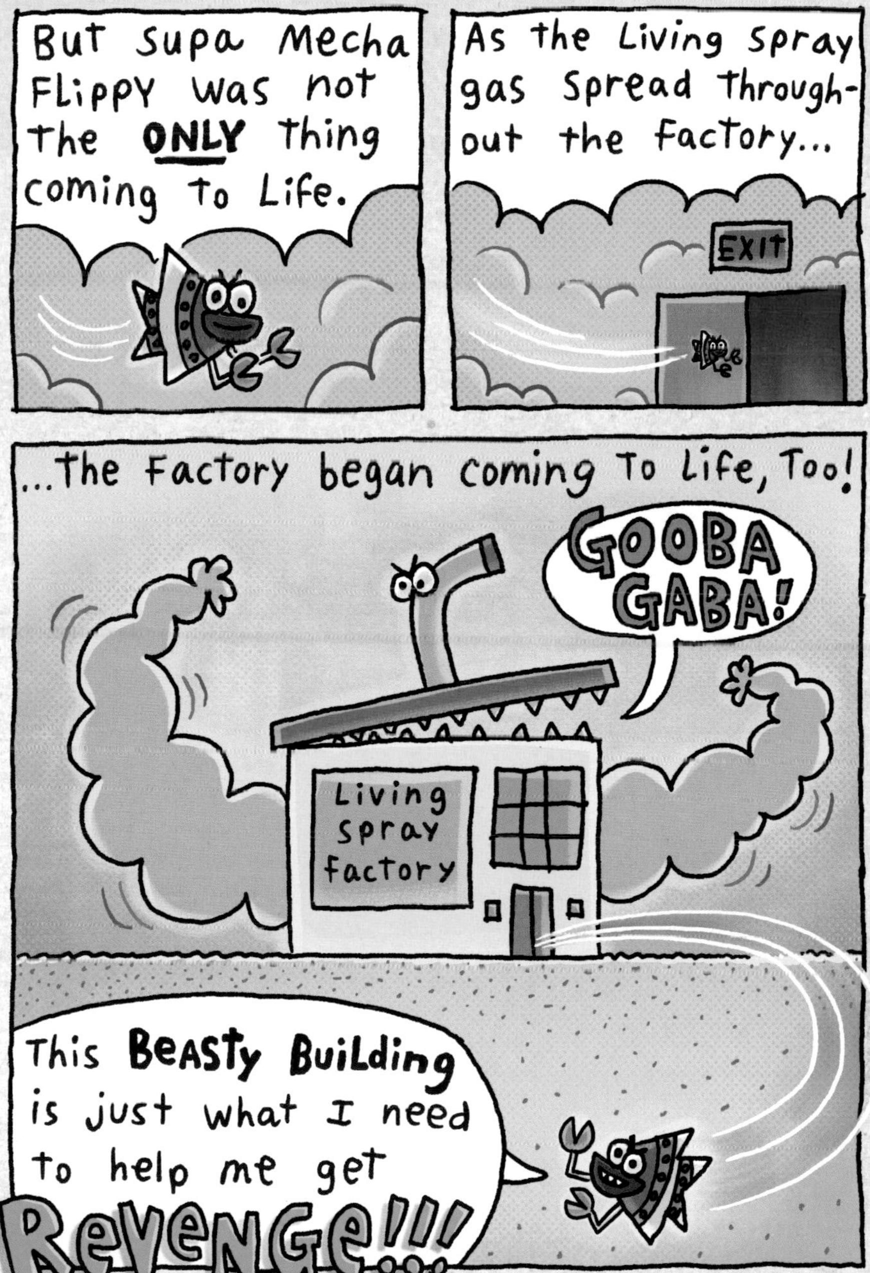
But Supa Mecha Flippy was not the ONLY thing coming to Life.
As the Living Spray gas spread through-out the Factory...
EXIT
...The Factory began coming to Life, Too!
GOOBA GABA!
Living Spray Factory
This BEASTY Building is just what I need to help me get REVENGE!!!...

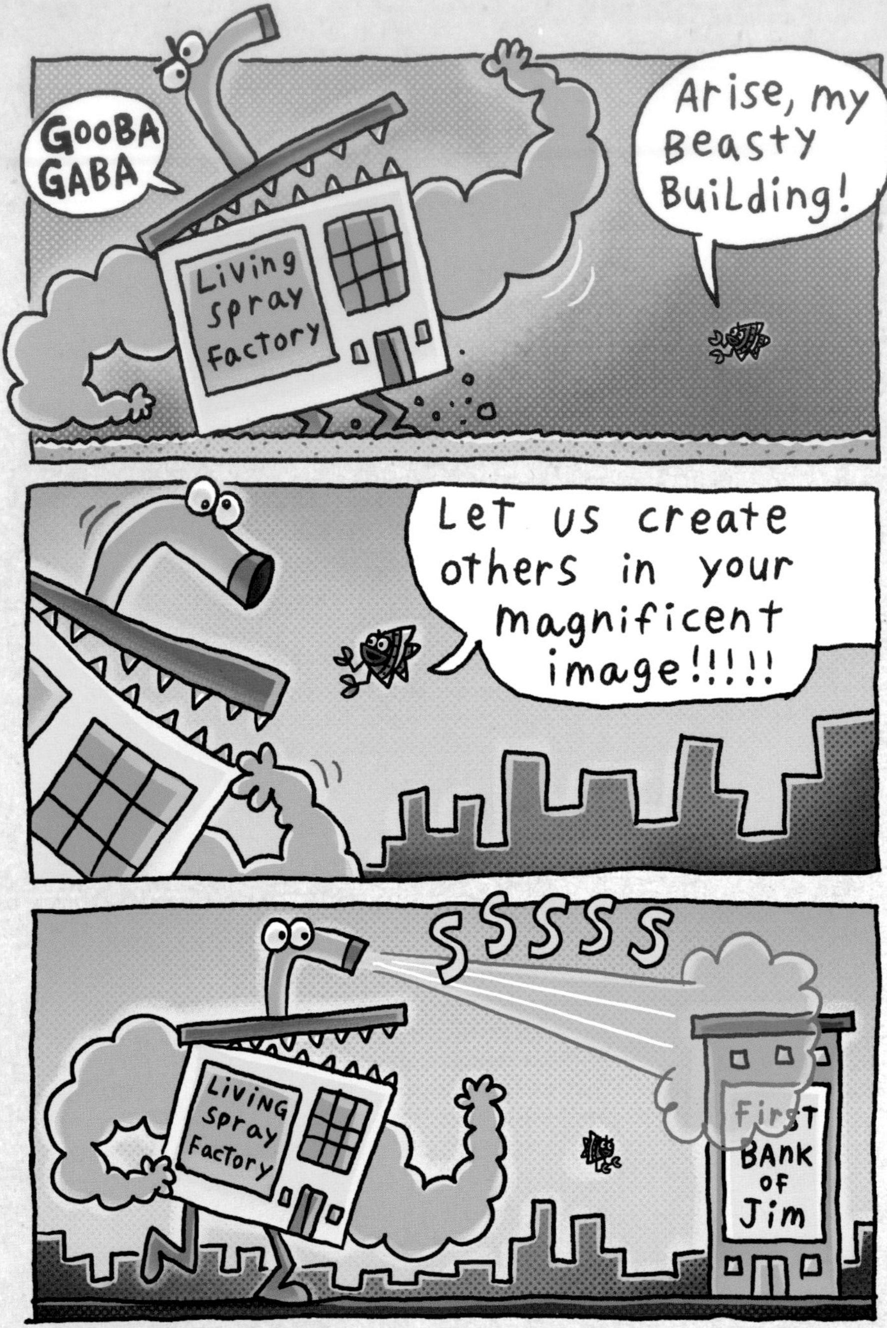
GOOBA GABA
Living Spray Factory
Arise, my Beasty Building!
Let us create others in your magnificent image!!!!!
SSSSS
LIVING Spray Factory
First BANK OF Jim

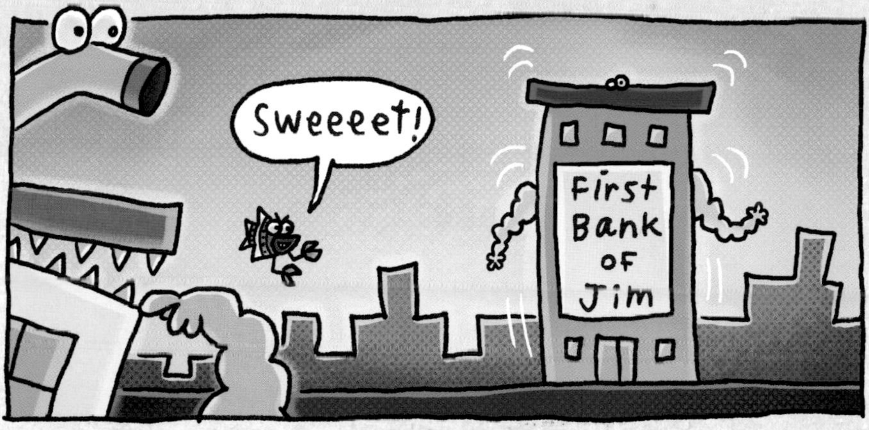
Sweeeet!
First Bank of Jim

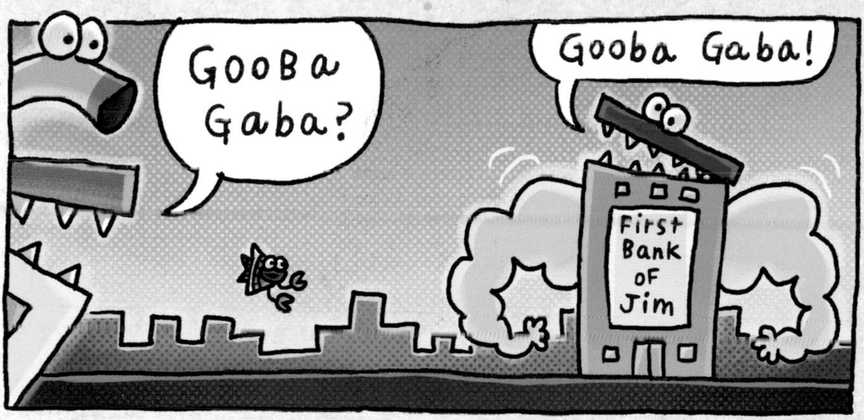
GOOBa Gaba?
Gooba Gaba!
First Bank OF Jim

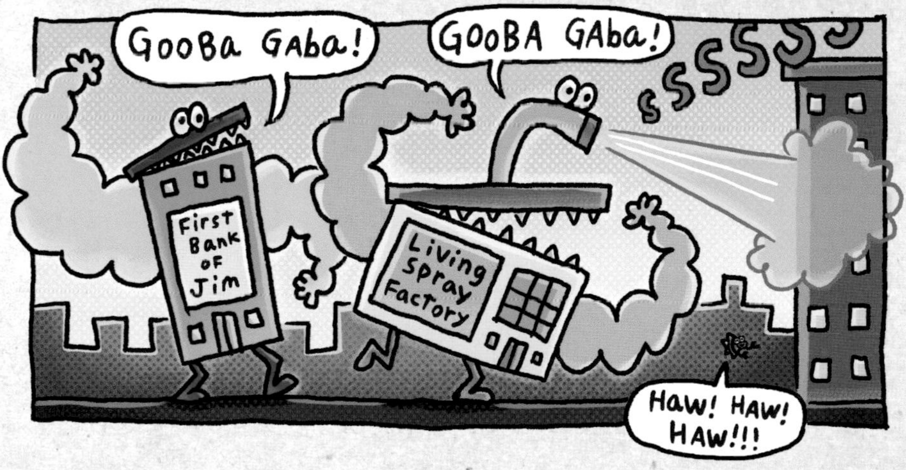
GOOBa GAba!
GOOBA GAba!
First Bank OF Jim
Living Spray Factory
HAW! HAW! HAW!!!

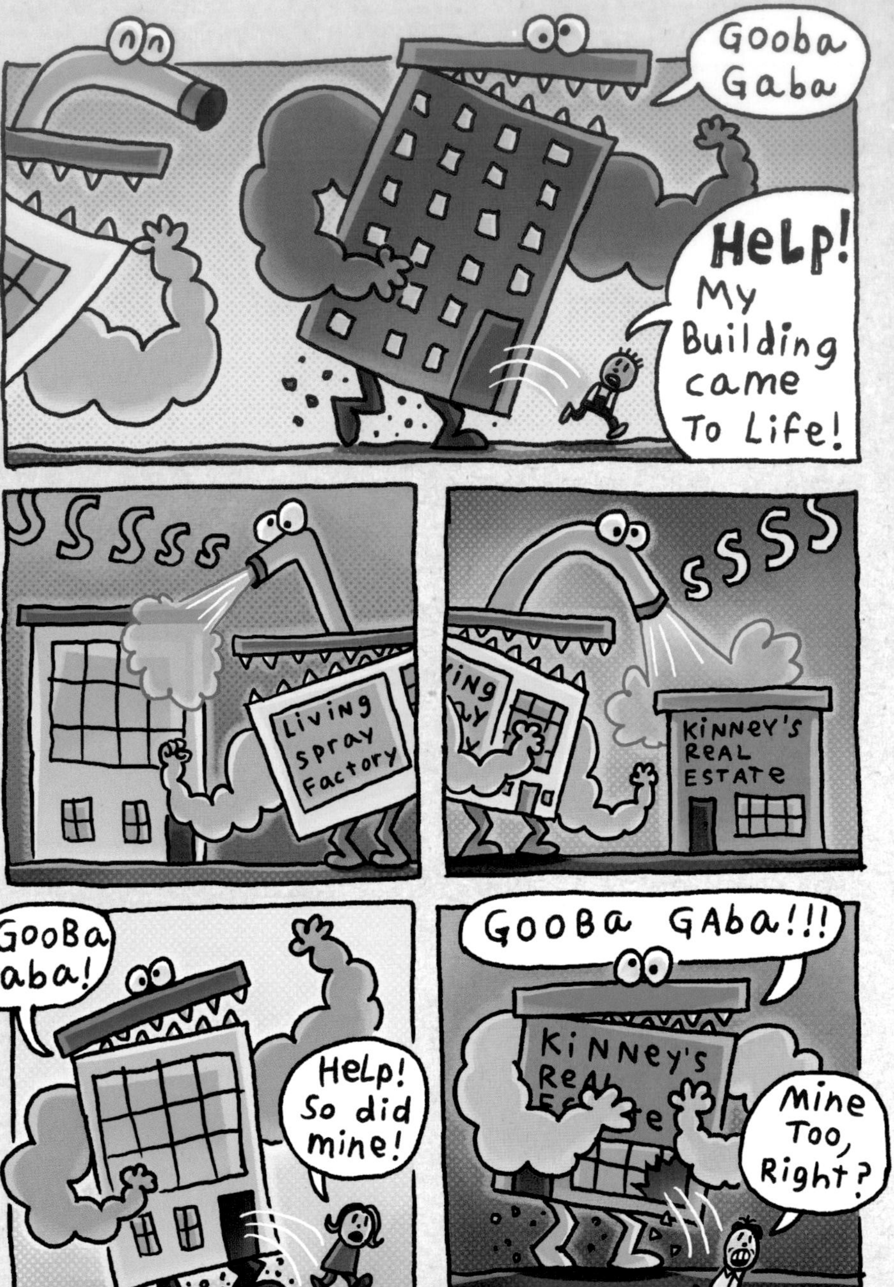
Gooba Gaba
HELP! My Building came To Life!
SSSSS
LIVING SPRAY FACTORY
SSSSS
KINNEY'S REAL ESTATE
GOOBA Gaba!
HELP! So did mine!
GOOBA GABA!!!
KINNEY'S REAL
Mine Too, Right?

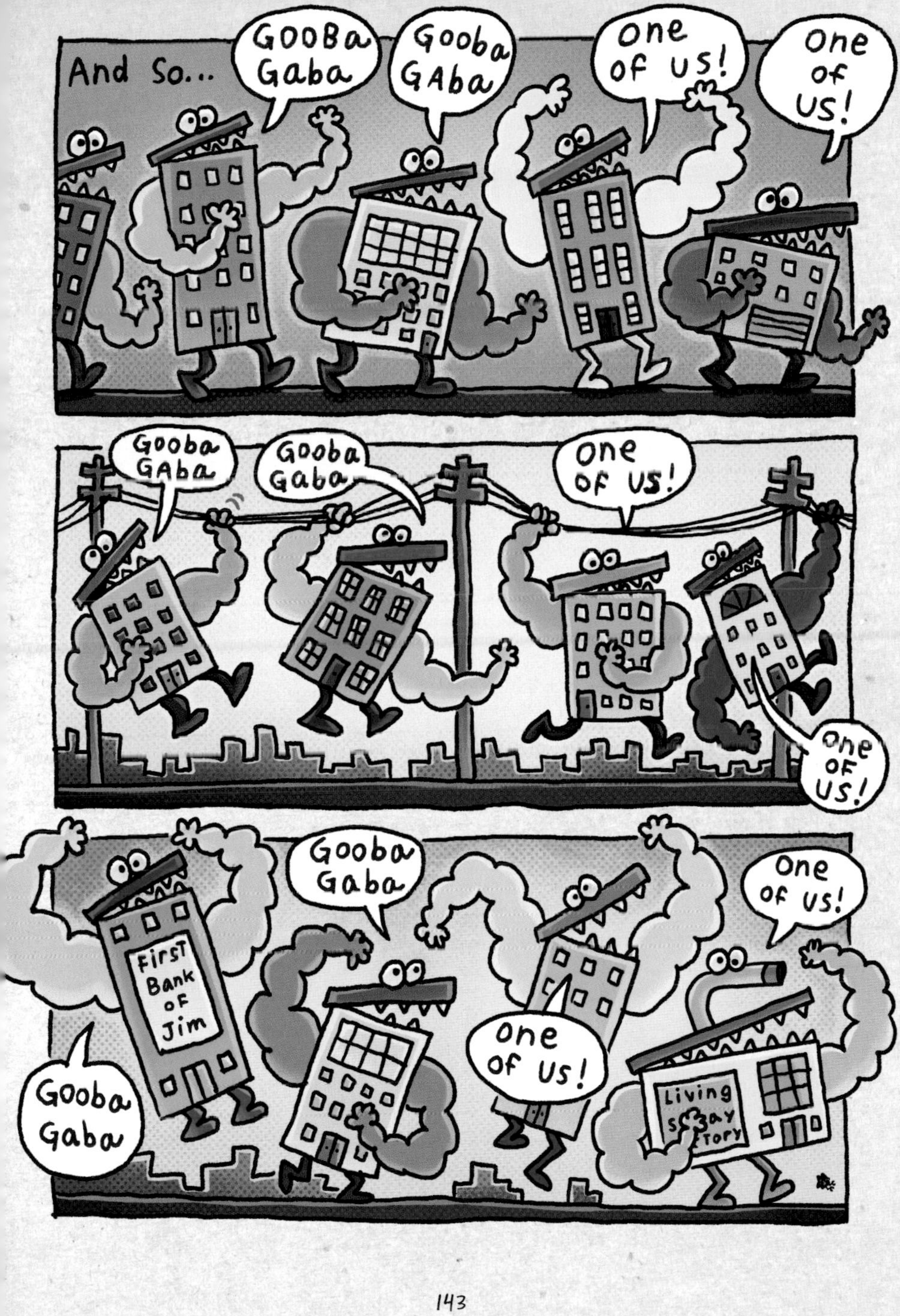

And So...
GOOBa Gaba
Gooba GAba
One of US!
One of US!
Gooba GAba
Gooba Gaba
One of US!
One of US!
Gooba Gaba
FIRST Bank OF Jim
Gooba Gaba
One of us!
One of US!

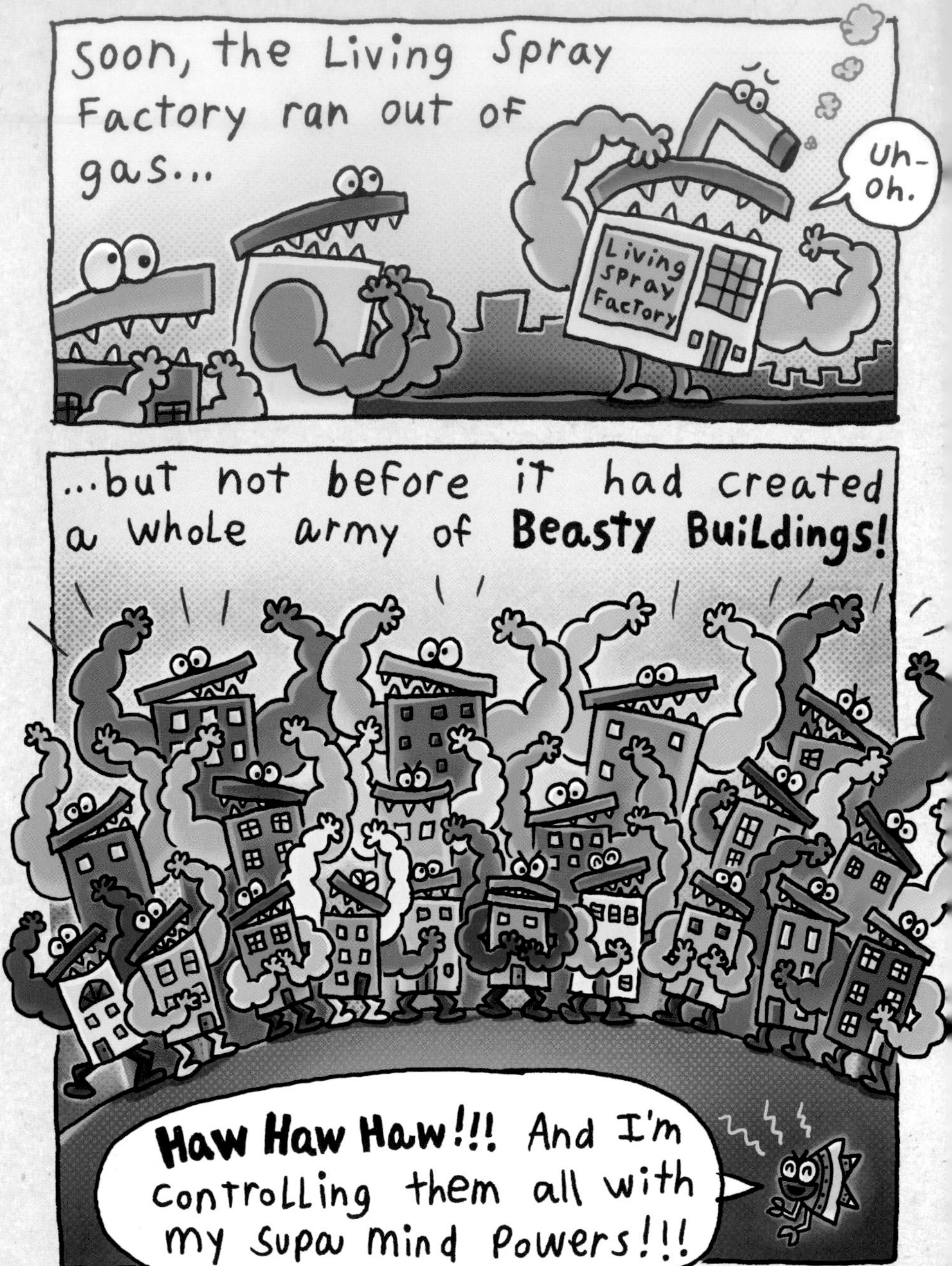
Soon, the Living Spray Factory ran out of gas...
Uh-oh.
Living Spray Factory
...but not before it had created a whole army of **Beasty Buildings!**
Haw Haw Haw!!! And I'm controlling them all with my supa mind powers!!!

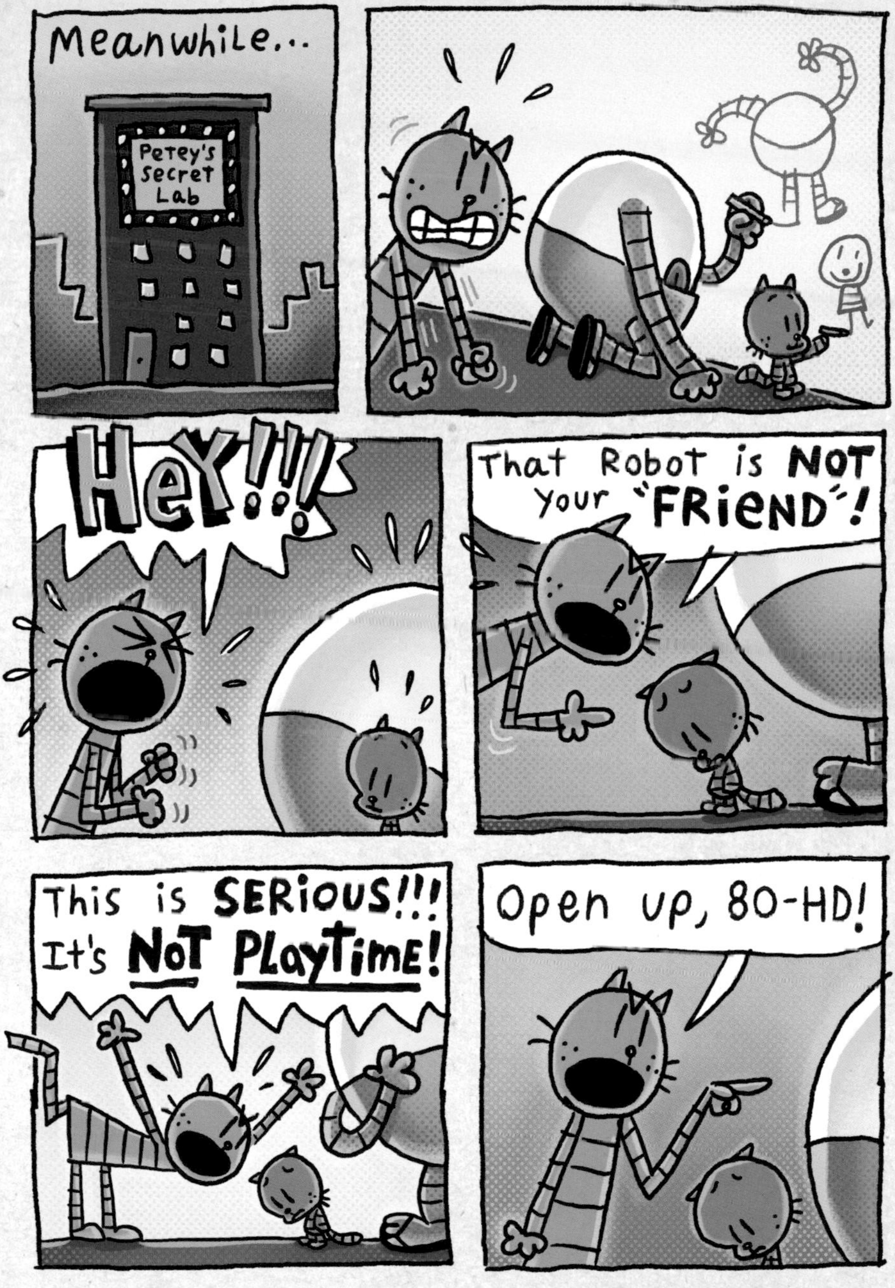
Meanwhile...
Petey's Secret Lab
HEY!!!
That Robot is NOT your "FRIEND"!
This is SERIOUS!!! It's NOT PLAYTIME!
Open up, 80-HD!

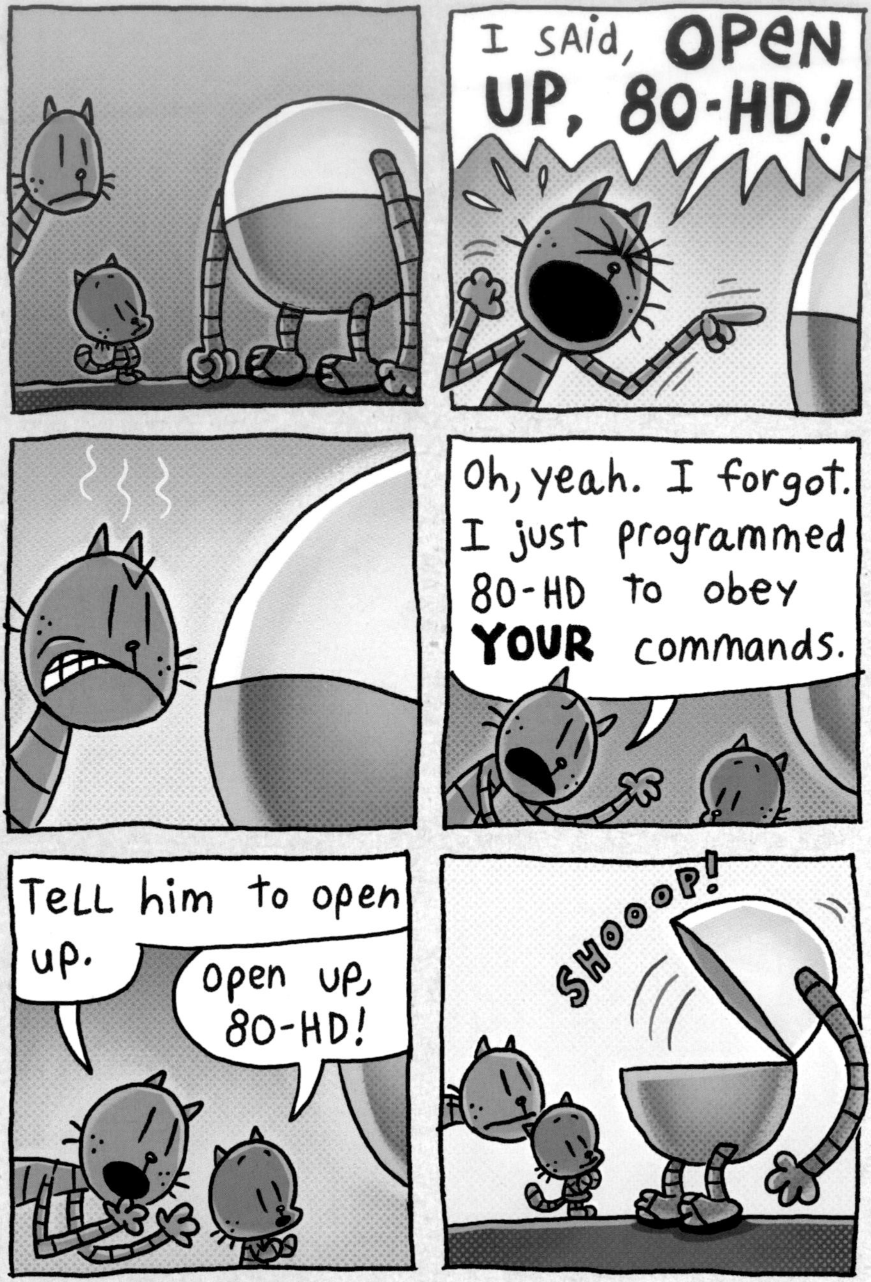
I SAid, OPEN UP, 80-HD!
Oh, yeah. I forgot. I just programmed 80-HD to obey YOUR commands.
TeLL him to open up.
Open up, 80-HD!
SHOOOP!

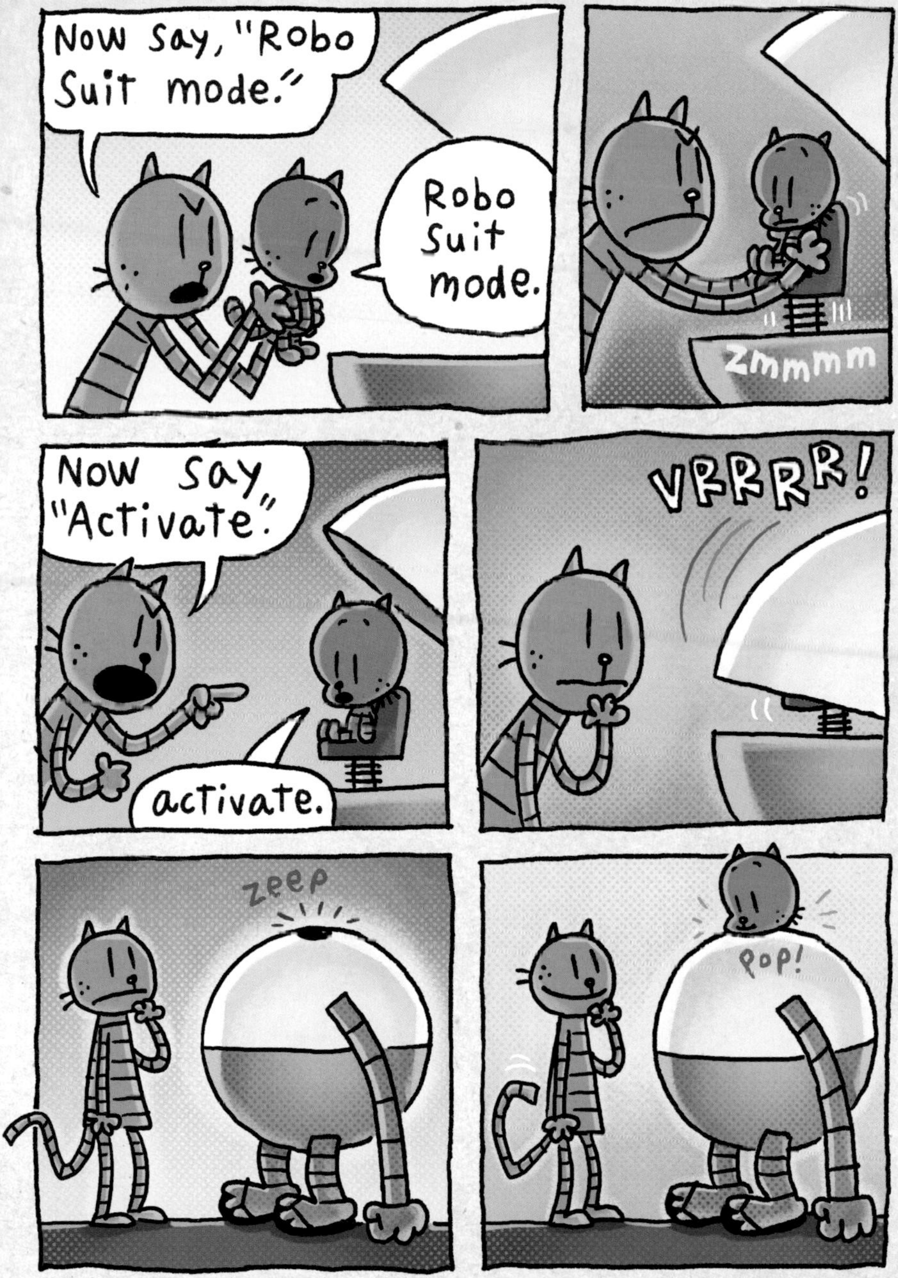
Now say, "Robo Suit mode."
Robo Suit mode.
zmmmm
Now say "Activate."
activate.
VRRRR!
zeep
pop!

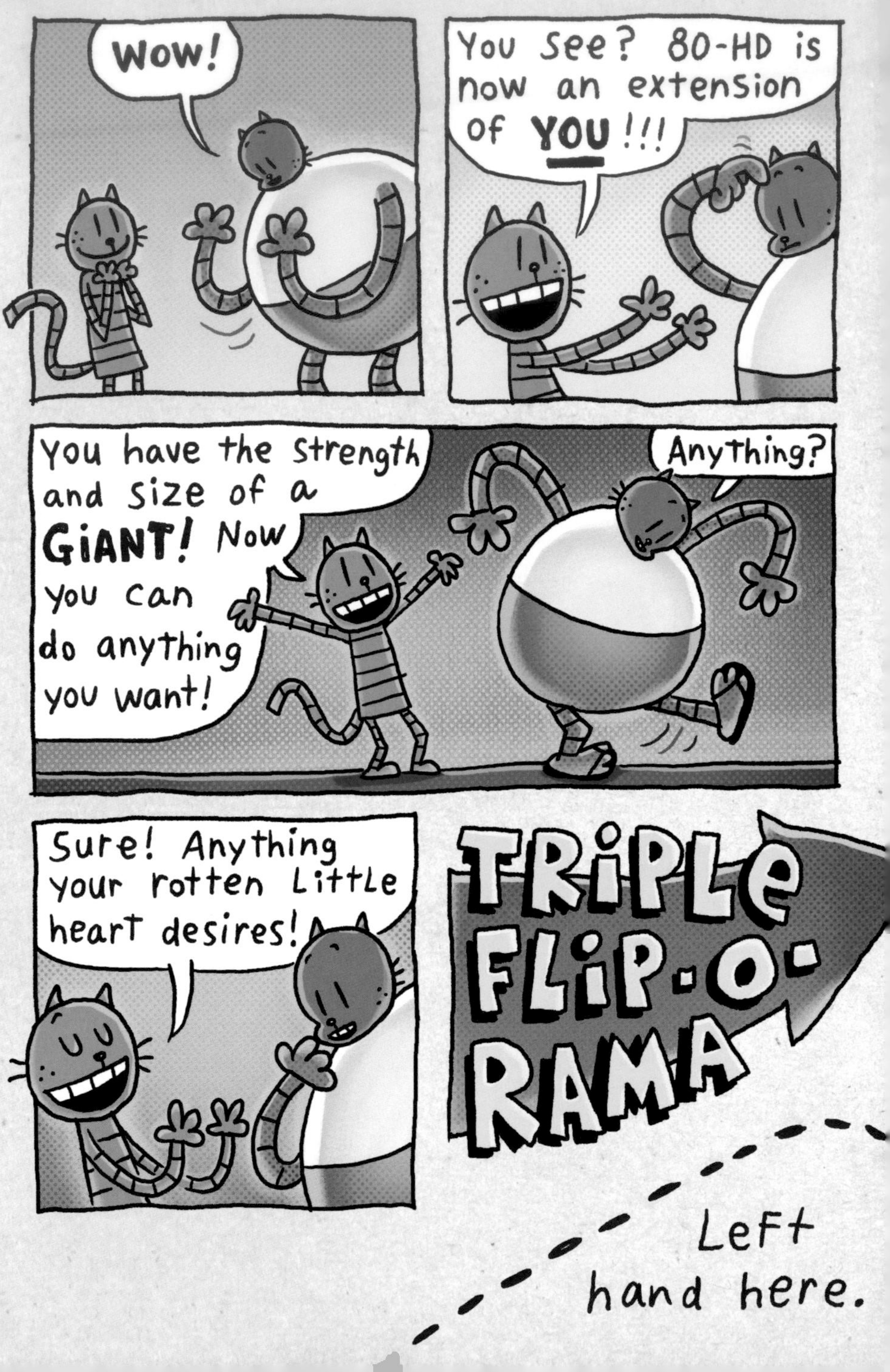
Wow!
You see? 80-HD is now an extension of YOU!!!
You have the strength and size of a GIANT! Now you can do anything you want!
Anything?
Sure! Anything your rotten little heart desires!
TRIPLE FLIP-O-RAMA
Left hand here.

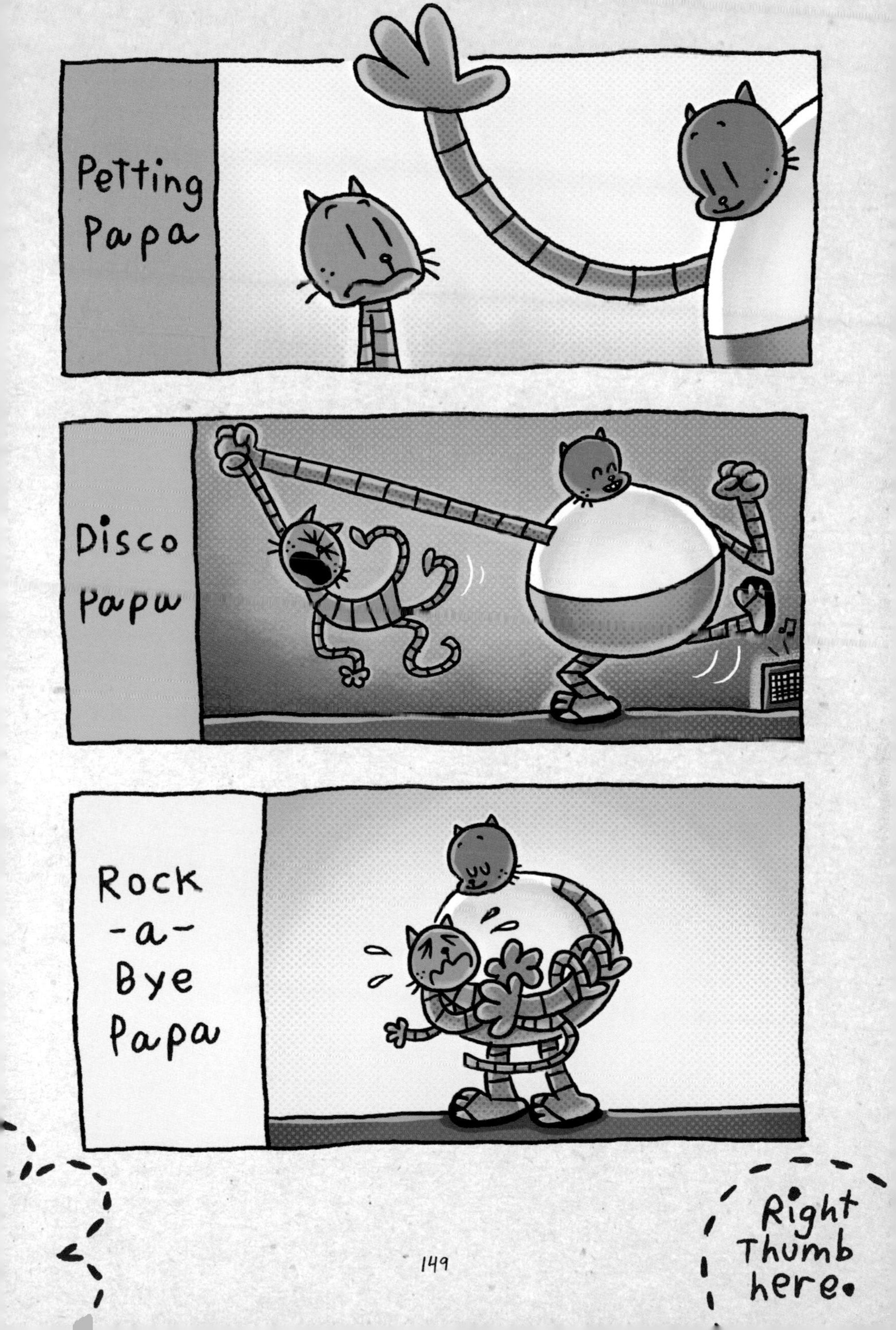
Petting Papa
Disco Papa
Rock -a- Bye Papa
Right Thumb here.

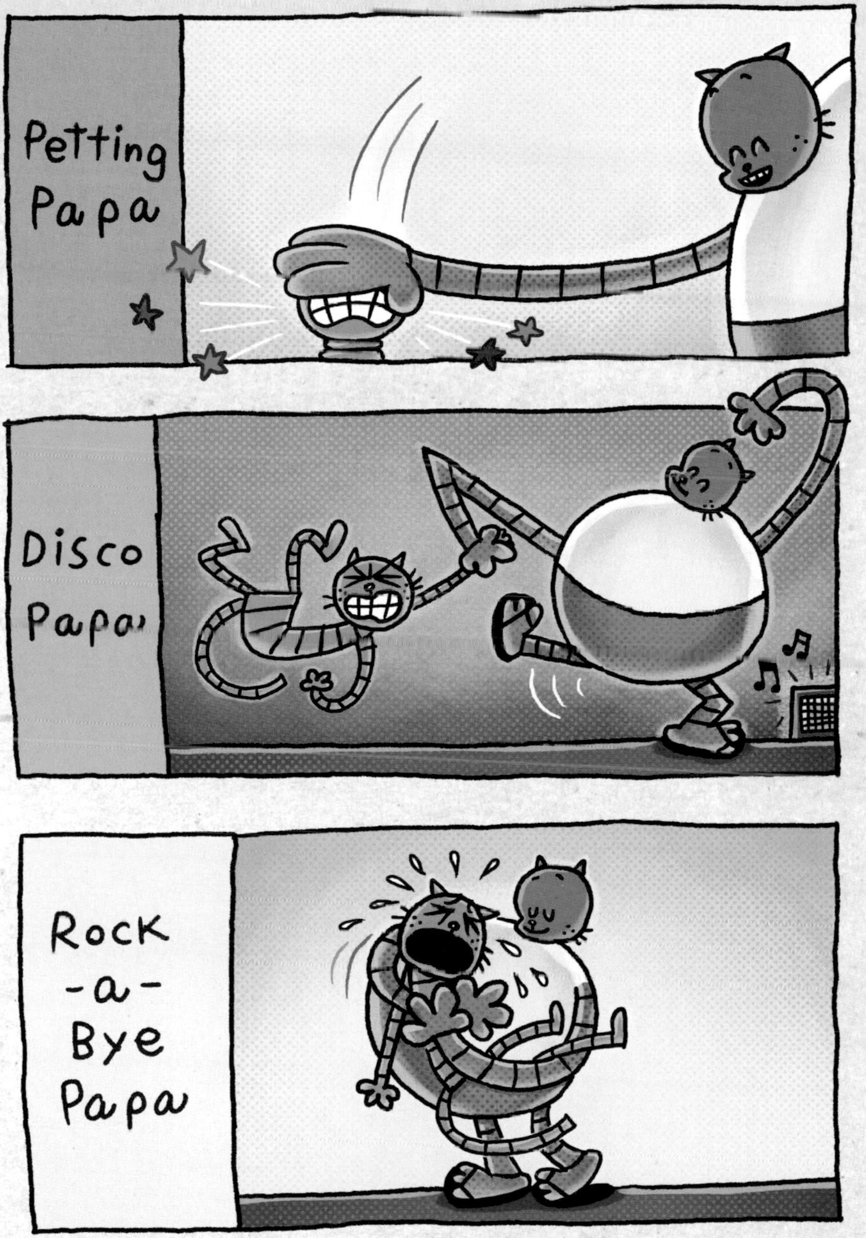
Petting Papa
Disco Papa
Rock -a- Bye Papa

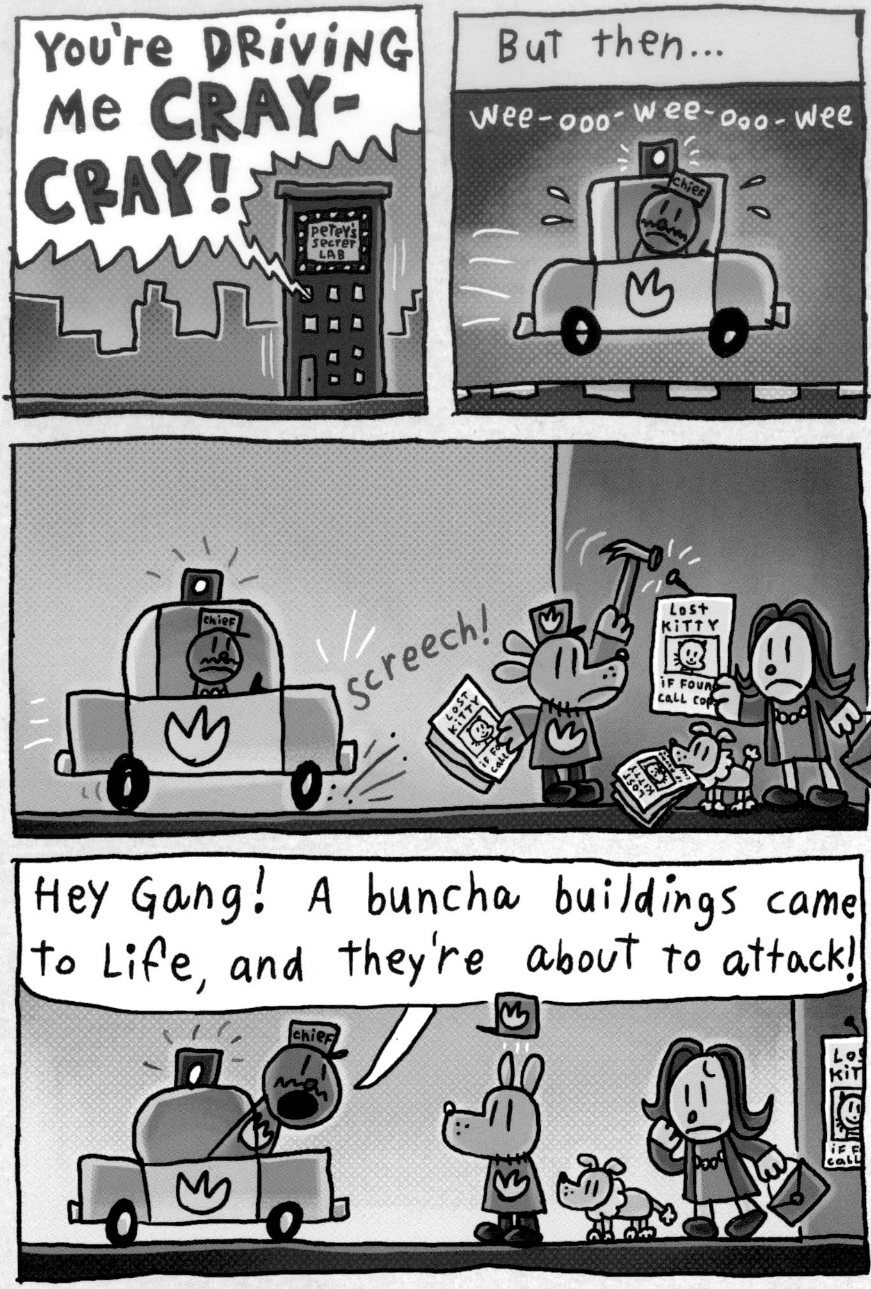
You're DRIVING Me CRAY-CRAY!
Petey's Secret LAB
But then...
Wee-ooo-wee-ooo-wee
chief
chief
screech!
LOST KITTY IF FOUND CALL COPS
LOST KITTY
Hey Gang! A buncha buildings came to Life, and they're about to attack!
chief

Here they come now! we gotta SPLIT, man!
chief
come on! what are you waiting for????
we mustn't run, Chief!
When the roof Shuts out the Sky...
WE MUST be The Light!

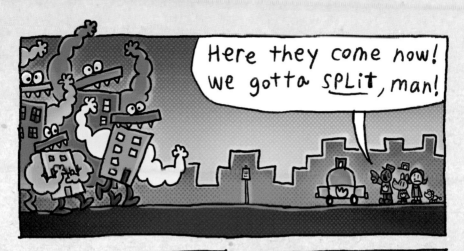

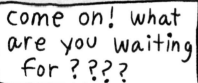

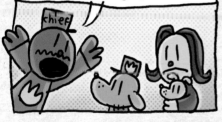

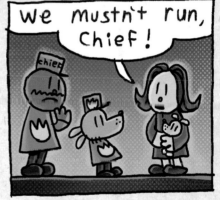

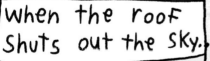

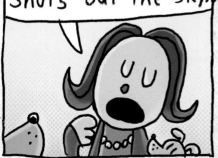

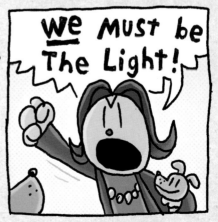

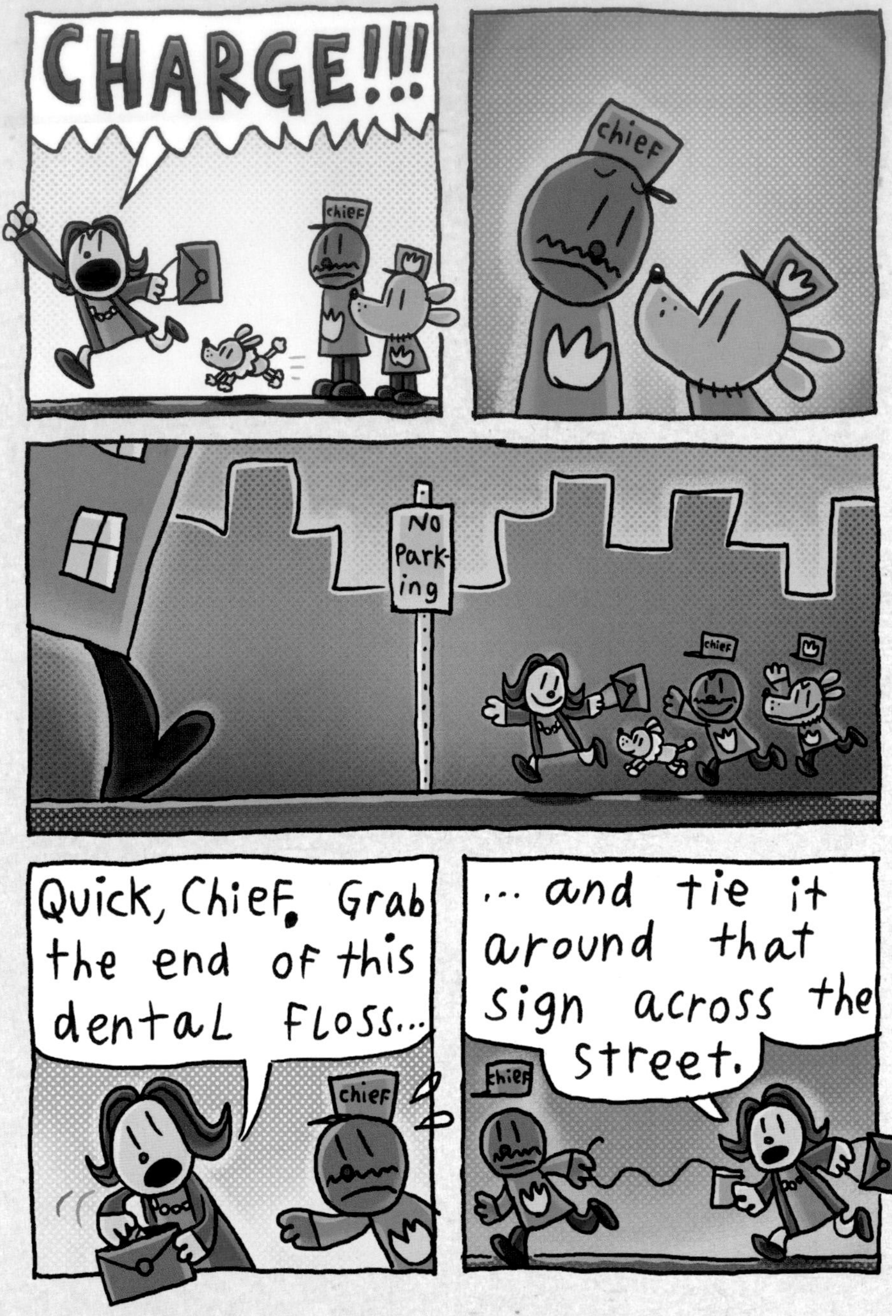
CHARGE!!!
chief
chief
No Parking
chief
Quick, Chief. Grab the end of this dental floss...
chief
... and tie it around that sign across the street.
chief

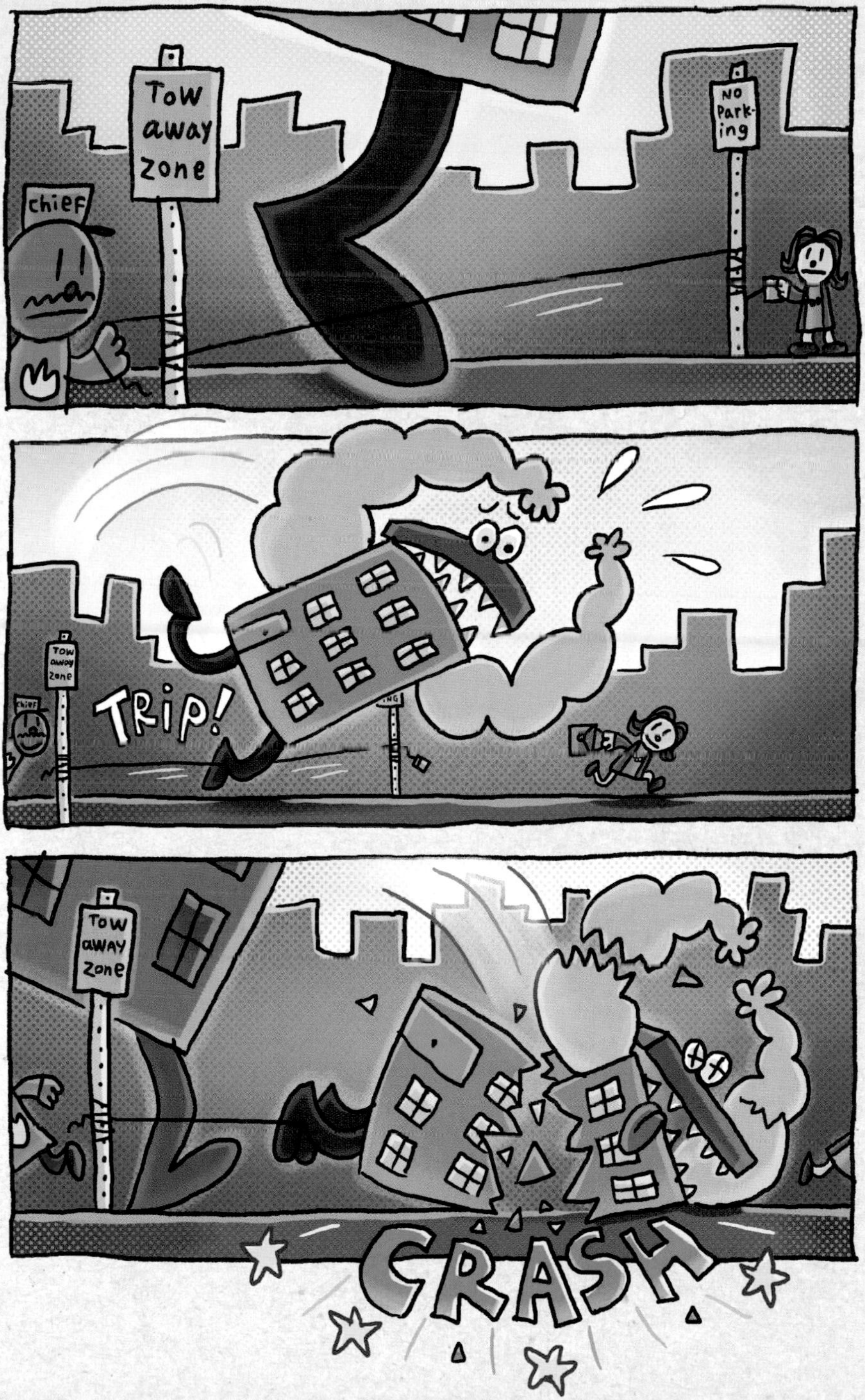

Tow away zone
chief
No Park-ing
Tow away zone
chief
TRIP!
Tow away zone
CRASH

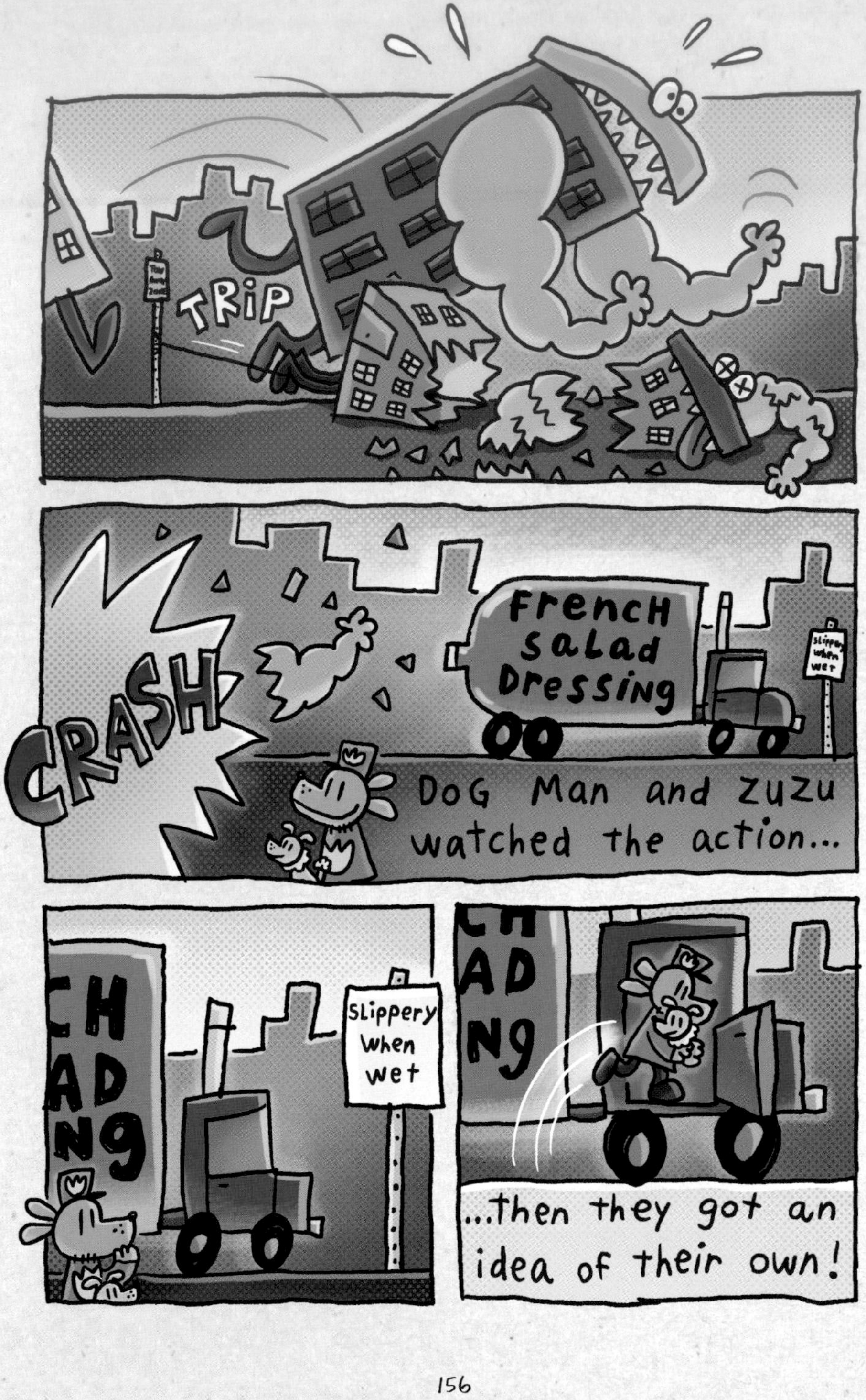
TRIP
CRASH
FRENCH SALAD DRESSING
Slippery when wet
DOG Man and ZUZU watched the action...
Slippery when wet
...then they got an idea of their own!

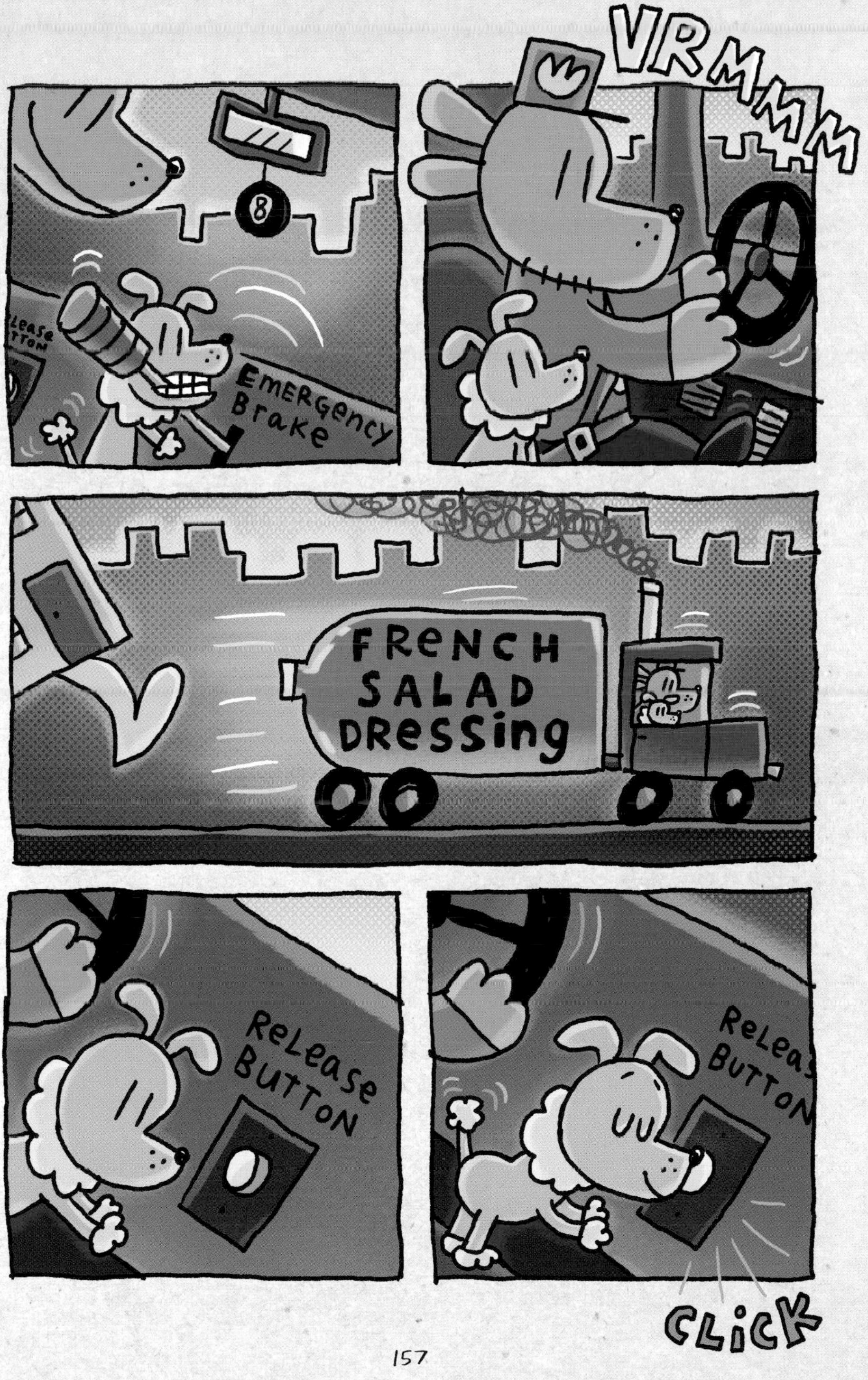

Release Button
Emergency Brake
VRMMMM
FRENCH SALAD DRESSING
Release BUTTON
Releas BUTTON
CLICK

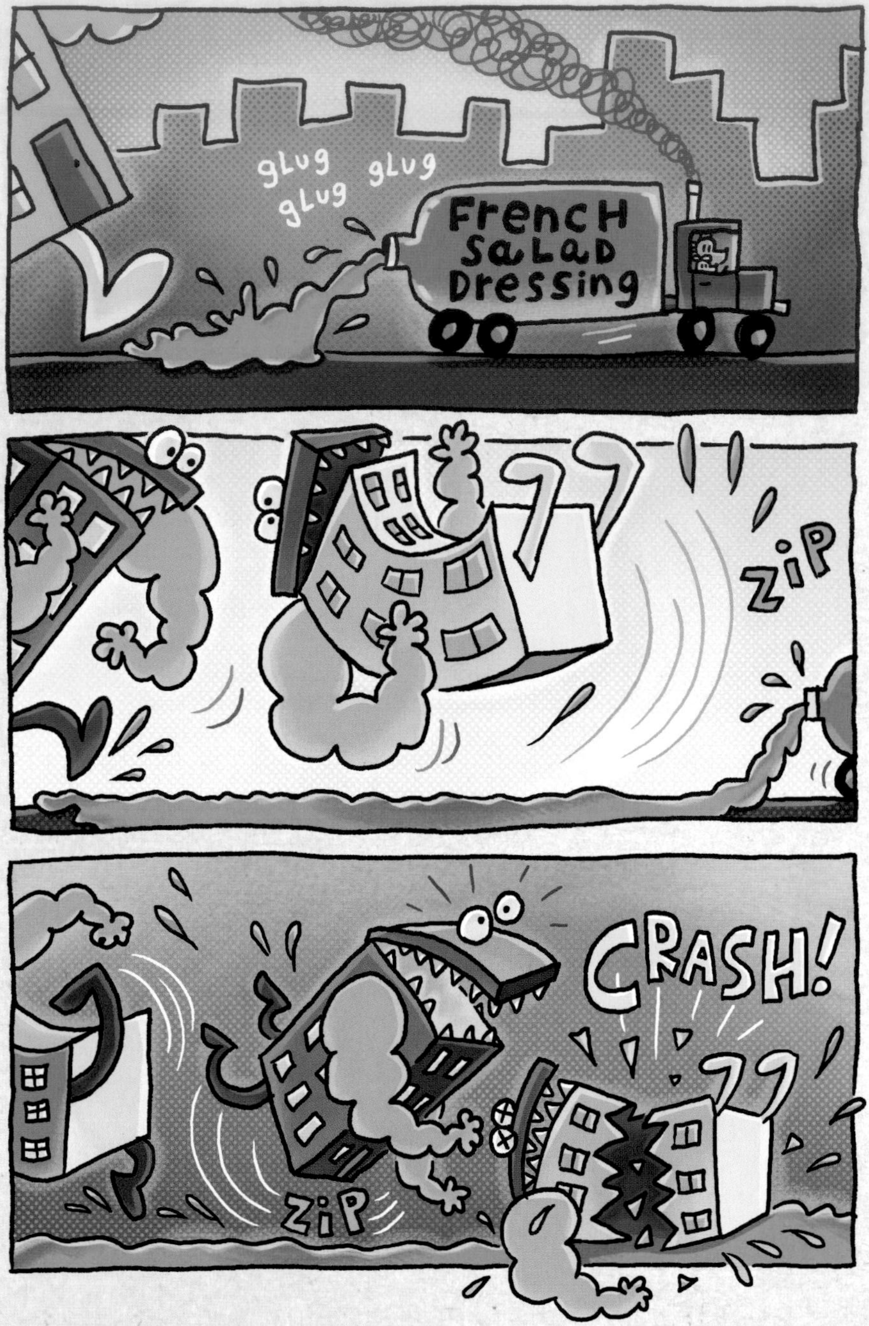
glug glug
glug
French Salad Dressing
ZiP
CRASH!
ZiP

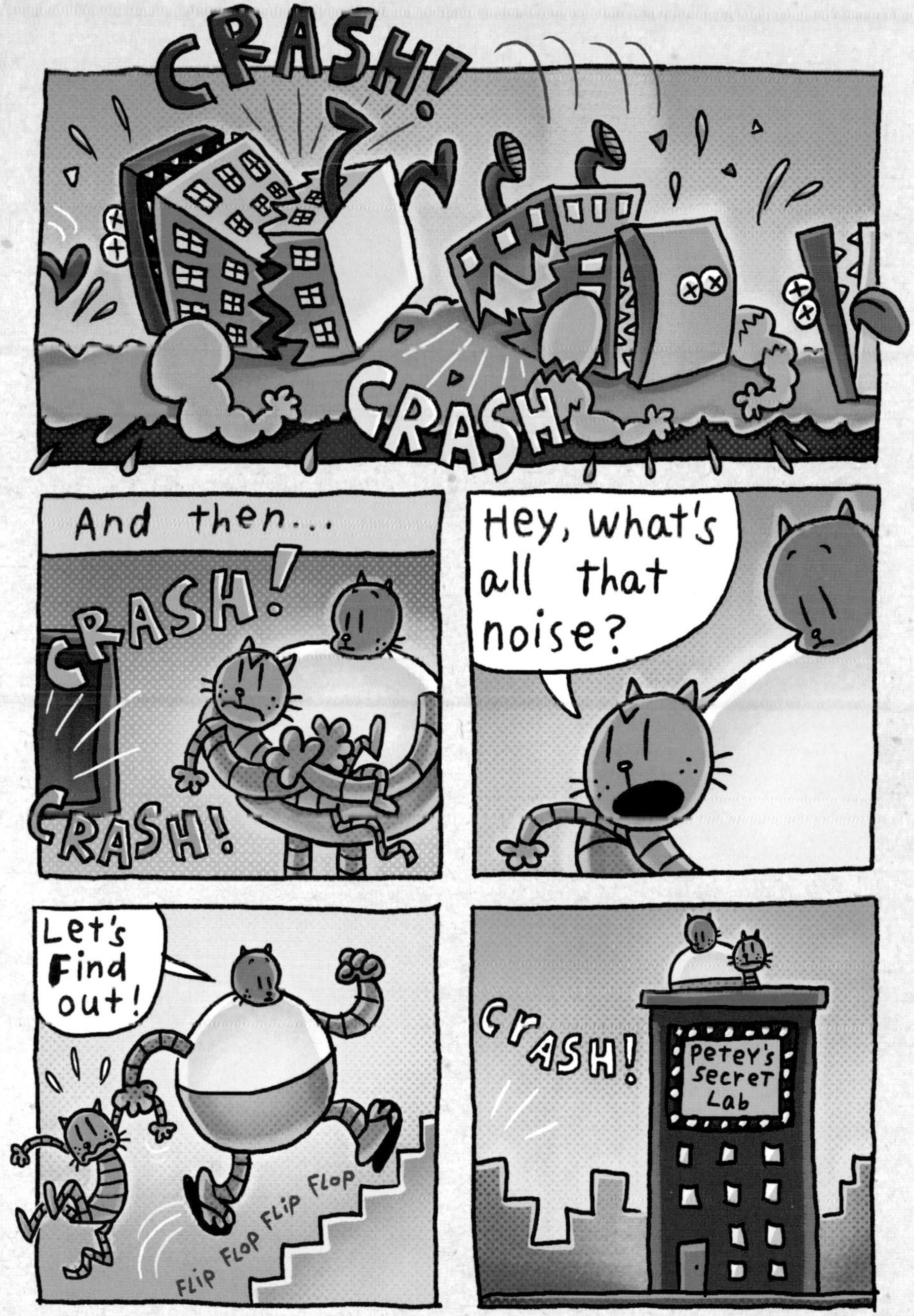
CRASH!
CRASH
And then...
CRASH!
CRASH!
Hey, what's all that noise?
Let's Find out!
FLIP FLOP FLIP FLOP
CRASH!
Petey's Secret Lab

I wish I could see Better!

PETEY

zummmmm

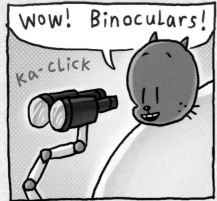

Wow! Binoculars!

ka-click

French SALAD Dressing

160

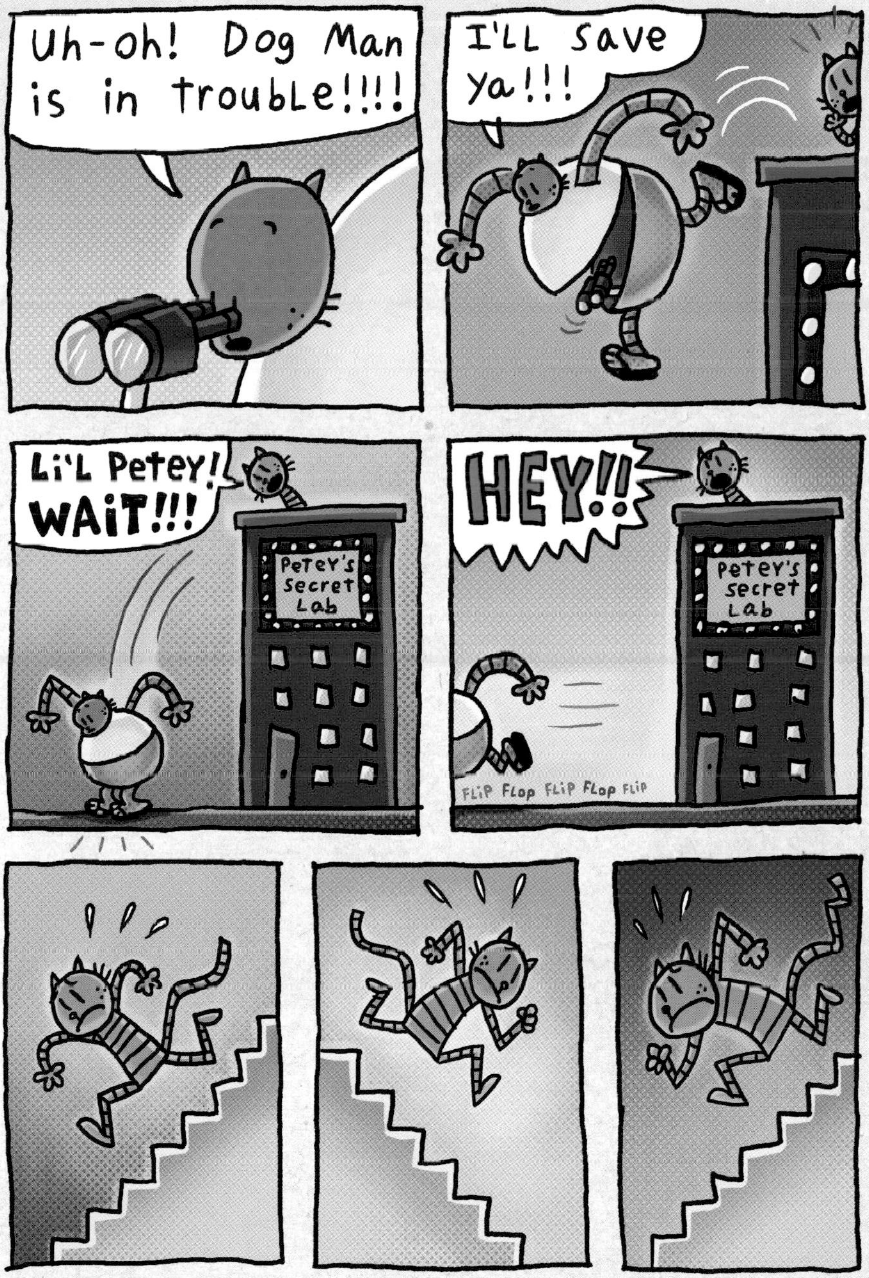

Uh-Oh! Dog Man is in trouble!!!!
I'LL Save ya!!!
Li'L Petey! WAIT!!!
Petey's Secret Lab
HEY!!
Petey's secret Lab
FLiP FLop FLiP FLop FLiP

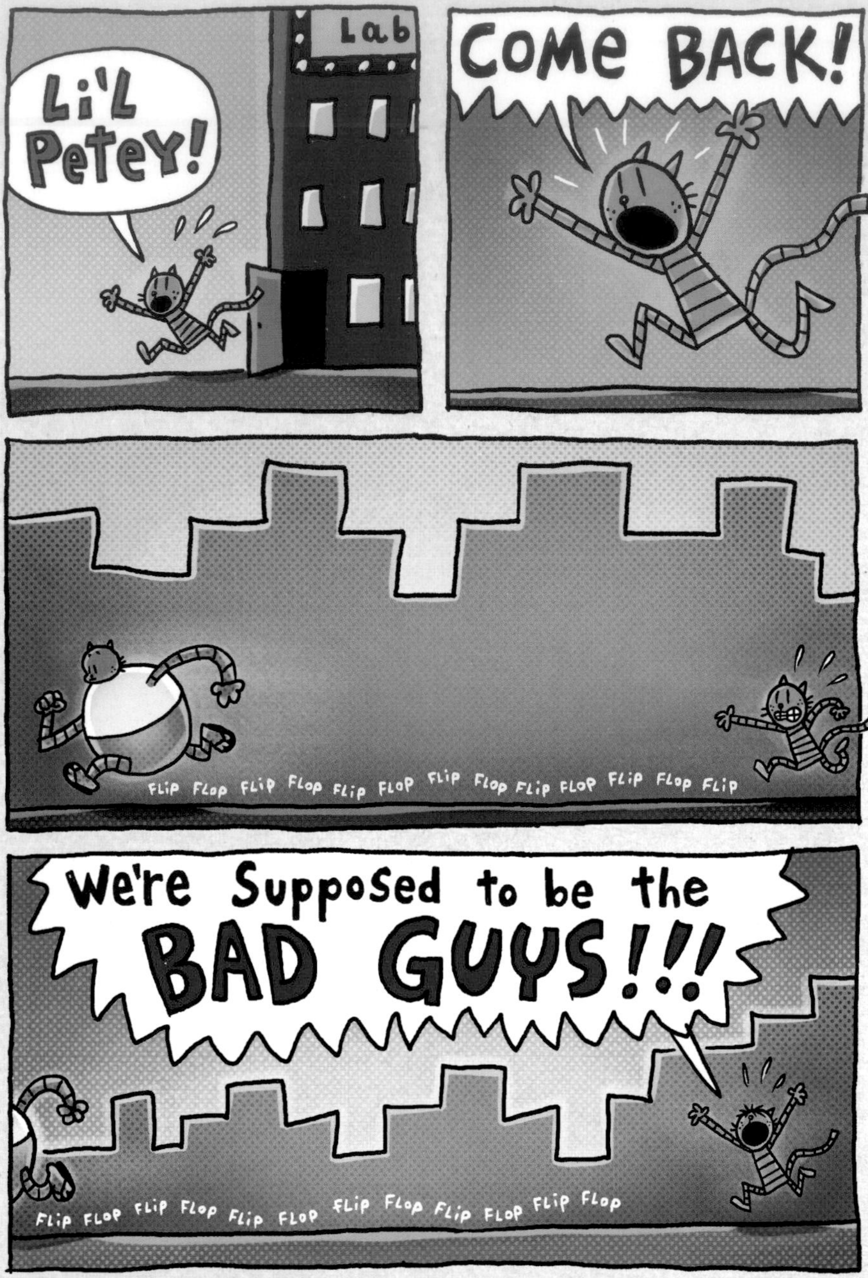
Lab
Li'L Petey!
COME BACK!
FLiP FLoP FLiP FLoP FLiP FLoP FLiP FLoP FLiP FLoP FLiP FLoP FLiP
We're Supposed to be the BAD GUYS!!!
FLiP FLoP FLiP FLoP FLiP FLoP FLiP FLoP FLiP FLoP FLiP FLoP

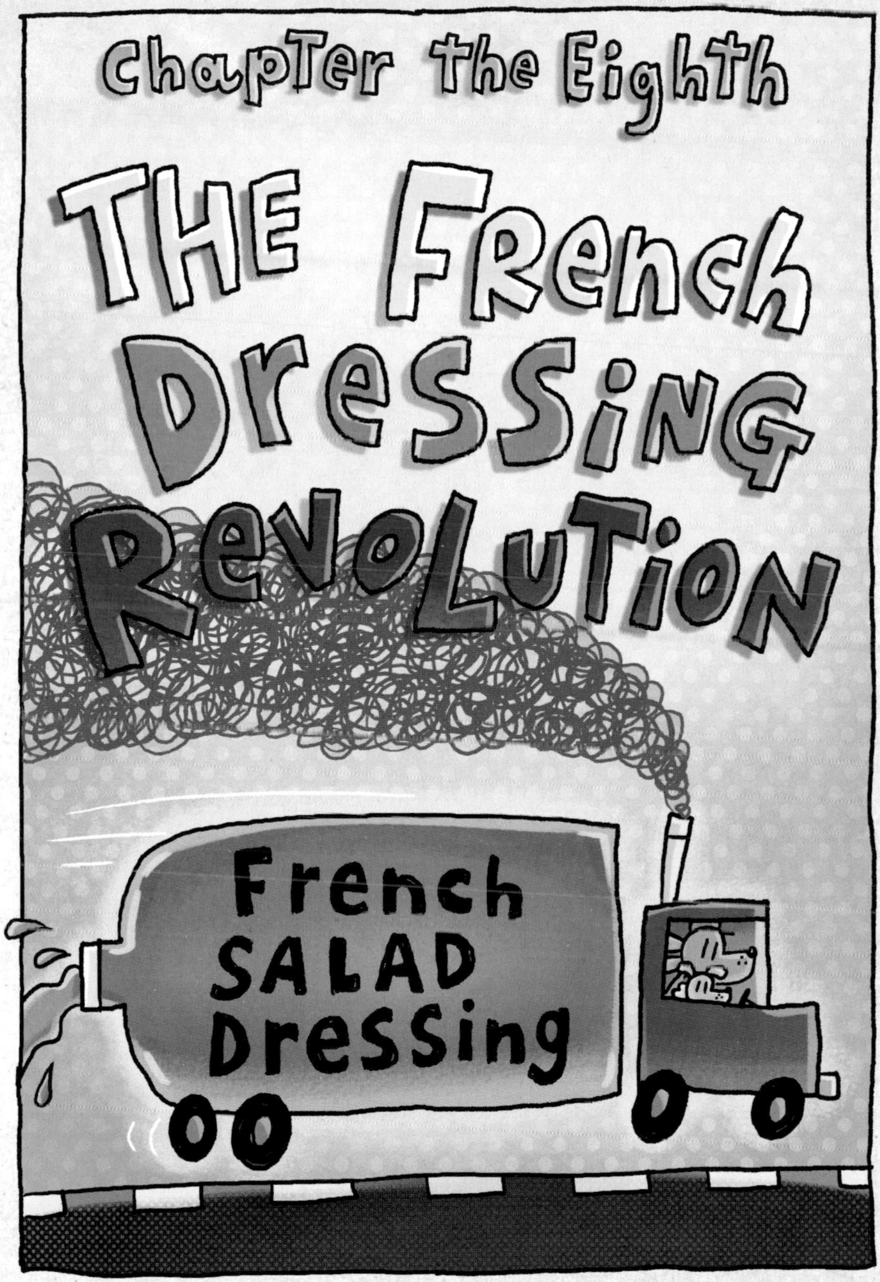
Chapter the Eighth
THE French Dressing Revolution
French SALAD Dressing

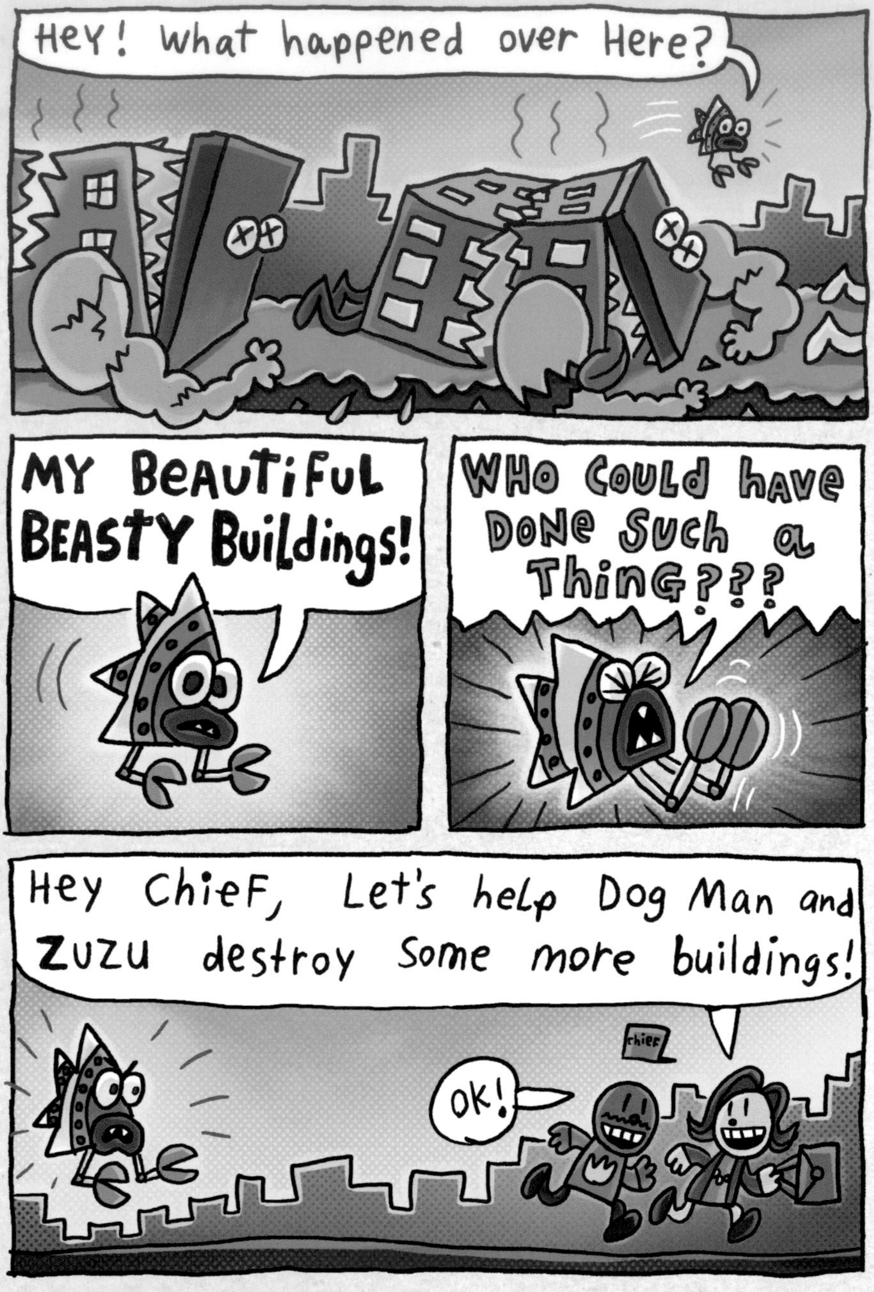
Hey! What happened over Here?
MY BEAUTIFUL BEASTY Buildings!
WHO COULD have DONE SUCH a THING???
Hey Chief, Let's help Dog Man and ZUZU destroy some more buildings!
chief
OK!

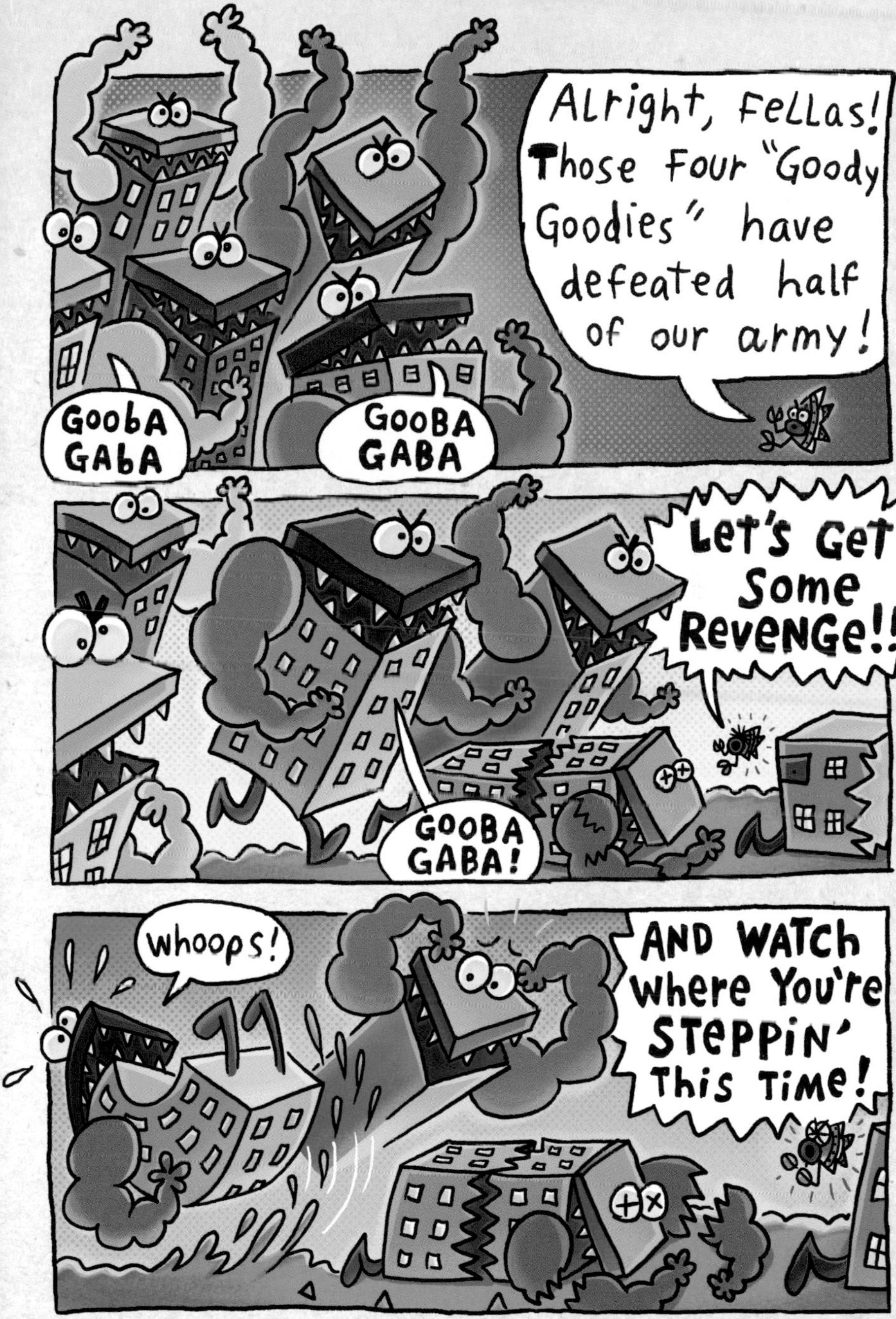

Alright, Fellas! Those Four "Goody Goodies" have defeated half of our army!
GoobA GAbA
GOOBA GABA
Let's Get Some RevenGe!!
GOOBA GABA!
Whoops!
AND WATCH Where You're STEPPIN' This Time!

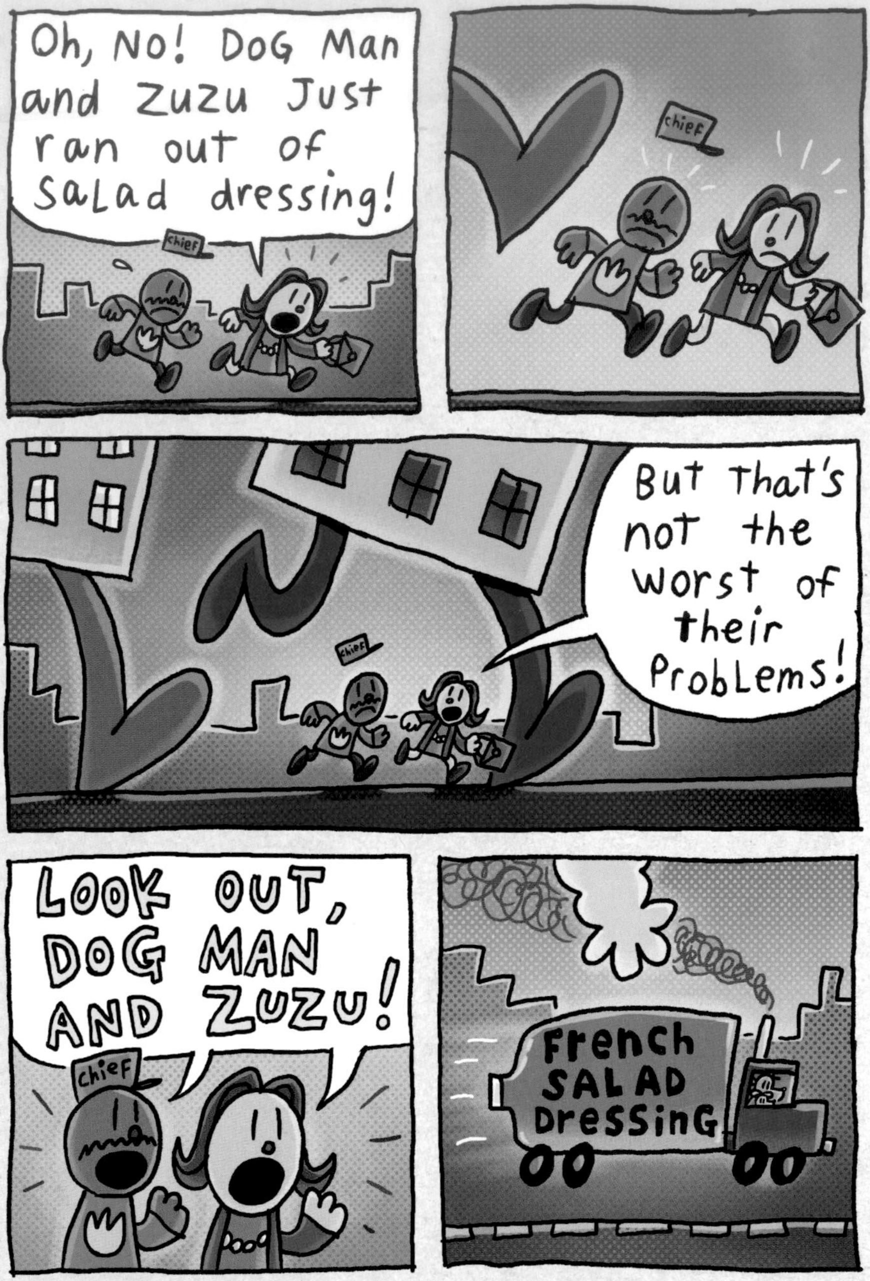
Oh, No! DoG Man and Zuzu Just ran out of SaLad dressing!
chief
chief
chief
But That's not the worst of their ProbLems!
LOOK OUT, DOG MAN AND ZUZU!
chief
French SALAD DresSinG

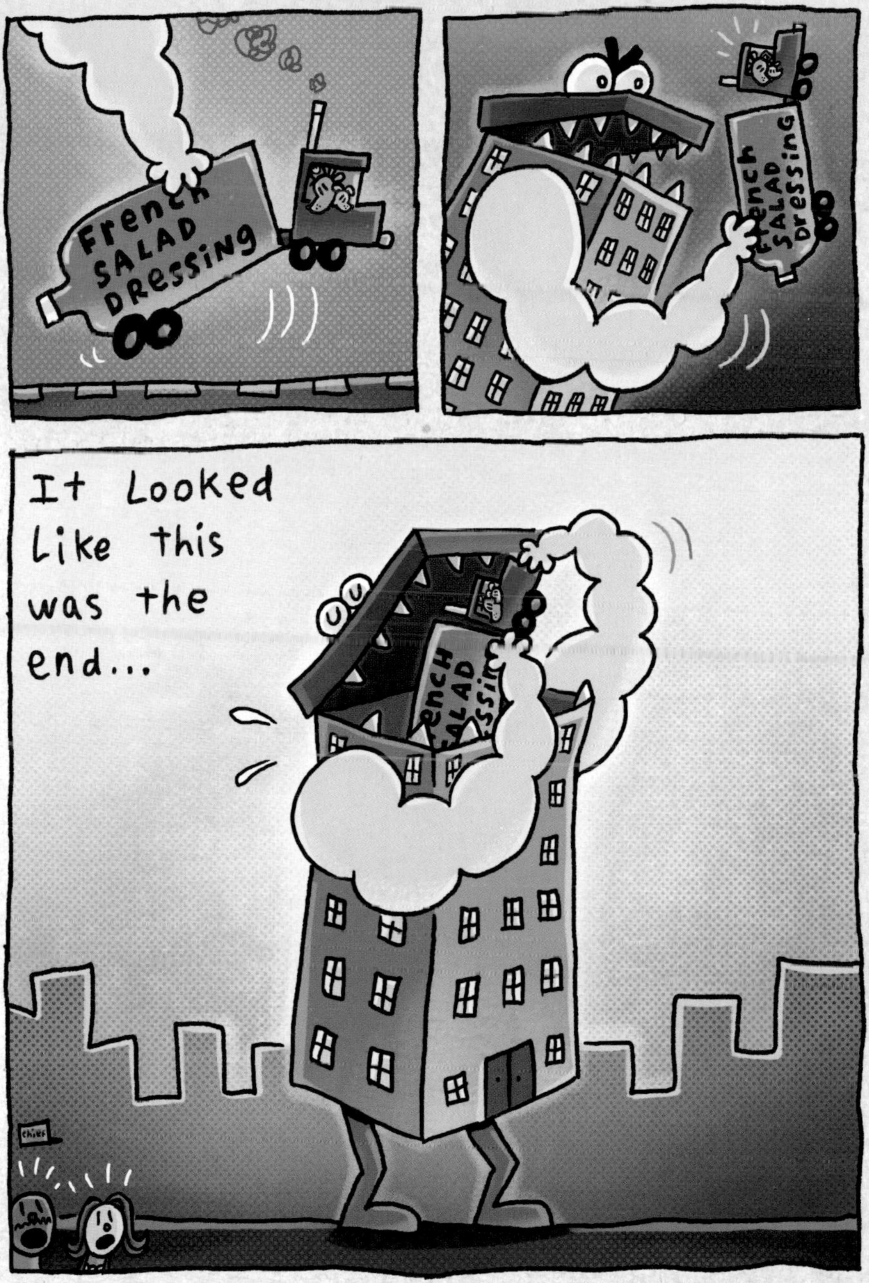
French SALAD DRESSING
French SALAD DRESSING
It Looked like this was the end...
chief

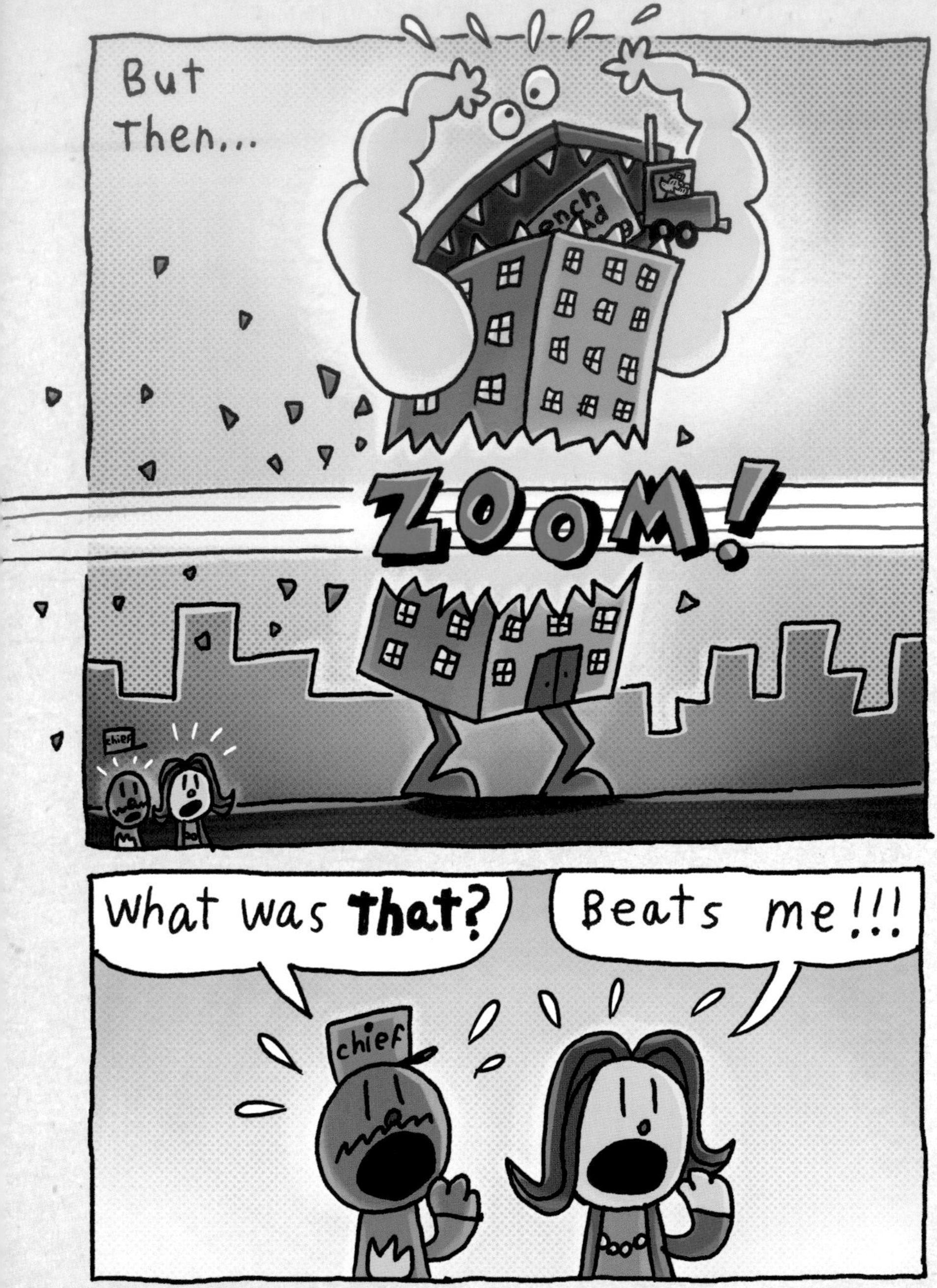
But Then...
ench
Ad
ZOOM!
chief
What was **that?**
Beats me!!!
chief

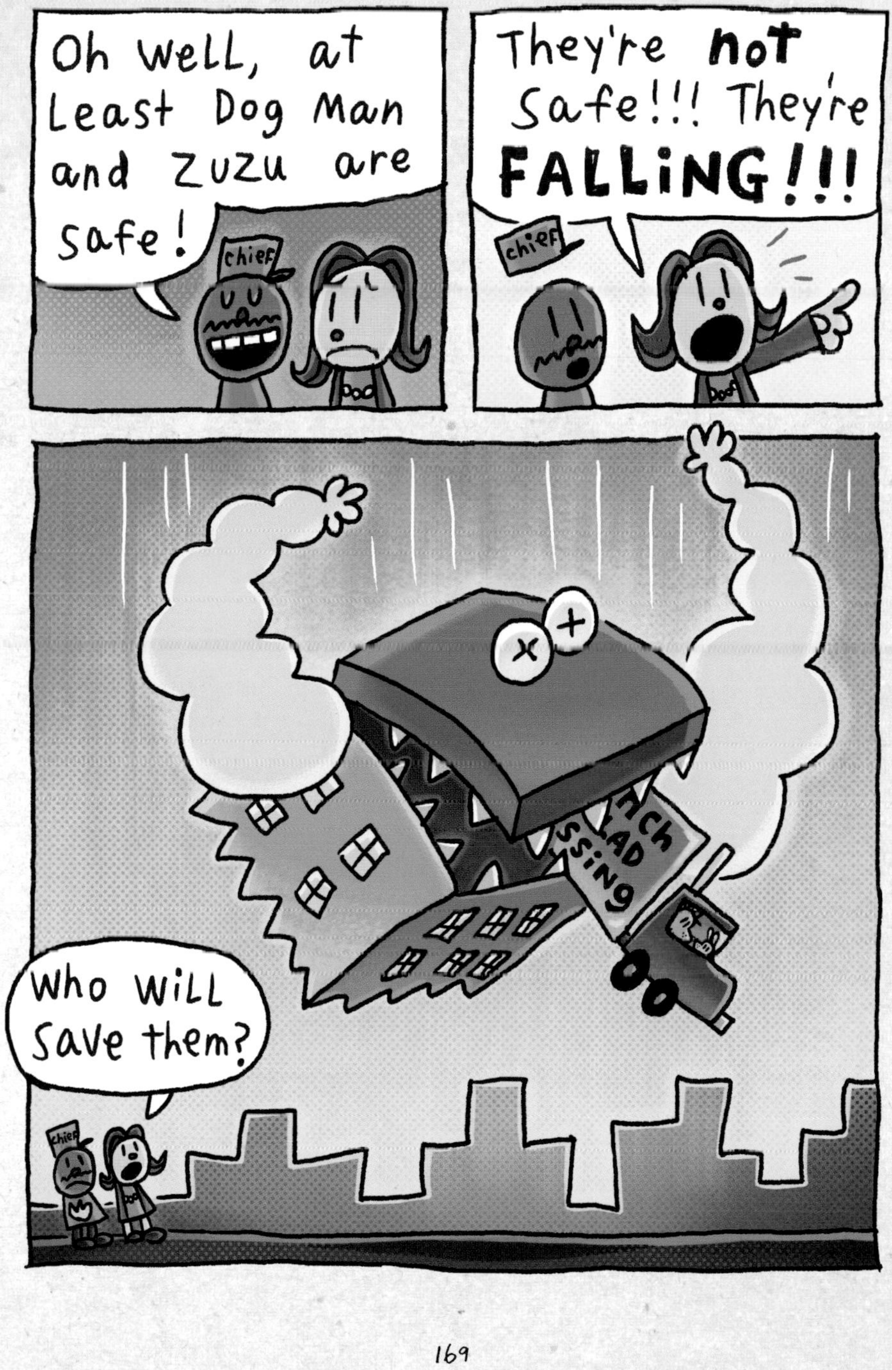
Oh WeLL, at Least Dog Man and ZUZU are safe!
They're **not** Safe!!! They're **FALLiNG!!!**
Who WiLL Save them?

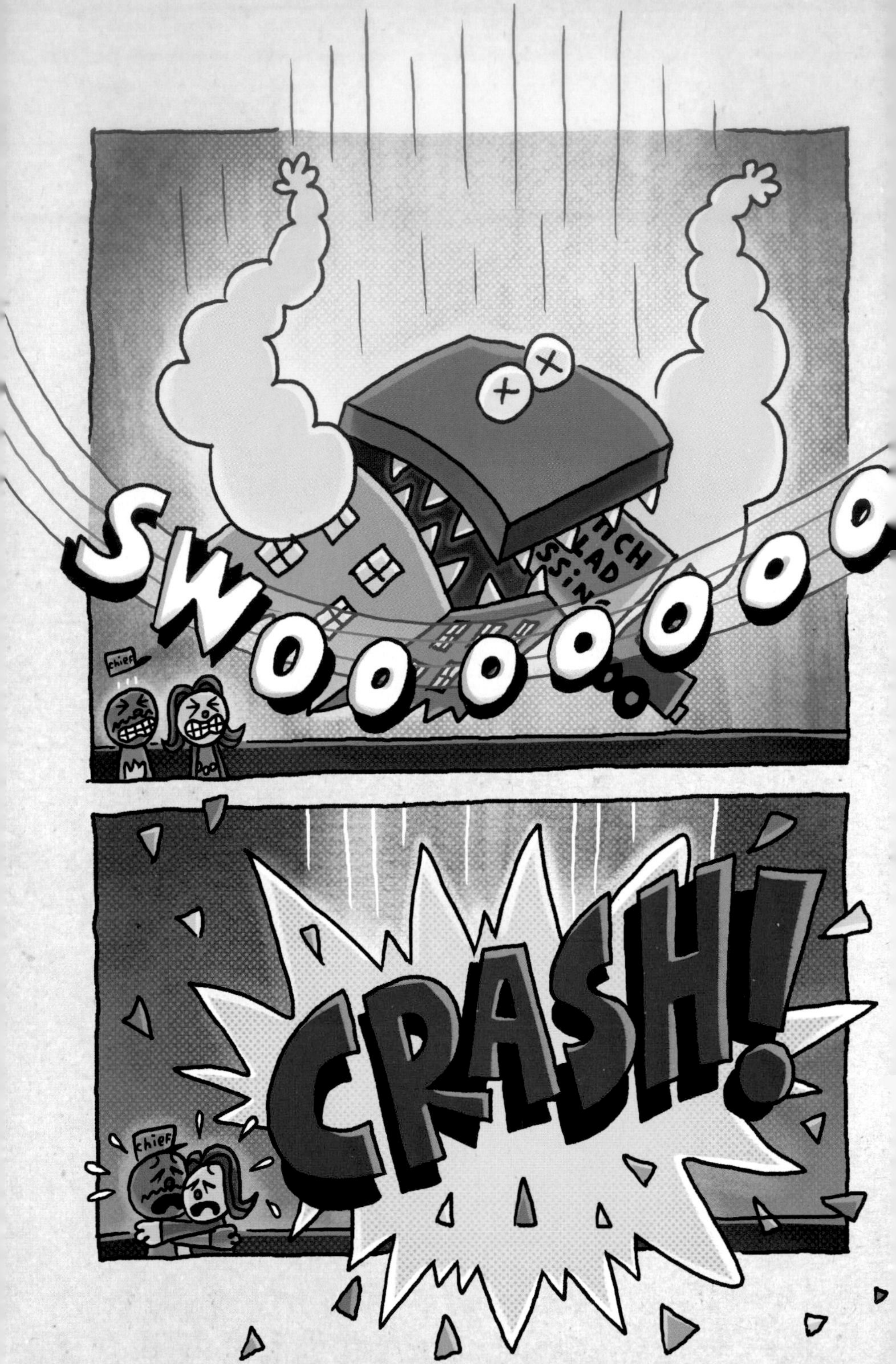

SWOOOOOOOOOOOOOO
chief
CRASH!
chief

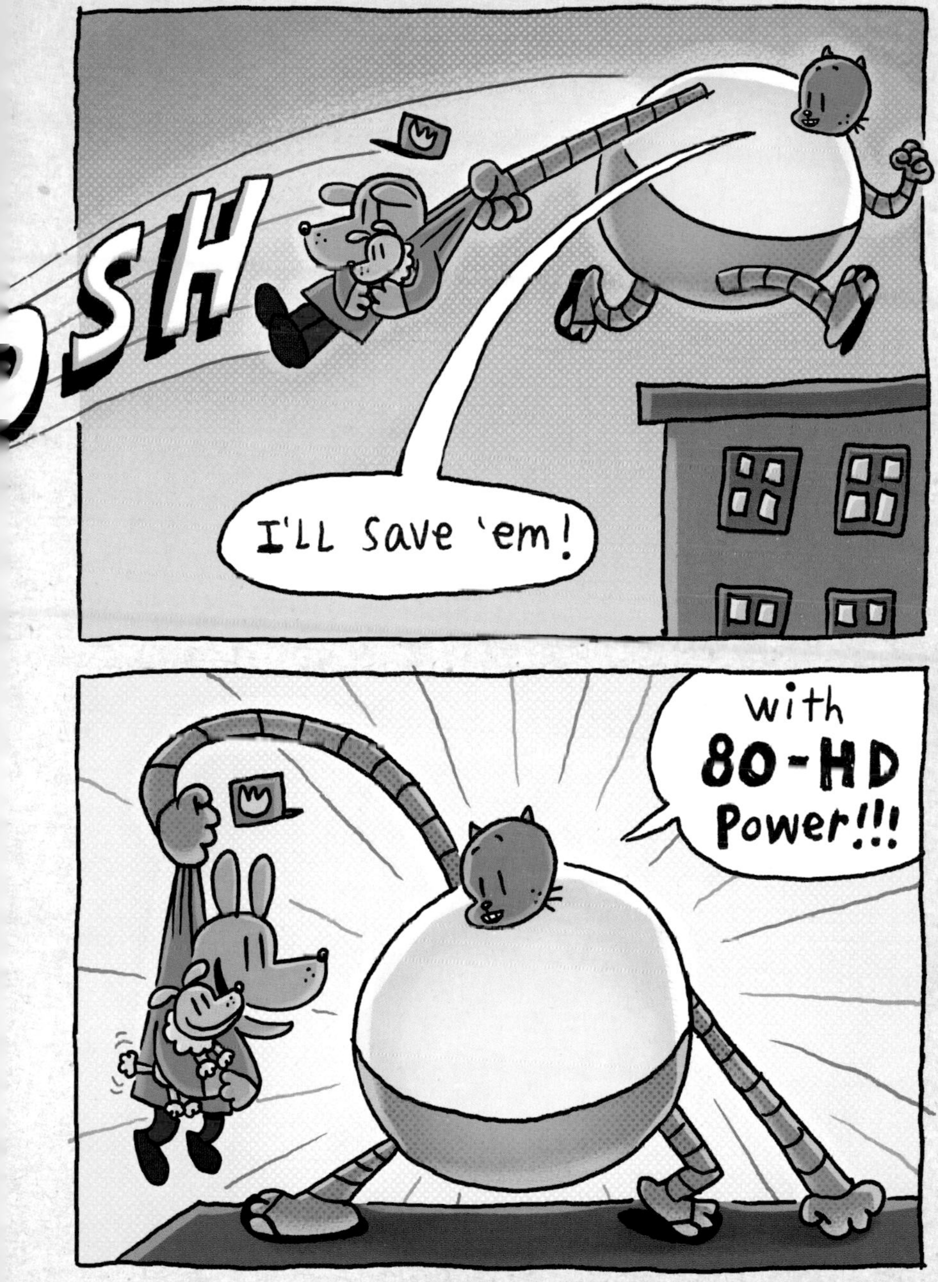
I'LL Save 'em!
with
80-HD
Power!!!

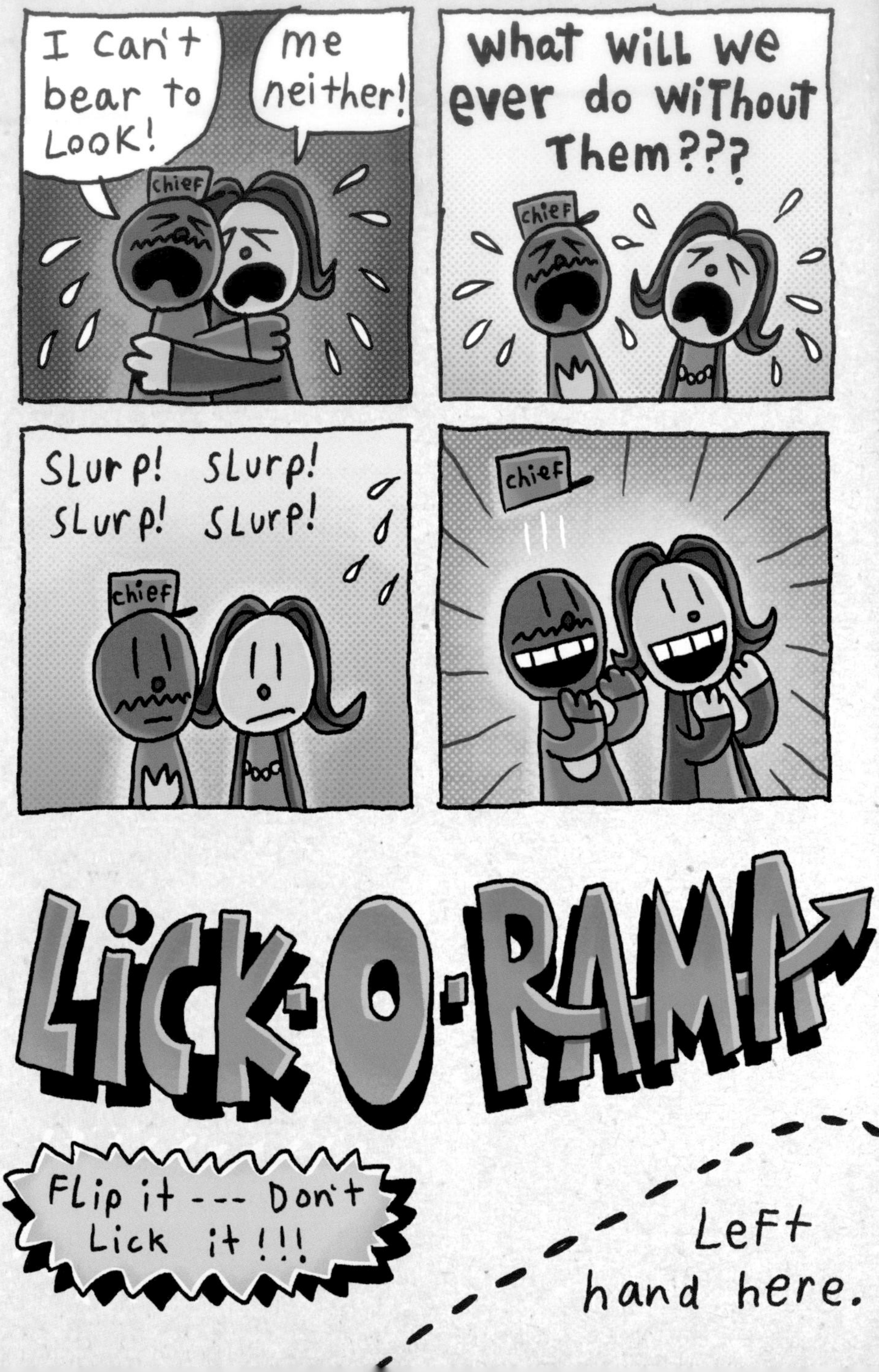

I can't bear to LOOK!
me neither!
what will we ever do without Them???
chief
SLurp! SLurp! SLurp! SLurp!
chief
chief
LICK-O-RAMA
FLip it --- Don't Lick it!!!
Left hand here.

He takes a Lickin'
and keeps on Tickin'!!!

Right
Thumb
here.

He takes a Lickin'
and keeps on Tickin'!!!

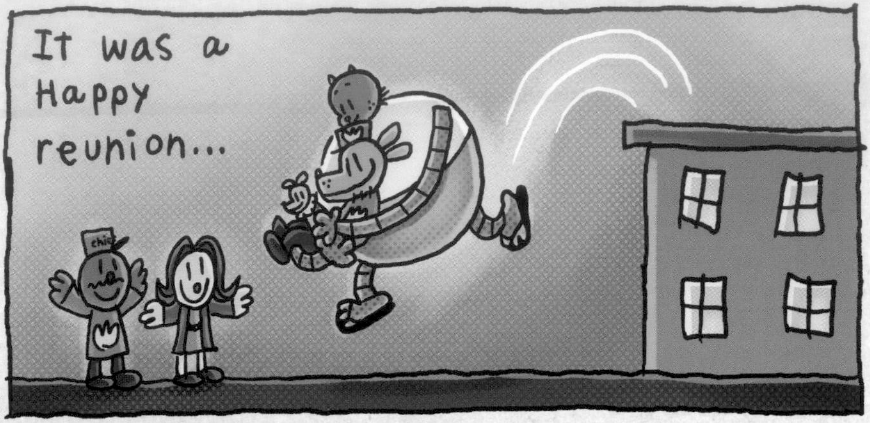
It was a Happy reunion...

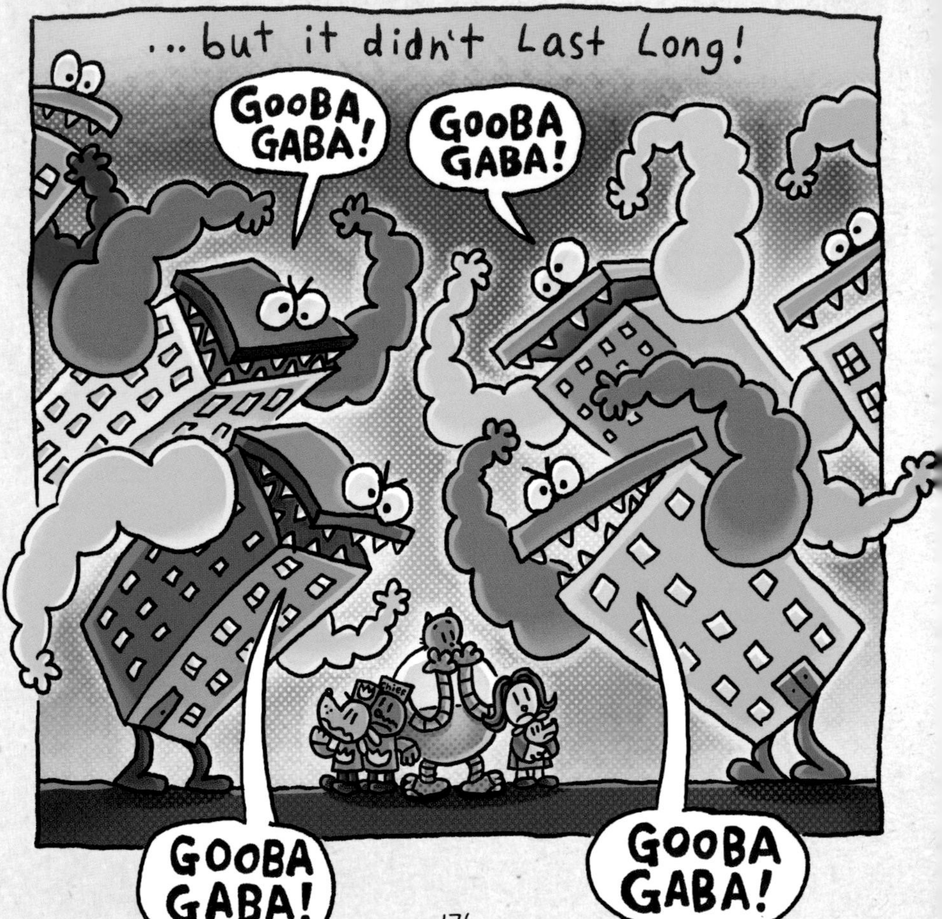
...but it didn't Last Long!
GOOBA GABA!
GOOBA GABA!
GOOBA GABA!
GOOBA GABA!

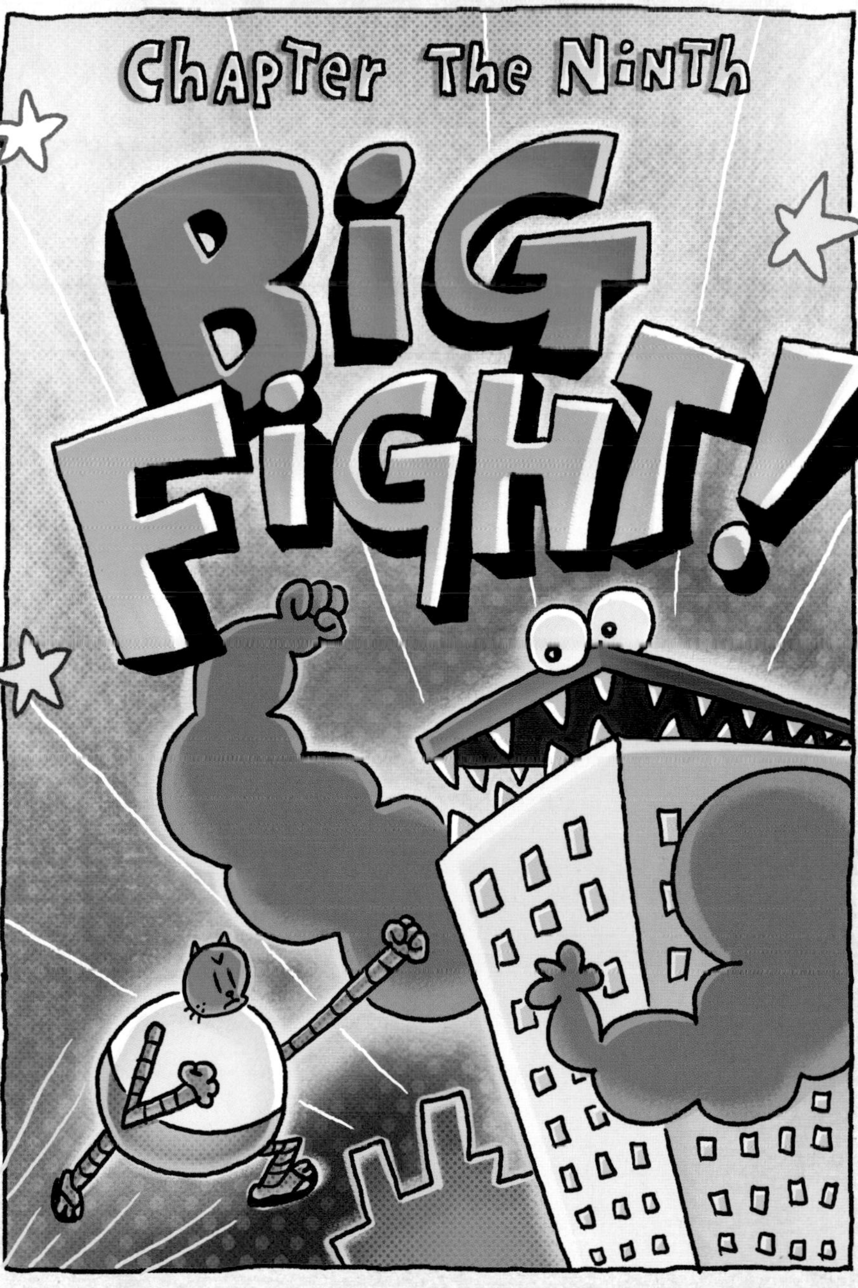
Chapter The Ninth
Big Fight!

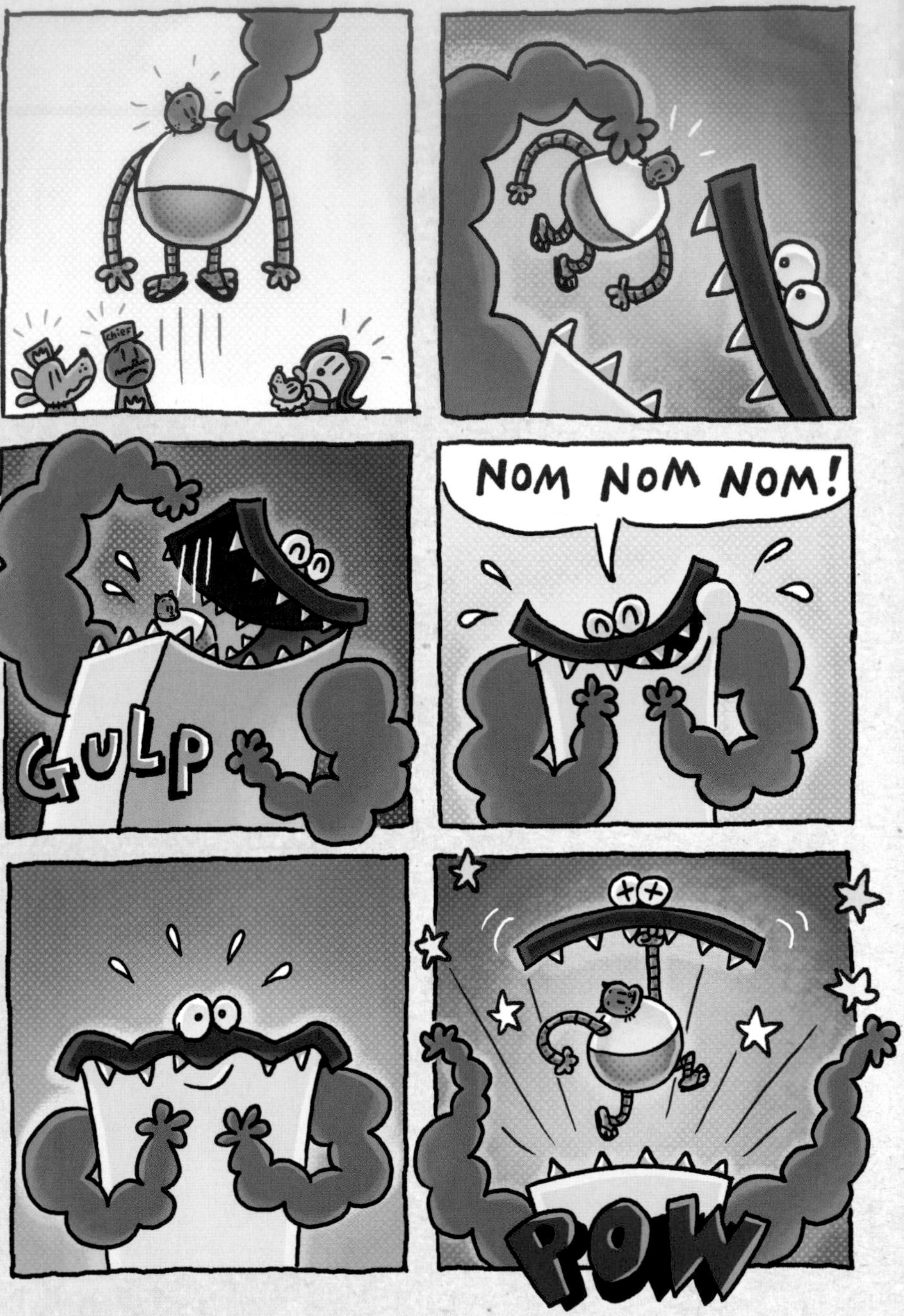
CHIEF
GULP
NOM NOM NOM!
POW

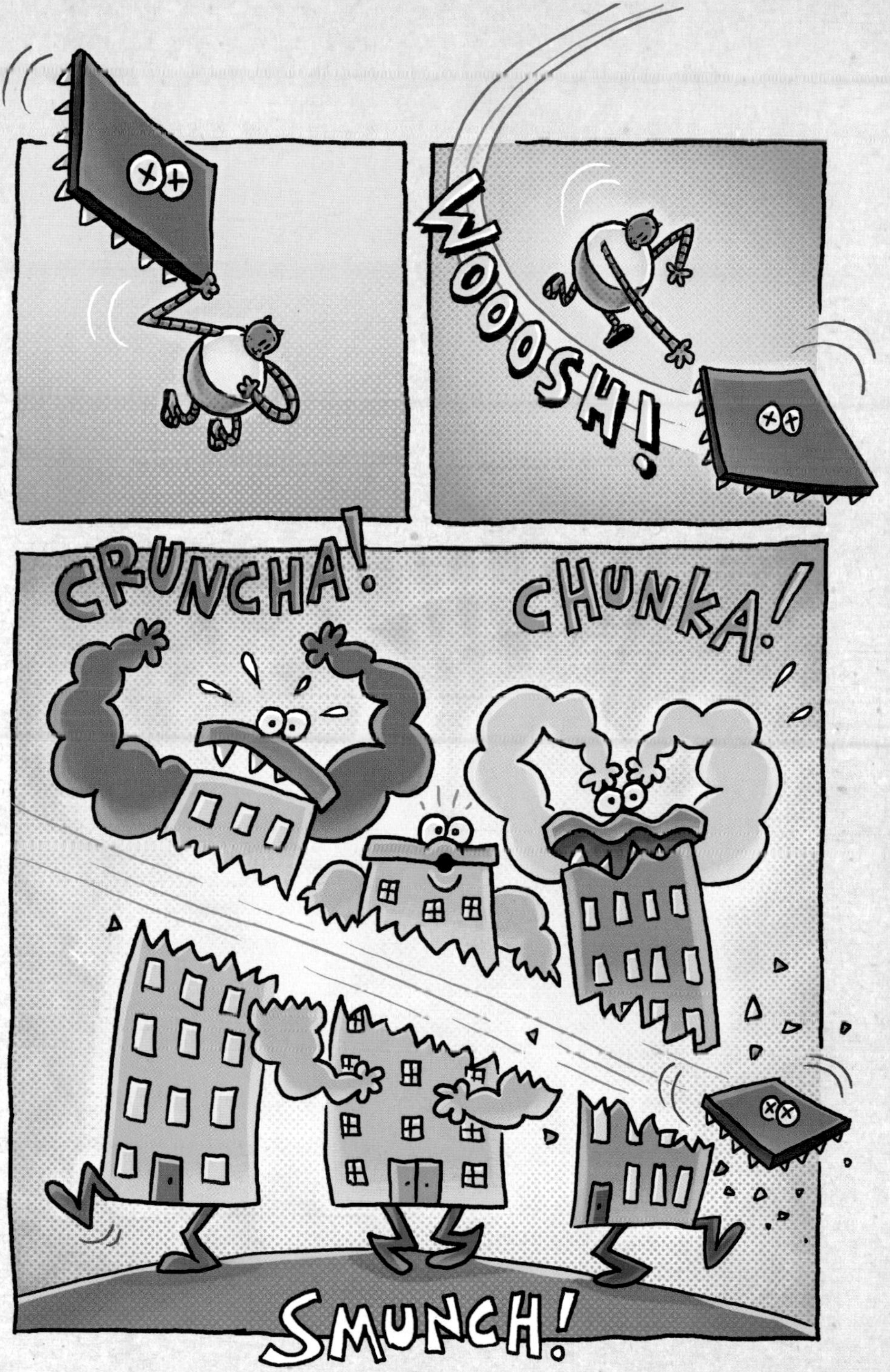
WOOOSH!
CRUNCHA!
CHUNKA!
SMUNCH!

GOOBA GABA!

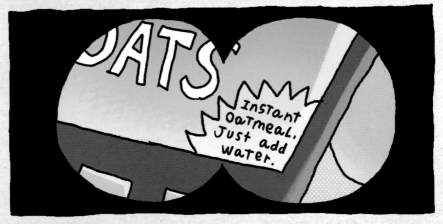

Instant Oatmeal. Just add water.

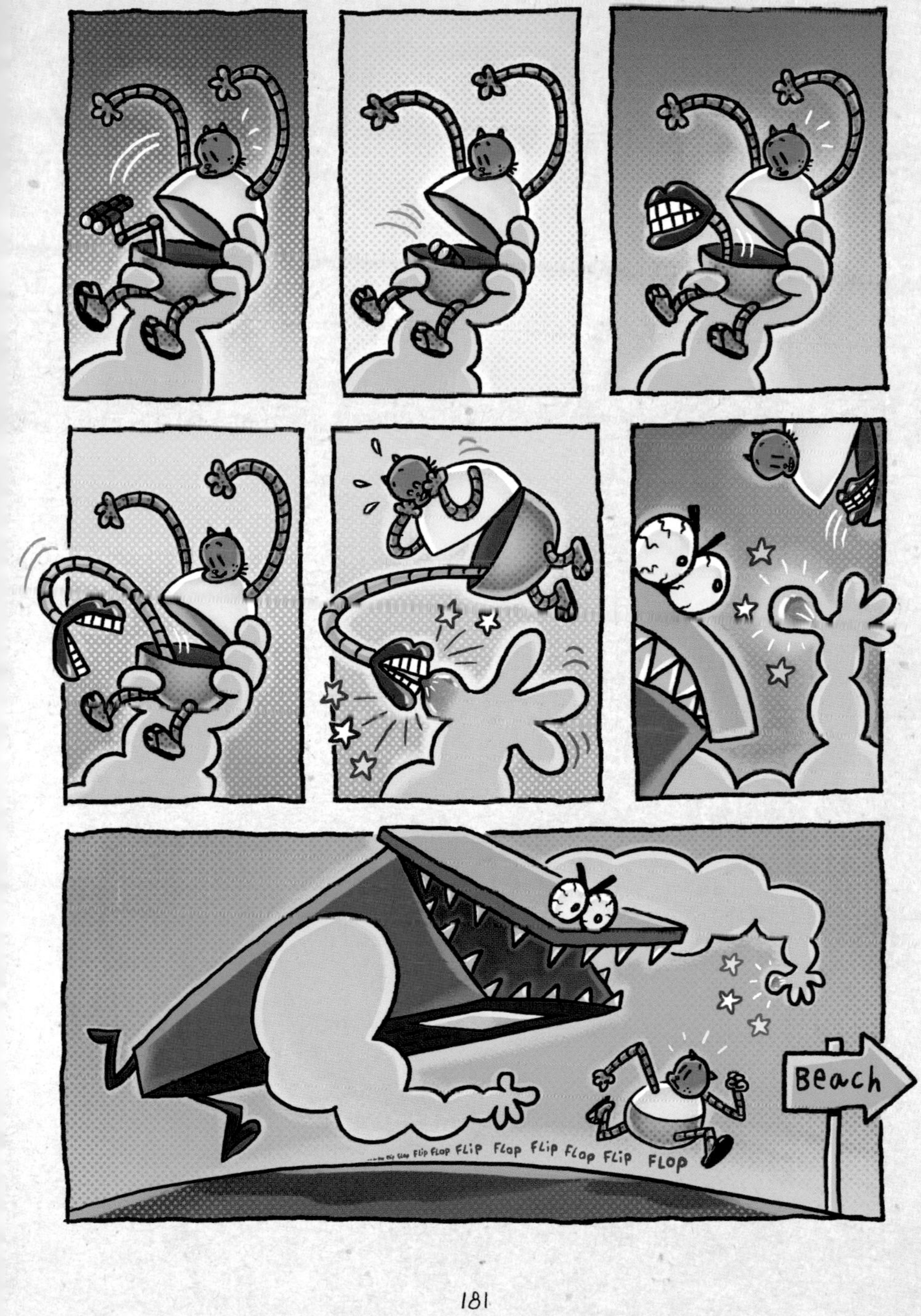
Flip Flop FLip Flop FLip Flop FLip FLOP
Beach

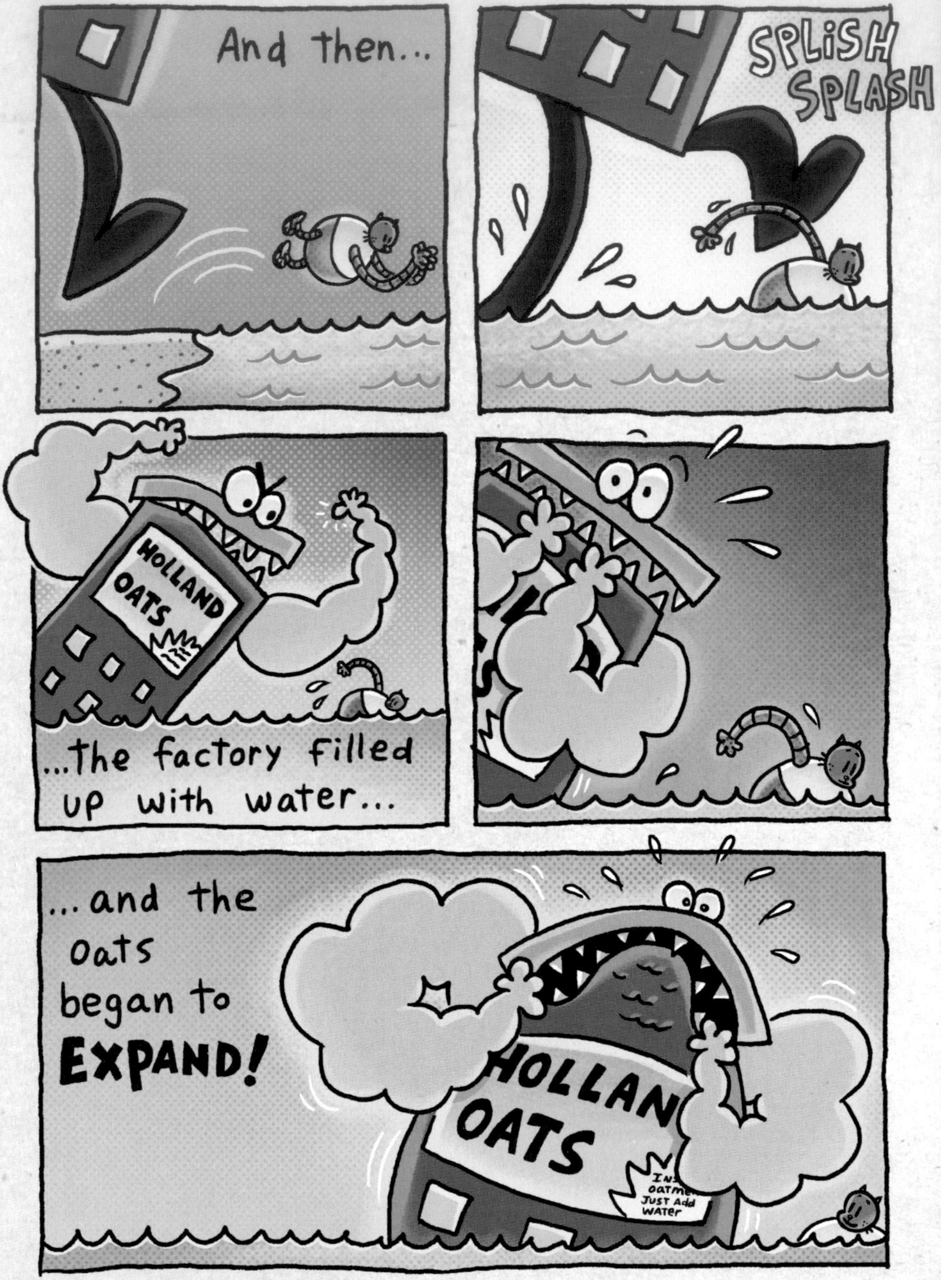
And then...
SPLISH SPLASH
HOLLAND OATS
...the factory filled up with water...
...and the oats began to EXPAND!
HOLLAN OATS
JUST Add WATER

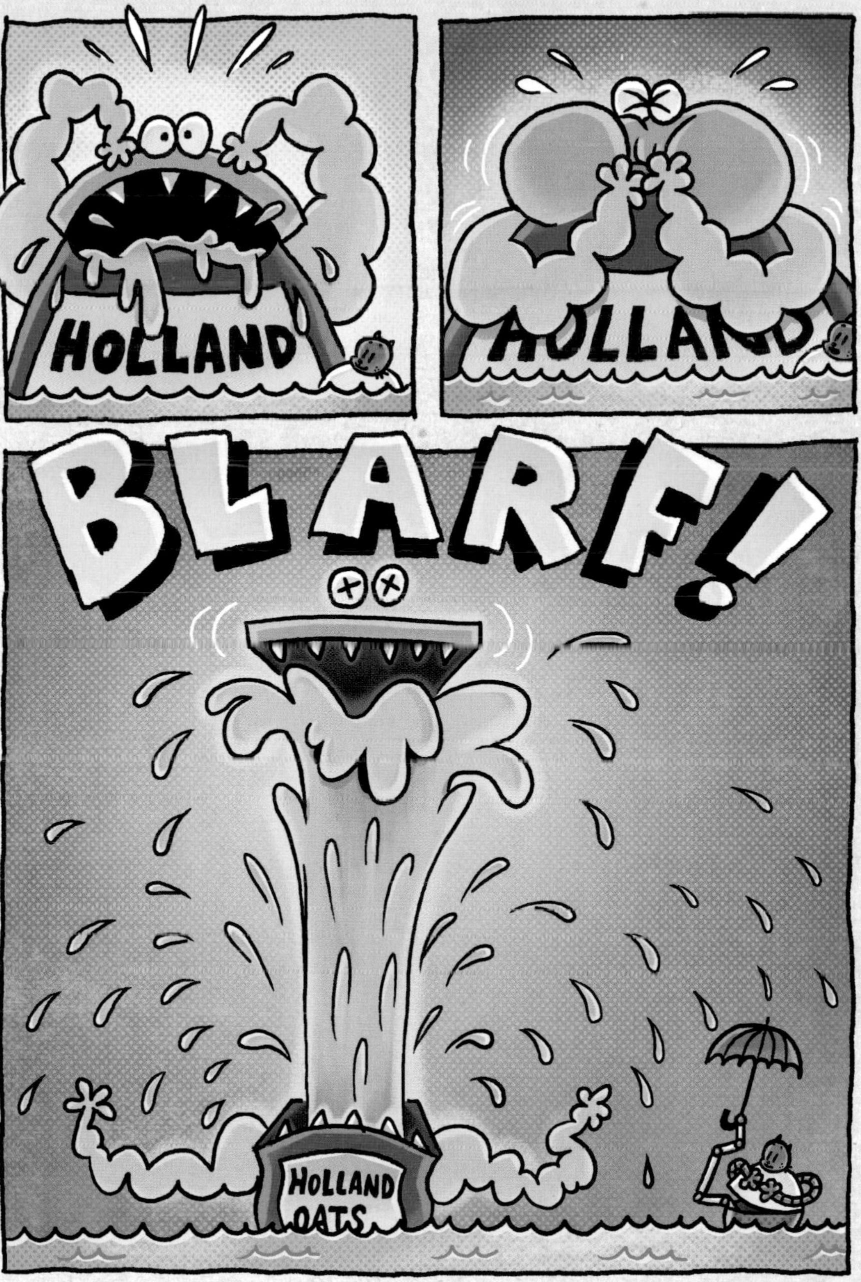
HOLLAND
HOLLAND
BLARF!
HOLLAND OATS

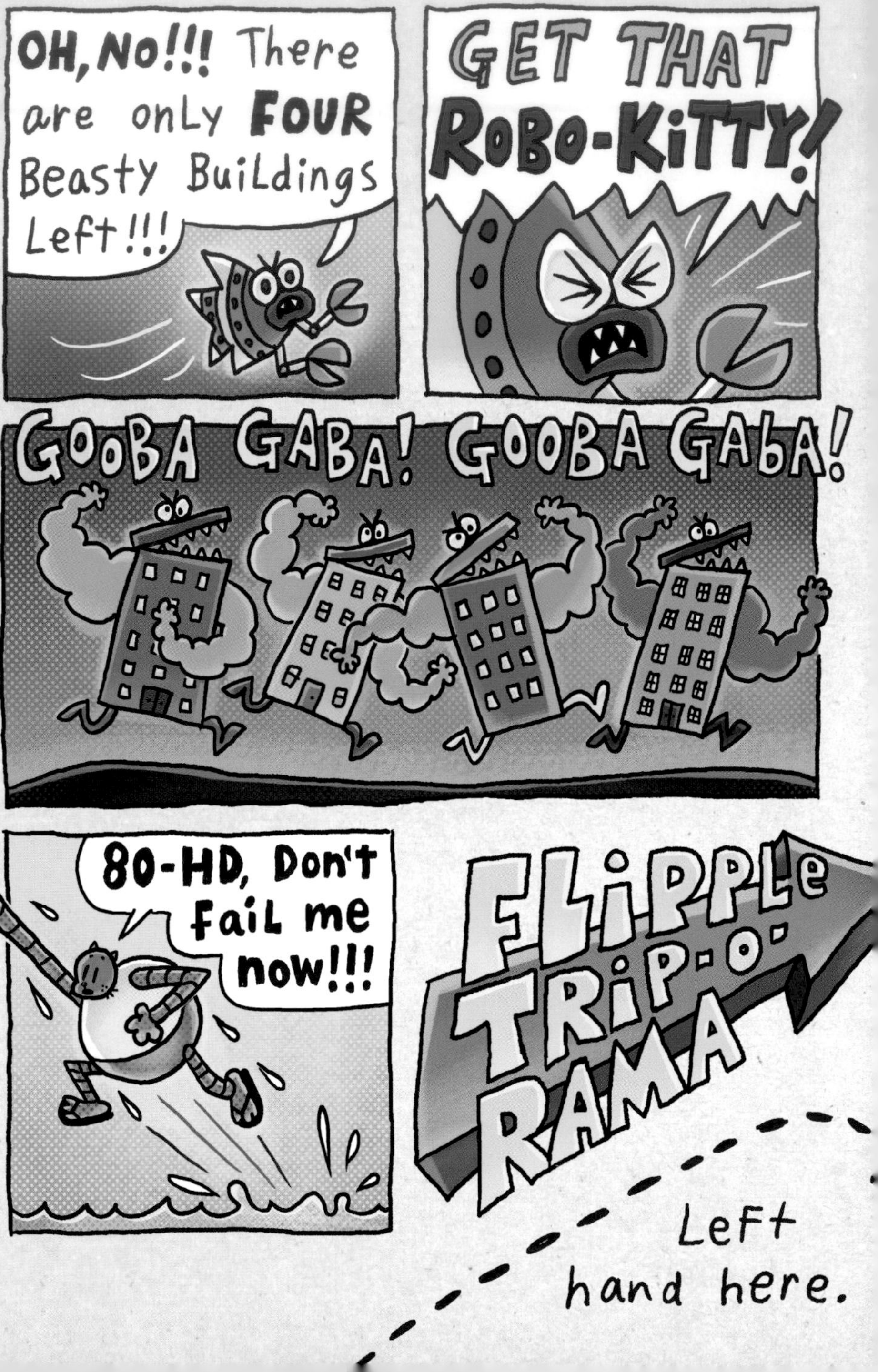
OH, NO!!! There are only FOUR Beasty Buildings Left!!!
GET THAT ROBO-KITTY!
GOOBA GABA! GOOBA GABA!
80-HD, Don't Fail me now!!!
FLIPPLE TRIP-O-RAMA
Left hand here.

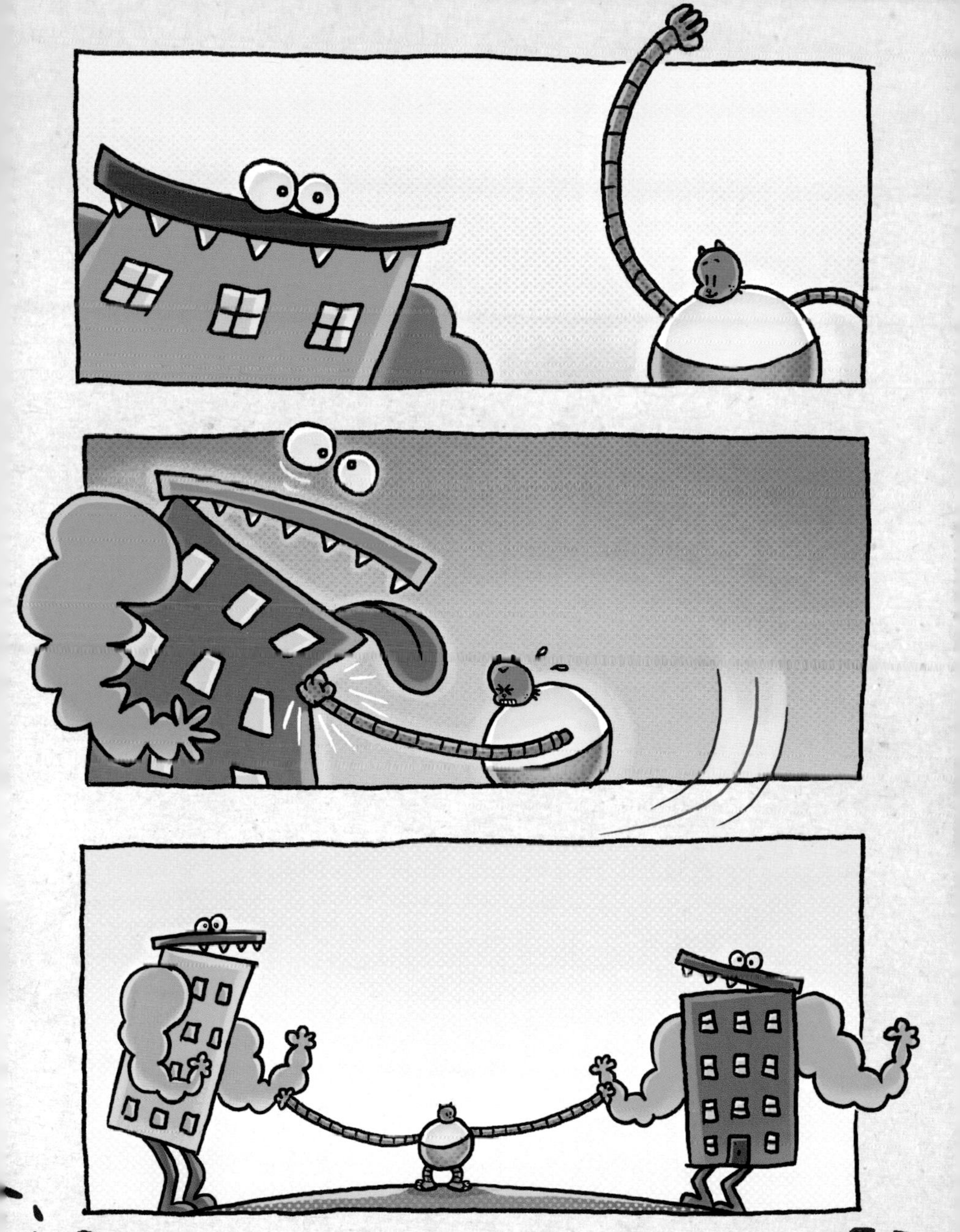

Right
Thumb
here.

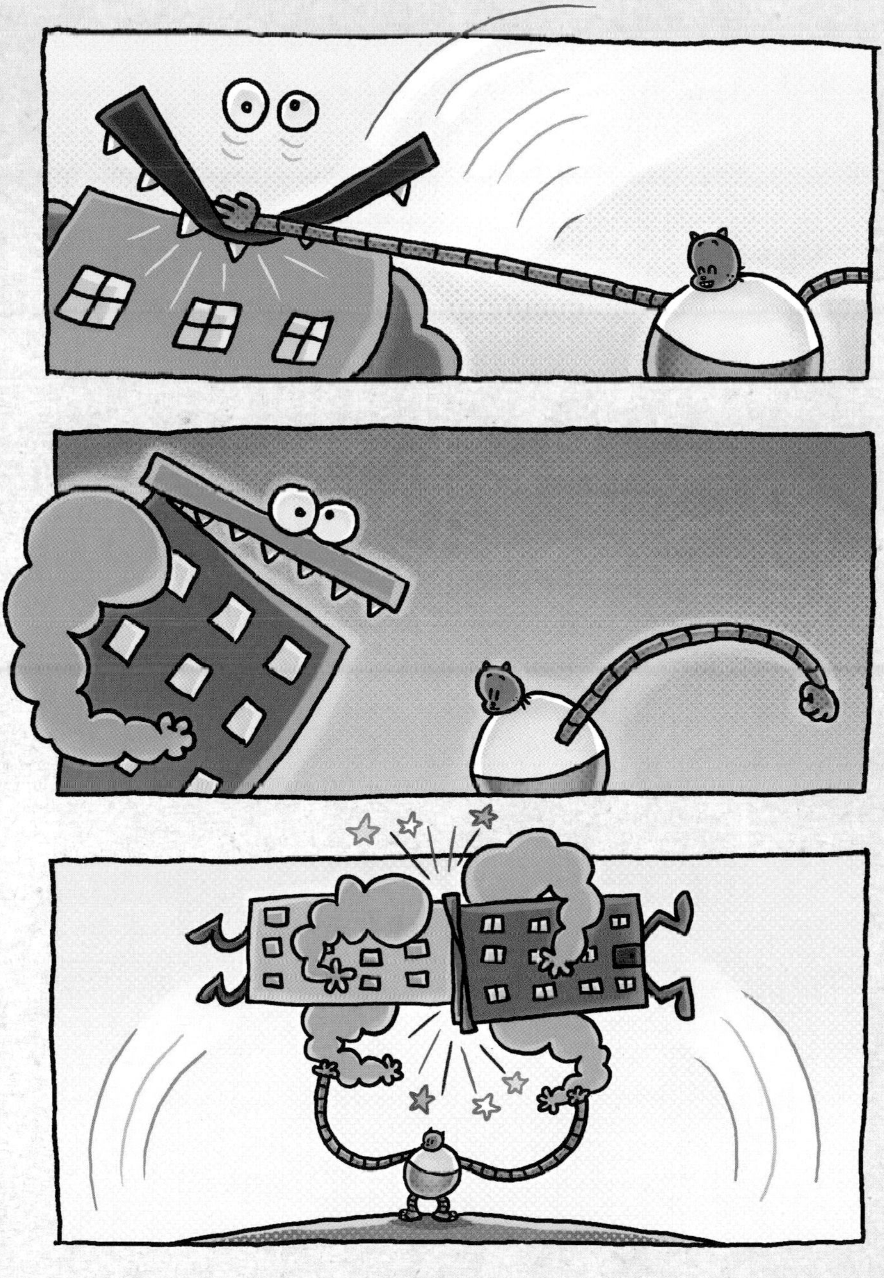

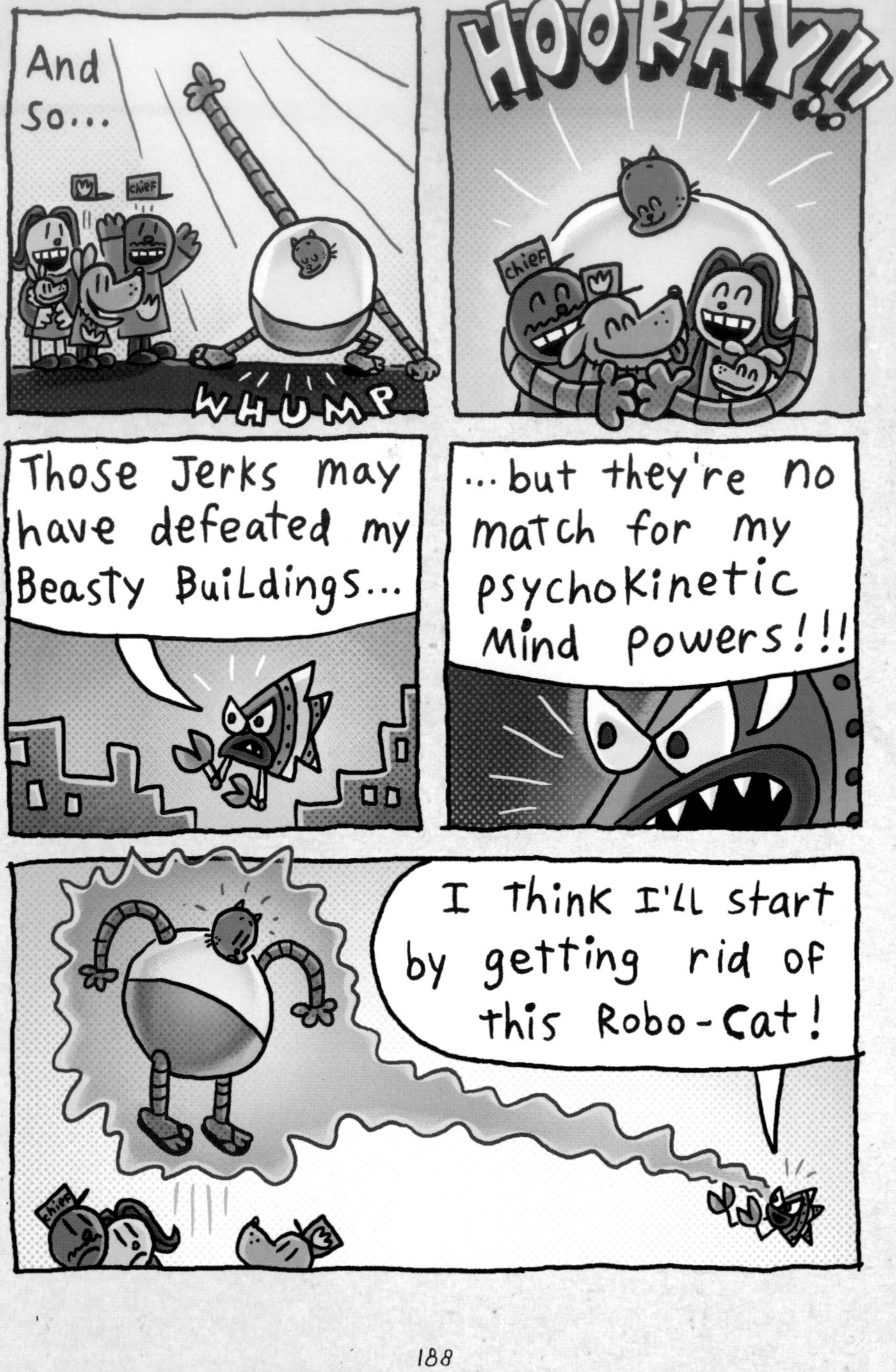

And so...
WHUMP
HOORAY!!!
Those Jerks may have defeated my Beasty Buildings...
...but they're no match for my psychoKinetic Mind powers!!!
I think I'll start by getting rid of this Robo-Cat!

Be GONE From Me!
FWOOOSH!
Li'L Petey!!!
I'm COMIN'

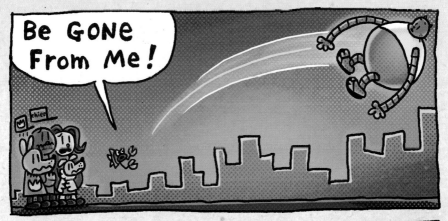

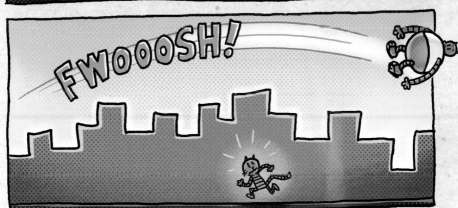

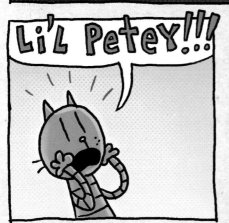

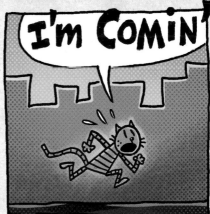

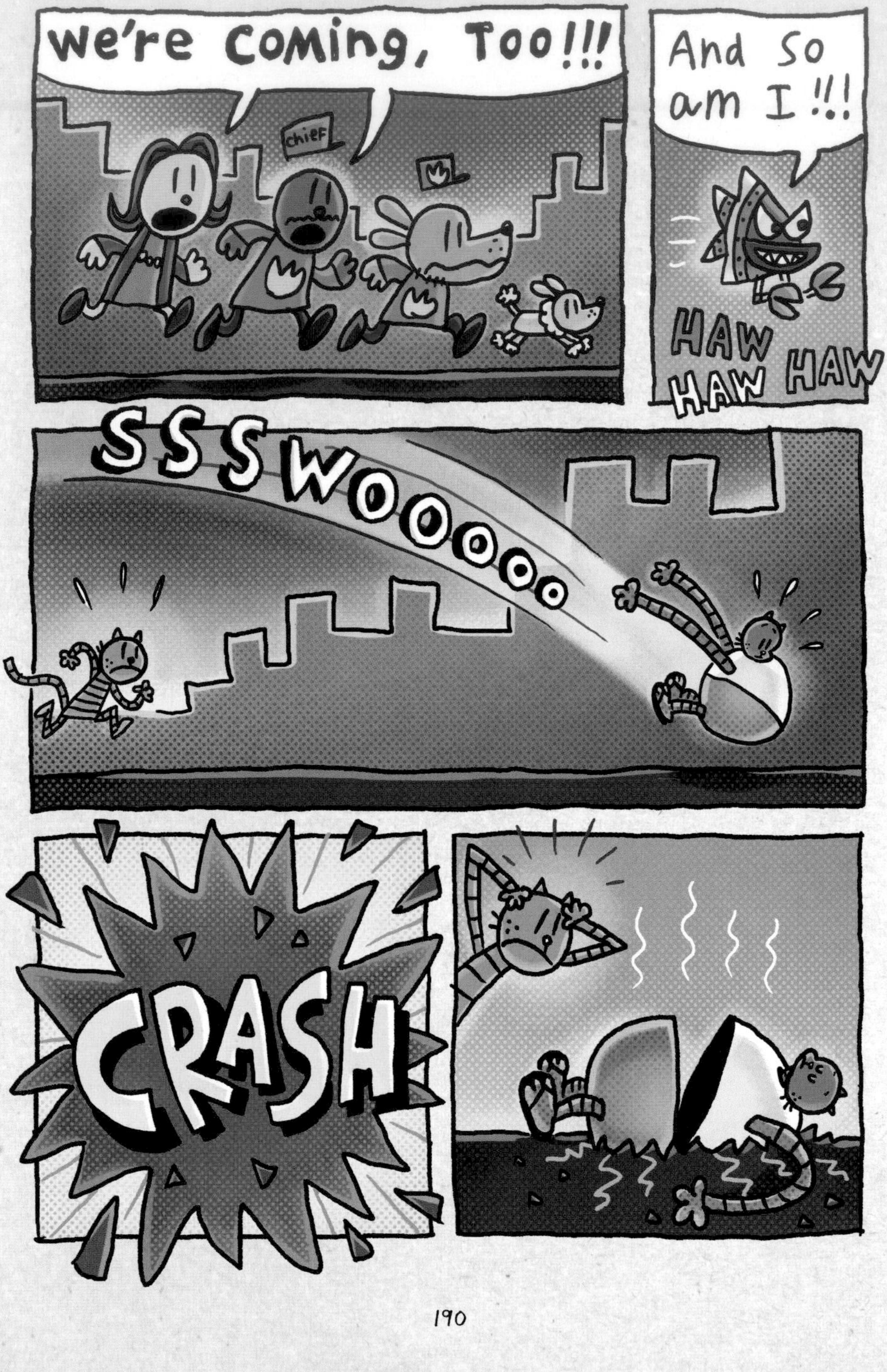
We're Coming, Too!!!
Chief
And So am I!!!
HAW HAW HAW
SSSWOOOOOO
CRASH

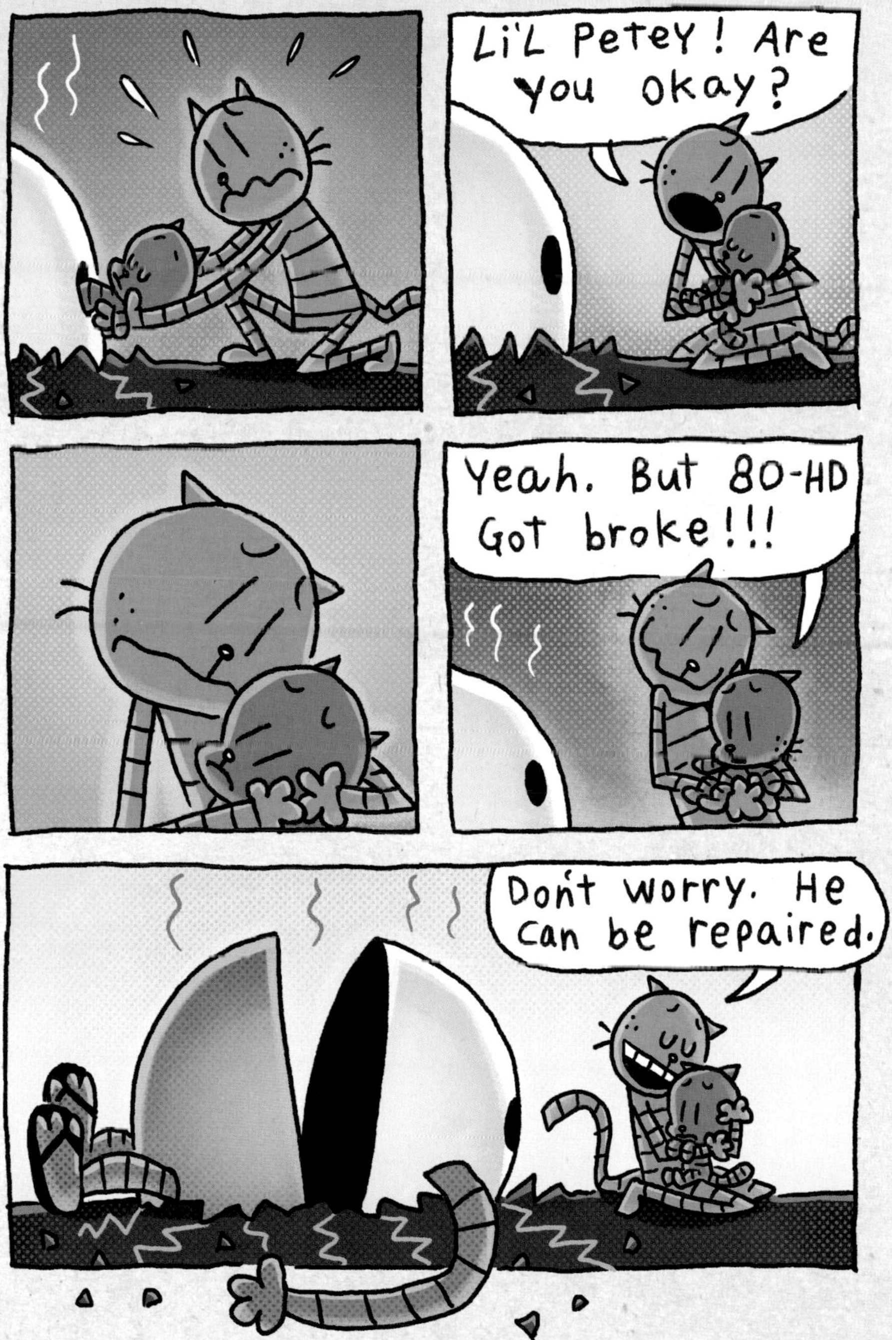
Li'L Petey! Are you okay?
Yeah. But 80-HD Got broke!!!
Don't worry. He can be repaired.

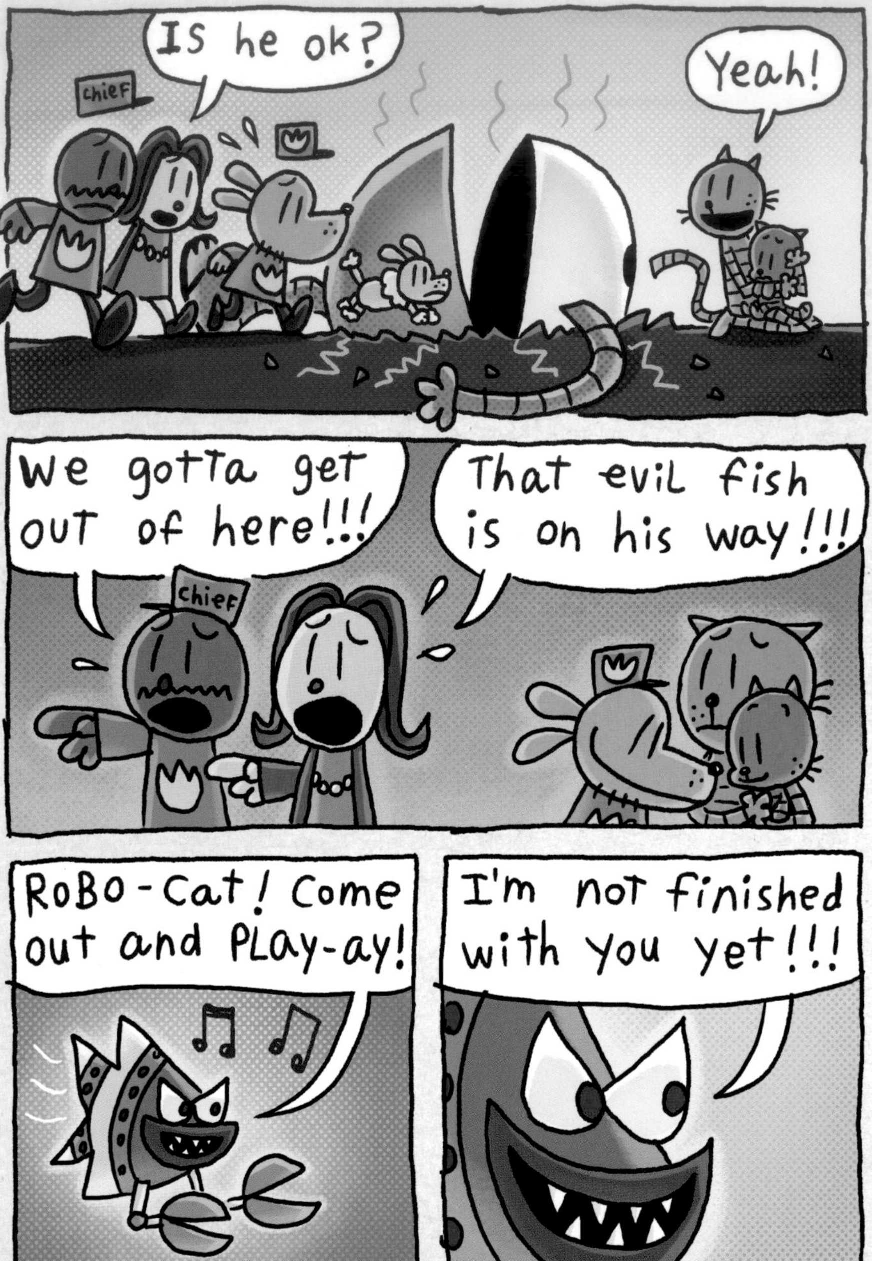
IS he ok?
Yeah!
chief
We gotta get out of here!!!
That evil fish is on his way!!!
chief
RoBo-Cat! Come out and PLay-ay!
I'm not finished with you yet!!!

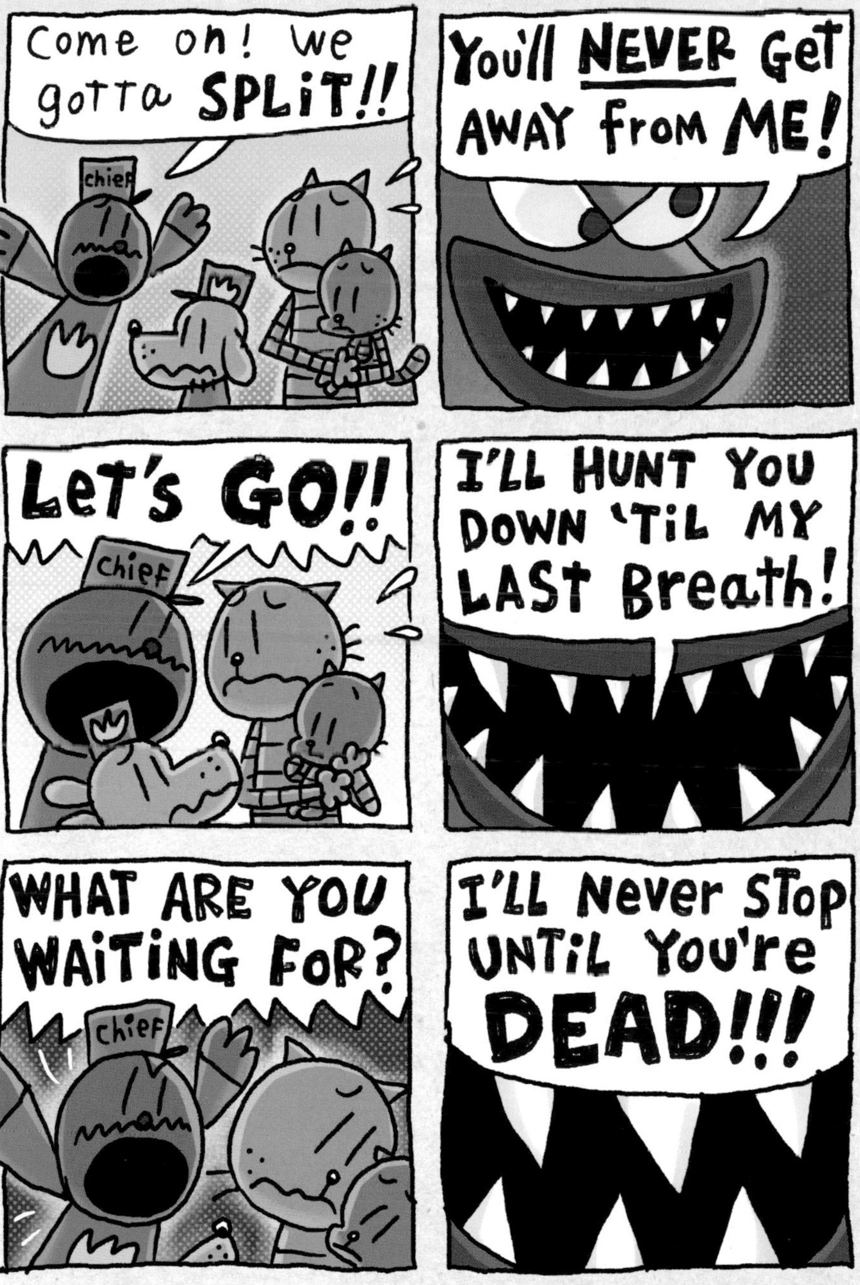
Come on! We gotta SPLIT!!
You'll NEVER Get AWAY from ME!
chief
Let's GO!!
I'LL HUNT YOU DOWN 'TIL MY LAST Breath!
chief
WHAT ARE YOU WAITING FOR?
I'LL Never STop UNTiL You're DEAD!!!
chief

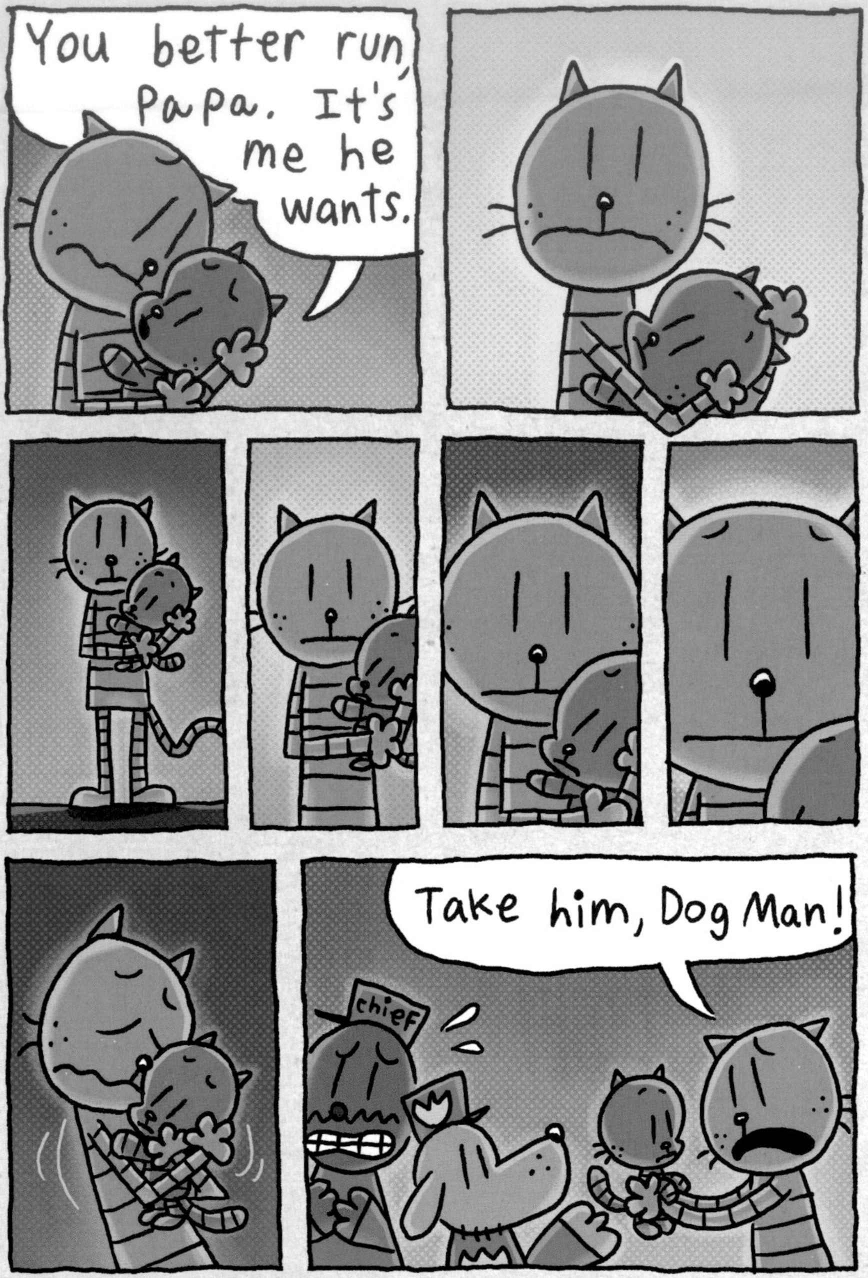
You better run, Papa. It's me he wants.
Take him, Dog Man!
chief

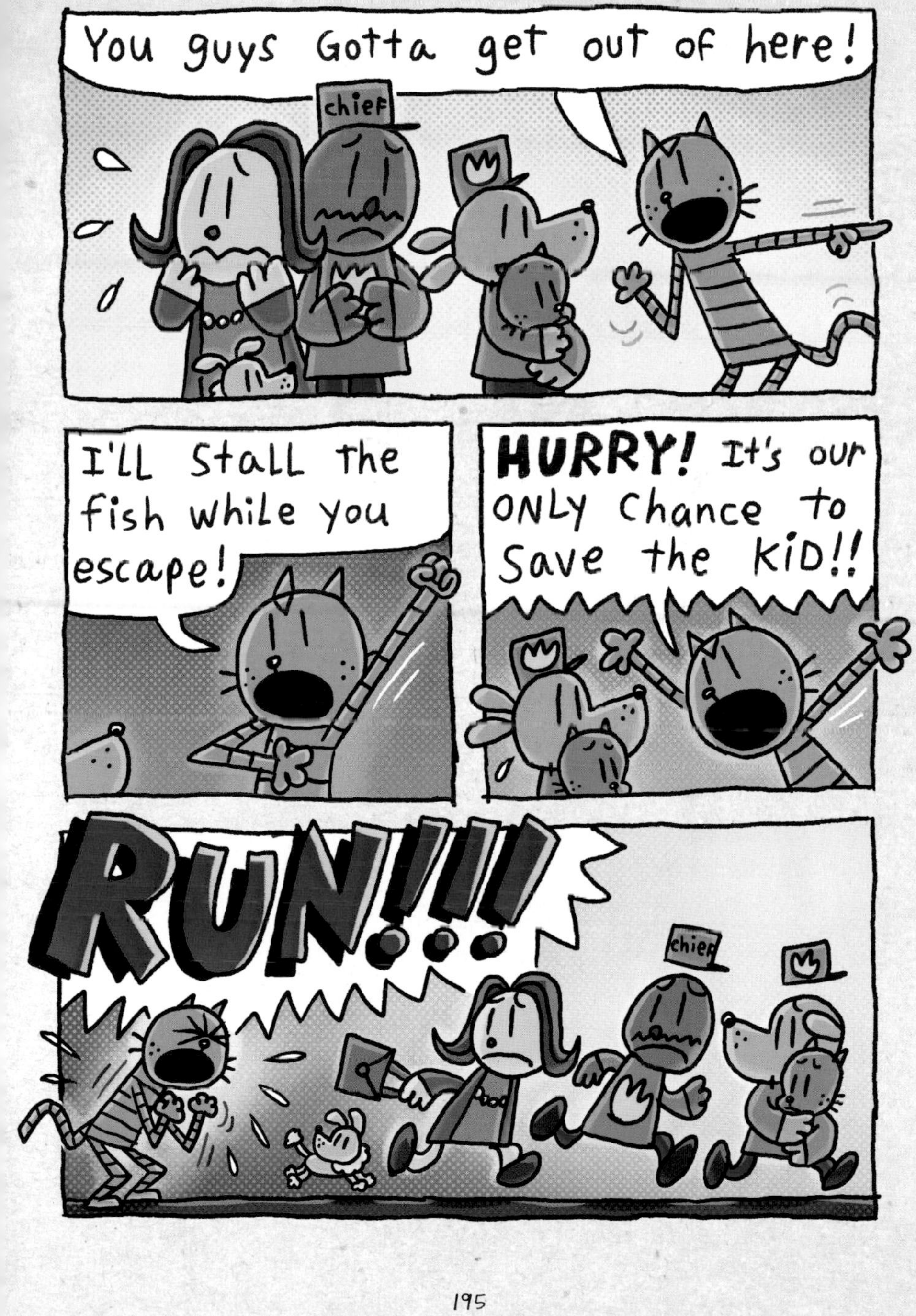
You guys Gotta get out of here!
chief
I'LL Stall the fish while you escape!
HURRY! It's our ONLY Chance to Save the KID!!
RUN!!!!
chief

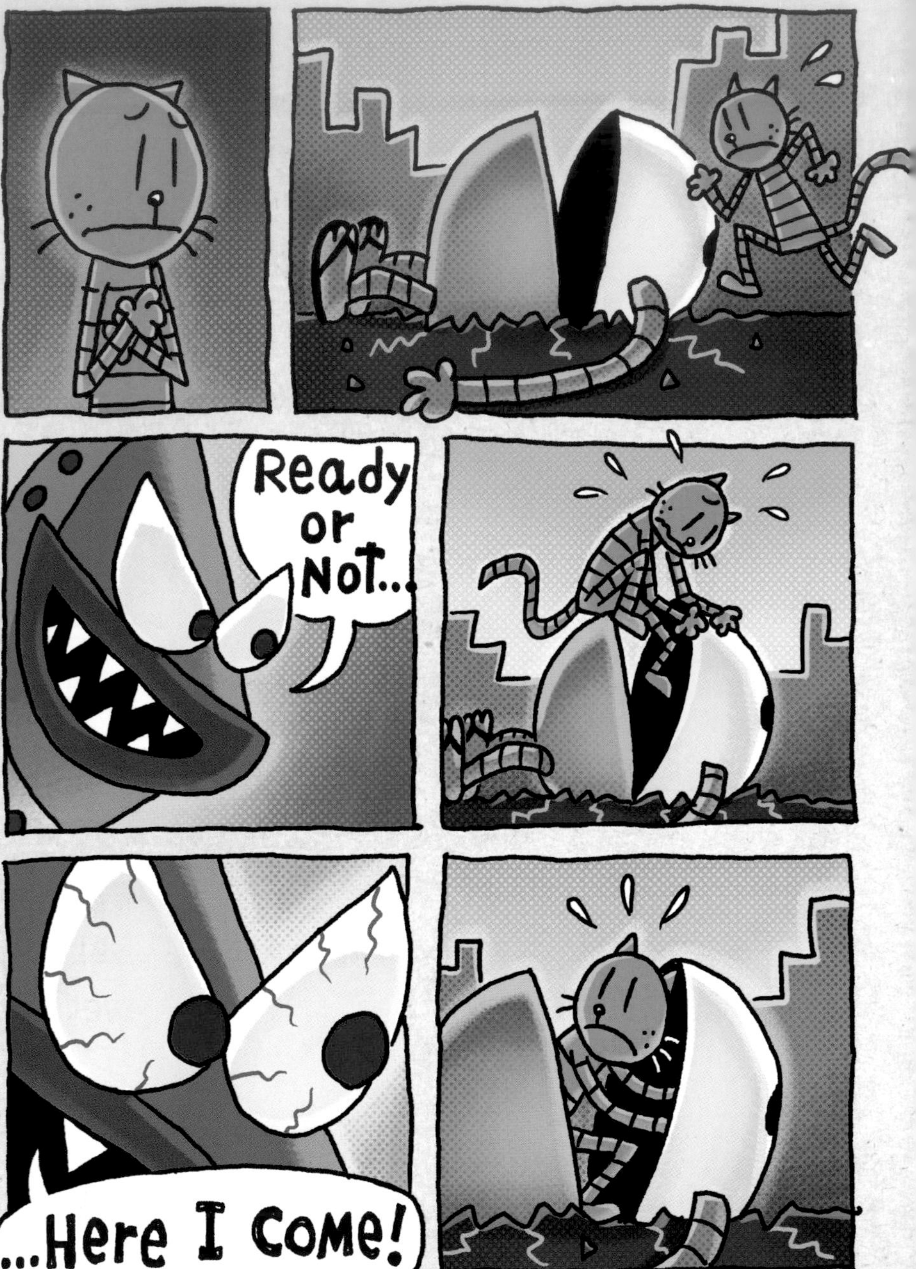
Ready or NOT...
...Here I Come!

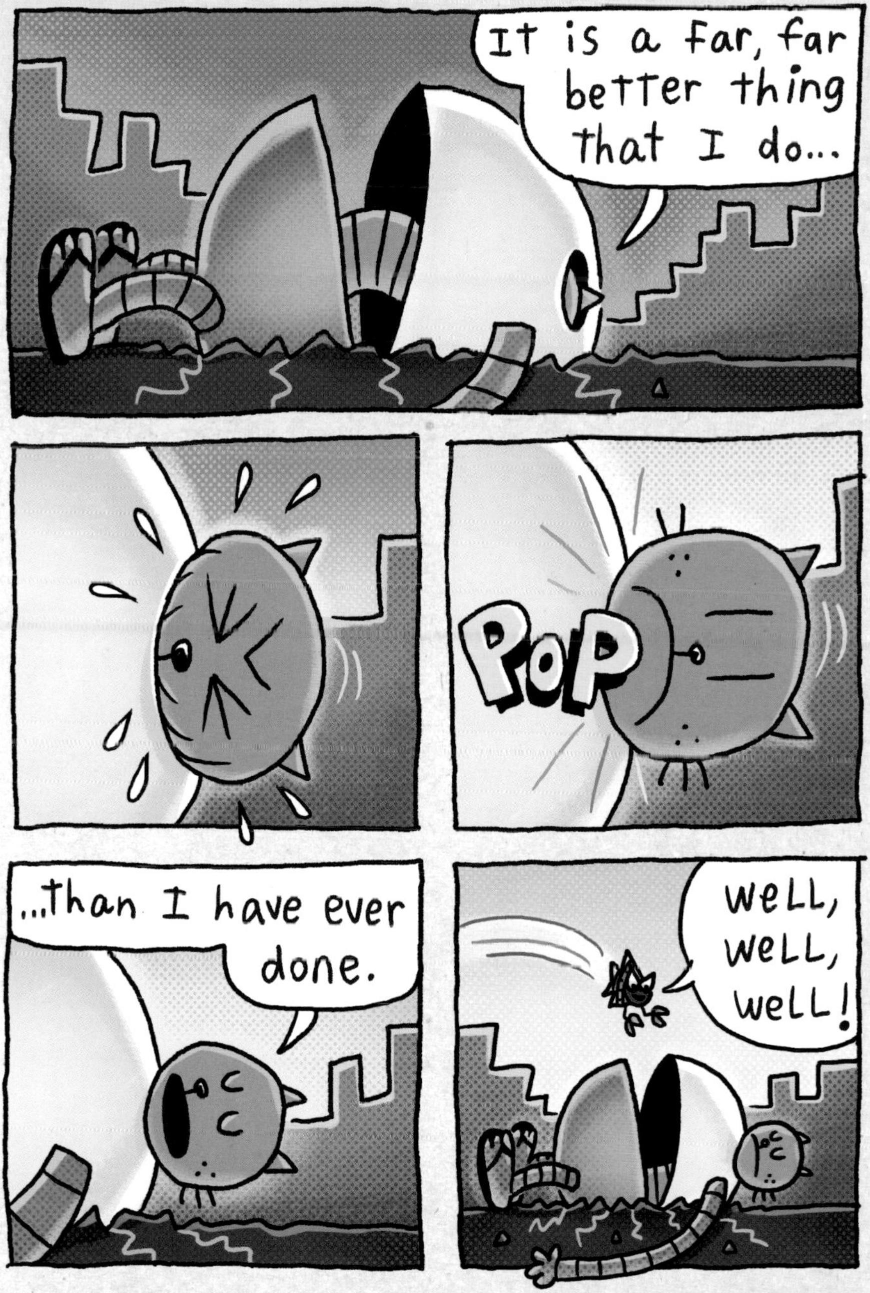
It is a far, far better thing that I do...
POP
...than I have ever done.
WELL, WELL, WELL!

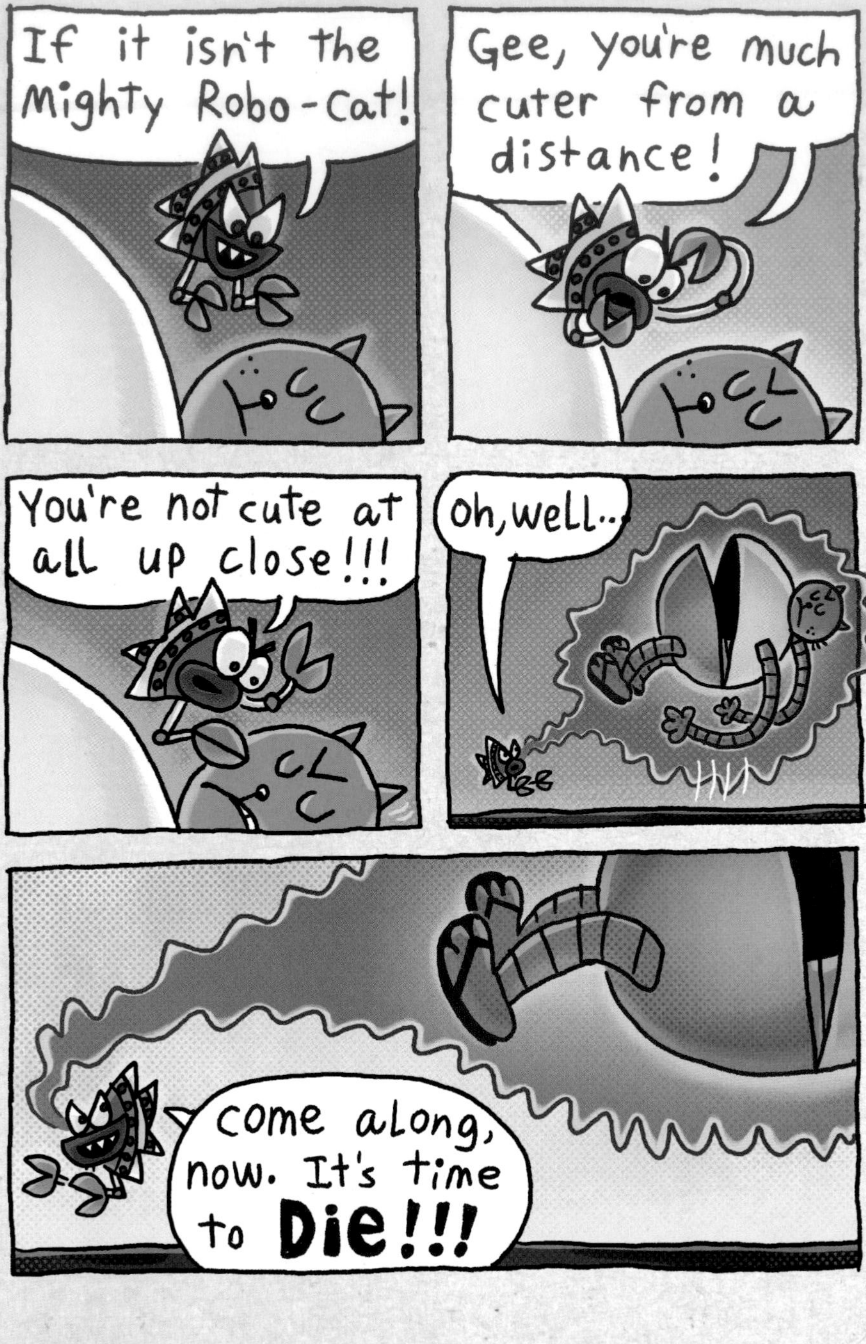
If it isn't the Mighty Robo-Cat!
Gee, you're much cuter from a distance!
You're not cute at all up close!!!
Oh, well...
come along, now. It's time to Die!!!

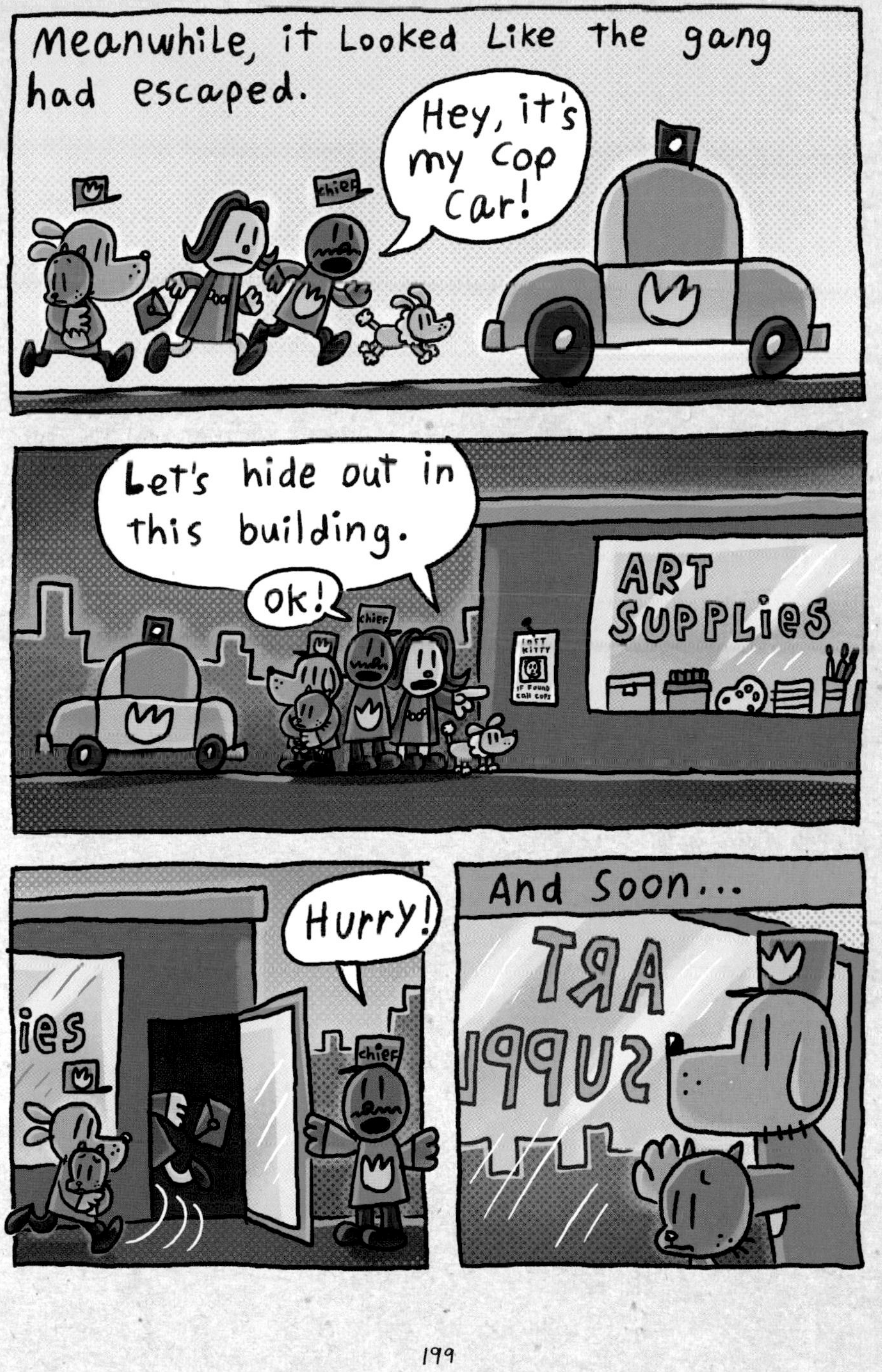
Meanwhile, it Looked Like the gang had escaped.
Hey, it's my cop car!
Let's hide out in this building.
Ok!
ART SUPPLies
Hurry!
And Soon...

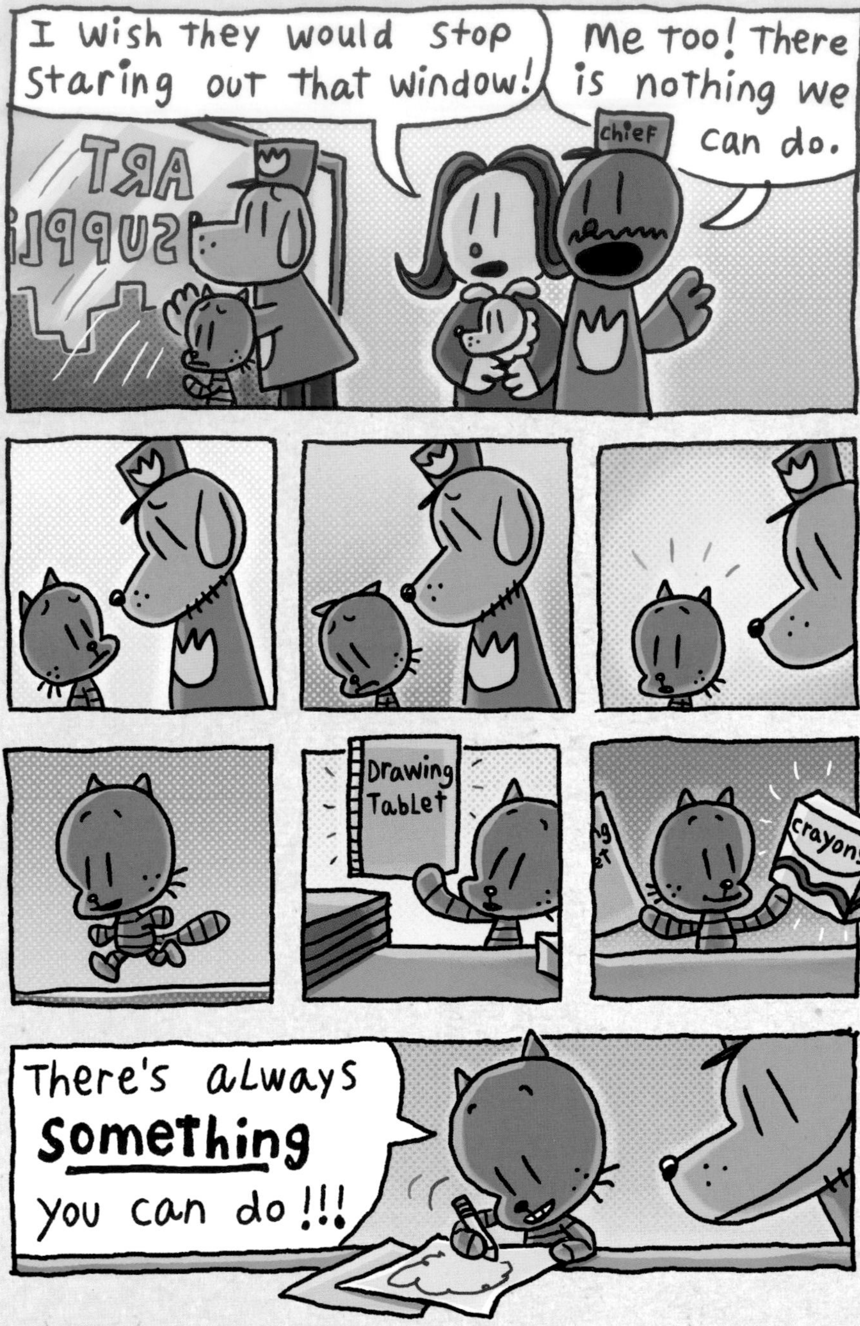
I wish they would stop staring out that window!
Me too! There is nothing we can do.
chief
ART SUPPLI
Drawing Tablet
crayons
There's always SOMETHING you can do!!!

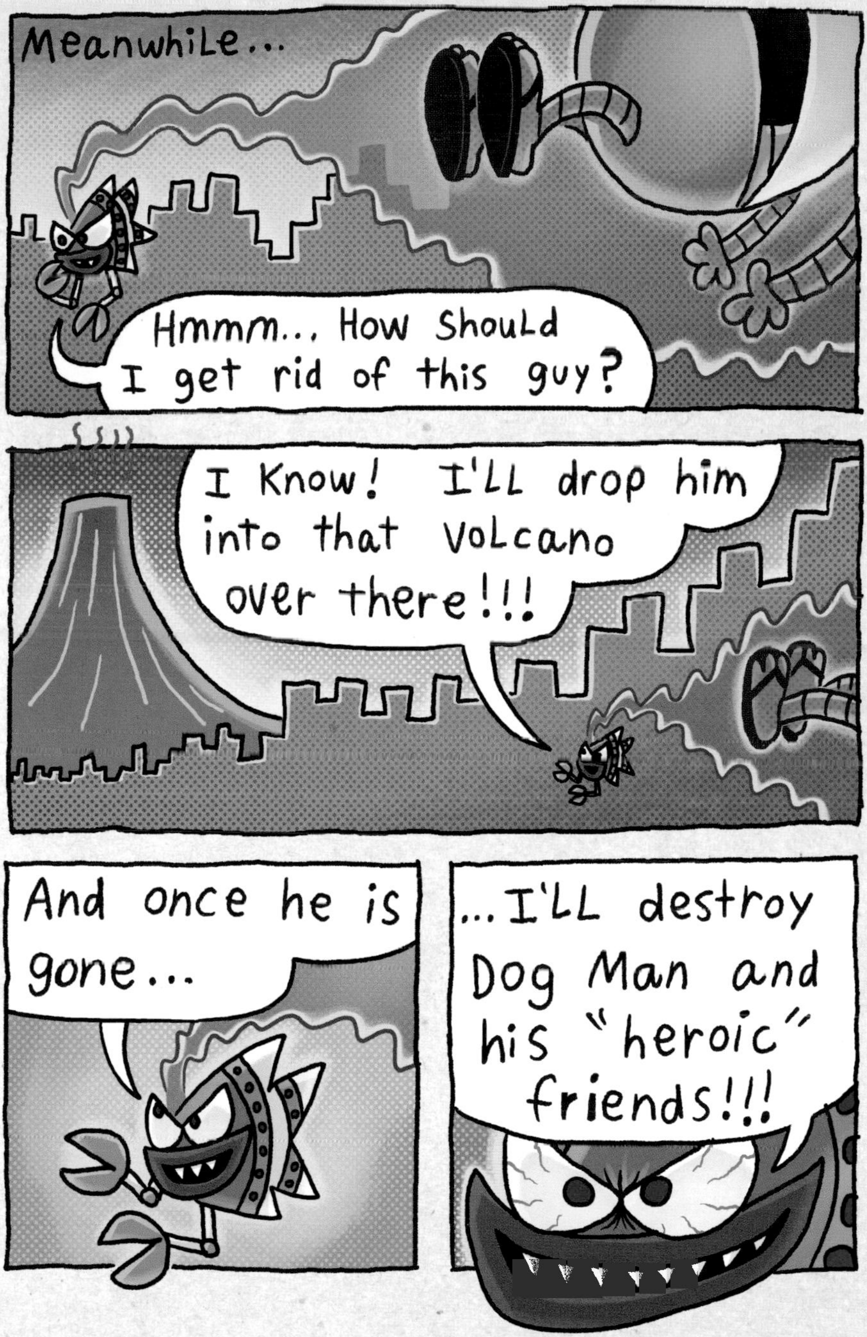
Meanwhile...
Hmmm... How should I get rid of this guy?
I Know! I'll drop him into that volcano over there!!!
And once he is gone...
...I'll destroy Dog Man and his "heroic" friends!!!

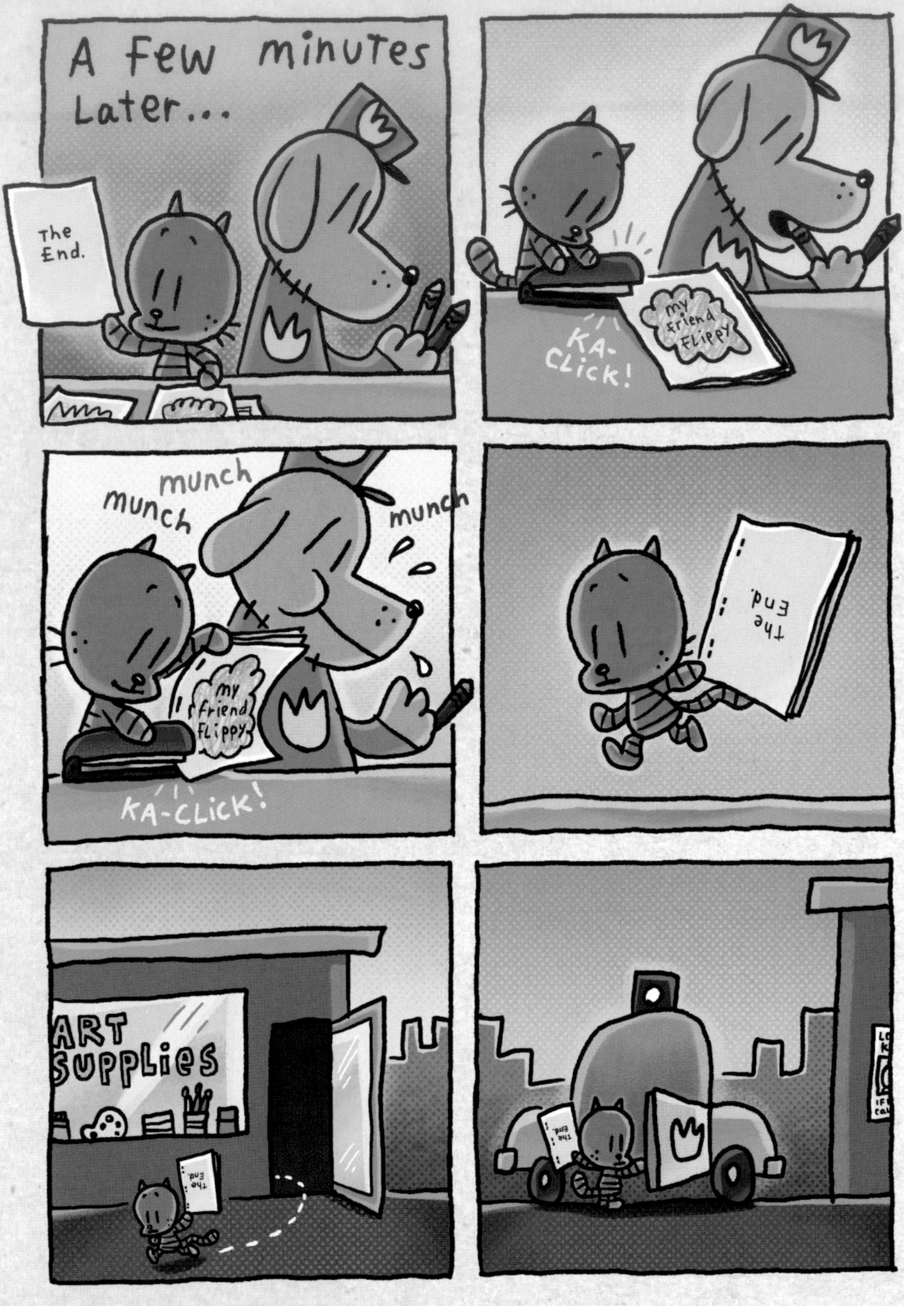
A few minutes Later...
The End.
KA-CLICK!
my friend Flippy
munch
munch
munch
my friend Flippy
KA-CLICK!
ART SUPPLIES

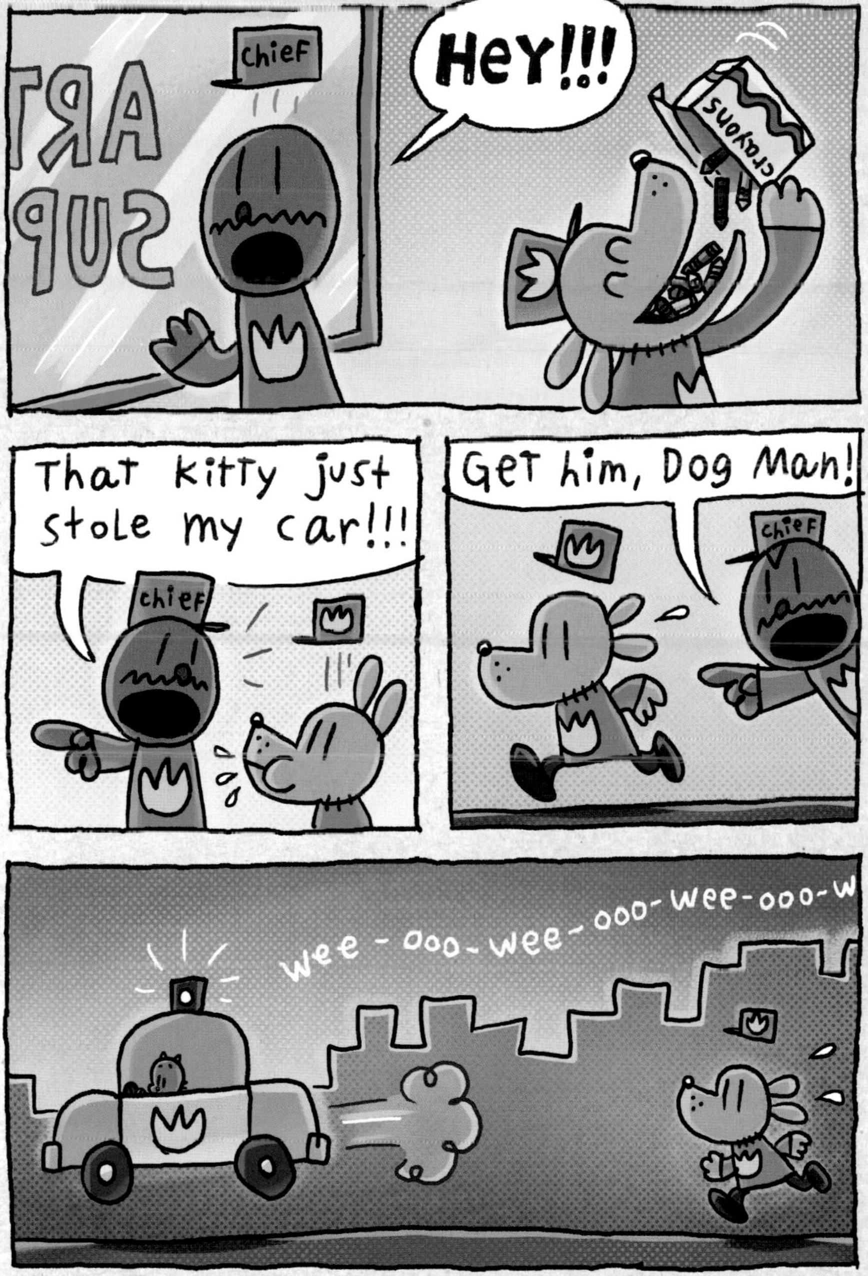
chief
ART
SUP
HEY!!!
crayons
That kitty just stole my car!!!
chief
Get him, Dog Man!
chief
wee-ooo-wee-ooo-wee-ooo-w

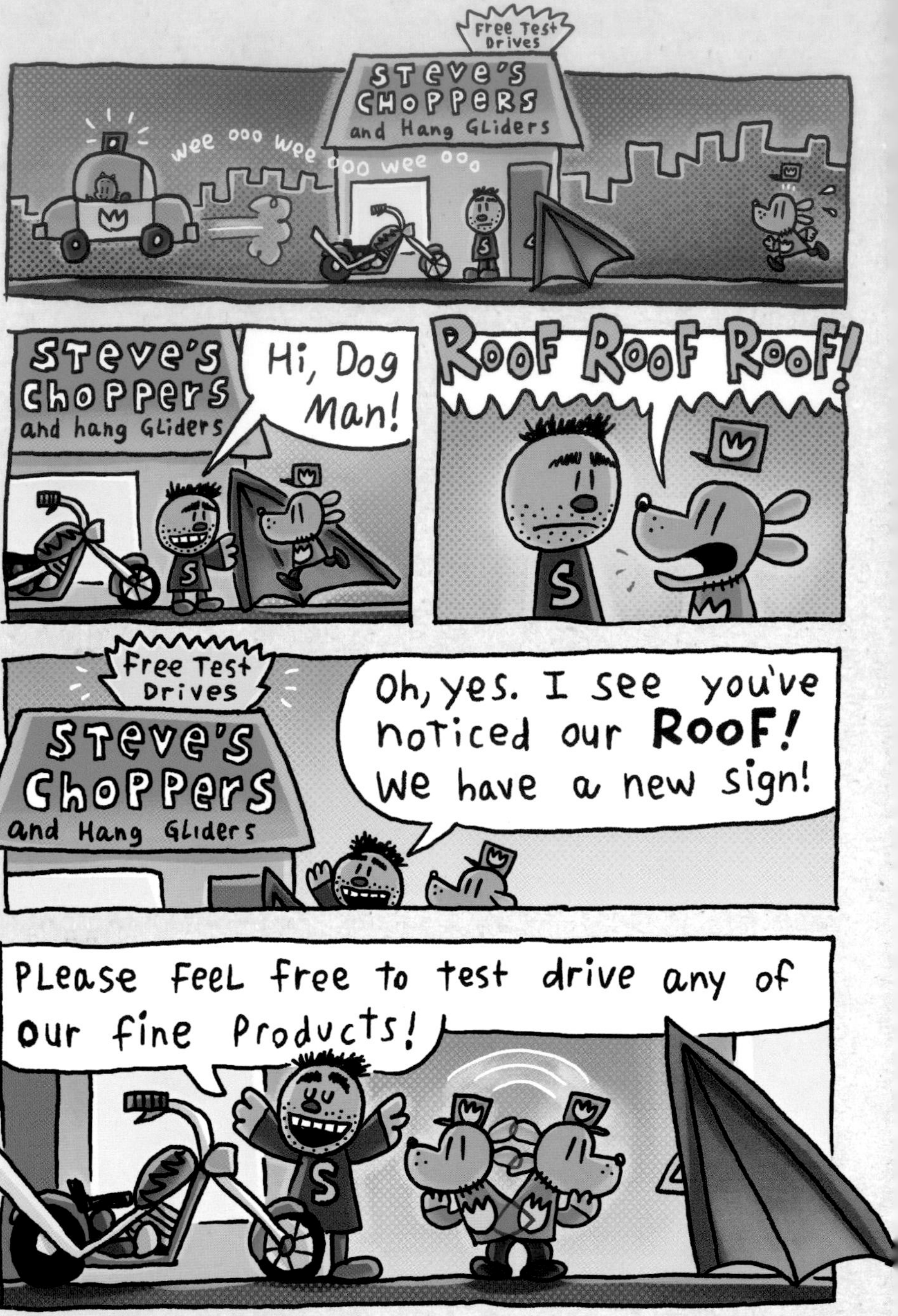
Free Test Drives
Steve's Choppers and Hang Gliders
wee ooo wee ooo wee ooo
Steve's Choppers and hang Gliders
Hi, Dog Man!
ROOF ROOF ROOF!
Free Test Drives
Steve's Choppers and Hang Gliders
Oh, yes. I see you've noticed our ROOF! We have a new sign!
Please feel free to test drive any of our fine Products!

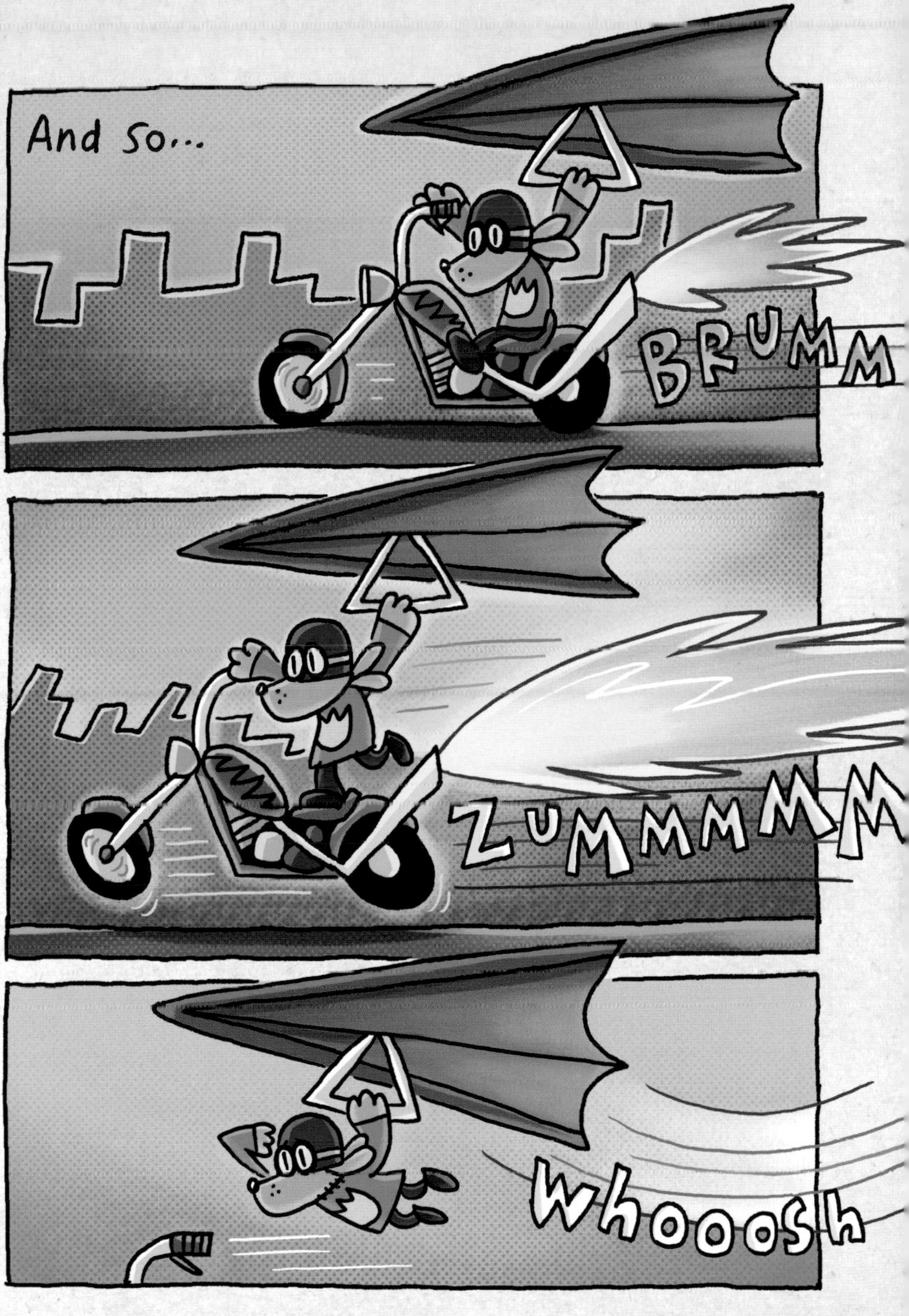
And so...
BRUMM
ZUMMMMM
Whoooosh

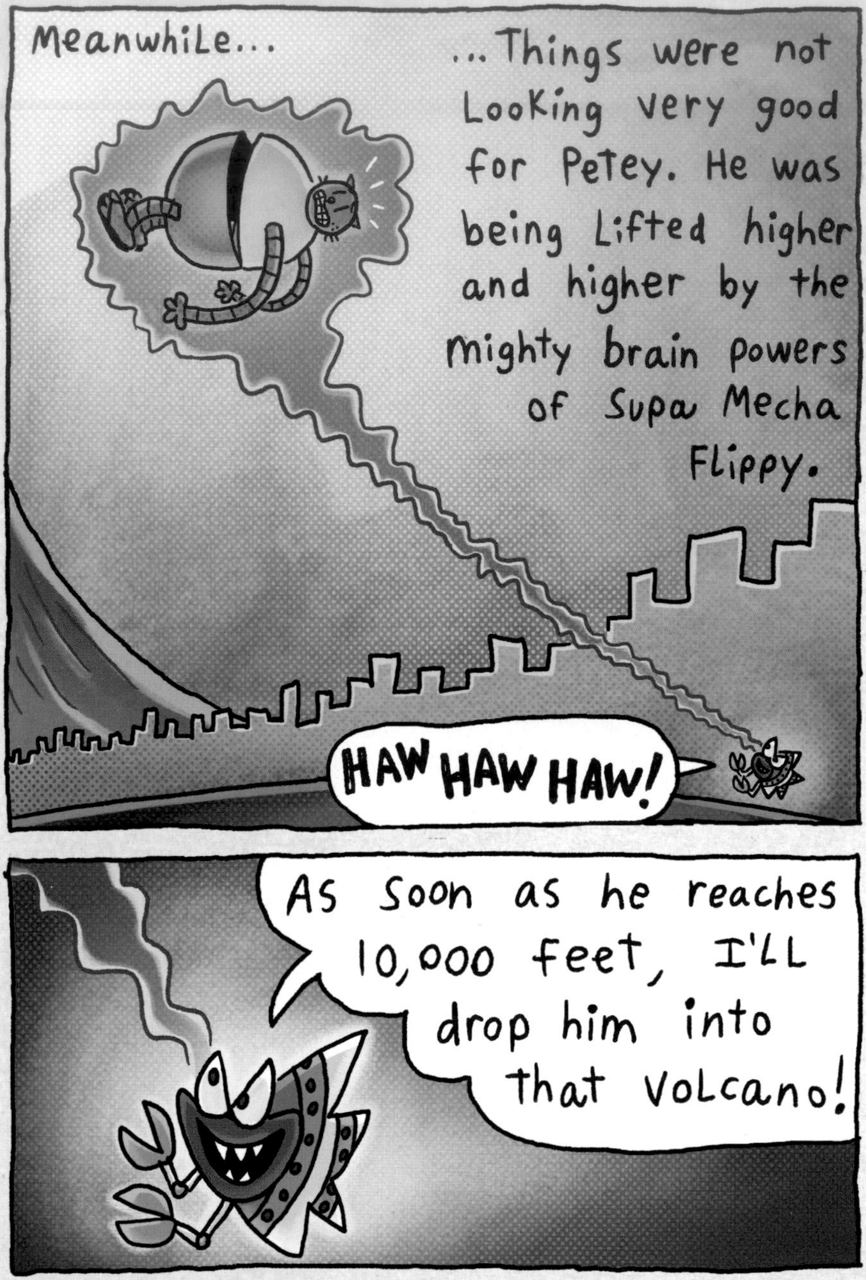
Meanwhile...
...Things were not Looking very good for Petey. He was being Lifted higher and higher by the mighty brain powers of Supa Mecha Flippy.
HAW HAW HAW!
As soon as he reaches 10,000 feet, I'LL drop him into that volcano!

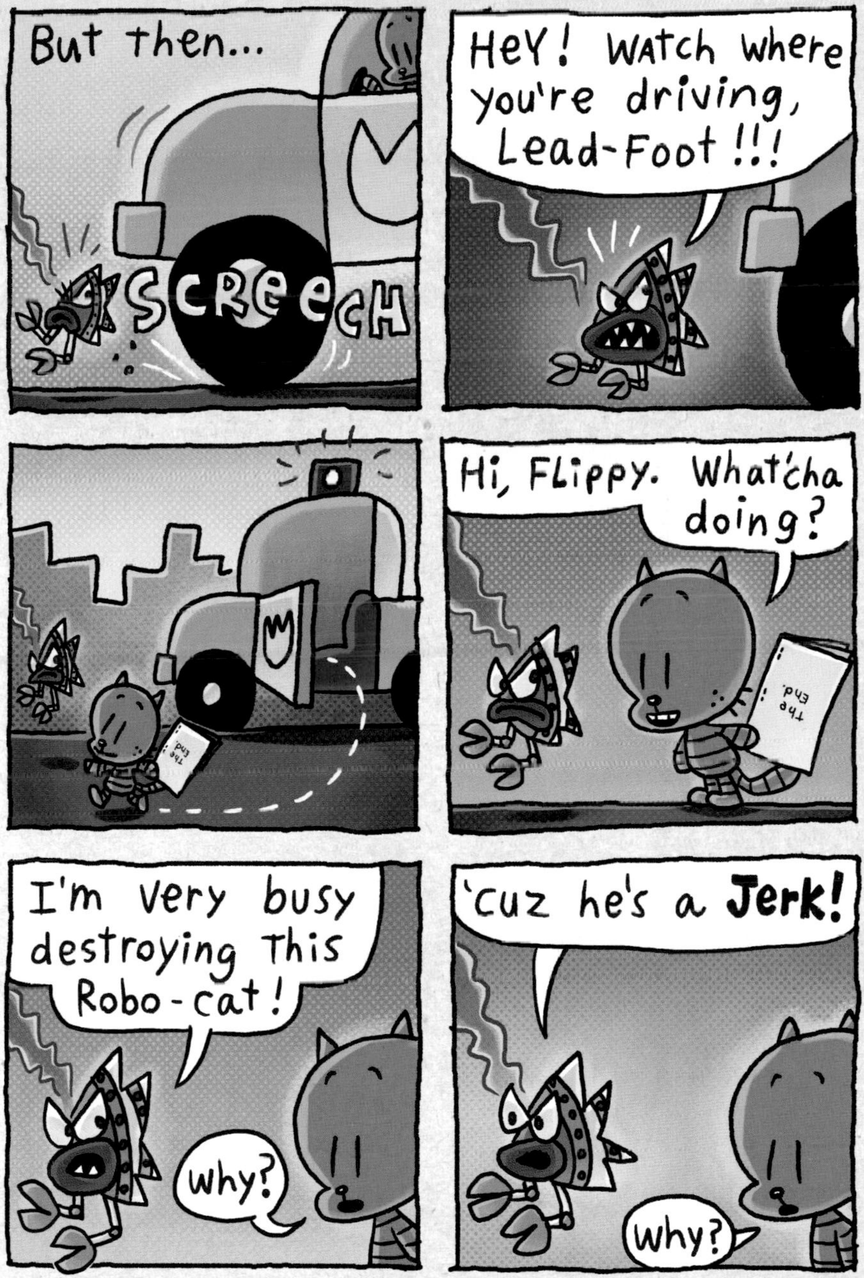
But then...
SCREECH
HEY! WATCH where you're driving, Lead-Foot!!!
Hi, FLippy. What'cha doing?
The End.
I'm very busy destroying This Robo-cat!
why?
'cuz he's a **Jerk!**
why?

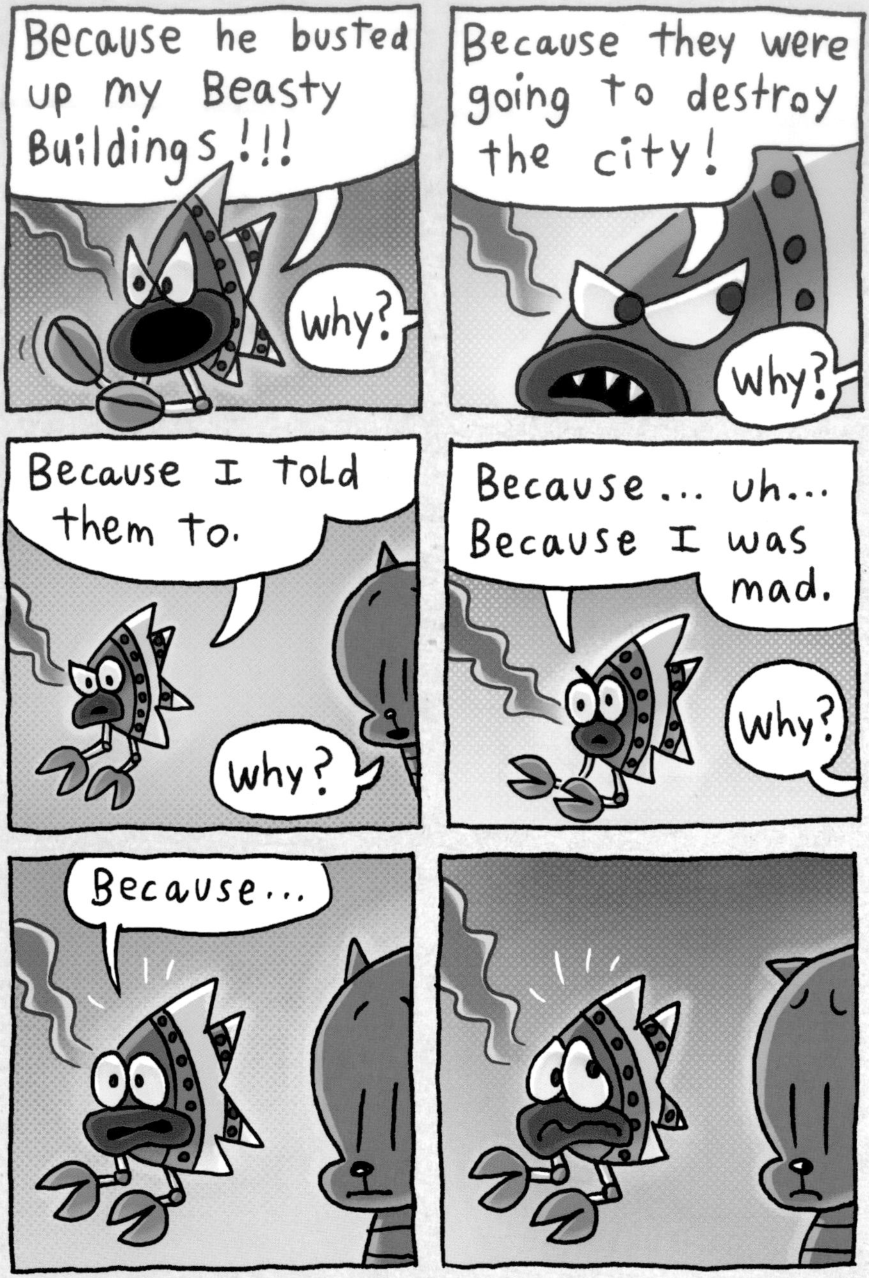
Because he busted up my Beasty Buildings!!!
why?
Because they were going to destroy the city!
Why?
Because I told them to.
why?
Because... uh... Because I was mad.
Why?
Because...

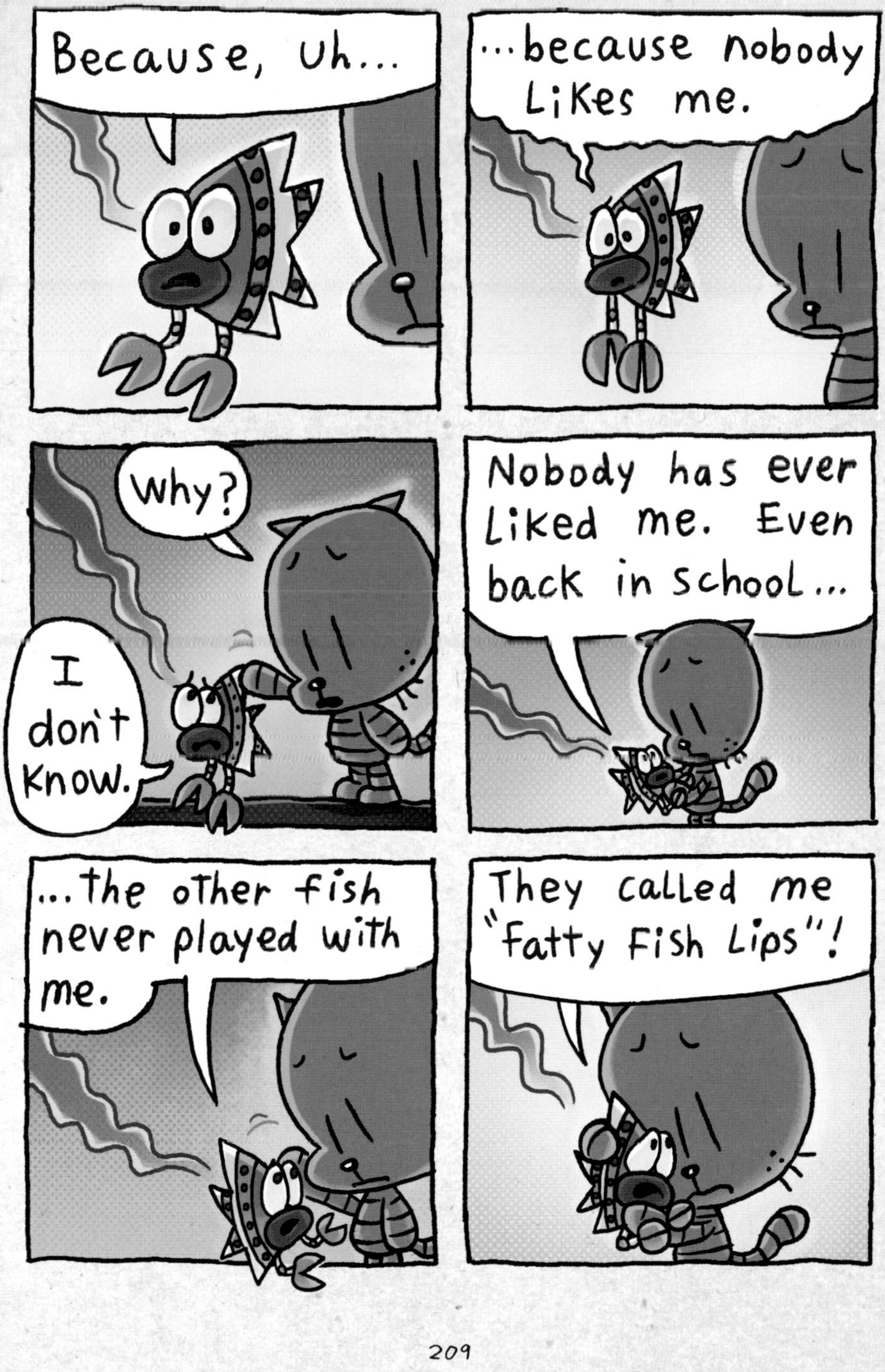
Because, uh...
...because nobody likes me.
Why?
I don't know.
Nobody has ever liked me. Even back in school...
...the other fish never played with me.
They called me "Fatty Fish Lips"!

I'm Sorry.
Hey, I know what will cheer you up!
The End.
Look! I made you a book!
my Friend FLippY
Do ya wanna read it?
OK.
And so...
The End.
my Friend FLippy

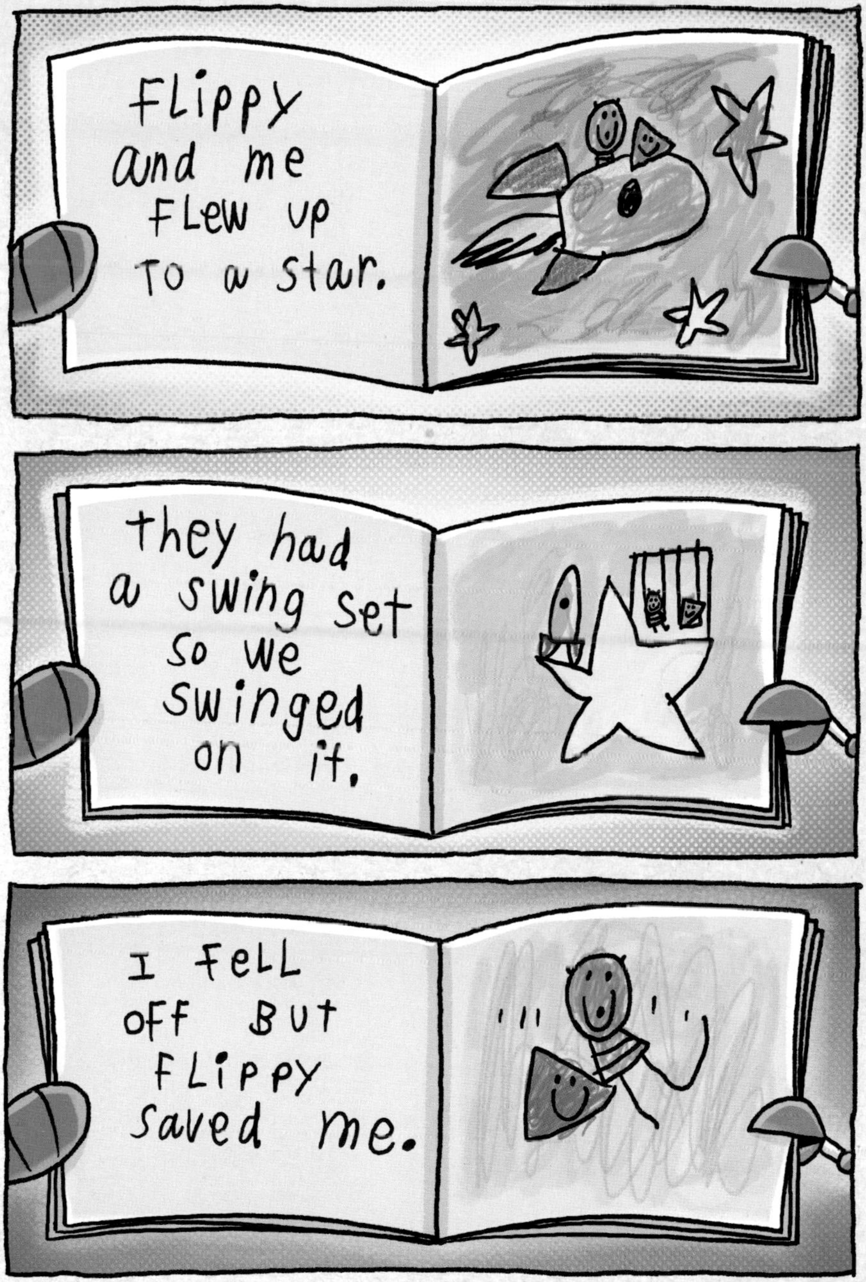
FLippy and me FLew up To a star.
they had a swing set so we swinged on it.
I feLL off But FLippy saved me.

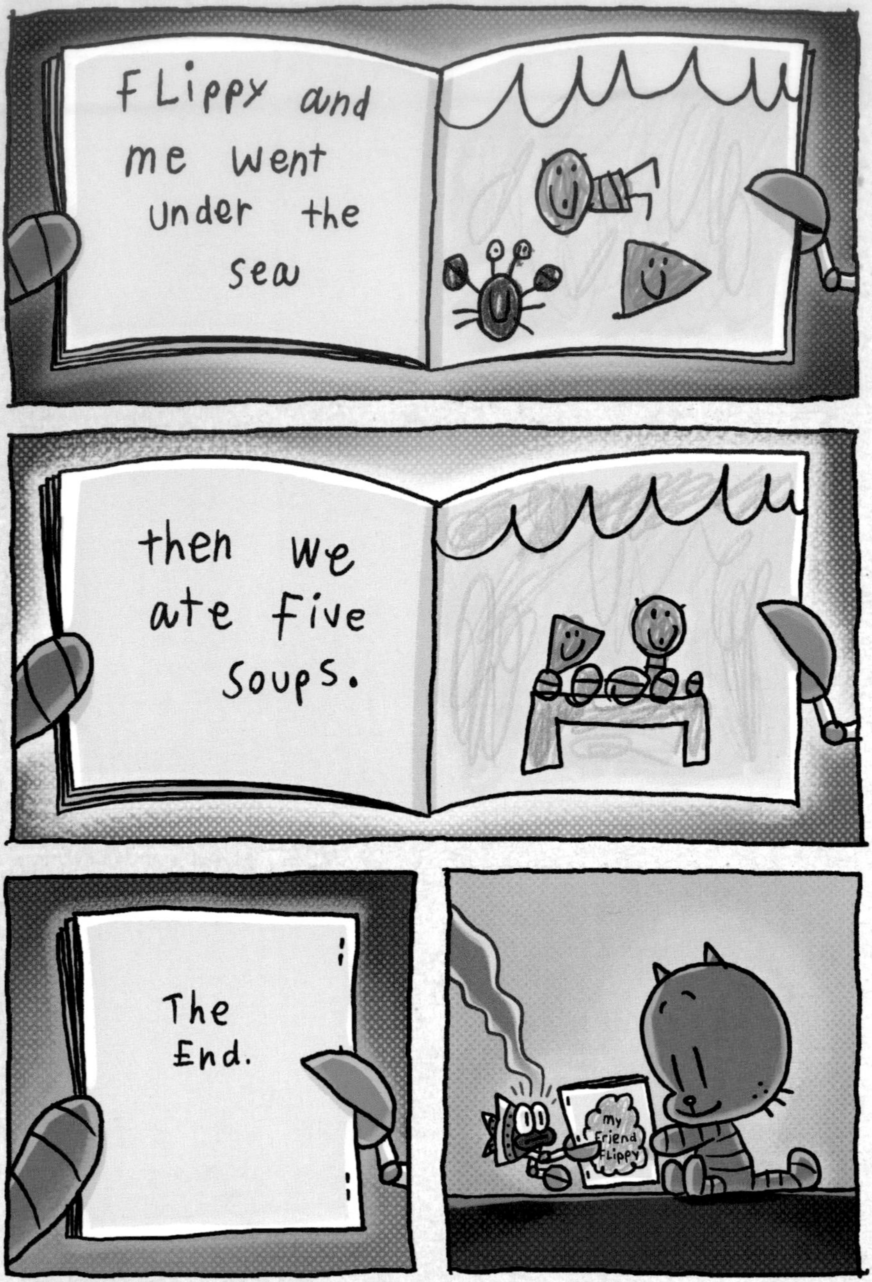
Flippy and me went under the sea
then we ate five soups.
The End.
my Friend Flippy

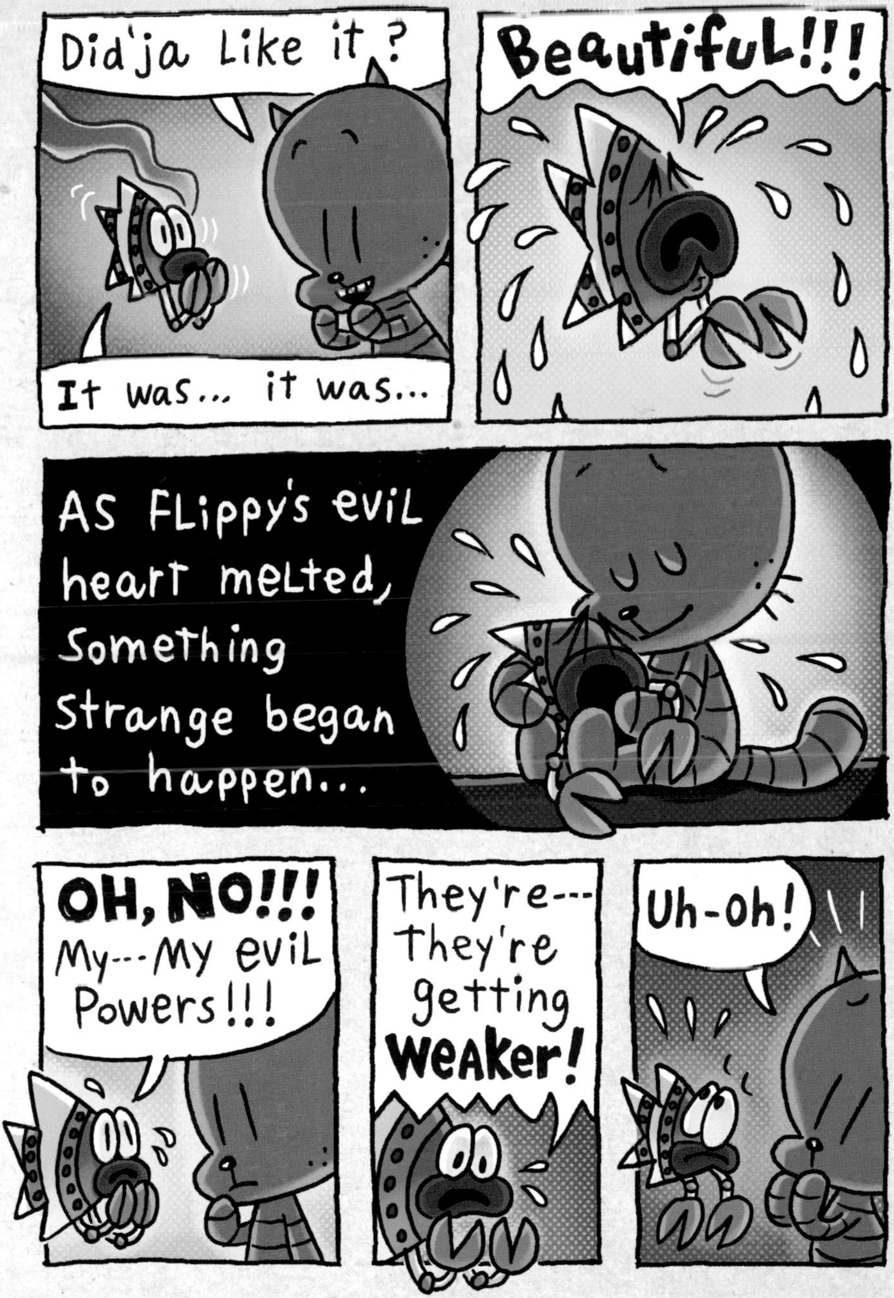
Did'ja Like it?
It was... it was...
Beautiful!!!
AS FLippy's eviL heart meLted, Something Strange began to happen...
OH, NO!!! My---My eviL Powers!!!
They're---they're getting WEAKER!
Uh-Oh!

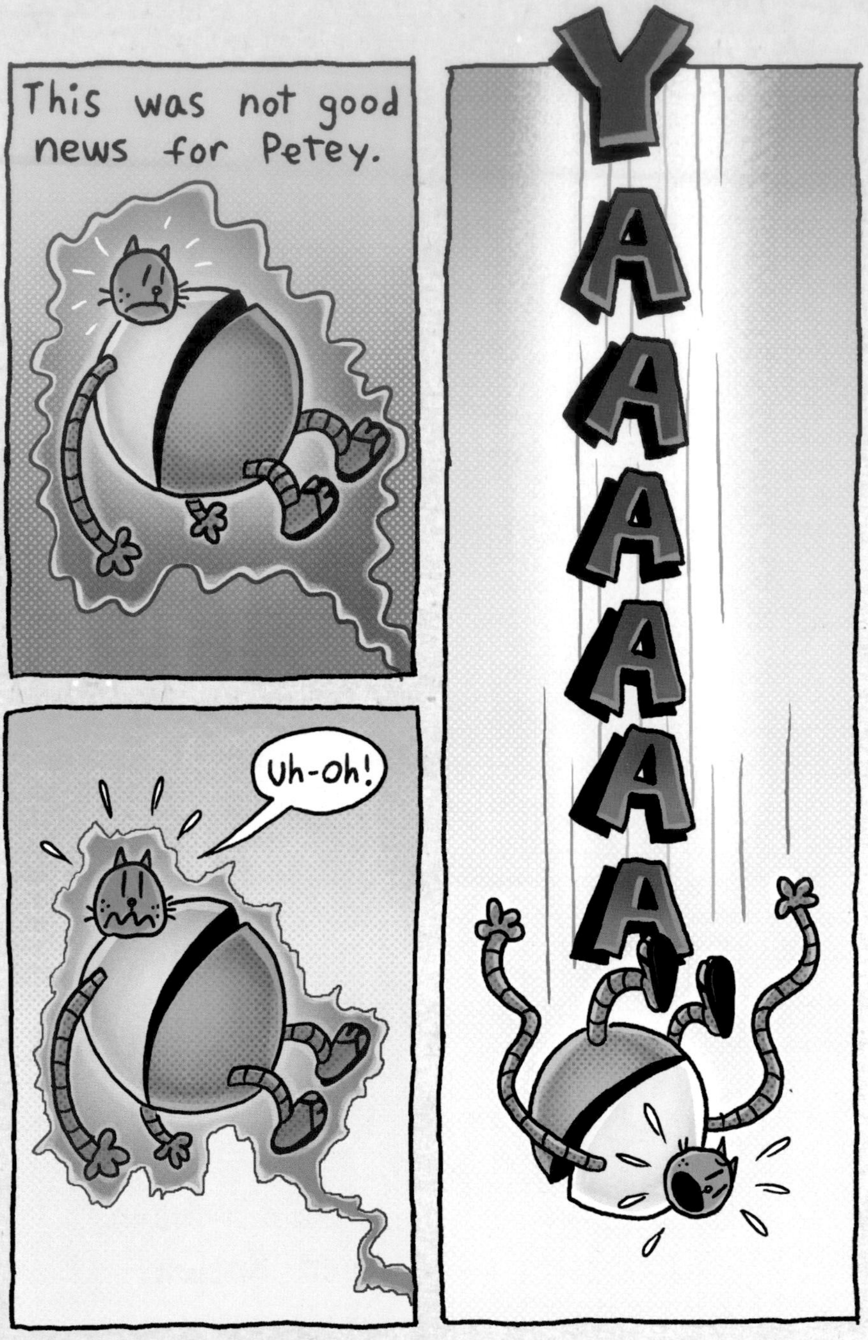
This was not good news for Petey.
Uh-oh!
YAAAAAA

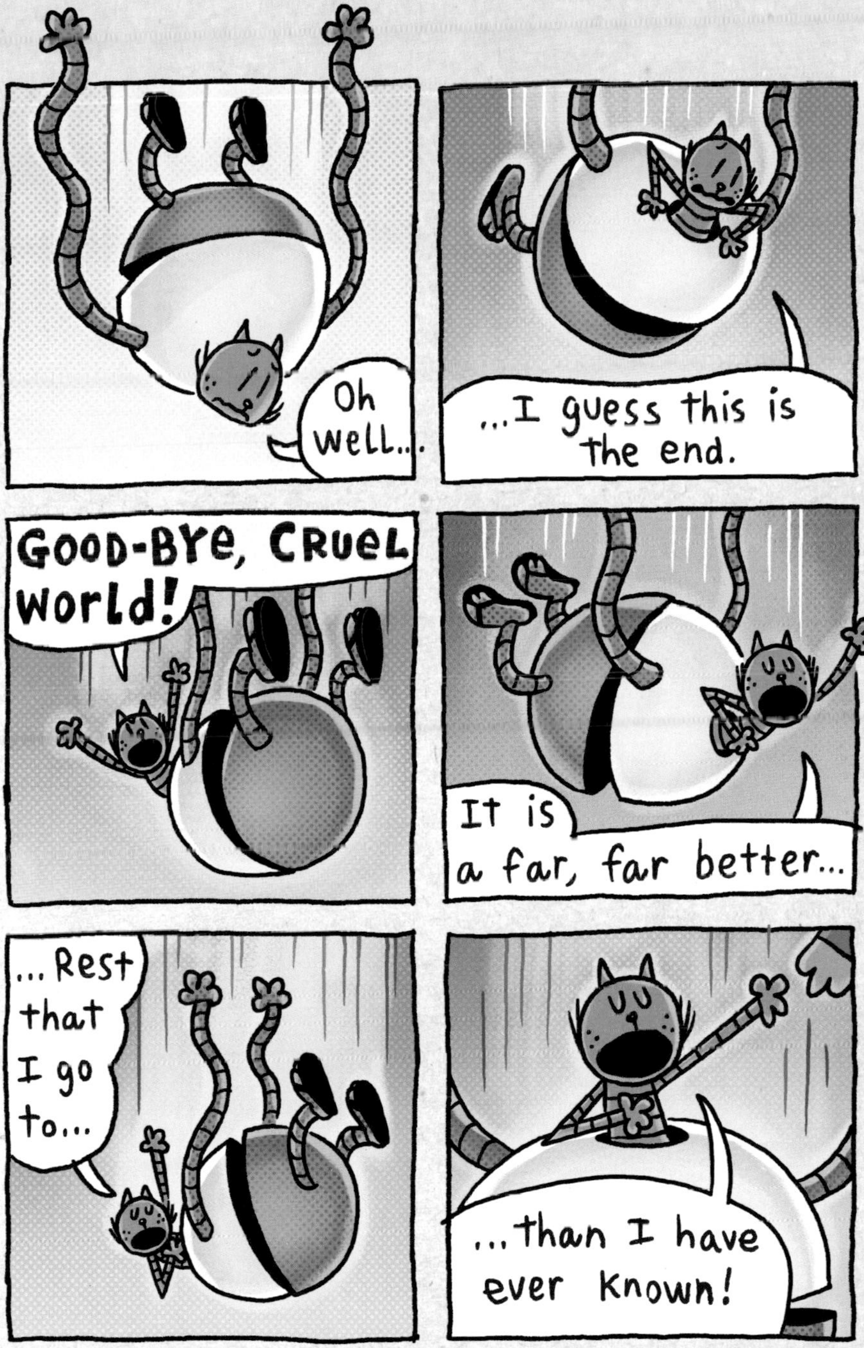
Oh well...
...I guess this is the end.
GOOD-BYE, CRUEL world!
It is a far, far better...
... Rest that I go to...
... than I have ever known!

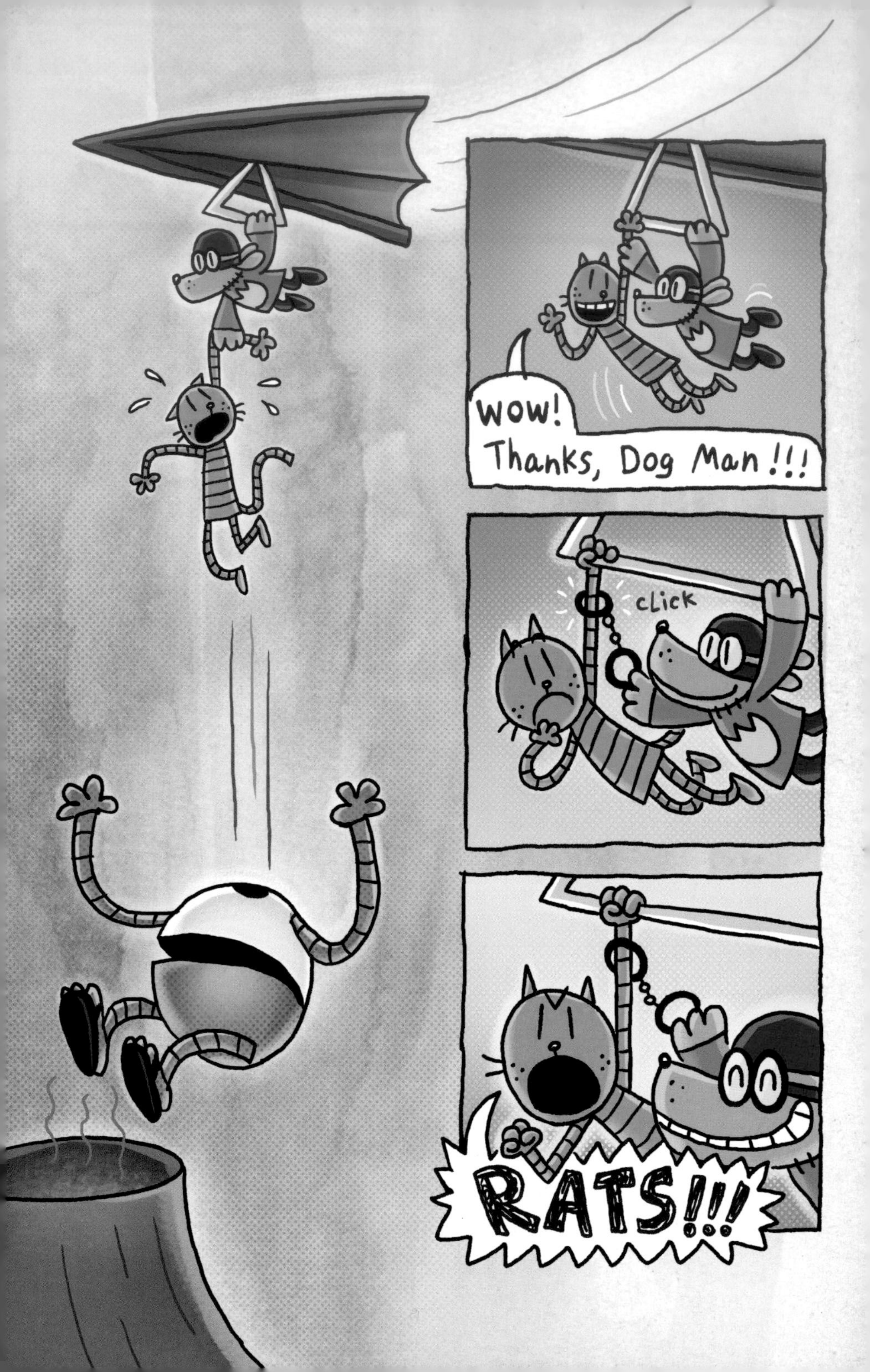
WOW!
Thanks, Dog Man!!!
cLick
RATS!!!

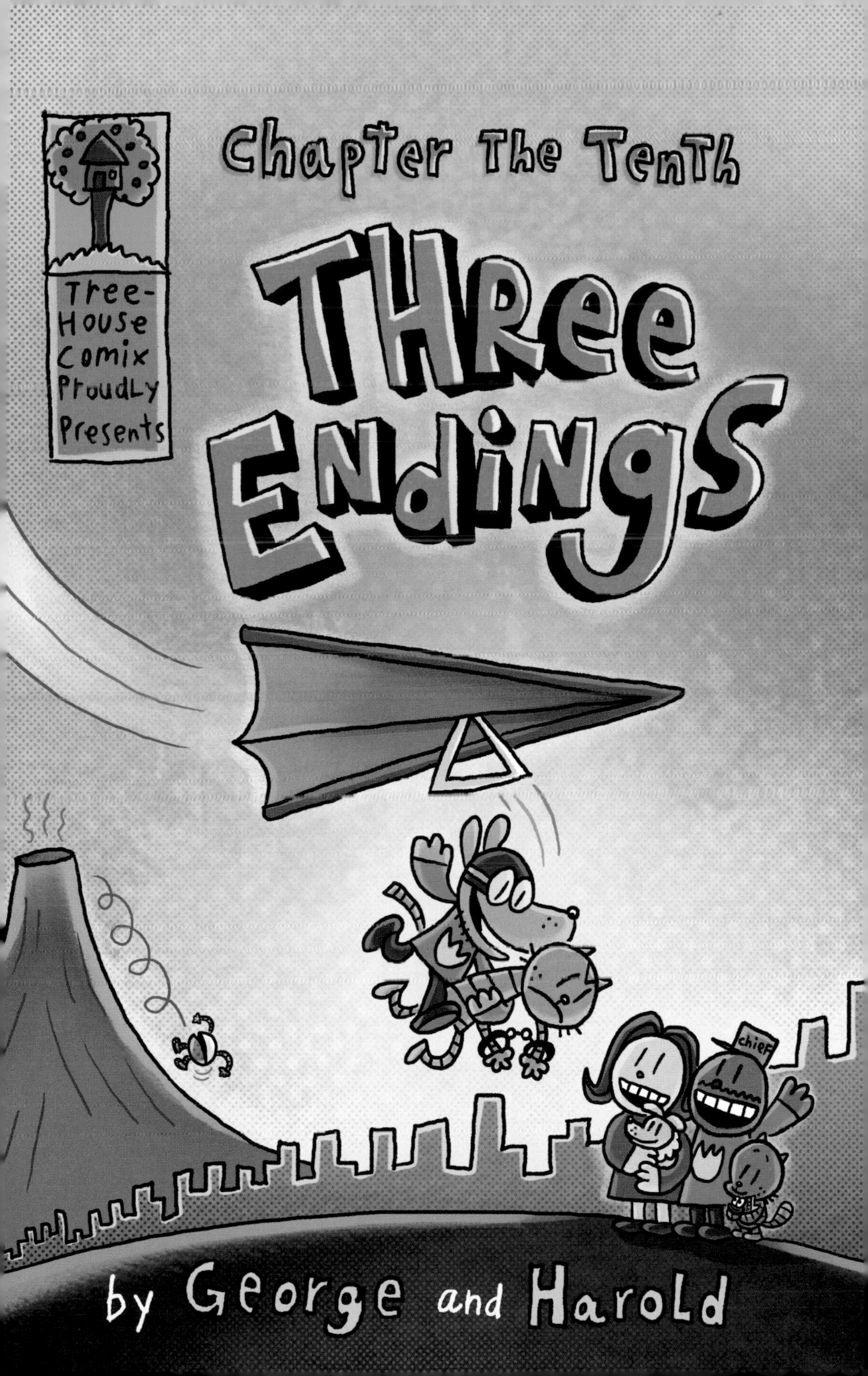
Tree-House Comix Proudly Presents
Chapter The Tenth
THRee EndingS
chief
by George and Harold

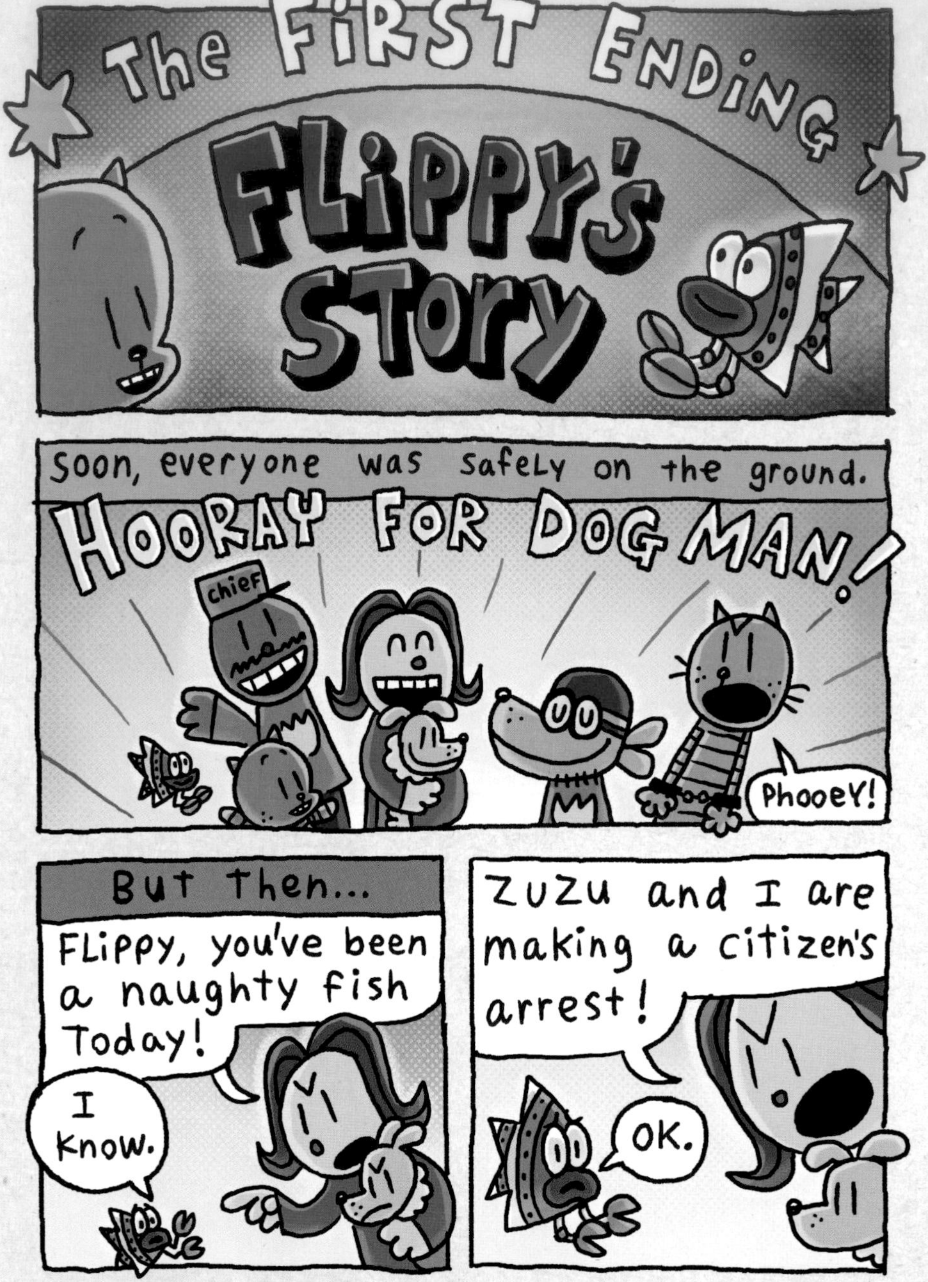
The FIRST ENDING
FLiPPY's STory
Soon, everyone was safely on the ground.
HOORAY FOR DOG MAN!
chief
PhooeY!
But Then...
FLiPPY, you've been a naughty fish Today!
I know.
ZUZU and I are making a citizen's arrest!
OK.

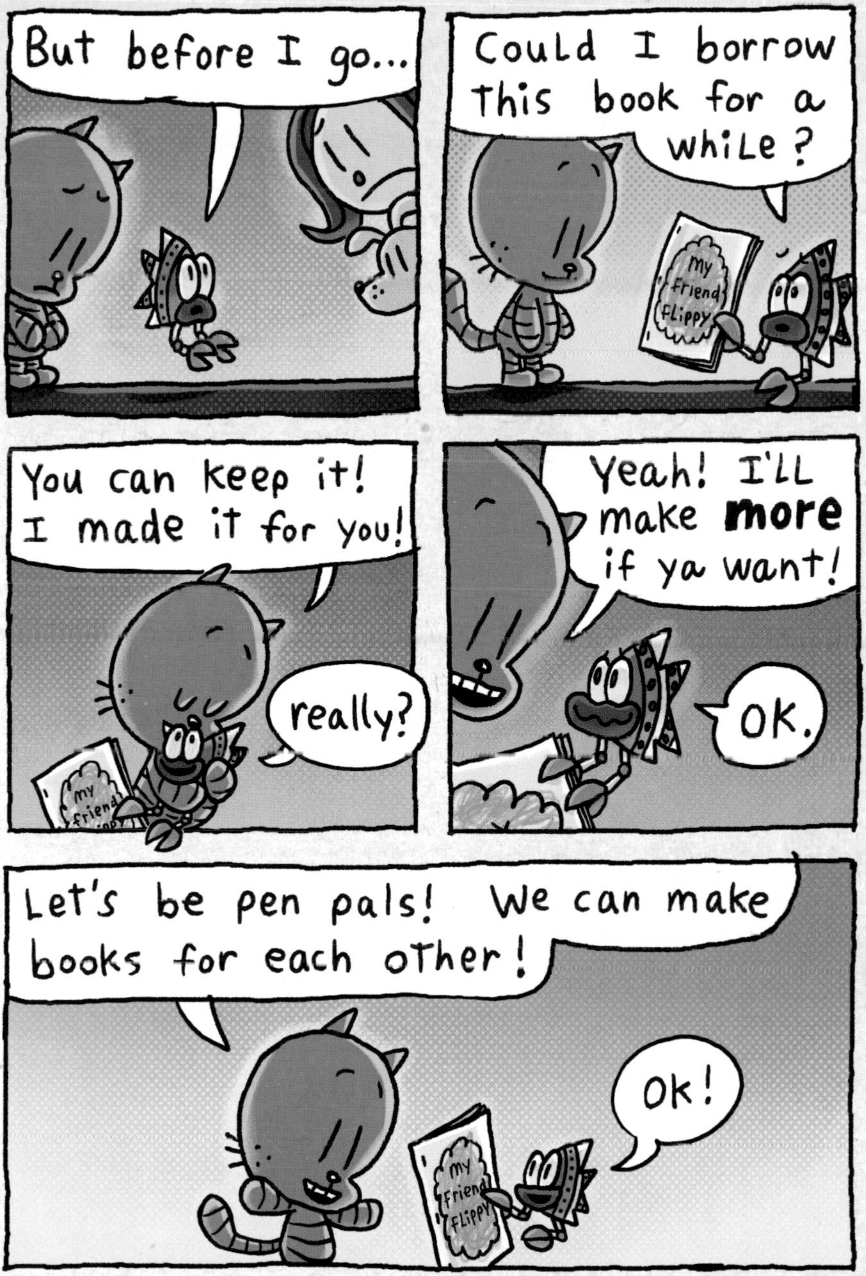

But before I go...
Could I borrow this book for a while?
my friend Flippy
You can keep it! I made it for you!
really?
Yeah! I'LL make **more** if ya want!
OK.
Let's be pen pals! We can make books for each other!
Ok!
my friend Flippy

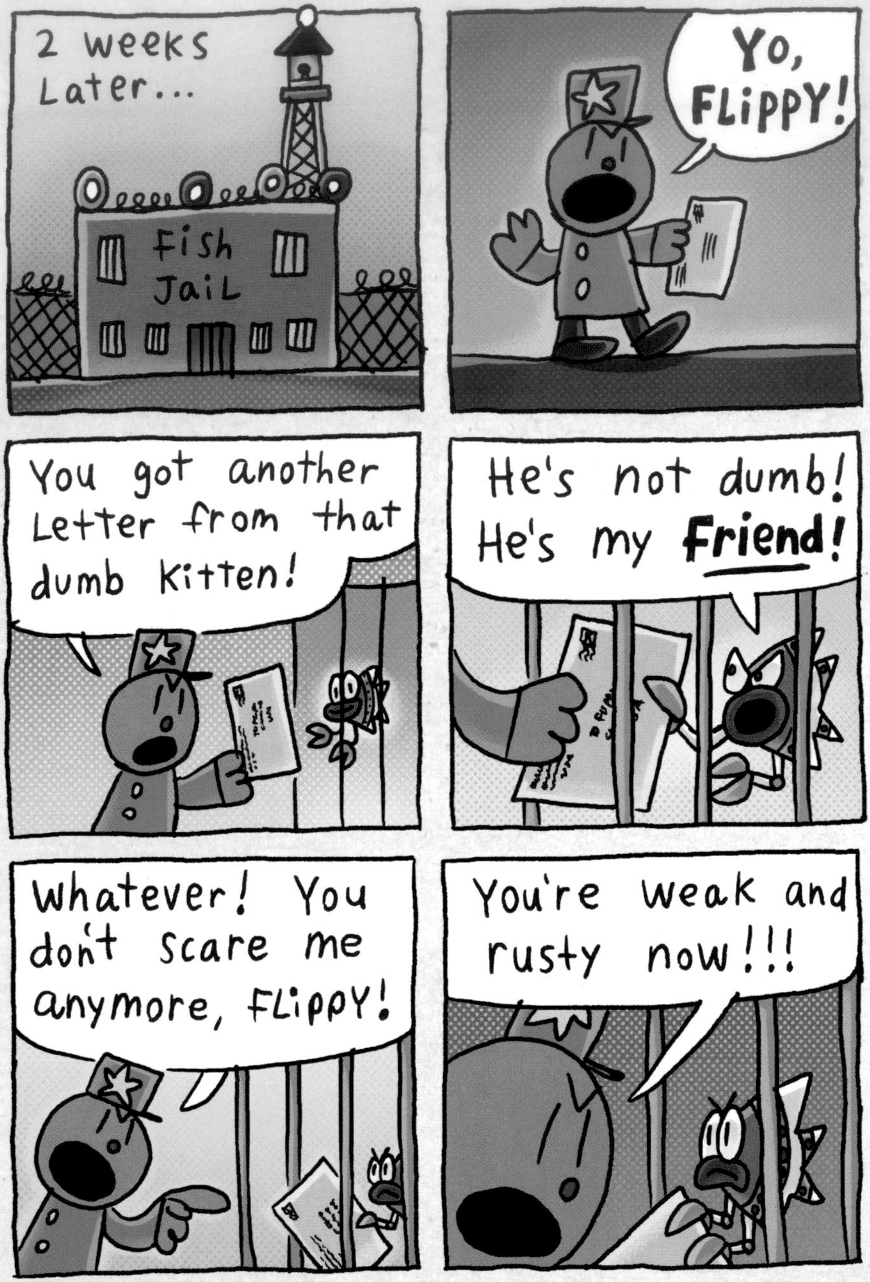
2 weeks Later...
Fish Jail
Yo, FLIPPY!
You got another Letter from that dumb Kitten!
He's not dumb! He's my **Friend**!
Whatever! You don't scare me anymore, FLiPPY!
You're weak and rusty now!!!

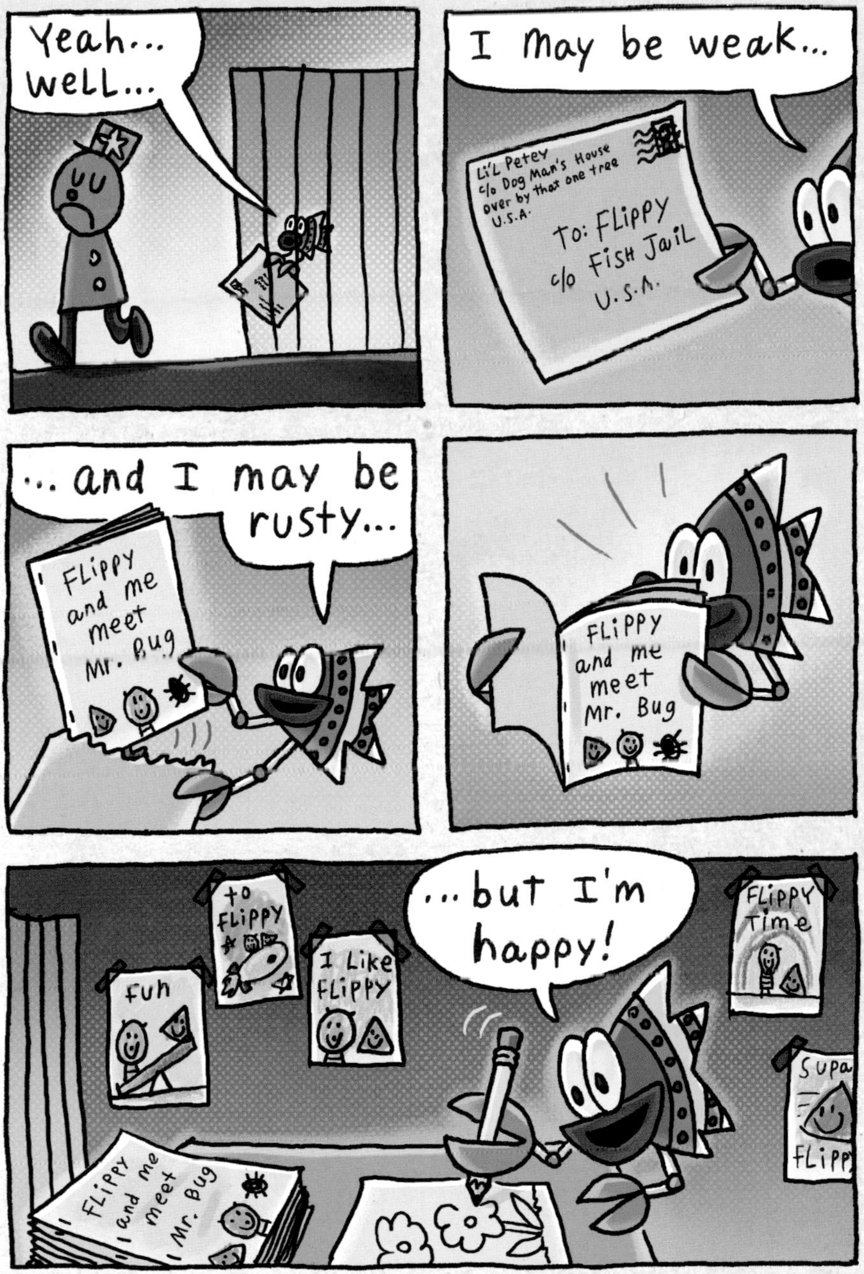
Yeah... well...
I may be weak...
Li'L Petey
c/o Dog Man's House
over by that one tree
U.S.A.
To: FLippy
c/o Fish Jail
U.S.A.
... and I may be rusty...
FLippy and me meet Mr. Bug
FLippy and me meet Mr. Bug
to FLippy
fun
I Like FLippy
... but I'm happy!
FLippy Time
Supa
FLippy and me meet Mr. Bug

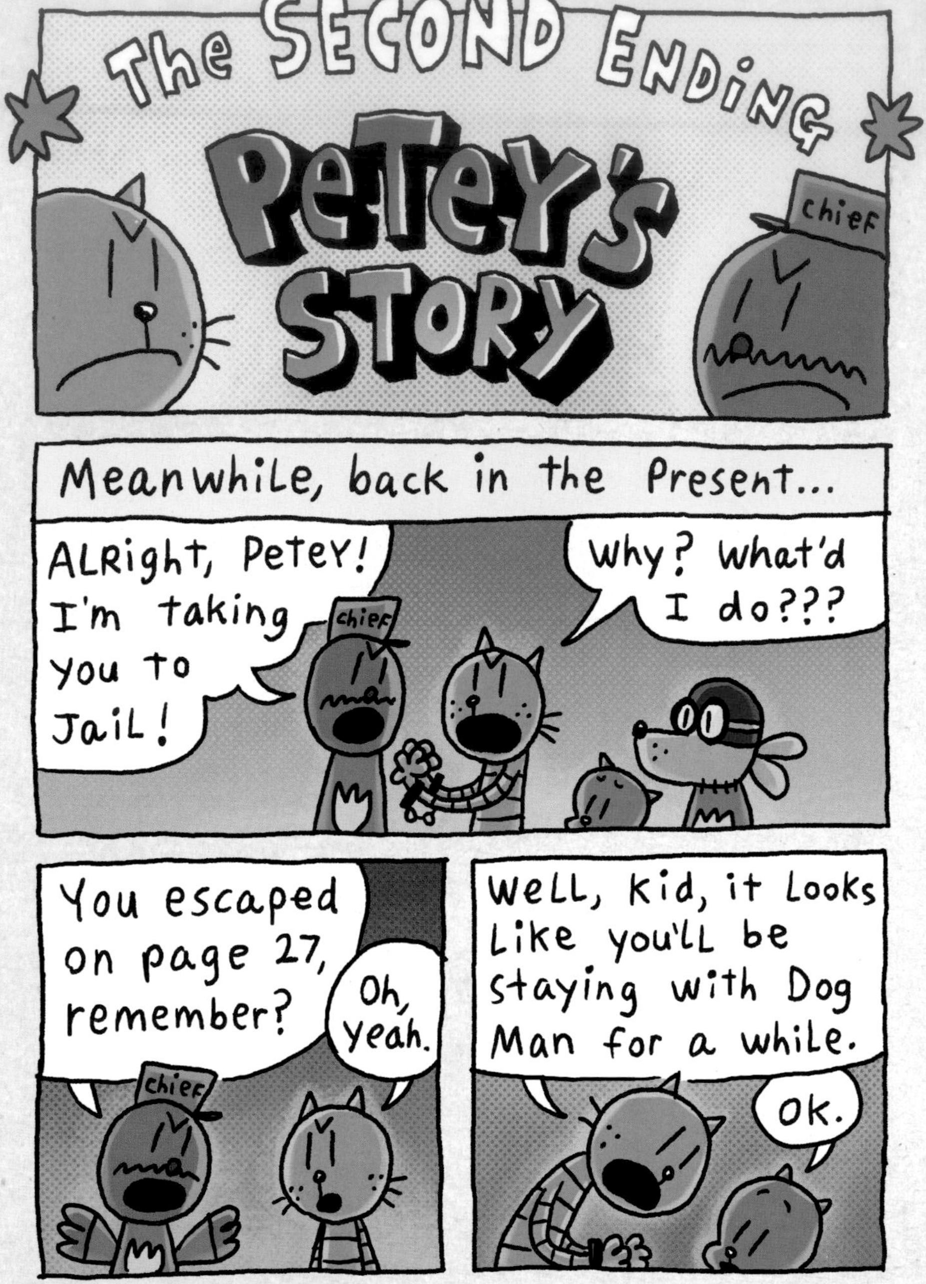
The SECOND ENDING
PETEY'S STORY
chief
Meanwhile, back in the Present...
ALRight, PeTEY! I'm taking you to JaiL!
chief
Why? What'd I do???
You escaped on page 27, remember?
Oh, yeah.
chief
WeLL, Kid, it Looks Like you'LL be staying with Dog Man for a whiLe.
OK.

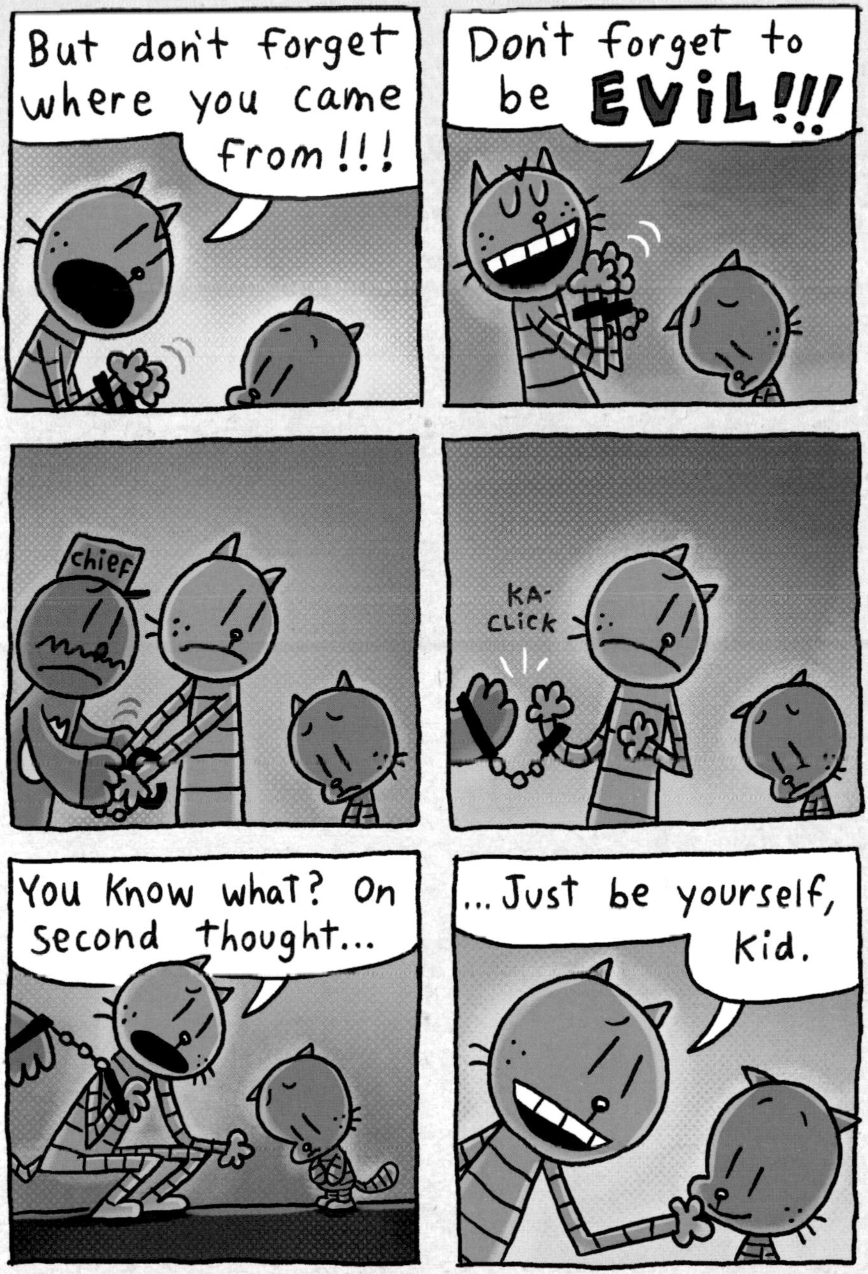
But don't forget where you came from!!!
Don't forget to be EVIL!!!
chief
KA-CLICK
You know what? On second thought...
...Just be yourself, kid.

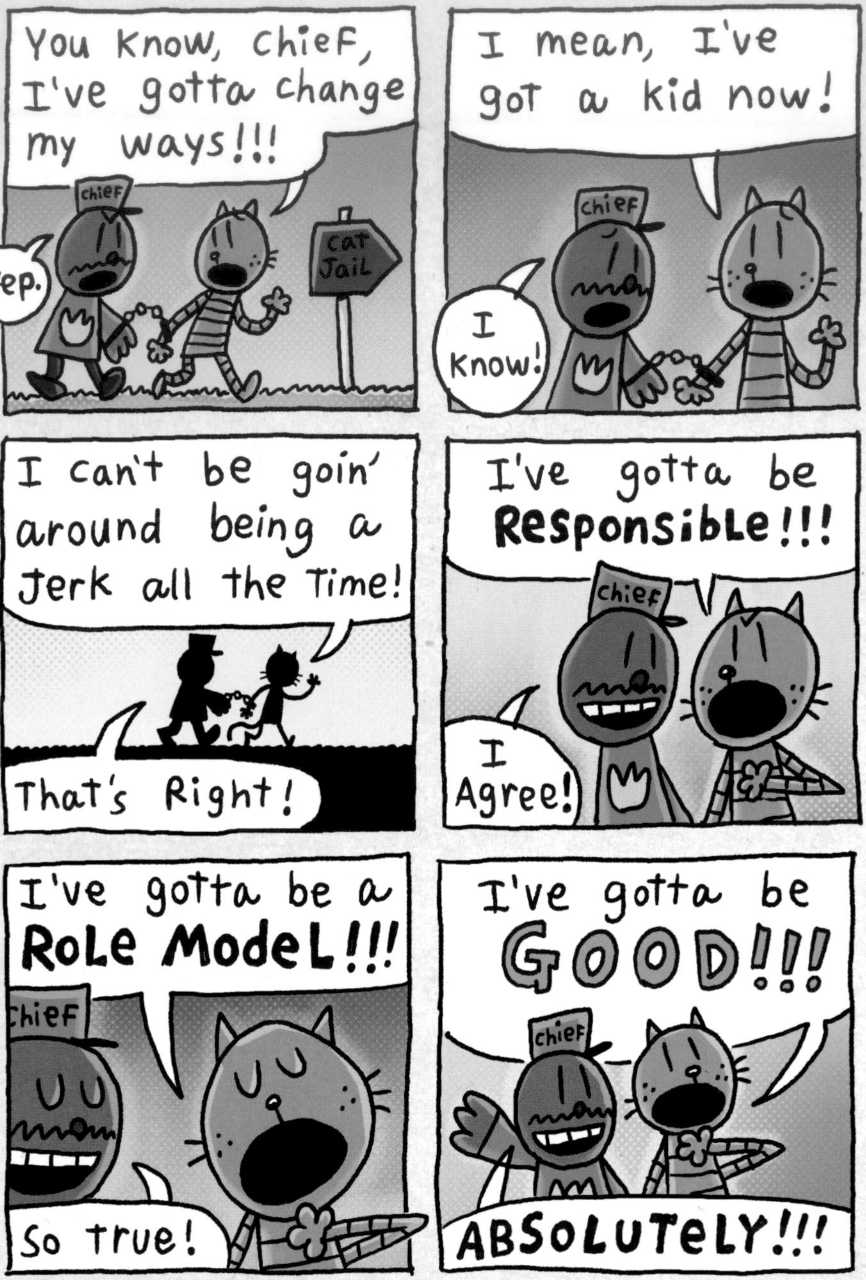
You know, chief, I've gotta change my ways!!!
chief
Yep.
Cat Jail
I mean, I've got a kid now!
chief
I know!
I can't be goin' around being a Jerk all the Time!
That's Right!
I've gotta be Responsible!!!
chief
I Agree!
I've gotta be a Role Model!!!
chief
So true!
I've gotta be GOOD!!!
chief
ABSOLUTELY!!!

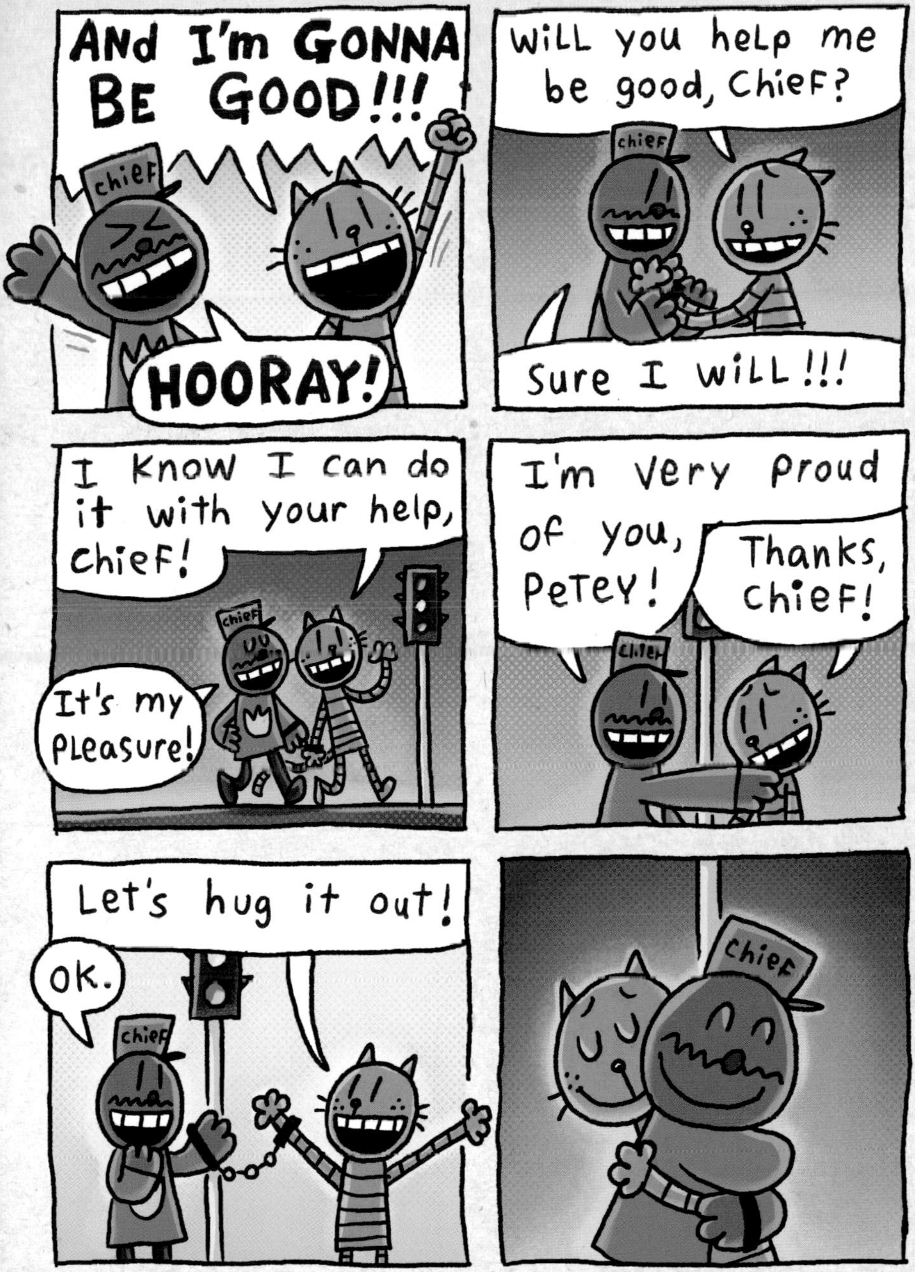
AND I'm GONNA BE GOOD!!!
HOORAY!
WiLL you heLp me be good, ChieF?
Sure I WiLL!!!
I Know I can do it with your help, ChieF!
It's my PLeasure!
I'm Very Proud of you, PeTeY!
Thanks, ChieF!
Let's hug it out!
OK.

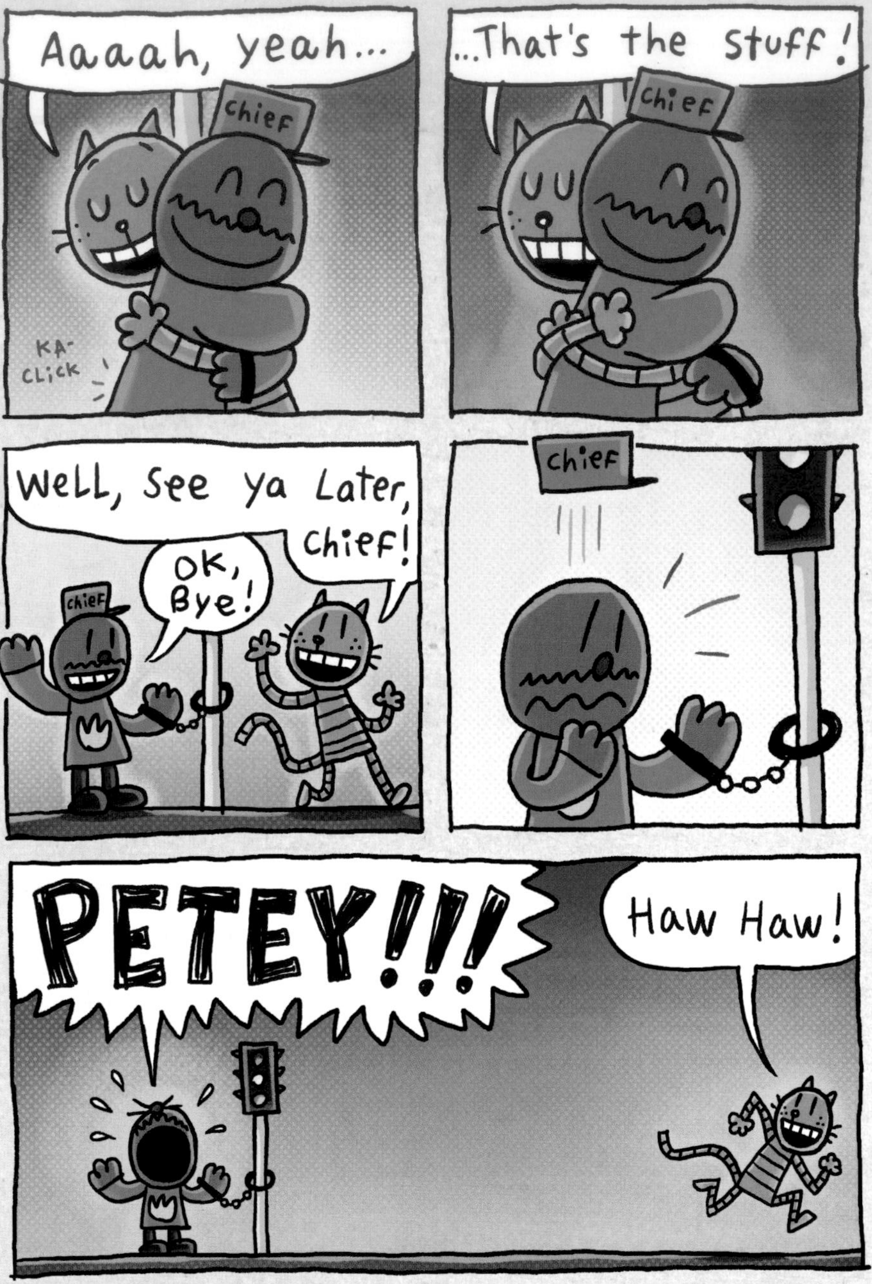
Aaaah, yeah...
Chief
KA-CLICK
...That's the stuff!
Chief
Well, see ya later, chief!
OK, Bye!
Chief
Chief
PETEY!!!
Haw Haw!

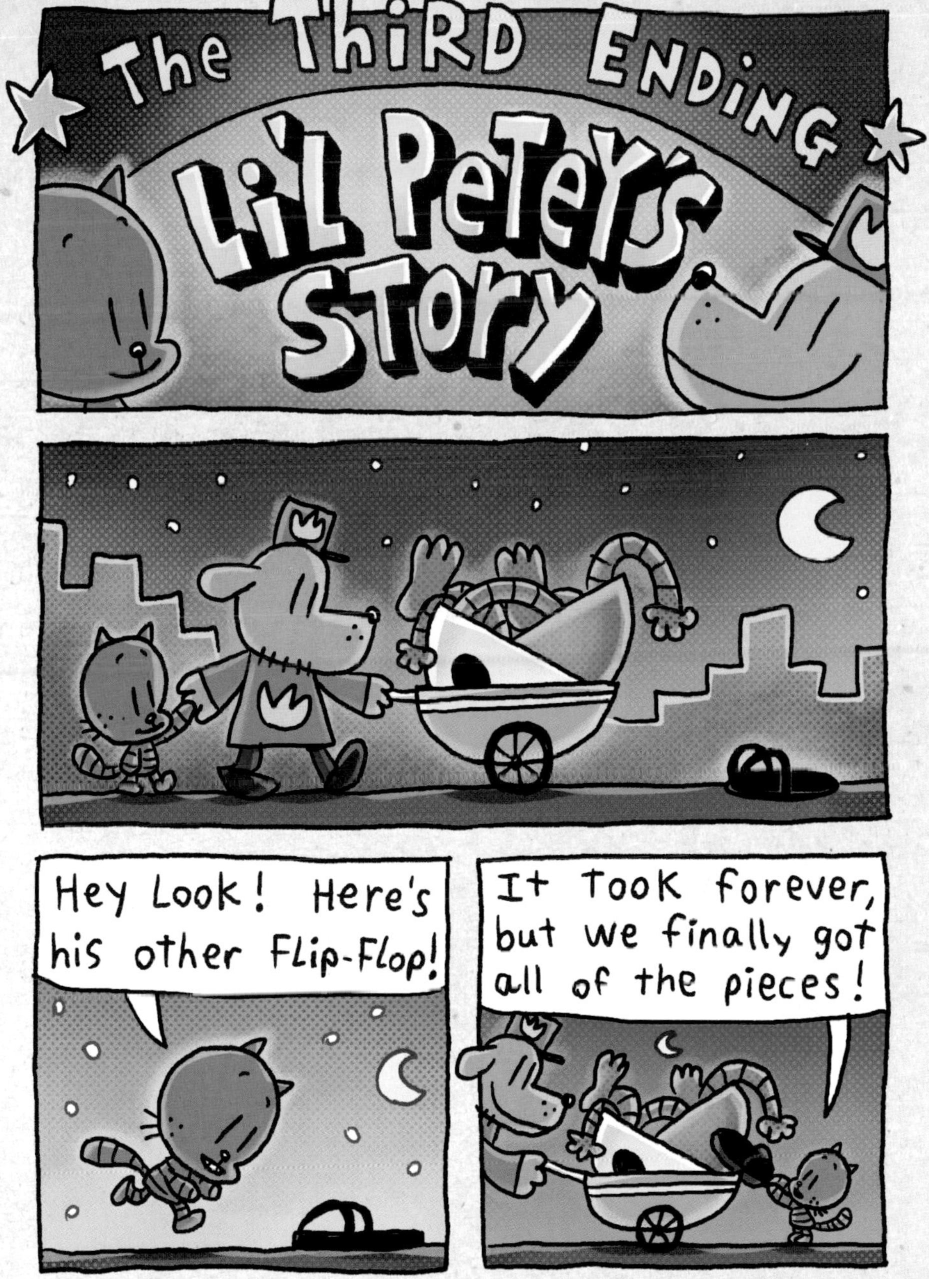
The Third Ending
Li'l Petey's Story
Hey Look! Here's his other Flip-Flop!
It took forever, but we finally got all of the pieces!

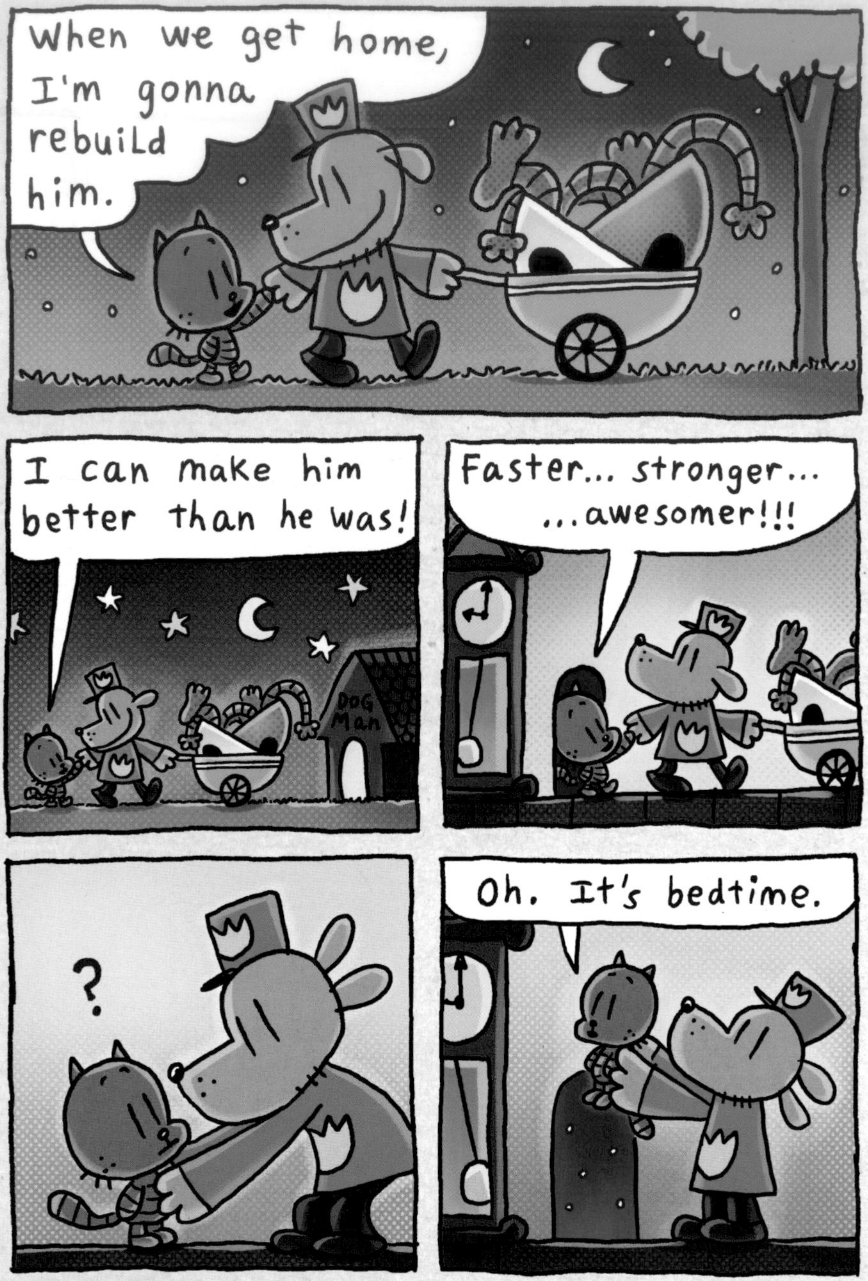
When we get home, I'm gonna rebuild him.
I can make him better than he was!
DOG Man
Faster... stronger... ...awesomer!!!
?
Oh. It's bedtime.

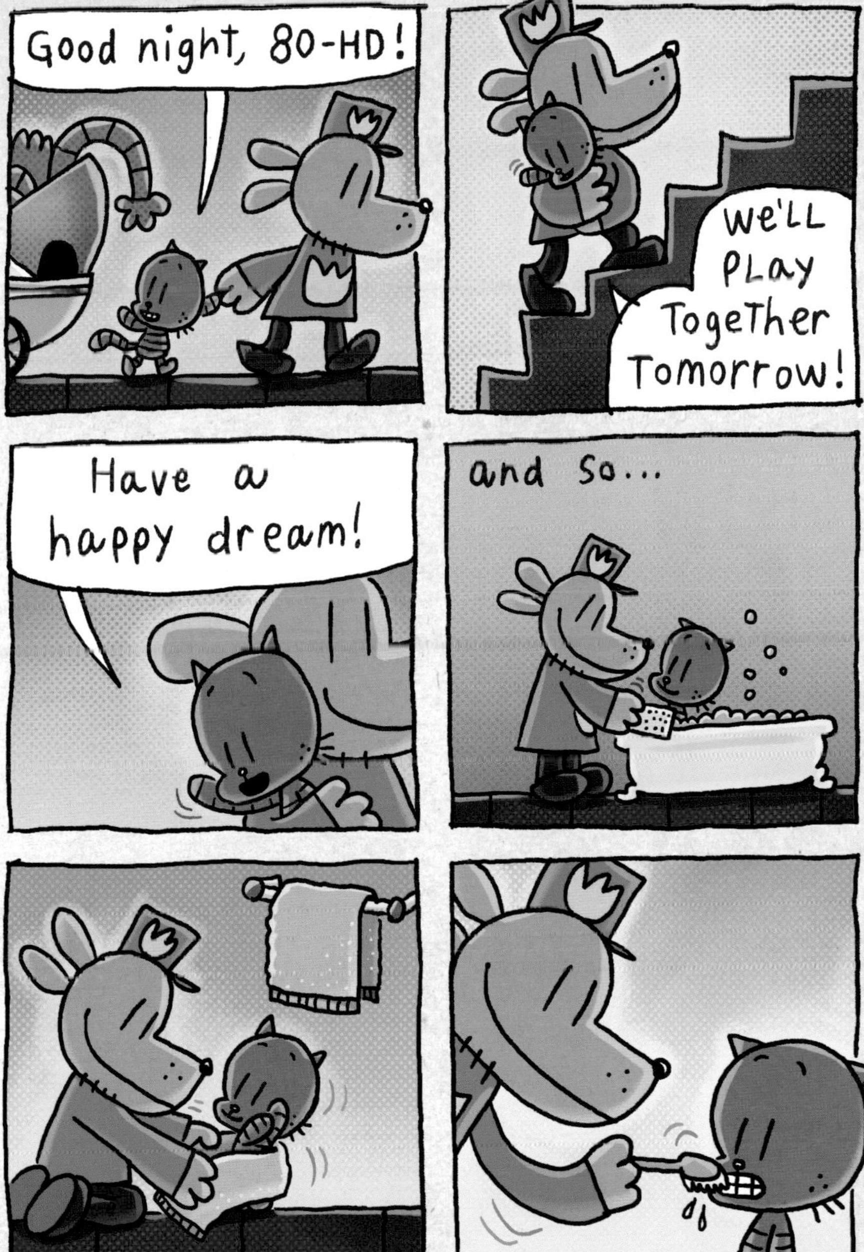
Good night, 80-HD!
We'LL PLay Together Tomorrow!
Have a happy dream!
and so...

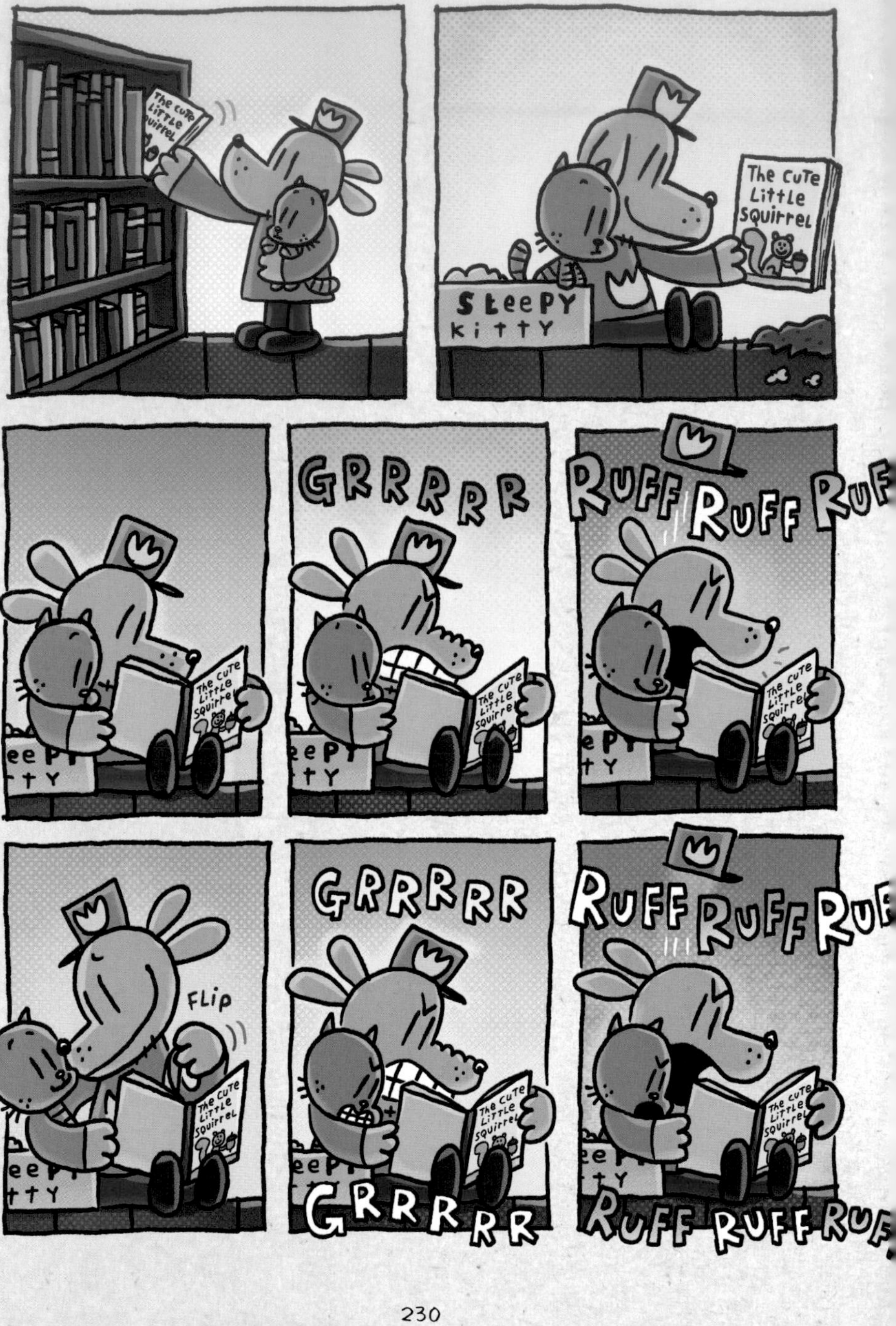
The Cute Little Squirrel
SLeepy Kitty
The Cute Little Squirrel
The Cute Little Squirrel
GRRRRRR
The Cute Little Squirrel
RUFF RUFF RUF
The Cute Little Squirrel
FLip
The Cute Little Squirrel
GRRRRRR
The Cute Little Squirrel
GRRRRRR
RUFF RUFF RUF
The Cute Little Squirrel
RUFF RUFF RUF

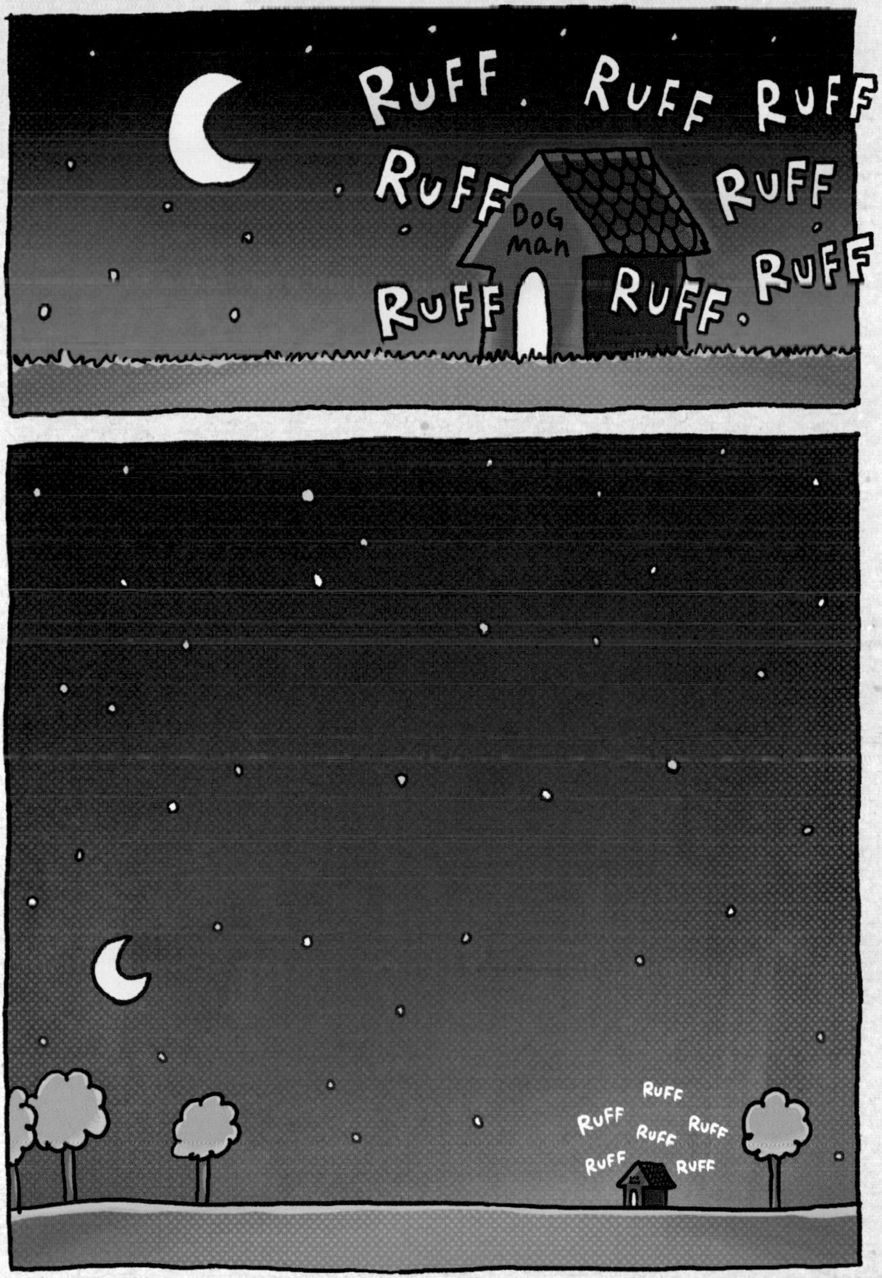
RUFF
RUFF
RUFF
RUFF
RUFF
DOG man
RUFF
RUFF
RUFF
RUFF
RUFF
RUFF
RUFF
RUFF
RUFF

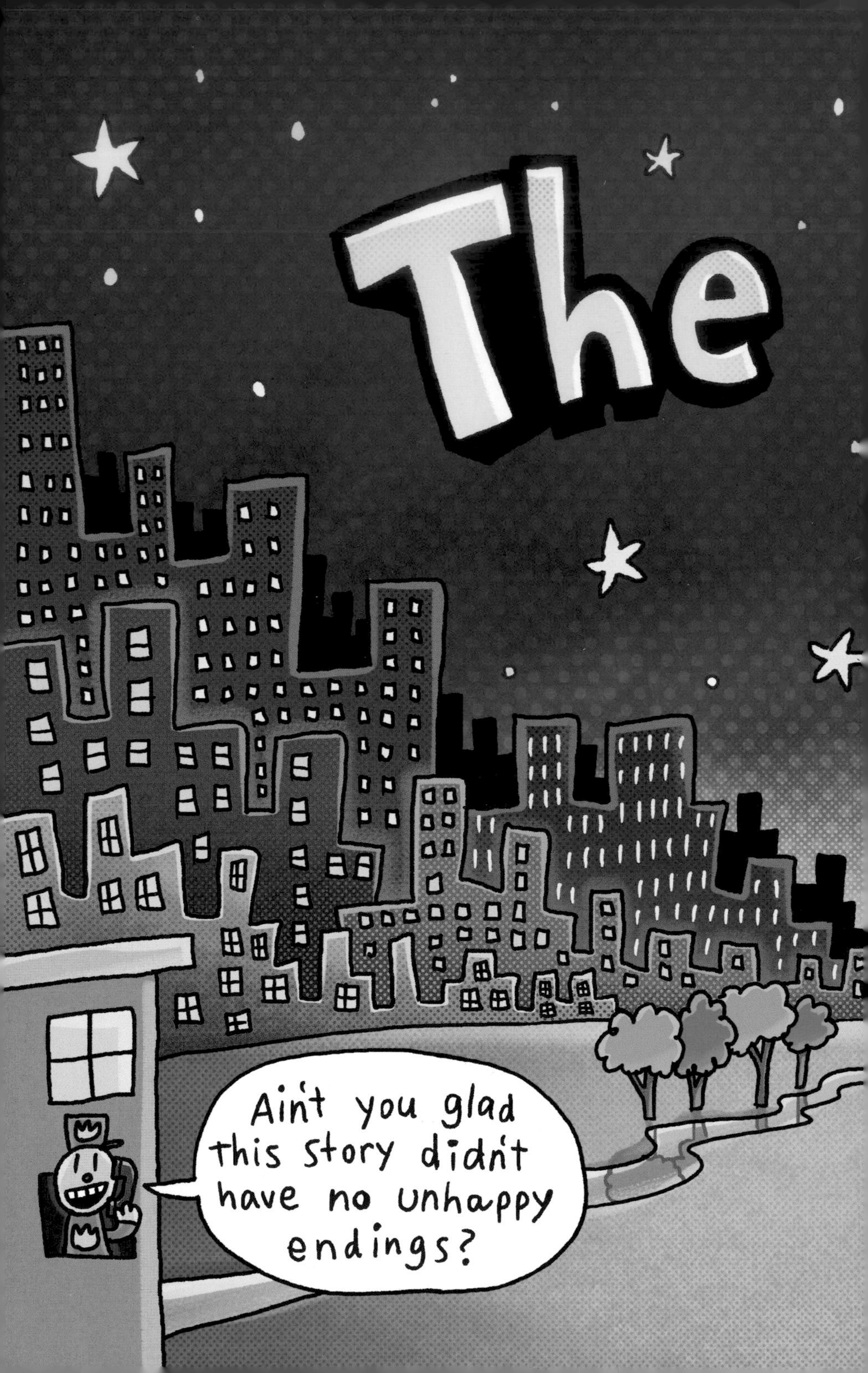
The
Ain't you glad this story didn't have no unhappy endings?

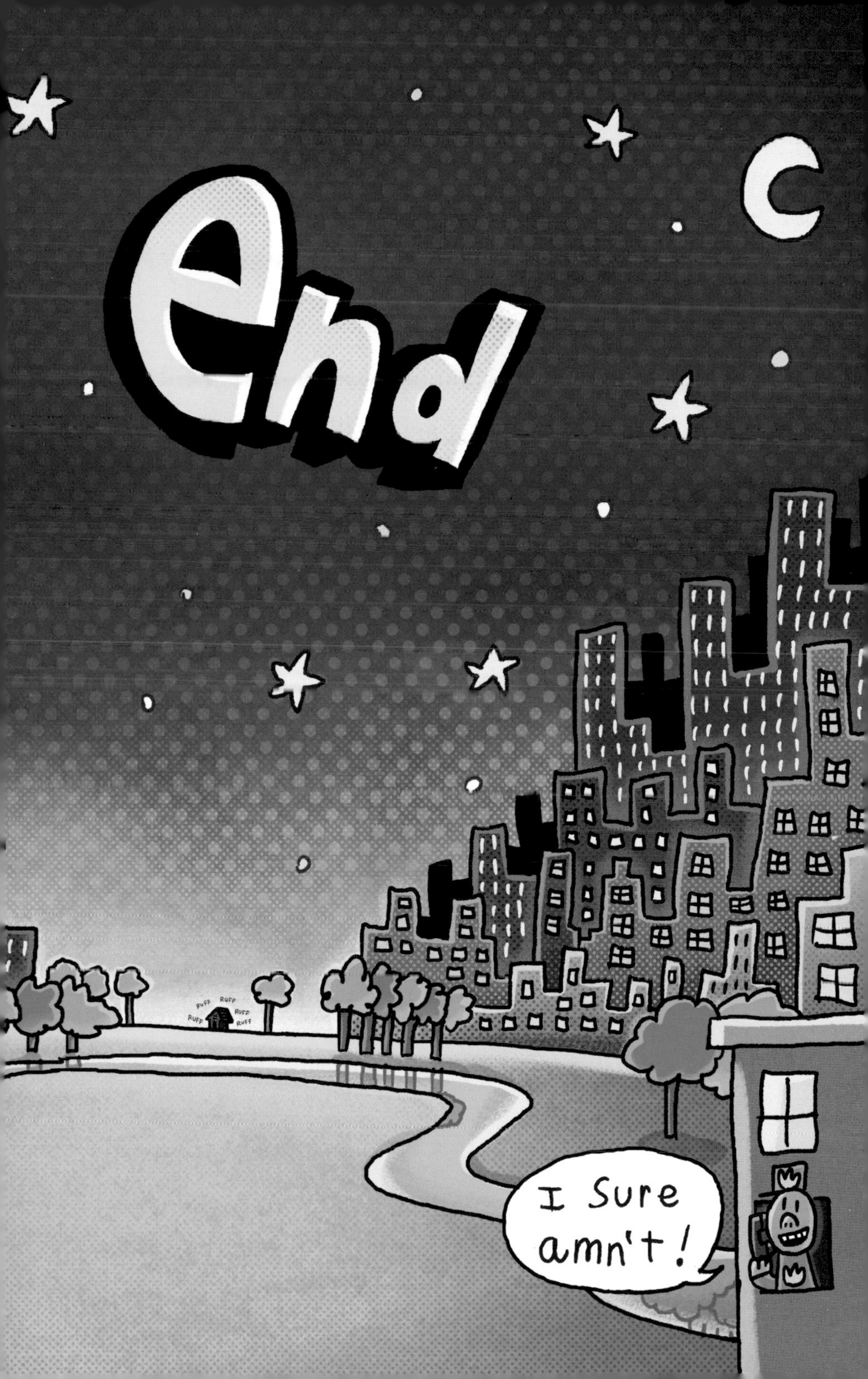
end
RUFF RUFF
RUFF RUFF RUFF
I sure amn't!

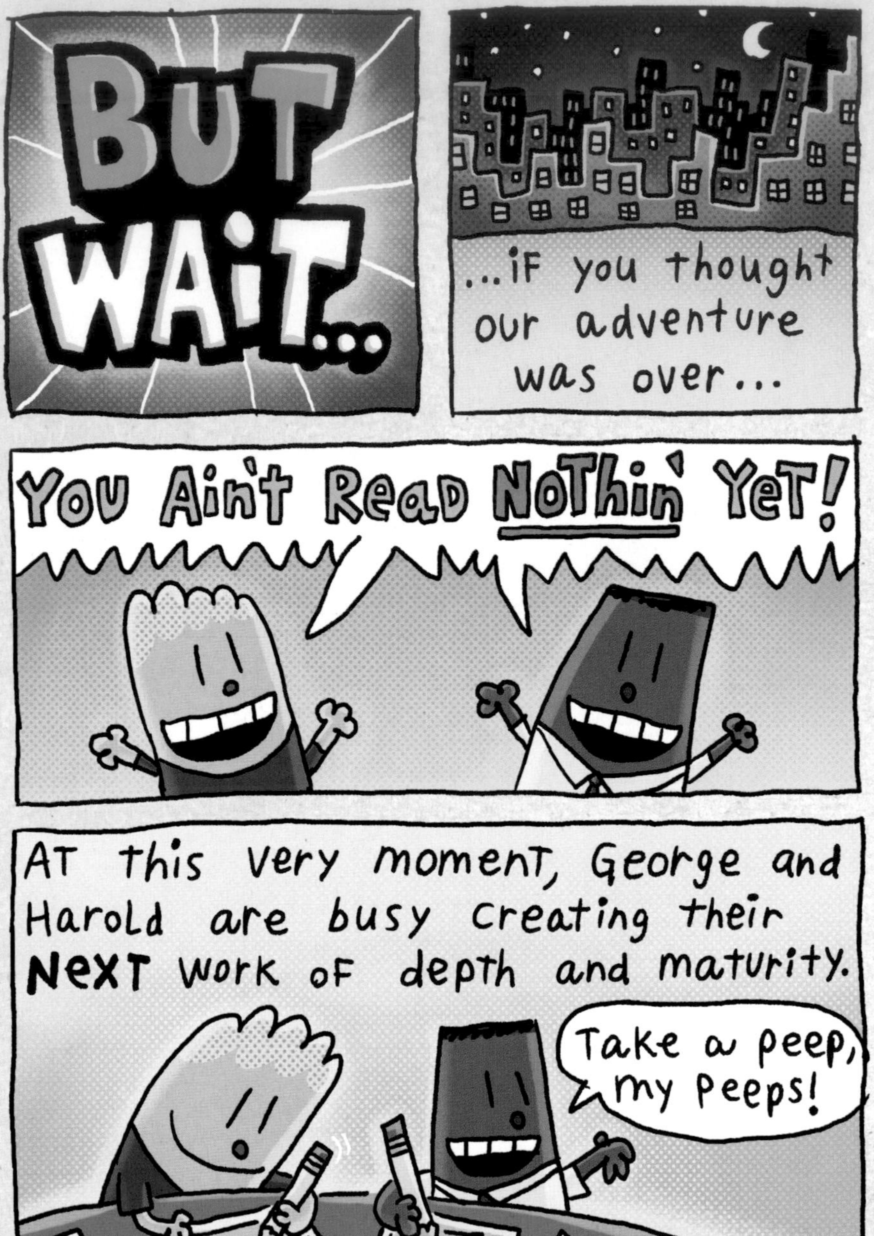
BUT WAIT...
...if you thought our adventure was over...
YOU AIN'T READ NOTHIN' YET!
AT this very moment, George and Harold are busy creating their NEXT work of depth and maturity.
Take a peep, my peeps!

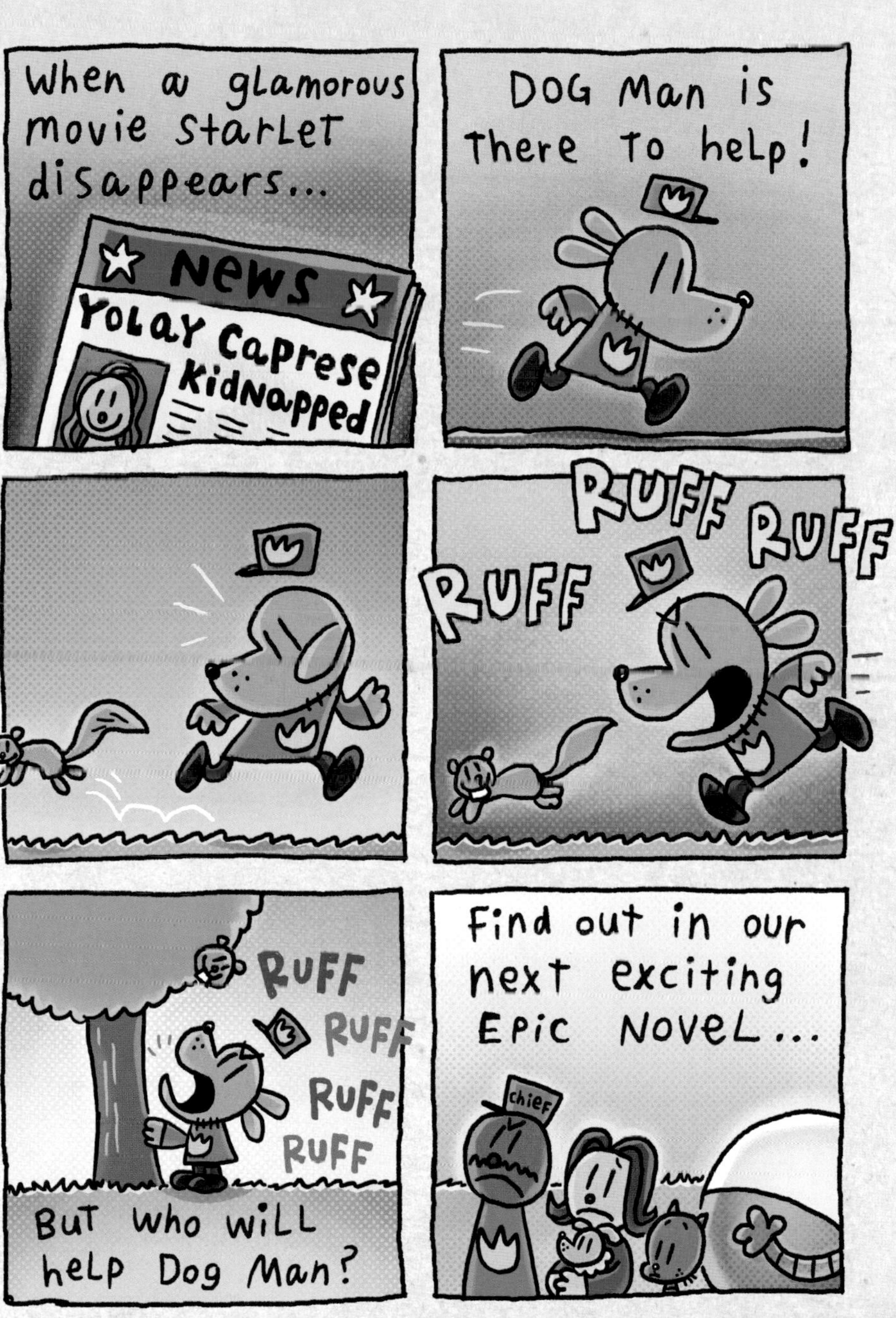

When a glamorous movie starlet disappears...
NEWS
YOLAY CAPRESE KIDNAPPED
DOG MAN is there to help!
RUFF
RUFF
RUFF
RUFF
RUFF
RUFF
RUFF
But who will help Dog Man?
Find out in our next exciting Epic Novel...
CHIEF

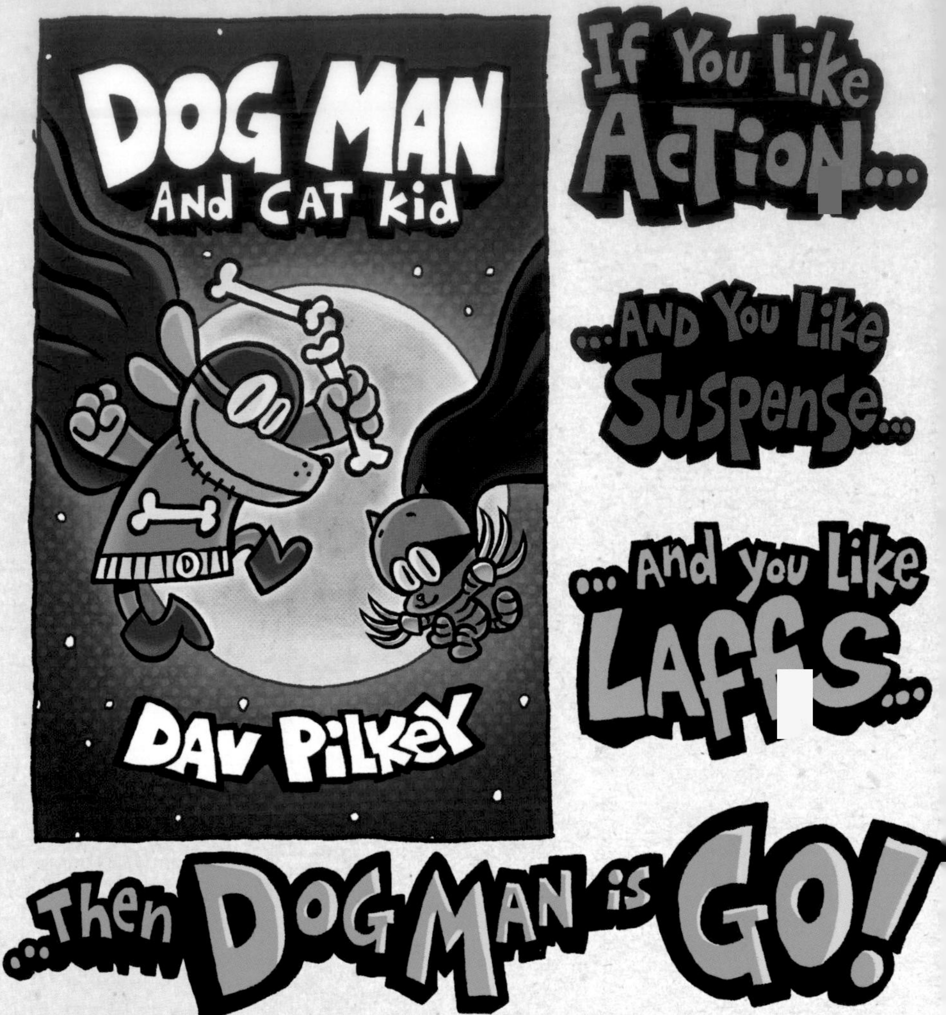
DOG MAN
AND CAT kid
DAV PILKEY
If You Like ACTION...
...AND You Like Suspense...
...And you Like LAFFS...
...Then DOG MAN is GO!
DOG Man is GO? That don't make no sense!
BUT we Like it!

HOW 2 DRAW

Li'L PeTeY

in 20 RidicuLousLy easy steps!

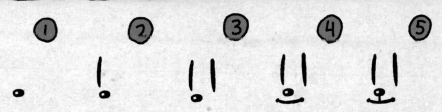

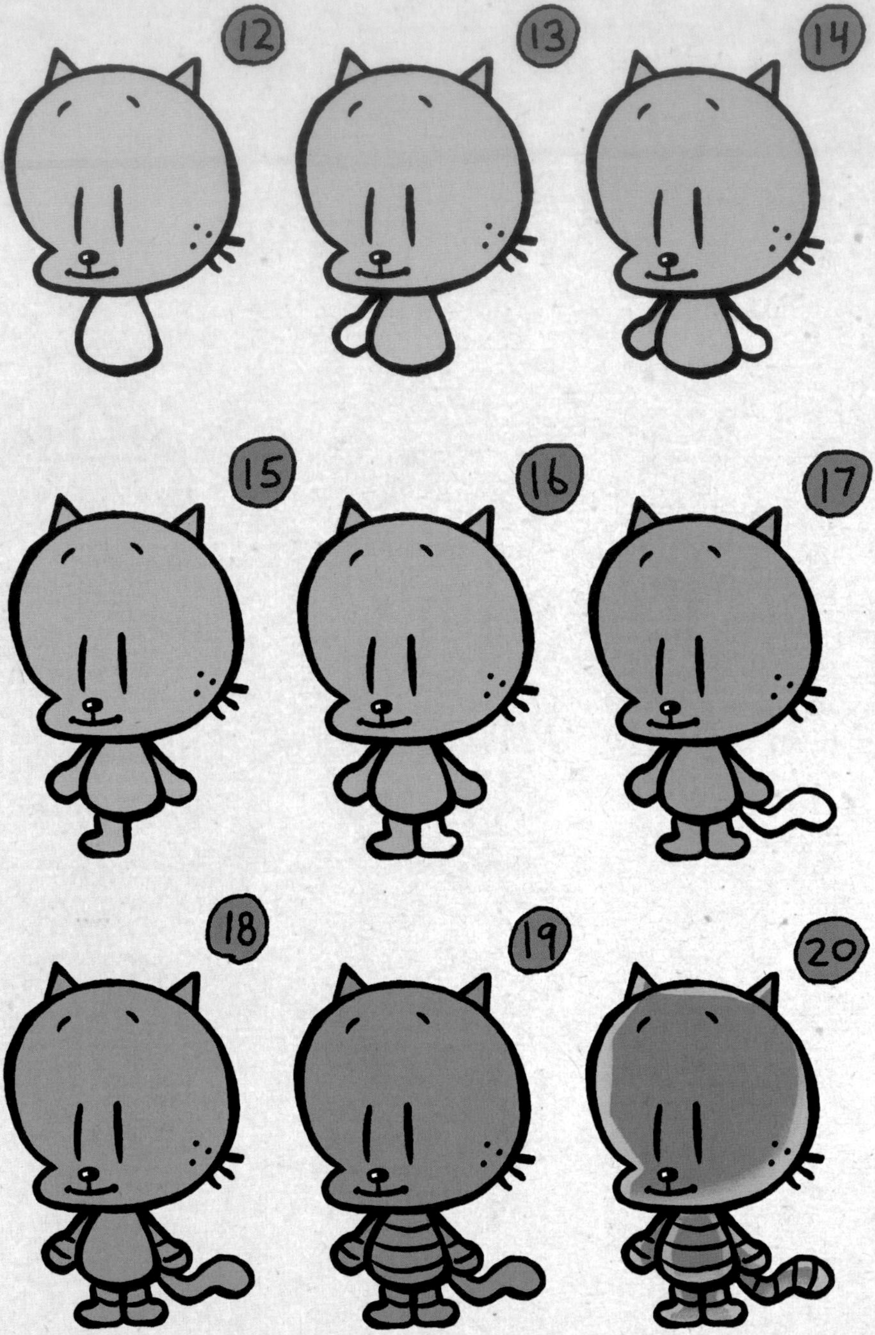
12
13
14
15
16
17
18
19
20

80-HD

in 18 Ridiculously easy Steps!

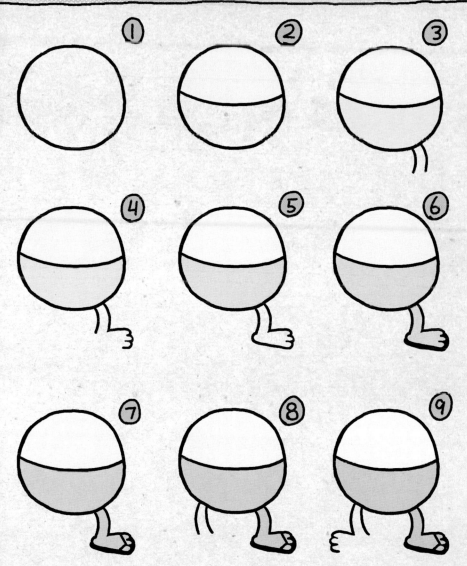

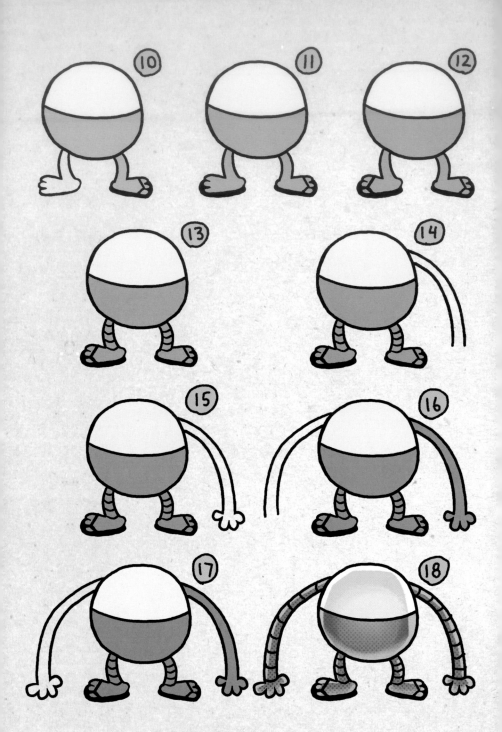

HOW 2 DRAW A BEASTY BUILDING

in **21** Ridiculously easy steps!

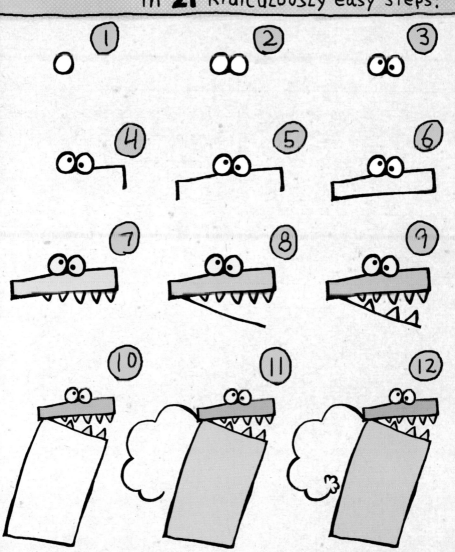

241

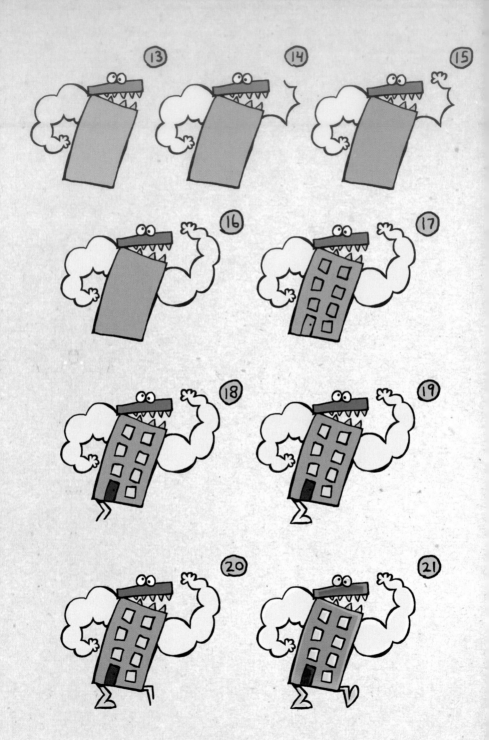

HOW 2 DRAW PETEY

in 27 RIDICULOUSLY easy STEPS!

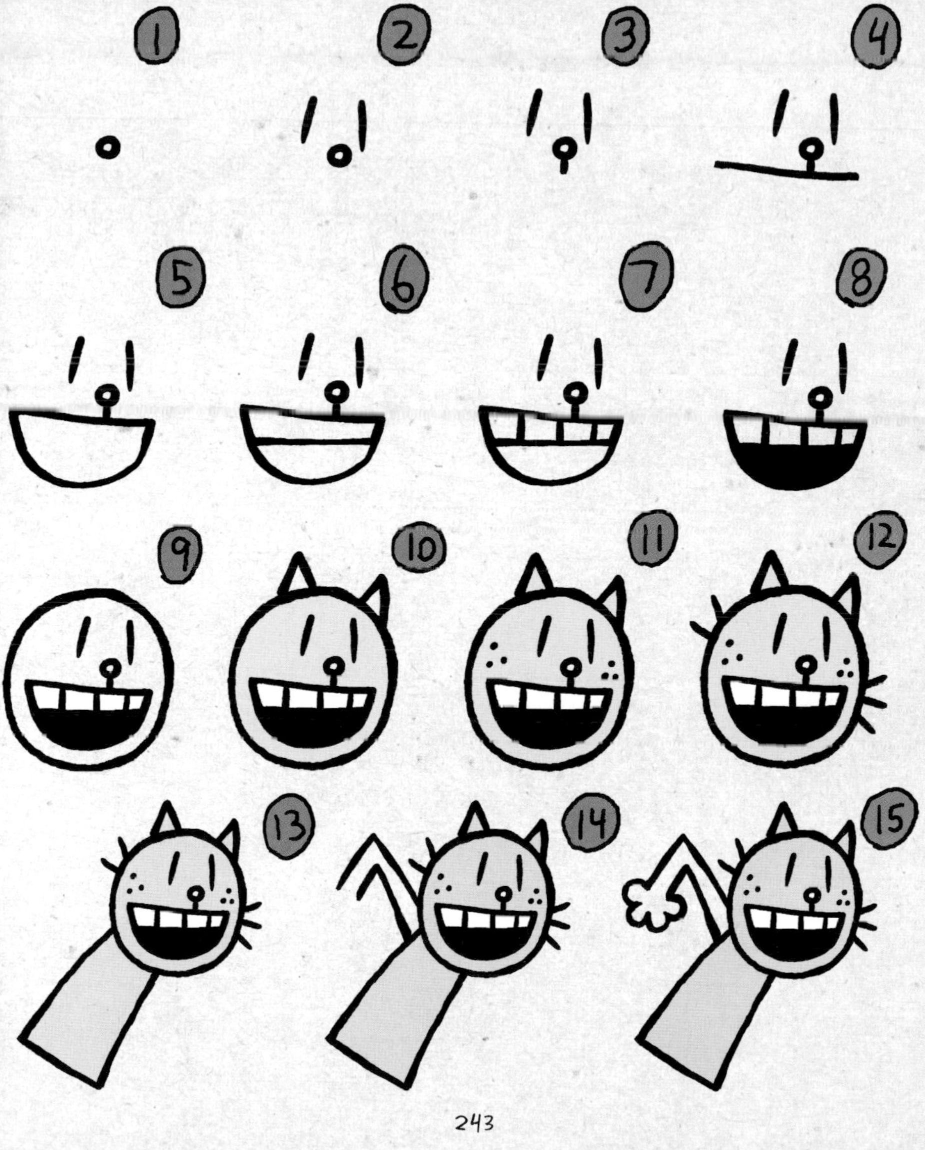
1
2
3
4
5
6
7
8
9
10
11
12
13
14
15

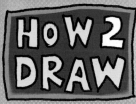

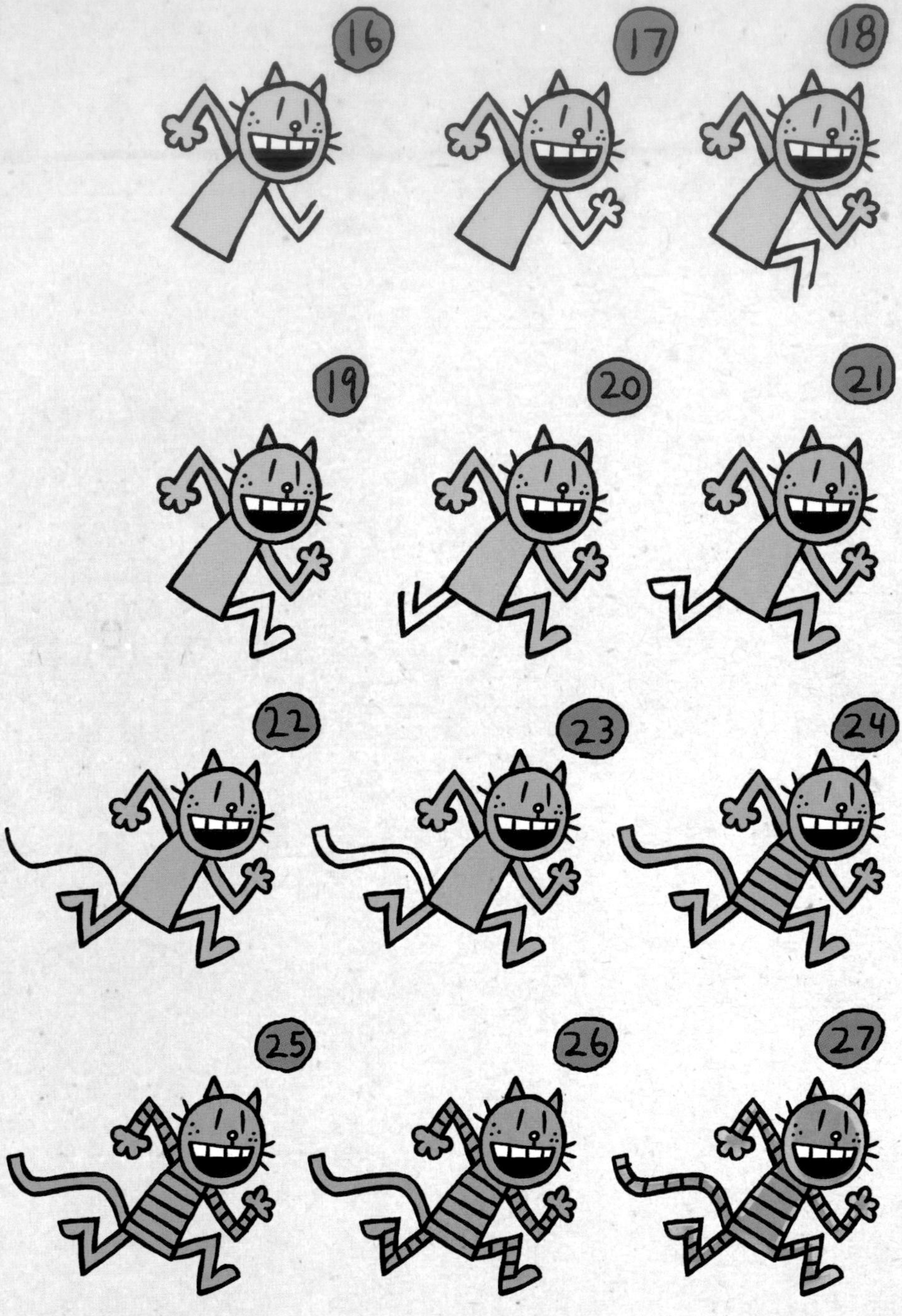
16
17
18
19
20
21
22
23
24
25
26
27

HOW 2 DRAW DOG MAN

in 34 Ridiculously easy Steps!

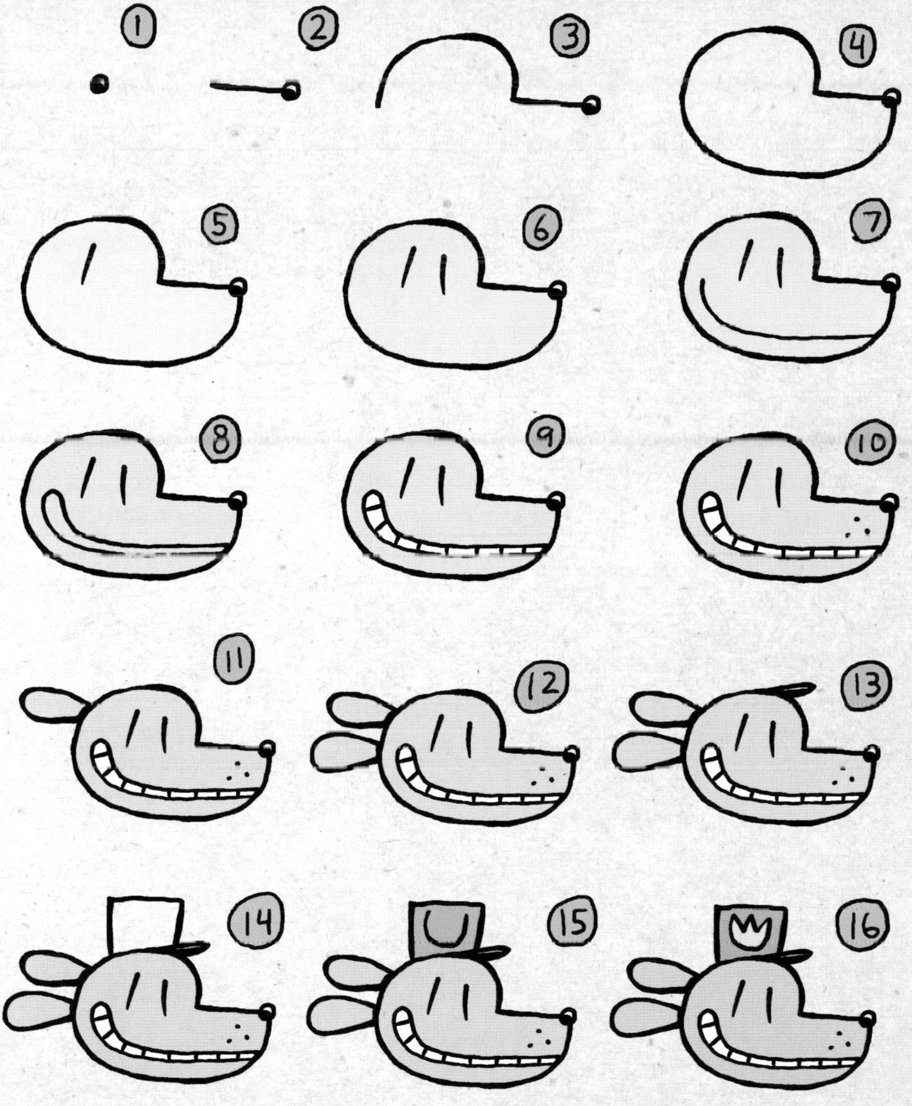
1
2
3
4
5
6
7
8
9
10
11
12
13
14
15
16

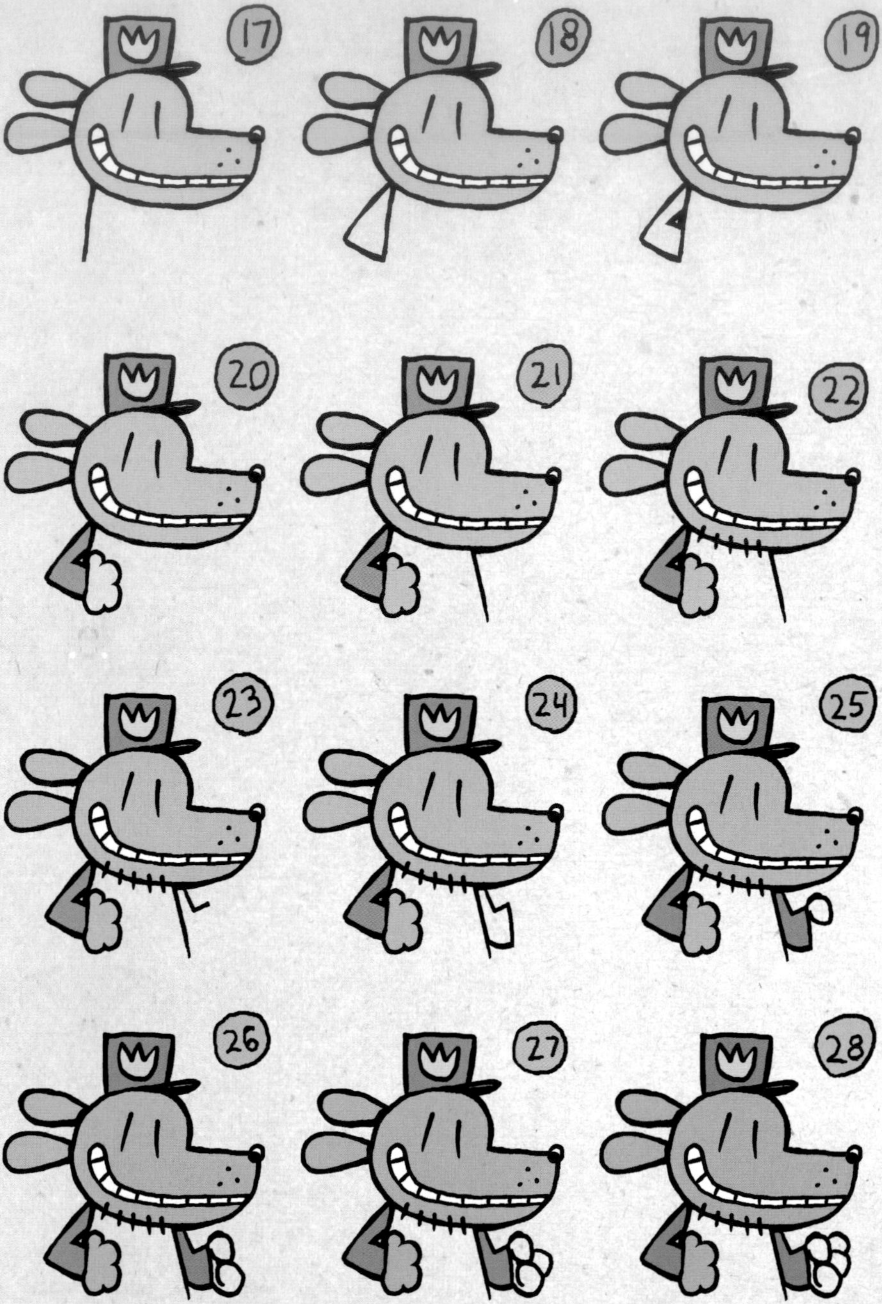
17
18
19
20
21
22
23
24
25
26
27
28

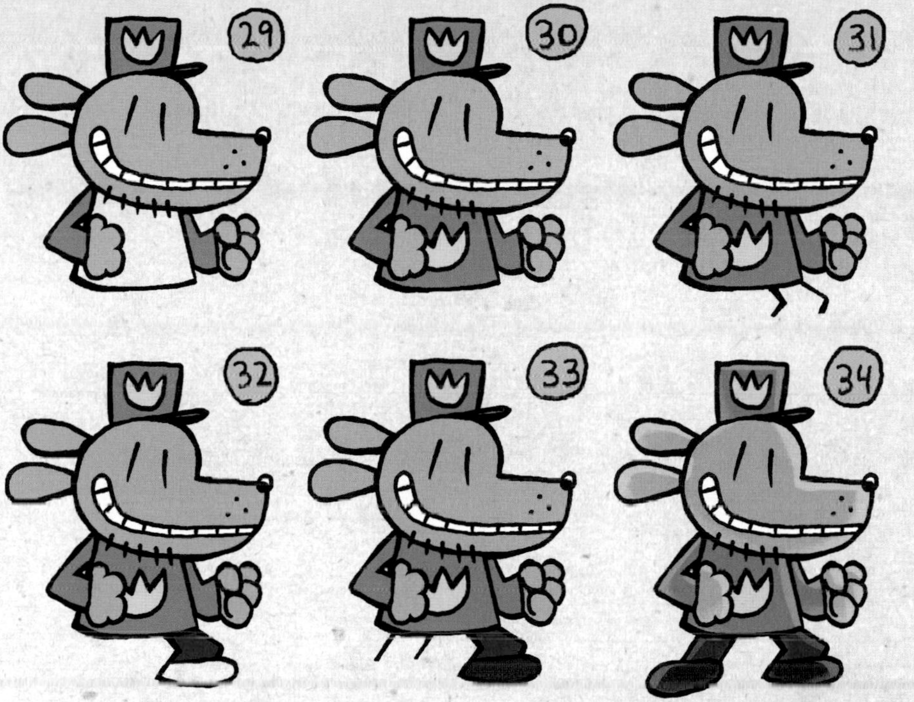
29
30
31
32
33
34

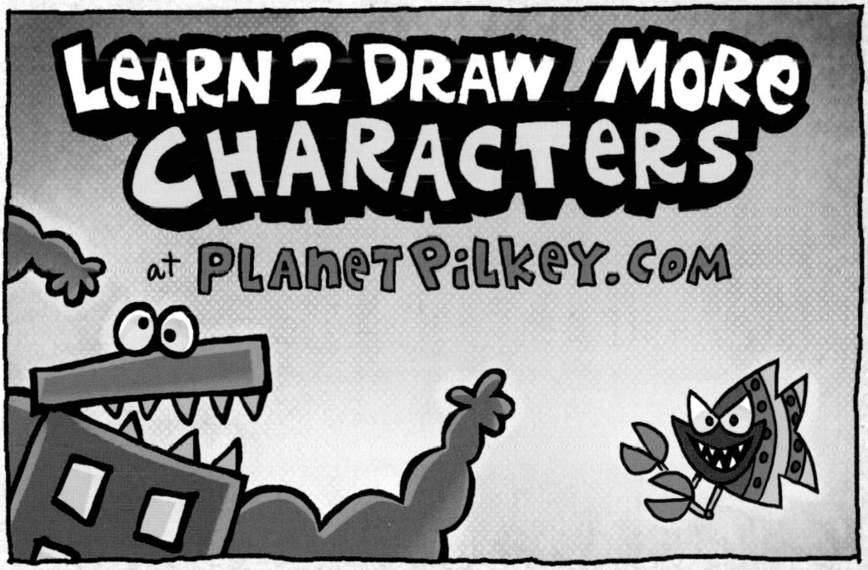
LEARN 2 DRAW MORE CHARACTERS
at PLANETPILKEY.COM

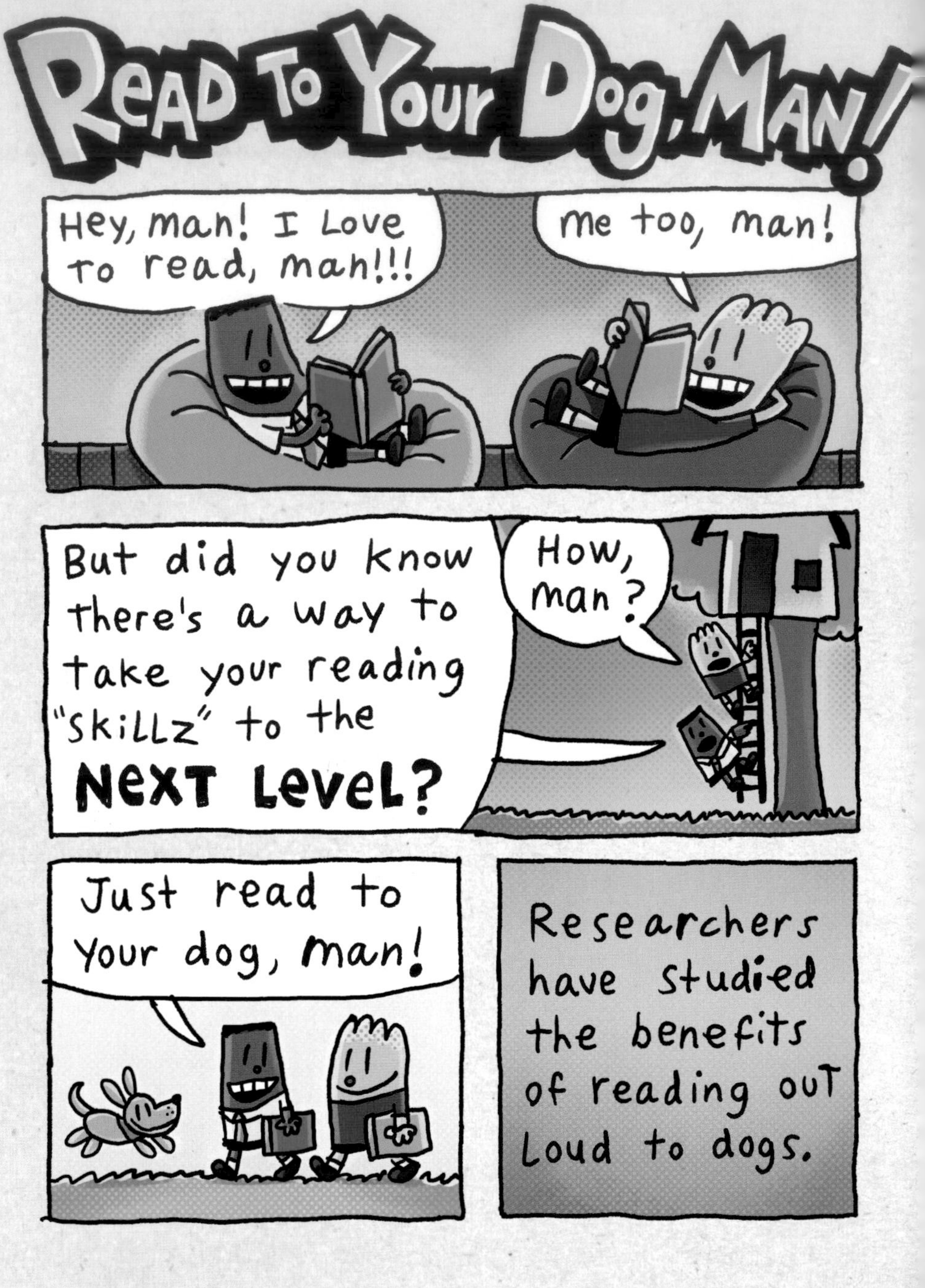
READ TO YOUR DOG, MAN!
Hey, man! I Love to read, man!!!
me too, man!
But did you know there's a way to take your reading "SkiLLz" to the NEXT LeveL?
How, man?
Just read to your dog, man!
Researchers have studied the benefits of reading out Loud to dogs.

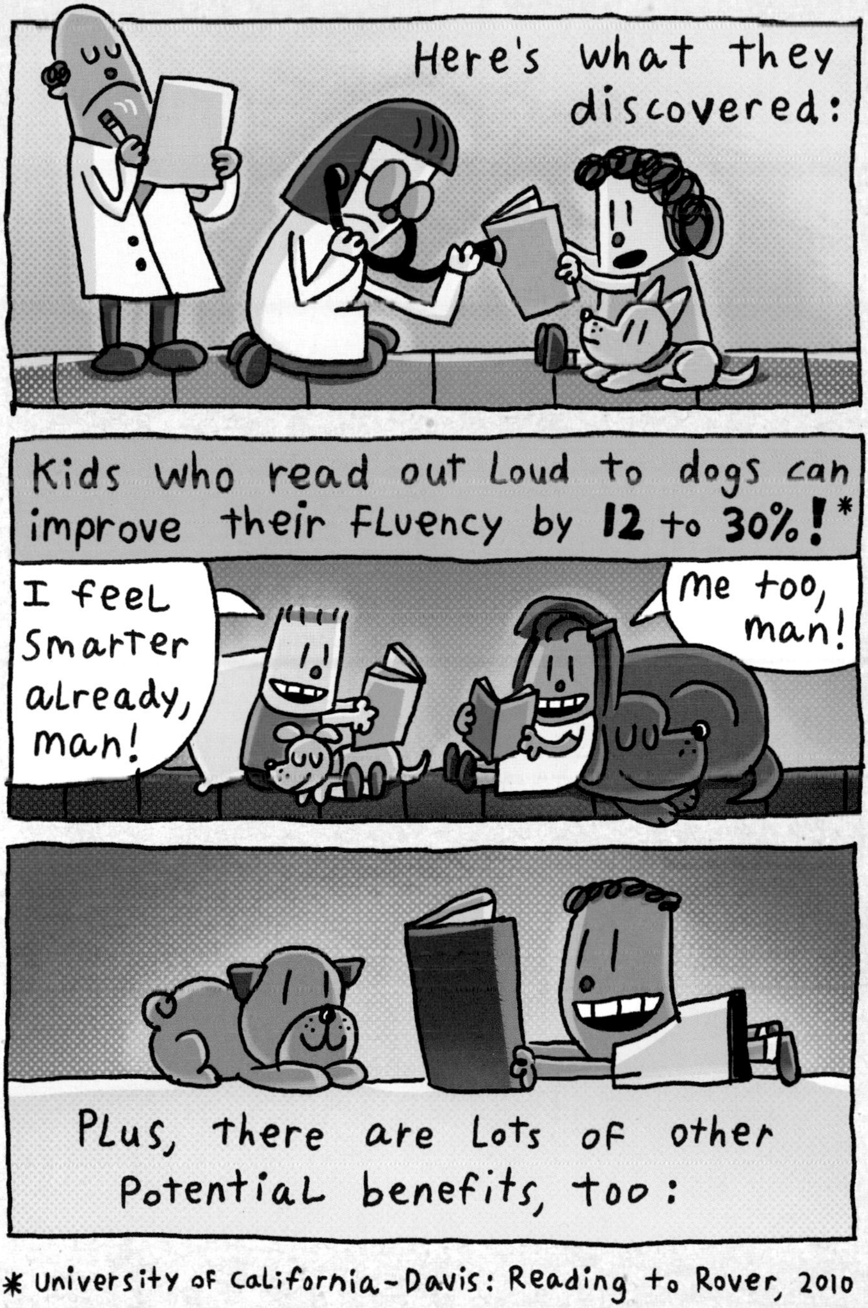
Here's what they discovered:
Kids who read out Loud to dogs can improve their FLuency by 12 to 30%!*
I feeL Smarter aLready, man!
me too, man!
PLus, there are Lots of other PotentiaL benefits, too:

* University of CaLifornia-Davis: Reading to Rover, 2010

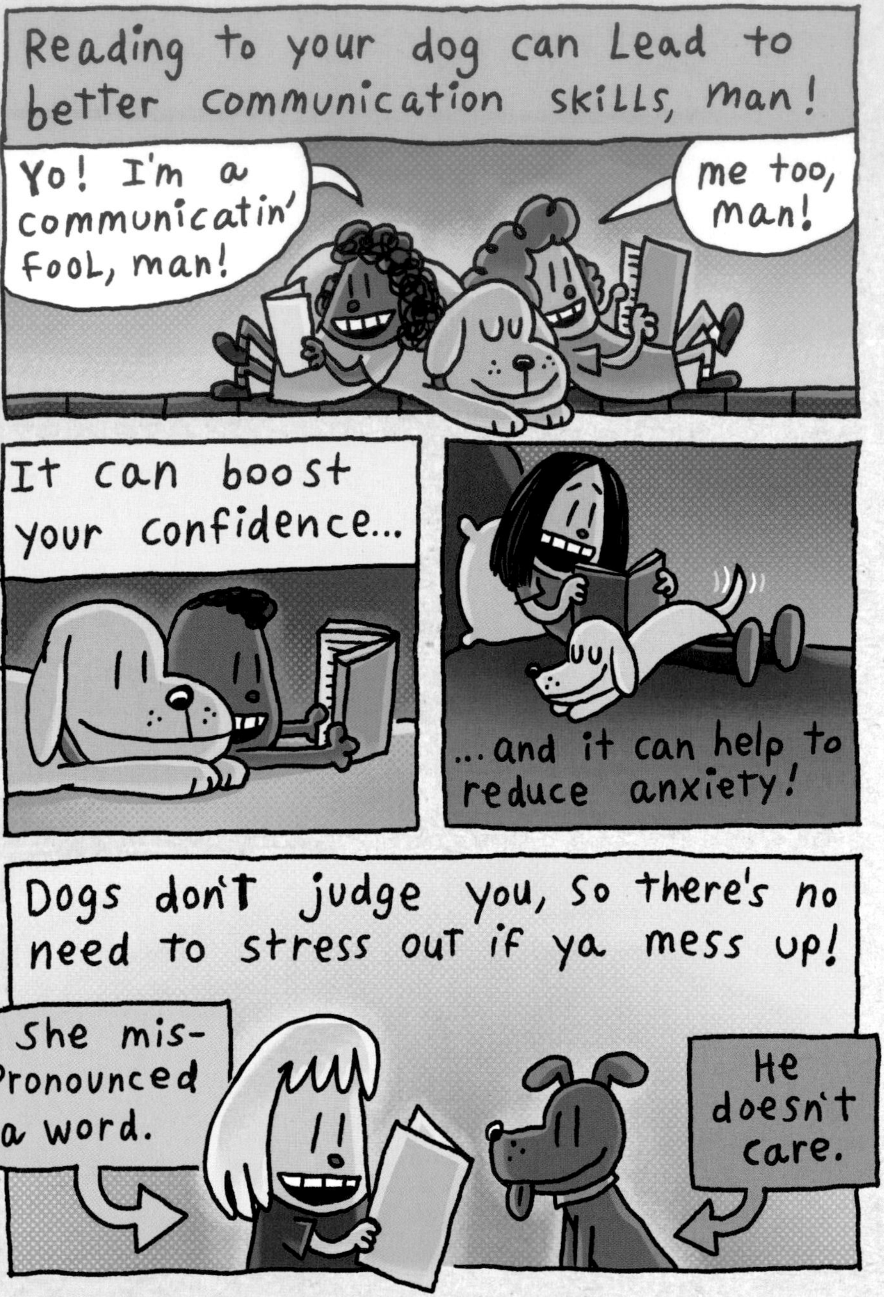
Reading to your dog can Lead to better communication skills, man!
Yo! I'm a communicatin' fool, man!
me too, man!
It can boost your confidence...
...and it can help to reduce anxiety!
Dogs don't judge you, so there's no need to stress out if ya mess up!
She mis-pronounced a word.
He doesn't care.

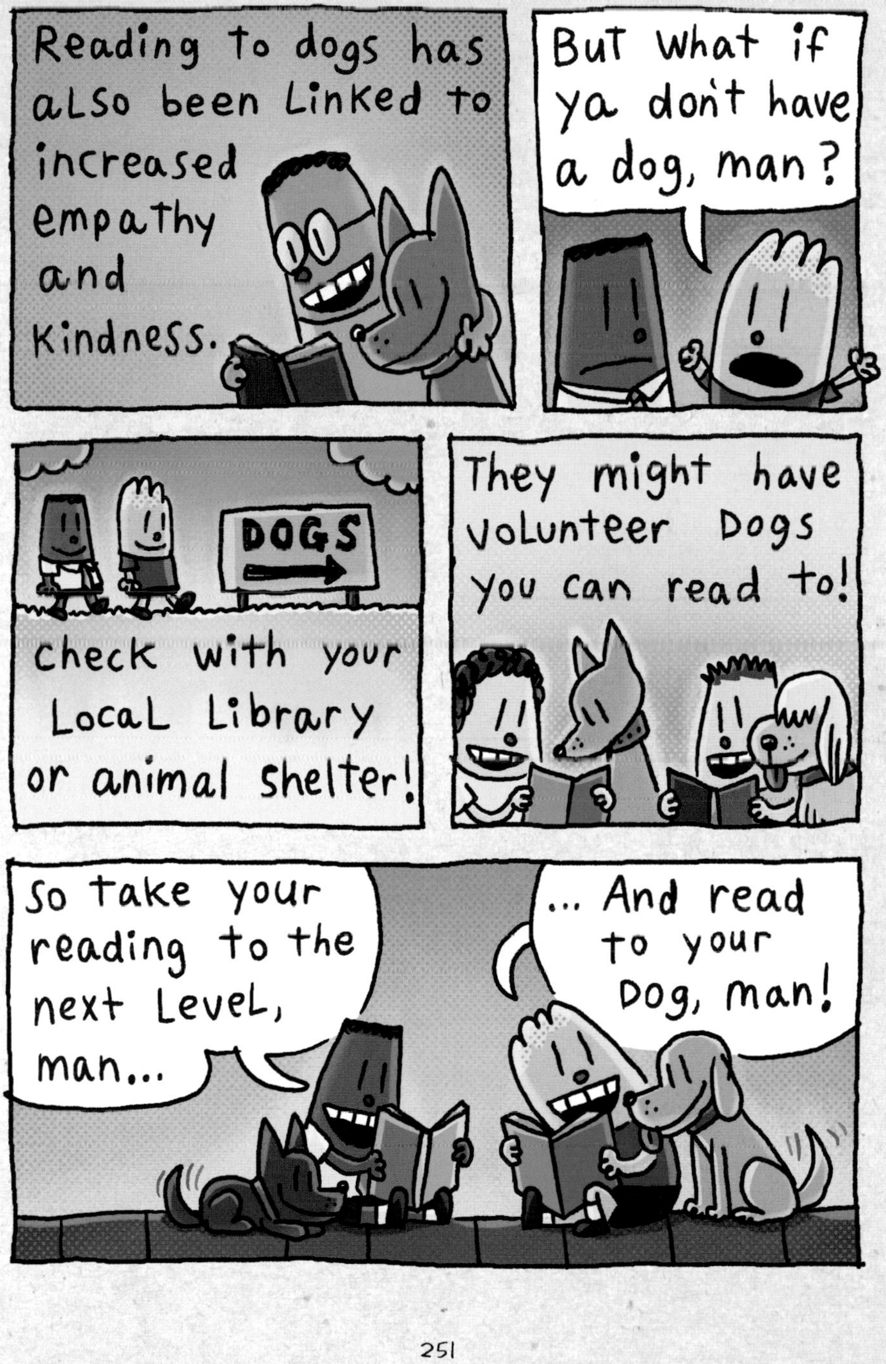

Reading to dogs has also been Linked to increased empathy and Kindness.
But what if ya don't have a dog, man?
DOGS
Check with your Local Library or animal shelter!
They might have volunteer Dogs you can read to!
So take your reading to the next Level, man...
... And read to your Dog, man!

READING TO YOUR DOG IS ALWAYS A PAWS-ITIVE EXPERIENCE!

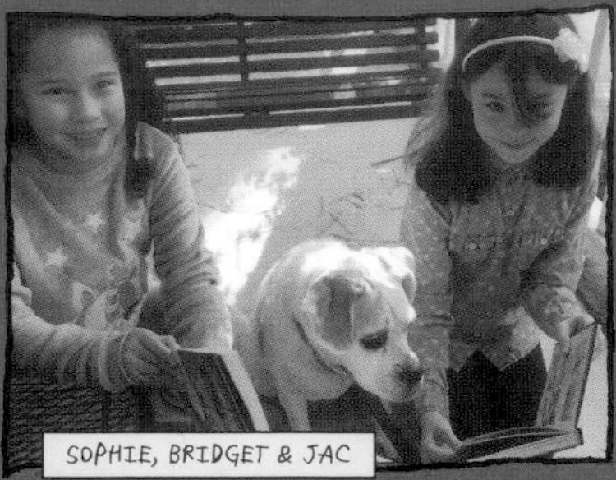
SOPHIE, BRIDGET & JAC

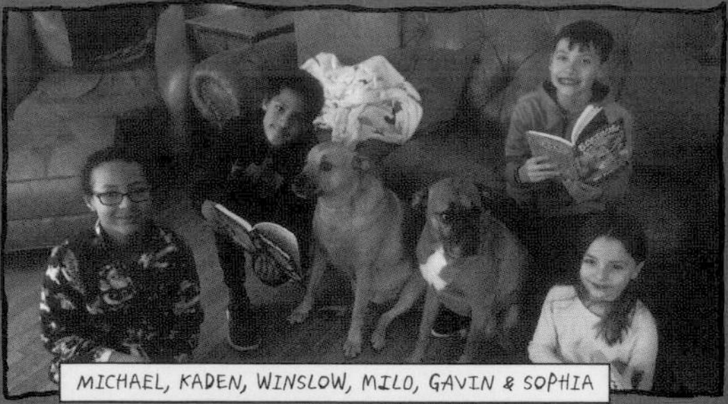
MICHAEL, KADEN, WINSLOW, MILO, GAVIN & SOPHIA

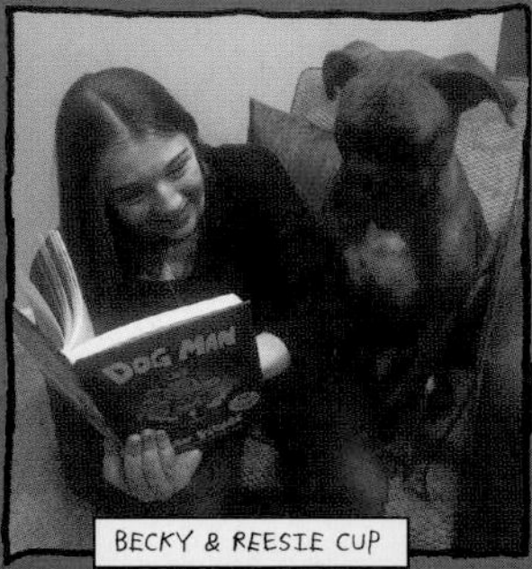
BECKY & REESIE CUP

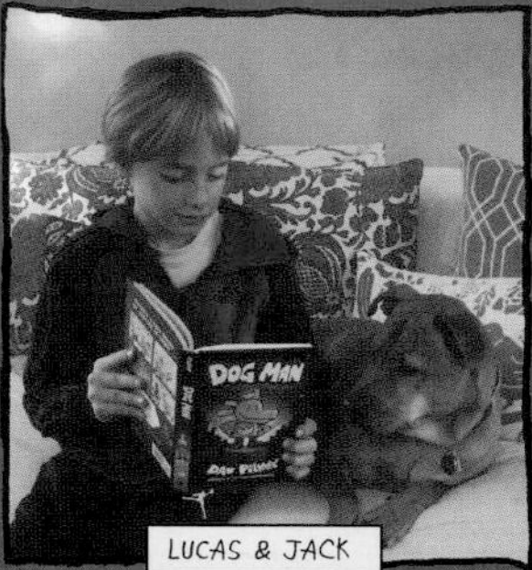
LUCAS & JACK

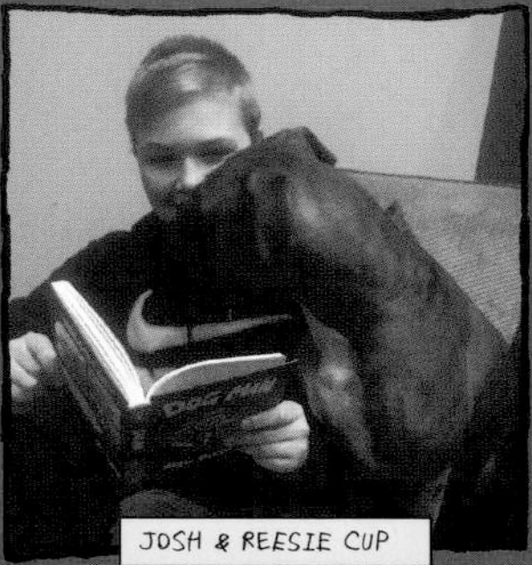
JOSH & REESIE CUP

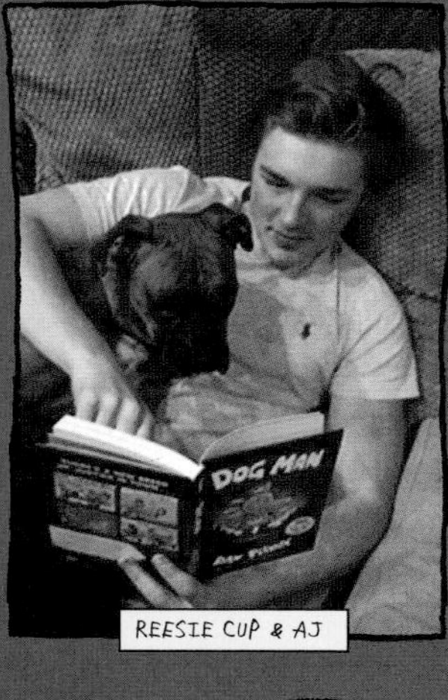
REESIE CUP & AJ

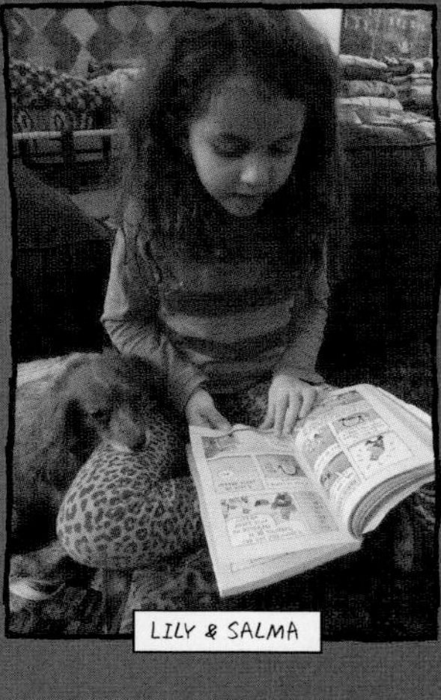
LILY & SALMA

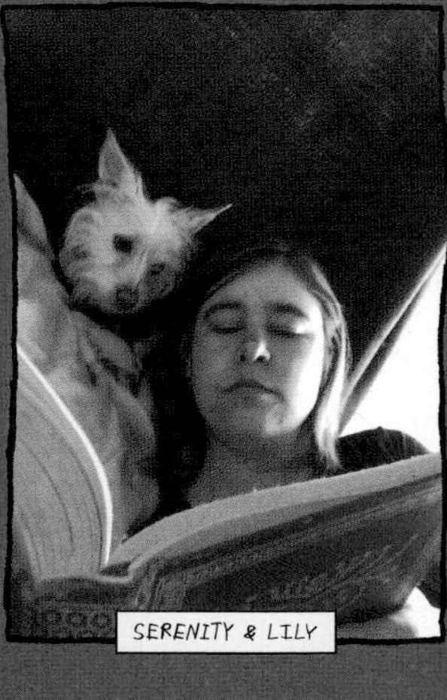
SERENITY & LILY

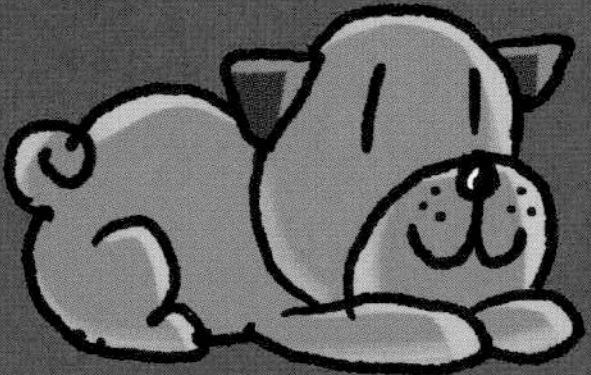

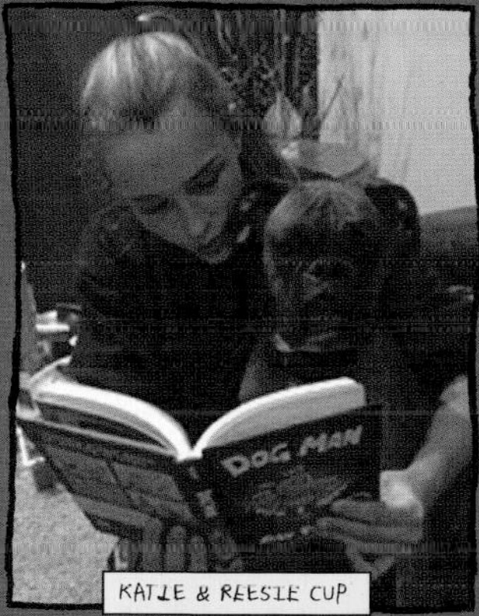
DOG MAN
KATIE & REESIE CUP

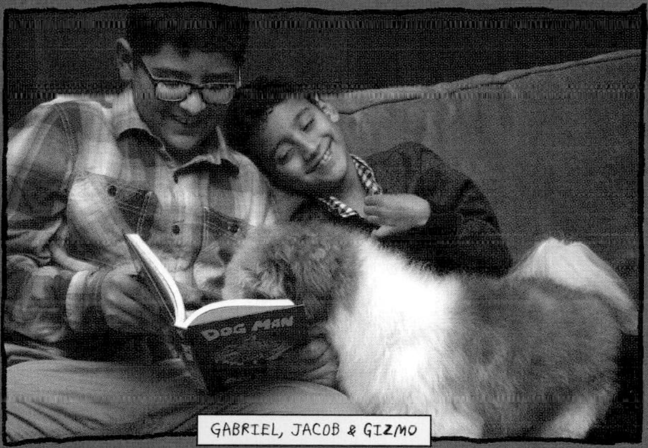
DOG MAN
GABRIEL, JACOB & GIZMO

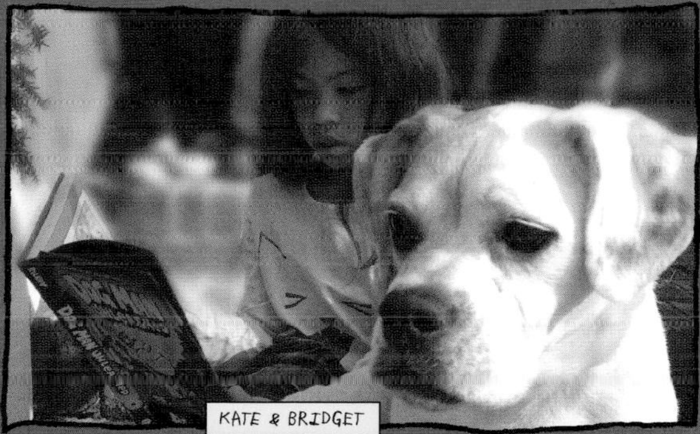
KATE & BRIDGET

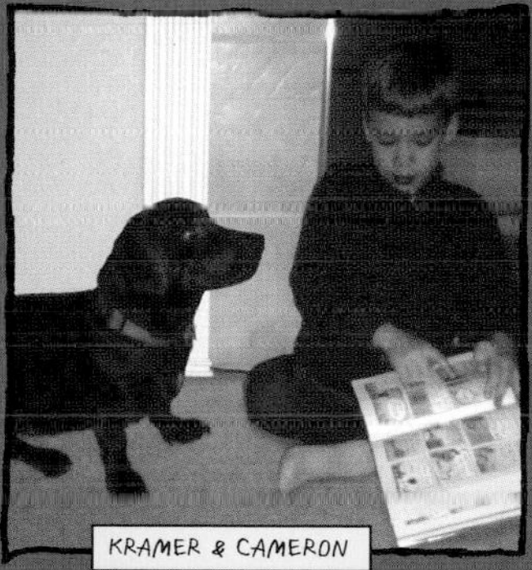
KRAMER & CAMERON

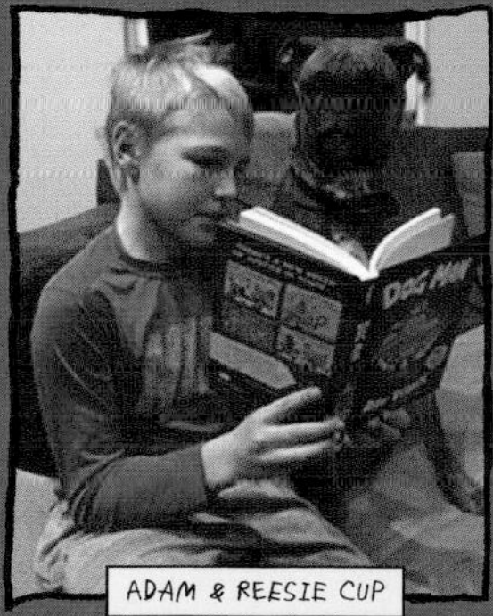
DOG MAN
ADAM & REESIE CUP

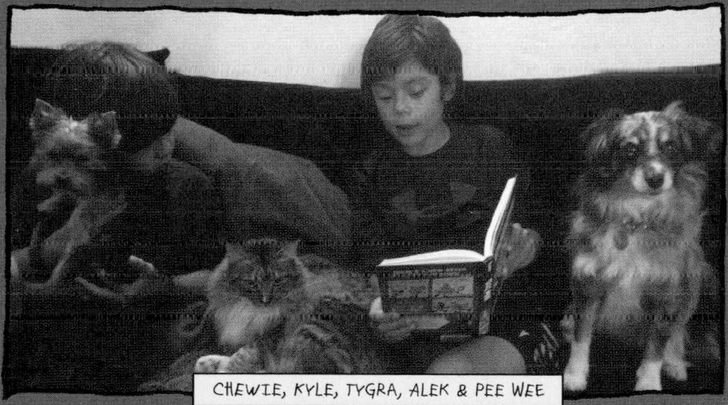
CHEWIE, KYLE, TYGRA, ALEK & PEE WEE

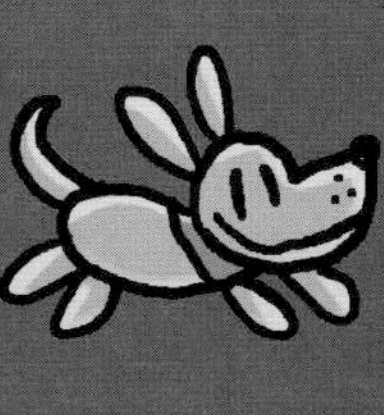

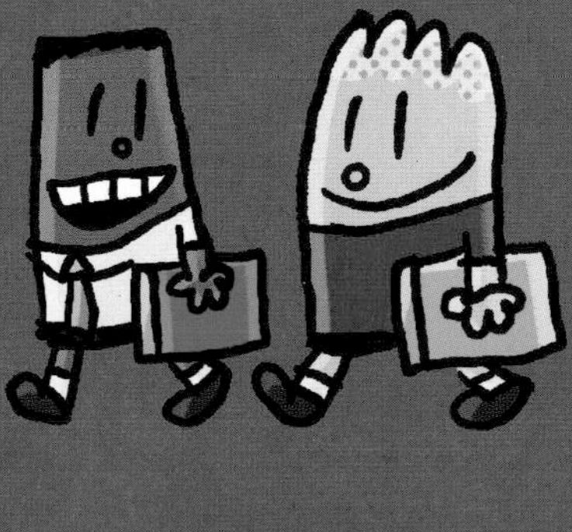

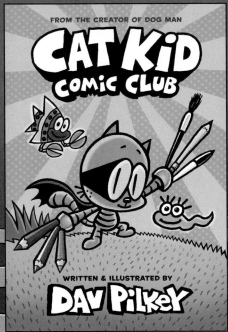

TH DAV PILKEY!

The Adventures of
CAPTAIN UNDERPANTS
FULL COLOR
THE FIRST EPIC NOVEL BY
DAV PILKEY
CALDECOTT HONOR ARTIST

FULL COLOR
CAPTAIN UNDERPANTS
AND THE ATTACK OF THE TALKING TOILETS
THE SECOND EPIC NOVEL BY
DAV PILKEY
CALDECOTT HONOR ARTIST

FULL COLOR
CAPTAIN UNDERPANTS
THE THIRD EPIC NOVEL BY
DAV PILKEY
CALDECOTT HONOR ARTIST

FULL COLOR
CAPTAIN UNDERPANTS
AND THE PERILOUS PLOT OF PROFESSOR POOPYPANTS
THE FOURTH EPIC NOVEL BY
DAV PILKEY
CALDECOTT HONOR ARTIST

FULL COLOR
CAPTAIN UNDERPANTS
AND THE WRATH OF THE WICKED WEDGIE WOMAN
THE FIFTH EPIC NOVEL BY
DAV PILKEY
CALDECOTT HONOR ARTIST

FULL COLOR
CAPTAIN UNDERPANTS
AND THE BIG, BAD BATTLE OF THE BIONIC BOOGER BOY
THE SIXTH EPIC NOVEL BY
DAV PILKEY
CALDECOTT HONOR ARTIST

FULL COLOR
CAPTAIN UNDERPANTS
AND THE BIG, BAD BATTLE OF THE BIONIC BOOGER BOY
THE SEVENTH EPIC NOVEL BY
DAV PILKEY
CALDECOTT HONOR ARTIST

FULL COLOR
CAPTAIN UNDERPANTS
AND THE PREPOSTEROUS PLIGHT OF THE PURPLE POTTY PEOPLE
THE EIGHTH EPIC NOVEL BY
DAV PILKEY
CALDECOTT HONOR ARTIST

FULL COLOR
CAPTAIN UNDERPANTS
AND THE TERRIFYING RE-TURN OF TIPPY TINKLETROUSERS
THE NINTH EPIC NOVEL BY
DAV PILKEY
CALDECOTT HONOR ARTIST

FULL COLOR
CAPTAIN UNDERPANTS
AND THE REVOLTING REVENGE OF THE RADIOACTIVE ROBO-BOXERS
THE TENTH EPIC NOVEL BY
DAV PILKEY
CALDECOTT HONOR ARTIST

FULL COLOR
CAPTAIN UNDERPANTS
AND THE TYRANNICAL RETALIATION OF THE TURBO TOILET 2000
THE ELEVENTH EPIC NOVEL BY
DAV PILKEY
CALDECOTT HONOR ARTIST

FULL COLOR
CAPTAIN UNDERPANTS
AND THE SENSATIONAL SAGA OF SIR STINKS-A-LOT
THE TWELFTH EPIC NOVEL BY
DAV PILKEY
CALDECOTT HONOR ARTIST

DOG MAN
The Musical
Original Cast Recording

The epic musical adventure is now available from Broadway Records!

PLANET PILKEY

Go to planetpilkey.com to read chapters, make comics, watch videos, play games, and download supa fun stuff!

Download on the App Store

HOME BASE

SCHOLASTIC

GET IT ON Google Play

ABOUT THE
AUTHOR-ILLUSTRATOR

When Dav Pilkey was a kid, he was diagnosed with ADHD and dyslexia. Dav was so disruptive in class that his teachers made him sit out in the hallway every day. Luckily, Dav loved to draw and make up stories. He spent his time in the hallway creating his own original comic books — the very first adventures of Dog Man and Captain Underpants.

In college, Dav met a teacher who encouraged him to illustrate and write. He won a national competition in 1986 and the prize was the publication of his first book, WORLD WAR WON. He made many other books before being awarded the 1998 California Young Reader Medal for DOG BREATH, which was published in 1994, and in 1997 he won the Caldecott Honor for THE PAPERBOY.

THE ADVENTURES OF SUPER DIAPER BABY, published in 2002, was the first complete graphic novel spin-off from the Captain Underpants series and appeared at #6 on the USA Today bestseller list for all books, both adult and children's, and was also a New York Times bestseller. It was followed by THE ADVENTURES OF OOK AND GLUK: KUNG FU CAVEMEN FROM THE FUTURE and SUPER DIAPER BABY 2: THE INVASION OF THE POTTY SNATCHERS, both USA Today bestsellers. The unconventional style of these graphic novels is intended to encourage uninhibited creativity in kids.

His stories are semi-autobiographical and explore universal themes that celebrate friendship, tolerance, and the triumph of the good-hearted.

Dav loves to kayak in the Pacific Northwest with his wife.

Learn more at Pilkey.com.